Disco Witches
of Fire Island

Also by Blair Fell
The Sign for Home

Disco Witches of Fire Island

《 *A Novel* 》

Blair Fell

alcove
press

This is a work of fiction. All of the names, characters, organizations, places and events portrayed in this novel are either products of the author's imagination or are used fictitiously. Any resemblance to real or actual events, locales, or persons, living or dead, is entirely coincidental.

PUBLISHER'S NOTE: The recipes contained in this book are to be followed exactly as written. The publisher is not responsible for your specific health or allergy needs that may require medical supervision. The publisher is not responsible for any adverse reaction to the recipes contained in this book.

Copyright © 2025 by Blair Fell

All rights reserved.

Published in the United States by Alcove Press, an imprint of The Quick Brown Fox & Company LLC.

Alcove Press and its logo are trademarks of The Quick Brown Fox & Company LLC.

Library of Congress Catalog-in-Publication data available upon request.

ISBN (hardcover): 979-8-89242-239-0
ISBN (paperback): 979-8-89242-034-1
ISBN (ebook): 979-8-89242-035-8

Cover design by Jim Tierney

Printed in the United States.

www.alcovepress.com

Alcove Press
34 West 27th St., 10th Floor
New York, NY 10001

First Edition: May 2025

10 9 8 7 6 5 4 3 2 1

For all the holy lovers, those who left us and those who remain and remember.

"I am the man, I suffer'd, I was there."
—Walt Whitman

Prologue

"Nothing deadens magic like the day-to-day onslaught of unrelenting grief."
　　　　　　　　—*Disco Witch Manifesto #134*

FIRE ISLAND PINES

May 3, 1989 . . . early morning

As Howie Fishbein searched the drizzly Great South Bay, his headphones blasted Sylvester's "You Make Me Feel (Mighty Real)." Flames of long silver hair whipped his weathered face, while his velvet bathrobe, the color of thick raspberry jam, billowed in the wind behind him. From a distance it appeared as if the island was bleeding.

There had been several omens indicating "a being of significance" would be arriving by water. What exactly the *significance* was, he did not know.

"We'll just have to wait," Howie said to a passing double-crested cormorant he thought might very well be the reincarnation of one of his many dead friends. "It's all we can do."

1.
Joe and Ronnie

"When stuck in her blues, a Disco Witch can always boogie to another part of the dance floor."
—*Disco Witch Manifesto #23*

THE FERRY

May 3, 1989 . . . 3:30 PM ferry

Where the hell is it? Excited by the prospect of crossing the Great South Bay for the very first time, Joe Agabian was struggling to see Fire Island through the ferry's rain-splattered window. It seemed as if the universe had purposely employed the fog and drizzle (and the scratched plexiglass window) to hide his past and future under a thick veil of secrecy.

He pulled the first mixtape Elliot had ever made for him from his backpack and inserted the well-worn cassette into his Sony Walkman. It was nearly four years ago when Joe first noticed his future lover sitting in those red banquettes upstairs at Woody's Bar in Philly. When Elliot looked over at Joe, it was as if a thousand blue-green dragonflies had swarmed his young heart. Elliot had sandy-brown hair, shining hazel eyes, and a strong (but not showy) body—a result of playing baseball as a teenager. And then there was his strong, resonant voice, which had launched a thousand hours of smart, funny banter. Elliot cared about the poor, hated Reagan and worshiped Fleetwood Mac. He was the one Joe had been waiting for his whole life.

Then the bad news . . .

"It'll be a challenge," Elliot warned after explaining that he had recently tested positive for the HIV virus. "You sure you're up for it?"

"I'm in love with you," Joe said, "and that's all that matters."

The cassette sleeve bore the handwritten title *Mixtape: Love Songs 1*. Joe could still feel Elliot's touch in the scrawl of the fine-tip blue marker. He had made a total of seven mixtapes for Joe during their relationship. Six had been lost to moves, mechanical accidents, or the flood in Joe's mother's basement the previous winter—which had also destroyed most of his and Elliot's photos together. *Love Songs 1* was the only cassette left, and Joe cherished it more than any other object in his life. It would be the perfect soundtrack for laying eyes on Fire Island for the first time.

He pressed "Play." Suddenly, the percussive jolt of Peter Gabriel's "Kiss of Life" jackhammered against the fog.

Six months earlier

"Yo, Chachi," Ronnie Kaminski shouted into the ear of a stunned, damp-eyed Joe on the night they first met. "You got some real nice dark eyes, and a sexy tan complexion. You Italian?"

Ronnie was six foot two, with a Chippendale's body and Fabio hair. He was strikingly handsome despite encroaching crow's feet and the errant gray nose hair. Joe knew who Ronnie was, of course—everyone loved to talk about him, Philly's number one gay-bar star. Some said he was the lover of a Channel 10 weatherman; others, that he was the illegitimate son of Paul Newman; and another that he was the aging "kept boy" of an antigay local politician. True or not, Ronnie clearly relished the gossip.

"Armenian m-mostly," Joe stammered, his anxiety about talking to hot guys instantly obliterating his already feeble ability at bar banter.

"Ah. Nice. I'm twenty percent Swede and eighty percent Polack, which is probably why I keep looking for meatballs in other guys' pants."

Joe realized that when someone is really, really hot, other people will automatically laugh at their terrible jokes—just as he was doing at that very moment. "Well, it was nice meeting you," he said, figuring Ronnie would soon disappear to do whatever mysterious, magical things really hot blond guys do on a Saturday night.

"Hold up a minute." Ronnie eyeballed Joe from head to toe. "You're a very interesting subject. I'm kind of a gay anthropologist—a 'gay-thropologist' I call it. I like to study other gay guys, and when I find one that isn't reaching his potential, I like to help him out. Like you, for example. Every weekend you come here all alone, looking like the worst sack o' sadness."

Joe's face flushed. That someone like Ronnie would even look at him was surprising, but that he claimed to have noticed him multiple times seemed unreal.

"You've been watching me?"

Ronnie winked and made one of those suave lateral clicks of the tongue à la Bogart. "Don't act so surprised. You got a *look*. Here's the thing: I've decided it's time you and me hit the dance floor and get to know each other."

Seconds later, he and Ronnie were dancing. It was the first time Joe had smiled in ages. In between Whitney Houston's "I Wanna Dance With Somebody" and Madonna's "Open Your Heart," he told Ronnie the sad story of Elliot—or rather, a facsimile of the true story. (Joe never told the whole truth about what had happened—not even to himself.) But everything else he said was fact, including how he was back to living at his mother's in the Philly suburbs (which he hated), and how he worked as an orderly at Friends Hospital on Roosevelt Boulevard (which he also hated), and how he wanted to move back to Center City and look into the organic chemistry course he needed in order to take the MCAT and maybe apply to medical school someday.

"But money is pretty tight," Joe said, "so I need to save up some cash."

"MCAT, huh?" Ronnie winked. "Brainy can be kinky."

"I guess." Joe was impressed at how Ronnie could turn a comment about a standardized test into something sexual. "But it's just an idea. I'm not really sure where I'll end up."

"Is that so? I get it. It took me all thirty-four years of my life to figure out my true destiny, but you're young. You'll get there." Ronnie squinted his eyes at Joe. "How old are you, anyway?"

Before Joe could say that he would be turning twenty-nine in March, Ronnie stopped him.

"Wait! Don't tell me! I'm really good at guessing ages. Let's see . . . baby face underneath that five o'clock shadow . . ." He peeped down the neck of Joe's shirt. ". . . Nice little hairy chest, but not a line around your eyes . . . still dresses like a clumsy straight guy . . . got it! You're twenty-three, right?"

Joe was happy he looked as young as that, but he also worried that Ronnie might look down on him, being that he was nearing thirty yet still worked a crap job, lived with his mom, and had literally nothing figured out. And what if he also discovered that Joe had been vowing to take that chemistry course for five years but still hadn't even looked at a catalog? So much for him thinking Joe had "potential." A bitter thought popped into Joe's head: *Life has been grotesquely unfair.* If it hadn't been for Elliot's sickness and death, he would have been able to make something of his life. He might already be in med school, and he and Elliot might already have been living in a townhouse they had bought together in Rittenhouse Square. Life *owed* Joe those five years back. *For just one night, I'm getting a do-over.*

"That's exactly right!" Joe said. "Good call. I'll be twenty-four in March."

"I knew it! Still a baby—and been through so much already." Ronnie pinched Joe's cheeks. "So, wanna go back to my place and fuck?"

"Sure," Joe said, though a middle-aged blond glam jock wasn't exactly his type.

"Stellar." Ronnie chugged the rest of his beer. "Let's get our coats."

The sex that followed was perfunctory and functional. Kiss, suck, condoms, fuck. Joe bottom. Ronnie top. Like the other three hookups Joe had experienced in the year and a half since Elliot's death, none of the men were as sexy or smart as his dead lover, nor were they the right size big spoon to Joe's little spoon. Every time he had sex, he'd leave his body, look down onto the bed, and watch himself betray Elliot.

After they toweled off, Ronnie lay back down and looked Joe in his big, sad brown eyes. "Let's face it, we both know *that's* not gonna happen again," he said, confirming to Joe that they were on the same page per their erotic incompatibility, "but I'm not done with you yet, Joey boy! I've decided you're gonna be my new project."

Joe's stomach squirmed. He hoped he hadn't inadvertently found himself hooking up with someone who was into EST or sold Herbal Life. "What do you mean 'new project'?"

Ronnie's eyes softened with pity as he took Joe's hand and spoke with a gentle firmness. "Face it, Joey boy. You're a mess. You looked like you were gonna cry the entire time we were having sex."

"I'm really sorry," Joe began.

"It's okay. I get it. We're living in hard times, but it's not just your broken heart that's the problem."

Joe got up from the bed, and pulled his Sears polo over his head. "What do you mean?"

"Look at yourself—the way you dress, how you cruise bars, even the way you keep your socks on during sex."

Joe glanced down at his white athletic socks; one was rolled down and one was up. He groaned.

"Here's the thing," Ronnie said. "I'm gonna teach you how to master this gay game and also help you get over your broken heart. Don't worry, kiddo, no charge. Sound good?"

While he doubted Ronnie would offer much of a solution to the paralyzing sorrow he had felt since Elliot's death, there was something about the gregarious, handsome jock that made Joe feel just a little hopeful for the first time in a long time. "You got a deal," Joe said.

After that, they hung out every weekend and quickly became best friends.

Ronnie gave Joe a mini-makeover, shaving a fire path through his Armenian unibrow, taking him to a better barber, and putting him in jeans that emphasized his muscular legs, cute butt, and *respectable* package. He taught Joe where to stand in a bar for the most flattering lighting and how to make small talk. Ronnie also told Joe of his own plans to marry rich and eventually become a motivational speaker like Norman Vincent Peale or Napoleon Hill—but a "gay-guy version," helping guys like Joe learn how to play the "gay game" and achieve their highest potential.

And it worked, up to a point. Joe started getting asked out by some quality men. Unfortunately, most dates ended with him choked up, talking about Elliot. After the men (politely) kicked Joe out, Ronnie would insist he come over for a post-date debrief. Almost always, Joe would end up in tears while Ronnie cuddled him until he fell asleep.

That Christmas, Ronnie got fired from his after-hours security job at the Holiday Inn for hooking up in unoccupied rooms. That's when he proposed that he and Joe get jobs on Fire Island for the summer.

"It's the opportunity of a lifetime!" Ronnie told Joe that frigid January night at Jim's Steaks on Philadelphia's South Street. "Last August, I met this rich old guy named Scotty Black. He owns this club called the Promethean—it's the hottest disco on Fire Island. If we go out there early enough, Scotty says he'll give us bartending gigs. He'll also provide housing, food, everything. We'll save a fortune!"

"Um . . . you know I don't know anything about bartending, right?" Joe said.

Ronnie waved his hand. "Nothing to it, especially in a gay bar. You just have to be cute, smile, flirt a little, and slosh some booze into a glass. A beagle could do it if he had thumbs and looked hot in a T-shirt!"

"I'm not sure I wanna be that far from Philly," Joe said, squirming in his chair as he poked at the crusts of his discarded cheesesteak roll. "My mom's getting older and—"

"Stop being a drama queen. Your mom is a big girl and wants you to be happy. She told me so. Look, my adorable little Armenian, you need to start having some F-U-N fast, or your heart and dick could get stuck in a sad, dark place. You don't wanna end up dead and alone in some studio in Fishtown with a cat named Little Sheba, do you?"

Ronnie had a point. Like many young men who had lost lovers to AIDS, Joe felt both like a frightened toddler and old beyond his years. It was his widowed mother, Evelyn, who had originally encouraged him to drive into Philly to meet new gay friends.

"Don't we have to interview or anything?" Joe asked Ronnie.

"Nope. Scotty said the jobs are basically ours if we want 'em. We're in like Flynn!"

"I don't know . . ." Joe scrunched his eyebrows.

"What have we got to lose?" Ronnie said. "I've slept with everybody worth sleeping with in Philly. Just think, an entire island of hot, rich gay men looking for love. Also there's no cars or even bikes allowed, so it's really safe—especially if you're gay. You can just walk down the boardwalk in your Speedo, holding hands and kissing in public, and no one's gonna beat the shit out of you or set your house on fire. It's Gaytopia!"

Gaytopia? Could any place feel that safe or free? How many nights had Joe pretended to be straight as he walked home from the bars while groups of hetero assholes shouted threats at the more obvious gays? How many times had he wished he could have held Elliot's hand as they walked South Street without worrying some Philly lug-head might mutter under his breath, "AIDS carriers"?

"That all sounds amazing, but how about we do it next year?"

"Enough with the stalling!" Ronnie shouted over Madonna's new hit "Live to Tell," which was blasting from the sound system. "Listen to Madonna! She's telling us to do it *now*! You turn twenty-four in March! I turn thirty-five in September. We only get to stay at the top of the homo-food chain for a short time—and that's the best-case scenario. Look what happened to Elliot. Look what's happening to nearly fifty percent of our friends over thirty. Who knows when any of us are gonna bite the big bad dick of death!"

"Jesus, Ronnie. Keep it down!"

"You know I'm telling the truth."

Maybe it was the third beer Joe drank that night, or maybe it was his finally acknowledging how small his life had become, or maybe it was the eight tons of despair clogging his stomach (along with the Jim's cheesesteak with Whiz), but he looked up at Ronnie and said, "Fuck it. I'm in!"

2.

Land Ho!

"Life will surprise you. Let it."
—*Disco Witch Manifesto #83*

May 3, 1989 . . . twenty-one minutes later

Peter Gabriel was singing "Kiss of Life" into Joe's ears as Joe zipped up his raincoat and climbed the slippery stairway to the ferry's upper deck. It was all so peaceful: the ferry's vrooming engine, the seagull's call, the shush shush of the parting water. He pressed "Fast Forward" on his Walkman. The mixtape whirred past Peter, past Joni, past Ricki Lee, until it hit the perfect song—Bonnie Raitt's slow, bluesy "Opening Farewell." Joe closed his eyes and listened to Bonnie's raspy alto. The spray of the Great South Bay gently stung his face. *It's a baptism,* he thought. *A cleansing of what had been, and a welcoming of what might be.*

"Ah-ha ha ha!" The barrage of loud laughter shoved Bonnie over the railing of Joe's serenity. He clicked off his Walkman and saw the two deckhands wearing yellow rain slickers, leaning against the captain's cabin and staring at him.

Were they laughing at him? He knew their type from high school—the sort that would play on the lacrosse team and snap wet towels at bare backsides. One was thick, a pimply-faced teenager, the same height as Joe. The other one was taller and lean, with a stubbly face that bore the flush of a young man who spent his life outside. Handsome—for a straight guy. He looked around the same age as Joe—or rather the same age Joe lied about being—early twenties. Even from across the boat, Joe was stunned by the incandescent blue of the man's eyes. The deckhand clocked Joe looking at him and whispered something to his coworker, then . . . more laughter.

Straight assholes. So much for this place being Gaytopia.

He wished Ronnie and he could have at least traveled out to the island together. Instead, Ronnie had arrived a week before, to make sure everything was set up, while Joe had to finish his last week at Friends Hospital in Philly.

Joe was about to head downstairs when he saw it—the fog was lifting, and Fire Island appeared like a long inky brushstroke across the horizon. As the ferry moved closer to the coastline, mansions emerged from the trees. *They have to be worth millions!* Joe's heart drummed excitedly. He recalled all that Ronnie had told him—the parties, the men, the feeling of nonstop wealth and hedonism. But then, as the ferry slowly sloshed its way into the harbor, disappointment overcame him. The totality of the business district was nothing more than a handful of squarish buildings with nautical decorations haphazardly slapped onto their cinderblock surfaces—a total contrast to the mansions he'd seen along the coast. Worst of all, only a handful of people were waiting for the ferry, tugging small red wagons filled with groceries or pots of flowers like old people play-acting children. It was like a gay ghost town.

And there was no sign of Ronnie. He checked the other side of the boat, looking off toward the eastern end of the harbor. It was just more gray emptiness except for a single sunbeam splitting the clouds and shooting a natural spotlight onto the very middle of the far dock. Into that illuminated patch of dock walked the most gorgeous hunk of man Joe had ever seen.

Who in the hell . . . ?

The man had to be six foot four at least, with broad shoulders. His bulging pectorals pushed against the word "Titans" on his damp gray sweatshirt. He appeared to be in his mid-thirties to early forties, with dark, close-cropped hair and a perfect salt-and-pepper beard that emphasized the squareness of his jaw. He looked like a *Colt Men* magazine model or one of those buff actors wearing a leather thong in a 1960s Italian gladiator movie.

Then it happened: the man turned his head just slightly, and despite the distance, he appeared to be staring directly at Joe with an expression of both desire and danger. Or perhaps sexual hunger and mortal threat? Whatever it was, Joe's skin began to vibrate at the thought of being touched by him. Then the Gladiator Man began to wave.

Joe nervously lifted his arm to wave back, his heart drumming *Boléro* against his ribs. Then, just as he flashed one of his glowing Armenian American smiles, a large yacht pulled between him and the Gladiator Man. When it finally cleared the view, the Gladiator Man had vanished.

Dammit, Joe thought. As his eyes scanned the far side of the harbor in hopes of seeing him again, he felt the ferry bump into the dock. The deckhands flew into action—ropes tied, gangplank set, passenger door slid open. Joe hurried below and was last in line to disembark. All the other passengers had someone waiting ashore with a red wagon and a hug. Soon, they'd all been whisked off down tree-covered walkways.

Joe stood alone with his duffel, on the lookout for Ronnie (and for that Gladiator Man). Five minutes passed, then ten, then fifteen. Still no sight of either of them. Every so often the two annoying deckhands would look over. Not wanting to appear as if he'd been abandoned (even if he had been), Joe walked over to the small strip of gray wooden shops, waiting for the deckhands to lose interest. They didn't. The taller one, who had remarkably blue eyes, wouldn't look away. Trying to gay-bait him, no doubt. Joe considered wandering off down one of the walkways and risking getting lost. But how far was he supposed to take the charade? Did he really need to prove to some good-looking, homophobic straight guy that he hadn't been pathetically forgotten by his only best friend? A "best friend" he had only known for six months before following him to an island he knew nothing about.

Dragging his duffel over to the lone pay phone in the harbor, he picked up the receiver before realizing he had neither change nor a phone number he could call. If Ronnie even had a phone; it was unlikely he'd be listed in any directory yet. Hanging up, Joe looked back toward the landing, wondering when the ferry would return to the mainland and whether he should return with it. Just then, he saw two funny-looking older men arrive at the dock and begin loading boxes into their two extra-large wagons. The taller of the two wore an old-fashioned maroon bathrobe and a Yankees baseball cap decorated with fake flowers on the brim. His long silver hair was tied in a ponytail that hung from the back of his cap. His wrists, fingers, and neck were heavily adorned with silver jewelry, including what looked like an entire catalog of religious icons—an Irish cross, a Hamsa, an ankh, a ying-yang symbol, a tree of life, and a winged heart with an Islamic crescent moon and star in its center. His shorter friend resembled a pint-sized member of the Village People, wearing black leather chaps and vest, with just a rim of dark hair around his bald pate and a little mustache dyed coal black.

The man in the maroon bathrobe looked at Joe with an overly familiar gaze. "Young man! Are you okay? You appear lost!"

He had a warm singsongy voice with an accent that was distinctly New York but with an almost fake mid-Atlantic twang—Katherine Hepburn if she had been born in Queens. His warm and silly presence instantly made Joe feel calmer.

"I'm okay!" Joe said as he walked ten paces closer so they could stop yelling. "Where are all the people?"

"It's too early in the season," the funny tall man said. "In just a few weeks, you won't recognize the place. Is it your first time?"

"It is."

"How wonderful! I'm Howard Fishbein, but everyone calls me Howie." He pointed to his little bald friend. "This is one of my housemates, Lenny D'Amico. Beneath his tough leather-man exterior is a very small, wounded heart of gold . . . with a stent."

"Nice to meet you. I'm Joe Agabian."

Howie whispered something to Lenny, who angrily whispered something back. Then Howie said to Joe, "Are you absolutely sure you don't need help?"

Joe scanned the harbor again. Still no sign of Ronnie or the hot Gladiator Man—or anyone else for that matter. "Um . . . I guess I *could* use some help. You wouldn't know a guy named Ronnie Kaminski, would you? He moved here last week?"

"You mean the tall hottie with long blonde hair?" Lenny asked with a voice like a nasally Brillo pad. "The one who dresses like a college jock and looks like a Chippendales stripper?"

"That's him." Joe laughed. "He's bartending at the Promethean—"

"You must be mistaken," Howie said. "If it's who we think, he's cleaning rooms over at the Flotel."

"The Flotel?" Joe said, perplexed as to why they'd ask a bartender to clean. "Is that a different bar?"

"The Flotel *Motel*," Lenny said. "Your buddy is the housekeeper. We saw him picking up cleaning supplies yesterday at Mulligan's Grocery. Howie and I clean houses out here too—among other things."

Anxious bees swarmed inside Joe's chest. "But he's supposed to be bartending."

Howie squinted his eyes again. "Bluish-indigo... hmm. Curious."

"What's wrong?" Joe looked to see if anything was on his shirt.

"Oh, nothing," Howie said, looking like he was trying to figure out a puzzle. "By the way, Joe, what age would you be?"

Joe had no idea why Howie was asking him his age or looking at him so strangely. He almost blurted out his real age, but then, with the island being so small, he thought it best to continue with the lie he had told Ronnie. "I just turned twenty-four in March," he said.

"No, that doesn't feel right." Howie shook his head at Joe's response. "So strange."

"I told you," Lenny mumbled to Howie, then nudged Joe's arm to get his attention. "So, you gonna be working out here too?"

"Yeah. We both came out here from Philly to bartend at the Promethean."

"Two hot cheesesteaks from *Philly*, huh?" Lenny imbued his words with extra salaciousness and then snorted. "I'll tell the island medic to stock up on penicillin."

Howie shot him a withering look. "Let me apologize for my crude housemate. He's a bit like the tiniest of kidney stones—can be extremely painful but eventually will pass. As for your friend

Ronnie, check the Flotel, room number one around back. That's where the porter usually sleeps."

"Which hotel is the Flotel Motel exactly?" Joe asked.

"There's only one hotel, my dear." He pointed down the left side of the harbor toward a shabby, three-story, cinder-block structure painted blue and white. "You can't miss it."

"That's a hotel?" Joe grimaced. "It's pretty . . . um . . ."

"Bleak?" Howie said, nodding. "With all the charm of a lobotomy."

"The greedy bastard who owns it still charges a fortune," Lenny added.

Joe thanked them, grabbed his duffel, and began walking toward the Flotel. Behind him, he heard Howie and Lenny bickering. Only bits and pieces reached his ears:

"Shouldn't you ask Max?"

"Just temporary . . ."

"Indigo blue! I sense it—"

"Probably the muck in your eye . . ."

"Joe, wait!" Howie called out.

Turning back, Joe saw Howie hobbling dramatically after him, waving his ring-covered hand, bracelets clacking. Lenny followed, looking peevish but resigned.

"These wet days are torture for my sciatica," Howie said. "Look, if you need anything, a hot meal, an ear to listen, or even a place to crash should an emergency arise, our house is on the next walk over. Just behind the Promethean."

Howie pulled out an old mimeographed flier from his fanny pack. In red marker he wrote his address and phone number over the graphic of a bare-chested man wearing a sailor hat.

"44 and ¼ Picketty Ruff?" Joe smiled as he read it aloud. "Why the one-fourth?"

"Forty-four just wasn't enough," Howie said with a wink. "Don't hesitate to reach out for help should you need it."

"Thanks," Joe said, folding the card up into a small stiff triangle and stuffing it into his back pocket. "That's super nice of you, but the Promethean provides room and board, so I'm all set."

"Wonderful," Howie said. "But don't be surprised if things work out a little differently than you planned. Fire Island is like that. Expect the unexpected—"

"And one or two STDs." Lenny snorted.

"She's being uncouth again," Howie said. "But *do* use condoms. And if you run into any problems . . . like the card says, we're at 44 and ¼ Picketty Ruff." Howie offered his hand. "And welcome to Fire Island."

3.
Hung Out to Dry

"Friends will let you down, even Disco Witch friends, but if you stick around for the next great song, you'll be glad you did."

—*Disco Witch Manifesto #37*

Thanks to Howie and Lenny's directions, it only took Joe two minutes to find Ronnie at the back of the Flotel Motel. When he saw his best friend's face, Joe knew something was up. But then Ronnie confessed why he had avoided meeting Joe at the ferry, and it was way worse than Joe could have imagined.

"No job or housing?" Joe repeated in shock, shivering in the cold of Ronnie's beer-cooler-sized room. "I don't understand. Didn't your friend Scotty Black say the bartending jobs and housing were definite?"

"Not exactly." Ronnie was wearing an Eagles tank top, greasy cut-off shorts, and a pair of yellow rubber cleaning gloves. "And he's not exactly my friend. I guess he meant the jobs were *like* a definite—"

"Jesus, Ronnie!" Joe's stomach clenched anxiously. "What am I going to do?"

"I swear I didn't mean for this to happen." Ronnie snapped off his rubber gloves and then made a cross with his finger atop his right pectoral muscle. "Scotty told me he was pretty sure there would definitely be jobs for us."

"'Pretty sure' or 'definitely'?"

"This is just how these gay vacation places work," Ronnie said. "Workers out here are like gay geese. They spend their summers here and then migrate to Miami or Key West for the winter. Scotty told me that every summer two or three regulars will head to P-town instead or fall in love with someone down at their winter gig; or, sad to say, some have been getting sick and . . . you know, whatever, they don't come back. So, Scotty invited a few more workers than he needs. He said he thought it was a near-sure thing."

"Are you serious?" Joe was livid. "This douche lied to us just in case his bartenders died of AIDS?"

"I guess you could say that's good news, right? Nobody died. We should be happy." Ronnie cast his eyes to the floor like a dog that had been caught chewing up a roll of toilet paper. "Okay, I feel like a twenty-four-karat dickbag," he said. "I shoulda told you it wasn't definite, but then you might not have come—"

"Exactly," Joe spat.

Ronnie looked down at the floor. "Okay, I'll admit it: I just didn't want to do this alone," he said in a way that made Joe know it was finally the truth. "I also worried that if we got separated, I'd lose your friendship, and you're the only best friend and mentee I've ever had. I'm really sorry."

It was pointless for Joe to try and make Ronnie feel any worse—despite it being a clear case of a half-truth. He knew his friend's intentions had been good. But still . . .

"Look, Ronnie, I get it. You were doing your wishful thinking thing again."

"It's called *creative visualization*! I read it in a book by Shakti Gawain. And it works . . . most of the time."

"Right. Cool. Whatever. So what am I going to do? I spent nearly every cent I had to move out here." Joe squeezed his eyes closed. Was this how a life of gay homelessness started?

"We'll figure something out," Ronnie vowed. "Let's keep our positive energies focused!"

"Do you think I could work here at the hotel too?" Joe asked. "I'm not proud. I've been cleaning bedpans for the last two years at Friends Hospital—"

Ronnie shook his head. "I already checked. Scotty said the Flotel only needs one porter. Otherwise, he's only looking for a bouncer at the moment—meaning someone who's huge and looks like a bull mastiff. You're way more beagle than mastiff, unfortunately."

Joe's fingers massaged the burgeoning migraine above his right eye. "I don't think I could even make it to my mom's house tonight. What time is the next ferry back?"

"Don't even think about it," Ronnie said quickly. "Look, I'm not supposed to have guests, but maybe you can crash here for the time being. The cot's too small for two, but we can take turns sleeping on the floor. It'll be a little hard, but I could steal some extra pillows from the supply closet. We just have to make sure you don't get caught. It's not exactly the Ritz, but it'll be fine."

Joe looked around the dank room. Its concrete walls were painted zinc white with cheap royal-blue accents. The tiny cot was shoved up against the wall with a threadbare blanket thrown across the top. A leak stain on the ceiling was ringed with black mold.

"On the floor, huh?" Joey slid down the wall onto the cold cement. A chill shot into his butt cheeks. "At least we'll be ready for them to transfer our bodies to a slab in the morgue."

That ever-present light in Ronnie's eyes dimmed as he flopped onto the cot in defeat. "I fucked up, okay? I wanted this to be our momentous transformational summer. Maybe my positive thinking was a little too positive, huh?"

Just as Joe was picturing himself sleeping on the beach, hair a tangled mess, begging muscle-bound men for sips off their protein shakes, he felt a sudden stab from the triangular folded club card stashed in his back pocket. "Oh, hey, I forgot." He pulled the flier out and unfolded it. "I met these two old guys when I got off the ferry. They said if I got stuck, I could crash with them. They wrote their address on this."

Ronnie's brow arched. "They literally just offered you a place out of nowhere?"

"Yeah. I know. Do ya think they were serious?"

Looking closer at the wrinkled mimeograph, Ronnie's eyes grew wide. "Holy crap, this club card has to be from the seventies.

Crisco Disco? Why the heck would he have something like this with him? And what the hell kind of address is that?"

"I have no idea." Joe took the flier back. "It could mean not sleeping on the floor, right?"

"I sure hope they aren't a couple of gay cannibals is all I can say."

Joe laughed. "Not these guys. They're really nice. A little like a Tom and Jerry cartoon—only older and gay. They clean houses and stuff."

"Crashing with two old house cleaners?" Ronnie said. "You gotta be careful who you associate with out here. You don't wanna be pegged as the *help*."

Joey picked up the toilet brush from Ronnie's cleaning supply caddy and waved it with his best Bea Arthur deadpan. "Seriously, Hazel?"

"As I said, it's temporary."

"Exactly. Same as me spending a couple of nights at Howie and Lenny's. Maybe they'll even know about other places I could stay or work. Where is Picketty Ruff anyway?"

Ronnie opened a map of Fire Island Pines that showed the grid of little walks and boulevards on the nearly vehicle-free island. "Hey, whad'ya know!" He pointed out his window to a tall wooden fence. "It's just on the other side of that. Like fifty feet away."

"That's bitchin'." Joe picked up his duffel bag, a fresh wind filling his lungs. "I mean I should at least go check it out, right?"

"I get off at four. I can go with you then—"

"Naw," Joe said. "I wanna go while they still remember they made the offer. Don't you always say I should never miss a good opportunity?"

"Yes, I do, l'il buddy." Ronnie placed his hand on Joe's shoulder. "Just be careful, okay? If stuff gets weird, just scream in this direction."

4.
44 and ¼ Picketty Ruff

"Beware the stranger and sinner, for their outlandish ways might transform you into the most glorious being known to the heavens."
—*Disco Witch Manifesto #14*

Unlike the predominant natural wood tones or pale neutrals of the other houses in the Pines, 44 and ¼ Picketty Ruff was the color of dried blood. To approach the front door one had to cross a ten-foot bridge over a moatlike drainage ditch and pass through a small gate that slammed closed like a gunshot, scattering the crows sitting in the nearby holly tree. On the front door was an ornate wreath with a laminated photo of Edith Piaf at its center.

Before Joe could even lift his hand to knock, he heard Howie's voice sing out from within, "Joe's here!" A second later the door opened to reveal Howie in a flowery caftan, beaming. "Come right on in, Joe! Take a seat. Relax—I'll make us a snack."

At first, the house's decor reminded Joe of his late Aunt Vartu's with all its mismatched 1970s colonial-style furniture and too many tchotchkes. But then he started to notice the differences, like the arty male nude photos and how the wall hangings and bric-a-brac, like much of the jewelry Howie wore, were mostly of religious icons from around the world: the elephant god Ganesha; the emaciated, fasting Buddha; one that looked half bird, half human; a bevy of extra-bloody

Christian martyrs; a goddess with snakes clutched in her upraised fists; and many more. Along with all this religious Grand Guignol kitsch, the stereo was blasting a cassette of 1970s-era disco music.

Lenny sat on a shabby, flower-patterned sofa, his eyes glued to Joe since the moment he walked in.

"Nice music," Joe lied, hoping to make a good impression.

"Do you like it?" Howie hollered from the kitchen.

"Yeah," Joe lied again. "It's great dinner music."

"It's actually morning music," Lenny corrected. "We're just starting late today."

"Oh," Joe said. "Wow, that'll sure wake you up."

"That particular track is 'La Vie en Rose' by Grace Jones. DJ Robbie Leslie finished his set with it at the 1978 Black Party at approximately eight thirty in the morning."

"Wow." Joe's eyes widened. "You remember that?"

Lenny raised one eyebrow. "I remember everything." He gestured to the shelves of bookcases lined with hundreds of homemade cassette tapes. "We keep bootleg recordings of all our favorite dance parties."

To demonstrate his enthusiasm and hopefully get on Lenny's good side, Joe looked through the cassettes, nodding and mmm-hmming. Unlike Elliot's *Love Songs 1*, Howie and Lenny's mixtapes were decorated with colorful ink drawings and handwritten calligraphic titles like *Beach Mix, 1979*; *DJ Roy Thode, the Saint, Opening Night, 1981*; and *DJ Leslie, the Saint Finale, May 2, 1988*; that particular tape's insert had hand-painted gold stars, moons, and a gravestone that said "R.I.P."

"You really went to all those parties?" Joe gushed. "That must've been something else." He felt slimy, faking it like that. The truth was, he had been totally clueless about music until he'd met Elliot, whose passion for the topic had been infectious. Joe found himself liking anything Elliot liked, from blues to contemporary rock, to world music and folk. Rikki Lee, Joni Mitchell, Pat Metheny. But when it came to dance music, Elliot had decidedly been of the "disco-sucks" school of thought. Joe had followed suit. But at that moment, to avoid sleeping on Ronnie's cold floor, he'd need to feign disco fandom. "This collection is seriously rad. All the greats. I really appreciate you letting me crash here."

"Who said we'd decided?" Lenny snipped. "Me and Howie have to have a little discussion first." He lowered his voice, leaning in toward Joe. "You know, our best friend, Max, will be coming out here eventually, so don't even think about trying to steal his spot. Capeesh?"

"I'm not here to steal anything." A ball of fear filled Joe's stomach. If he lost this opportunity, he'd be condemned to Ronnie's pneumonia-inducing floor—and even that wasn't a guarantee. "It would just be temporary. I promise."

"That's what they all say." Lenny's nasally whisper rose in irritation. "I know how you pretty boys like to roll."

"Pretty boy?" If he hadn't been so desperate, Joe would have laughed out loud. "I have no idea what you think I'm trying to do, but—"

"Oh, sure, play dumb, but if you think you're gonna—"

A large metal spoon smashed into the sink, startling Joe while Lenny fell silent. Howie rushed into the living room, his maroon bathrobe flying behind him, slamming down a plate of Hickory Farms cheese logs, grapes, and Ritz crackers on the coffee table.

"Leonardo Gennaro Vincenzo D'Amico!" he shouted, wagging his finger. "You're being your mother again!"

Lenny shrugged, scrunching what little neck he had, looking guilty. "I was just—"

Howie put his hand up to silence him. "As I said. You and I will talk and then decide. Meanwhile, Joseph darling, just ignore our bad seed here. She takes time to warm up to folks—"

"Said the necrophiliac," Lenny muttered.

Joe laughed, more out of nerves and a desire to win him over.

"Don't bother humoring him," Howie said. "Lenny's Sicilian. He hates change." Then, to Lenny, "Joe wouldn't be staying in Max's room anyway. Both of you, follow me!"

Howie opened what looked like a closet door between the kitchen and bathroom and pulled down a ladder. As he climbed, he hummed the melody to "Try to Remember" from *The Fantasticks*, singing out the words, "Follow, follow, follow!"

Remembering Ronnie's warning, Joe wondered if cannibals sang show tunes.

"Go on, no point in wasting time," Lenny said in an ominous whisper—or that's how Joe heard it. "*Follow*, like she just sang. Howie always gets his way."

Joe warily climbed up the ladder. As soon as he stepped into the attic, he was instantly hit with a burst of sauna-hot air. It smelled of cedar, dusty old insulation, and something else he couldn't name but vaguely recalled smelling before. There were shelves and boxes everywhere, and the walls and beams were covered with framed vintage photographs.

"Wow. Are all these photos of you guys?"

"Oh my, no," Howie said. "These shots go back to the forties. We're just the most recent in a long line of holy lovers who have occupied 44 and ¼ Picketty Ruff."

"Holy lovers?" Joe's eyes widened in realization. "I was trying to figure out if you two were boyfriends or not."

Both men did comedically dramatic retching sounds, indicating Joe had horribly missed his mark. "Boyfriends?" Howie laughed. "Of course, we've slept together. I mean we're gay and all. But now we've settled into one of those typical Boston marriages by way of *Who's Afraid of Virginia Woolf.*"

"When Howie says 'holy lovers,' he just means *homos*," Lenny quipped.

"Lenny!" Howie chided. "You know it's more than that." He touched the tips of his fingers together under his nose, like a professor. "We use the phrase to mean any person whose identity or desire for love lies outside the commonplace. We believe the Great Goddess Mother has blessed all inverts, queers, sissies, trans folk, dykes, two spirits, asexuals, bisexuals, pansexuals, and what-have-yous with extraordinary gifts and with the preternatural ability to love much more expansively."

"Oh," Joe said, pretending it was the most normal thing in the world. "Gotcha. And you two and Max all live and work out here the whole year?"

"Goodness, no," Howie exclaimed. "Lenny goes to Florida at the first hint of cold, and Max goes back to the city to stay with his boyfriend, Heshy. I'm the only one who hibernates out here during the offseason. But with the first sniff of spring, I emerge, pretty like a crocus and buzzing like a locust."

Joe gave a small laugh and wiped the beads of sweat on his forehead.

"You think *this* is hot?" Lenny warned. "Come midsummer, it's like a Turkish bath."

"We have fans he can use," Howie said. "And at night there's a wonderful cross breeze. We'll just need to shuffle things around a little. Lenny, help me."

They started moving boxes off the shelves, each labeled with their contents: feathers, rhinestones, leather scraps, dolls' heads, glass eyeballs, and more. At the front of the attic were two old sewing machines on a desk, two mannequins of different sizes, a handmade tree with branches festooned with hundreds of spools of colorful threads, organized by hue and shade—cool colors at the bottom, warm colors at the top. There were piles of lace, big jars of dolls' body parts, milk crates piled high with vintage fur—animal heads still attached.

"Max and I had been using the attic as our workroom," Howie said, huffing and puffing after the climb upstairs. "But I think, with a little elbow grease, it could be a very cozy bedroom. Now, if you'll pardon us, Lenny and I are going to the kitchen for a little tête-à-tête. Hold tight."

As soon as they were downstairs, Joe heard them bickering. Too nervous to listen, he turned his attention to the old photos covering the walls and beams. On the lower right corner of each was a white slip of paper bearing a handwritten date, location, or event where the photo was taken. Things like "Fire Island Party on the Beach, 1979," "Provincetown, August 1969," "Key West, 1962." Joe, who'd first had sex with a man in 1982, the year after the virus was identified, wondered how much the gay world had changed since the crisis began. How much fun had they had before making love turned into a death threat?

Several of the shots were of a much younger Howie Fishbein in crazy outfits and long brown hair, his head crowned with enormous, ornate hats featuring dioramas or not-so-miniature millinery installations. One hat featured an entire castle with an Elizabethan-costumed Barbie doll in the process of being decapitated. Was it? Yes, it was! Geneviève Bujold as Anne Boleyn in *Anne of a Thousand Days*. Lenny (with more hair) was dressed as the executioner, complete with leather apron and a mask, but otherwise naked. There were always several other men (and a few women) with them, all dressed outlandishly, including a Hispanic-looking man, dressed in beads and crazy headgear, who appeared at the center of every group photo. *Is this Max?* And why were they all dressed that way?

Joe had never dressed in anything close to flamboyant. Preferring to blend in, he'd get the straightest-looking haircut (no Flock of Seagulls for him), shirts from Sears, khakis from JC Penny. Ronnie was vehemently opposed to doing drag—he said it would destroy his image as a "sexy gay jock." For Joe, seeing Howie and Lenny wear their gayness with such abandon was both shocking and impressive. How freeing that must feel. For a few minutes he found himself lost in the photos, staring at the faces, searching for . . . something, but he didn't know what. It was almost like he could hear the music that must have been playing back then, smell the patchouli, feel the warmth of their vests, the chill of their love beads.

The darkest, hidden corner of the attic was filled with the most risqué photos of groups of naked men either having sex or just sitting around the house naked. These photos were much older, and all in black and white. But he experienced the same thing, finding himself unable to look away as if the men in the photos were casting a spell on him.

But then Joe heard footsteps on the ladder, and he quickly stepped away from the lurid photos.

"Don't worry!" Howie poked up his head through the floor hatch. "Those orgies were way before we moved into this house!" Stepping into the attic, he walked over and pointed to one very vivid image. "How nice to capture oneself in the midst of such passion! Sadly, most of those men are gone now . . . but not all. You'll meet a few this summer—though you may not recognize them. Such is the brutality of time and deliquescence."

Joe blinked, confused. "What?"

"Getting old," Howie clarified.

"Ah, okay," Joe said. "I love all these old pics . . . especially that Anne Boleyn one, and these over here." He gestured to the shots that had entranced him the most. "It's weird. It's almost hard to stop looking at them."

"Is that so?" Howie said, again in that strange, puzzling way.

"Yeah, they're really great." Joe pointed to another one of several clothed men jammed onto what looked like a newer version of the downstairs couch. Younger Lenny, sporting a bad comb-over, sat between a younger Howie and that wildly dressed Hispanic man. "Is that Max?" Joe asked.

"Indeed it is," Howie said. "Maximon Esteban Hieronymus De Laguna. He's the most important stooge in our Three-Stoogian triumvirate—the Moe of 'mos, we like to joke. You'll love him, and he'll love you. That photo is from our first year on the island, when we had dozens staying here. Our orgies, though un-photographed, lasted days. Bliss exploded everywhere, staining everything and everyone with joy."

"The cleaning bills were a fortune!" Lenny called from the base of the ladder before scampering up into the attic and pointing to a photo of a twenty-something man wearing a thong in a bodybuilder's pose. "See that one? I was a hot piece of mortadella, huh?"

"That's *you*?" Joe said, sounding far too surprised. Lenny sucked in his cheeks, his eyes narrowed bitterly. "I mean," Joe nervously added, "that's *obviously* you. It's uncanny . . . you've barely aged."

Howie then—in an obvious appeasement to Lenny—gently turned Joe's face to the light. "To be honest, Joseph, you remind me a bit of Lenny when he was your age."

The thought that he could he ever turn into someone like Lenny, with his bald head, dyed black mustache, and squat bowling-pin body distressed Joe more than a little. But then, when he saw Howie's wink, he quickly nodded. "Sure," he said. "I can see what you mean."

"You think?" Lenny smiled cockily, looking at both himself and Joe in a nearby mirror. "I was a little better looking at your age, of course—"

"Don't push it, Lenny," Howie muttered. "So shall we all agree that Joseph here, who looks practically like your son—brother, I mean, *little* brother—will be our temporary guest in the attic?"

Lenny sighed with resignation. "Okay," he said, "but he's got to pay rent and share the chores while he's here."

"Of course!" Howie gushed. "I'm sure young Joseph will be happy to help."

"Definitely," Joe agreed.

"Good! Then we want at least twenty-five dollars a night!" Lenny said.

Joe's heart sank. Twenty-five dollars was more than his budget. "I don't think I can afford that. I only brought seven hundred dollars with me. I need to stretch it until I get a job."

"Great work, Miss Fishbein." Lenny folded his arms while adding a harrumph. "Suddenly we've turned into a Bowery flophouse for indigent twinks."

"Oh, just stop," Howie said, brushing Lenny off. "Joe'll get a job as quick as you can spit. There's the Seahorse clothing store or one of the two liquor stores or . . . wait a minute. I'm an idiot! I've got a fabulous idea! Joe, wait up here one minute. Lenny, come with me."

Howie and Lenny scrambled down the ladder again. Joe heard the phone being dialed and then Howie talking to somebody. A few minutes later, the men scrambled their way back into the attic. At first, Howie looked dire but then quickly broke into a broad smile.

"You have a job interview at five PM today with Dory the Boozehound."

"A job interview?" Joe's heart bubbled with the news. "But how . . . I mean, with *who*?"

"Dory the Boozehound. You'll adore her. She's eighty years young, rich, and fabulous."

"Owns a bar called Asylum Harbor," Lenny added.

Howie pointed out the front window. "Adorable little bucket of blood just across and down the walk. Dory's part of our inner circle—a bodhisattva if there ever was one. So many people with AIDS have spent their final hours lying on her deck, watching the waves, listening to their favorite disco tracks until it's time for them to go."

"You mean"—Joe's voice cracked with an emotion—"they die in her house?"

"They do," Howie said. "Dory believes it's her responsibility to try and give those in need a beautiful place to cross over. Right now, one of our dearest friends, Saint D'Norman, is staying with her. He was terribly sick last year, but he's so much better now. Praise the Great Goddess Mother. I'll tell you more about Dory and Saint D'Norman later, but you should go get your things, and then get ready. Meanwhile, Lenny and I will get your room in shape. Let's say seventy-five dollars per week for now? A little more after you get established. Would that work?"

"Yeah . . . I mean . . . wow." Joe couldn't believe his bad luck was finally turning around. "So I can stay? Seriously?"

"Only until Max moves back," Lenny corrected.

"Of course," Howie replied, winking at Joe. "Something like that."

5.
Dory the Boozehound

"The lesbians, fag hags, and transsexuals shall save your wounded ass."
—Disco Witch Manifesto #12

Dorothy Lieberman-Delagrange, aka "Dory the Boozehound," had just celebrated her eightieth birthday with a luncheon feast of chicken paillard at the 21 Club. After a slice of candle-torched chocolate mousse, she and her granddaughter, Elena, took a car out to Sayville to catch the ferry to Fire Island Pines. "Saint D'Norman is thrilled you're spending the whole summer," she told Elena. "He's been fixing up your room all week."

"That's sweet of him," Elena said, half listening, as her finger drew a woman's teary face in the steamed-up ferry window. Huge, liquescent tears ran down its foggy cheek.

Elena was an unparalleled beauty—when she wanted to be. She had perfect caramel-brown skin and haunting green eyes that were preternaturally large. She often complained that she looked like a sloth when she didn't wear makeup, ignoring the fact of having been a successful model since the age of fourteen—the first Black girl ever to appear three times on the cover of *Twentieth-Century Girl* magazine. With all the trauma of the previous two years, including the two stints in Bellevue—which Dory had only found out about after the fact—it was no surprise that Elena was considering retiring at the ripe old age of twenty-three. When Dory suggested that she come out to Fire Island for the summer before making any serious life-altering decisions, Elena responded with one of her expressionless shrugs. "Why not?" she mumbled. "An island filled with men ignoring me sounds like the perfect oblivion."

Dory fingered Elena's lovely golden-brown curls tied into a bouquet atop her head. She loved her granddaughter more than anyone else in the world and was devastated at the thought that her precious girl had tried to end her own life—more than once.

Whatever caused her to feel this unhappy, I'm sure Fire Island can heal her, Dory thought. *If any place can . . .*

Dory's relationship to Fire Island Pines was far different from most residents'. Her roots in the community dated back to the 1920s, when her white, Jewish father Milty "Gutterjuice" Lieberman, at the behest of his Black, Seventh Day Adventist wife, stopped bootlegging and went into real estate, purchasing dozens of acres of the barrier island. Years after his death, Dory made a small fortune selling the bulk of the property. For sentimental reasons she kept a half-acre plot on Ocean Walk, though for decades she'd never set foot on it, turned off by Fire Island's notoriously racist, (mostly) white inhabitants.

But then in 1970, recently widowed Dory became involved with a mystical cabal of gay clubbers in Manhattan's nascent disco scene. During a night of intense dancing at the Loft, she had a vision where her late father, Milty, appeared to her and told her she should build a great house on the vacant Fire Island property and open a "sleazy little gay bar" in the Pines.

So she did. The house she built was a magnificent six-bedroom beachfront paradise, complete with floor-to-ceiling windows looking out on the great Atlantic. It became the perfect summer retreat for her club friends (of all races) to celebrate their annual three-day-long, highly decadent Summer Solstice Party. Dory, who had always been vociferously straight, became an even greater star of the gay community, and she set her sights on opening the gay bar.

Unfortunately, with the dearth of commercially zoned property in the Pines, she was forced to lease a sordid little upstairs bar space from Scotty Black—a greedy and unpleasant man whom she, and many others, detested. Scotty, wanting to pocket as much money as he could from Dory, proffered a completely unfair agreement for the bar: he not only was asking an exorbitant price, but the contract was stuffed like a capon with stipulations, caveats, and red flags. Despite her lawyer's pleas not to sign, she'd had no other options in the tiny harbor—Scotty Black owned everything. So, wanting to honor her father's otherworldly wishes, Dory went ahead with the agreement.

Within a month of signing, she opened Asylum Harbor, a quaint little rough-and-tumble "cruise bar" where one could grab a hot boy and cold beer all within a matter of minutes. Dory's bar quickly became a huge success, and by the late 1970s had been declared the best bar in Fire Island Pines. But then AIDS arrived, decimating the clientele and many of her dearest friends. With fewer and fewer customers showing up at Asylum Harbor, the threat of Scotty Black exercising some of those shady, contractual stipulations was becoming more and more real—including his right to close the bar for good.

Just as Dory and Elena arrived at her beach house, they heard the telephone ringing. Before they could get their shoes off, Saint D'Norman, a lean, fifty-something, gay Black man with a melon-bald head and a Steinway keyboard smile, walked over to Dory, dragging a receiver attached to an extremely long spiral telephone cord.

"It appears you have an important call, Dor." Saint D'Norman rolled his ennui-ridden eyes. His years having worked as a nurse, not to mention membership in Dory and Howie's secret dance coven, gave him an air of stoic amusement no matter what was before him, be it a burnt appetizer or the apocalypse. As he handed Dory the telephone, he raised a single very aristocratic eyebrow. "It's Howie. He sounds ... um ... overly excited."

"Of course, my dear." Dory shared a knowing smile with Saint D'Norman, her closest confident and, as needed, executive assistant/major domo. "Now, if you could show my granddaughter our dear Alan's old room. She'll adore the view."

"Of course." Saint D'Norman smiled and pointed to the stairs. "Just up there. I remember you when you were just a sneaky little dandelion. Look at you growing into a gorgeous sunflower!"

Once they were out of earshot, Dory lifted the phone. "Howie, darling, how are you?"

"I'm fine, thanks be to the goddess," Howie's voice buzzed through the earpiece. "It's preseason madness, natch. Lots of owners with their hair transplants on fire ..." He took a breath. "Dor, the reason I'm calling is, are you still looking for a bartender for Asylum Harbor?"

"I am. Do you know someone?"

"I think I do. Scotty Black pulled a fast one, and this poor kid named Joe found himself out here jobless, homeless, and with barely a penny to his name. We're temporarily sheltering him in our attic like Shirley Temple in *The Little Princess*."

Dory certainly needed a bartender. She also despised how the tyrannical Scotty Black reveled at playing goddess with other people's lives. Still, the bartender position was far too important to give away just for spite or to please one of her dearest friends.

"What's he look like?" Dory said, getting down to business. "I need a real five-star stud."

"Well, I haven't seen him shirtless or anything. But he looks like the love child of Sal Mineo and Montgomery Cliff. Eyebrows like two large, melancholy chinchillas about to mate."

"Mmm." Dory had always been a fan of overwrought eyebrows.

"Appears to have a furry chest too—which is like hens' teeth out here lately. His aura is all over the place—lots of blue and indigo among a torrent of dark bands. I sense something tragic happened in his past. What exactly—I can't see it. I'm hoping when Max gets out here, he'll be able to give him a solid read. The main thing is he's got this mesmerizing swirl of contradictions: butch but vulnerable, smart, sexy, sweet, and curious at the same time. He also yearns, Dory. He *yearns*."

"Ooh, I like that too," Dory said. "One can't be truly beautiful without yearning."

"Exactly. Customers will either want to fuck him or adopt him."

Dory lowered her voice. "What about the package?"

"Not that I've noticed . . ." Howie cleared his throat knowingly. "However, it appears as if he's hiding a liverwurst sandwich down the front of his Levi's. All the old geezers will be blowing their pensions on your best top-shelf liquor just to stare."

Dory closed her eyes as an image of her father flashed across her brain. He was nodding his head.

"Have him at my bar at five," Dory said. "If he's half of what you say, the job is his."

6.
A Room of One's Own

"Keep your dirty secrets in bedazzled boxes."
—*Disco Witch Manifesto #126*

"Try this," Ronnie said, handing Joe a skimpy, sleeveless Gold's Gym T-shirt that had been cut off at the midriff.

While Howie and Lenny were setting up the attic, Joe had run back to Ronnie's room at the Flotel to borrow something more appropriate to wear for his five PM interview.

"Where'd you get this?" Joe asked, squeezing himself into the shirt. "The kids' department at Woolworths?"

"It's not The First Pennsylvania Bank—it's a gay bar. They wanna see your guns and your tits."

Joe checked himself in the mirror. The shirt did make his arms looks bigger. It also exposed the furry treasure trail that perfectly bisected his stomach. "Wow . . . I look kinda good."

"More than *kinda*! You'd give Tony Danza a run for his money. Now, let me see your tightest jeans—we may need to rip 'em in the crotch."

When Joe got back to 44 and ¼ Picketty Ruff, the boys were still banging around upstairs, so he dragged his duffel into the bathroom to shower and get ready for his interview. When he emerged twenty minutes later, Howie and Lenny were on the couch, hands folded, smiling mischievously.

"Look at you!" Howie exclaimed. "So handsome!"

"Not bad." Lenny nodded approvingly. "Ripped crotch. Nice touch. Trampy, but not overboard."

"Ronnie is a genius at gay stuff," Joe said. "Can I see the attic yet?"

"We hope you like it," Howie said, winking at Lenny.

Joe climbed up the attic ladder with his duffel. As soon as his head cleared the hatch, he let out a Hollywood-worthy gasp. The attic had been completely transformed. All the boxes were gone, and the shelves had been rearranged, creating enough room for a bureau, a fully made-up queen-sized mattress, and a nightstand with a campy lamp featuring a male hula dancer and a stack of old books.

"Do you like it?" Howie asked from just below Joe on the ladder.

"It's incredible," he said, stepping up into the newly created bedroom.

"The mattress is practically new!" Lenny shouted up. "We stole it—I mean *commandeered* it from one of the houses we clean!"

"They won't mind," Howie added. "They're Merv Griffin rich. Besides, they switched to waterbeds. By the way, that afghan was knitted by a wonderful transsexual up in Provincetown. The wool is from a herd of holy Guatemalan alpacas. Feel the energy. It'll keep you safe from any terrible nightmares . . . or at least the useless ones."

Joe dropped his duffel and rubbed his hands across the soft orange and brown afghan before letting his exhausted body fall onto the giant angel-food-cake mattress. "This is the most comfortable bed I've ever been in," he said. "Thank you so much. You really didn't need to do all this."

"Oh, poo!" Howie waved his hand. "We're gay. We'd redecorate the inside of a milk carton given the chance."

Joe got up from the bed to explore all that was new in the room, including a just-bought shiny padlock on the crawl space next to the ladder. "Is that where you stashed all your stuff?" he asked, stepping toward the small door. "Maybe I could also use it for a closet."

Lenny leaped in front of Joe, blocking him. "You can't go in there," he snapped.

Joe jerked backward, noticing the anxious look in Lenny's eyes. "But I was just—"

"What Lenny means is"—Howie tittered as if he were embarrassed by Lenny's overly dramatic response—"we keep some very important things in there: old supplies, relics, and whatnot."

"Relics?" Joe asked.

"Unfortunately, we've lost a number of friends over the past few years," Howie said.

"One hundred and six in total," Lenny chimed in glumly. "Eighty-two of 'em were close friends."

"*Eighty-two?*" A lump of pain filled Joe's throat. He had lost only Elliot, and the grief had paralyzed him. To have lost that many seemed unfathomable. "I'm so sorry."

"Thank you, Joe." Howie looked over to one of the group photos. "When we helped clean out their apartments, we wanted to keep what was most precious to them."

"Or sometimes we just kept *them*." Lenny shrugged.

Joe offered a small laugh, assuming it was a joke. Lenny, however, did not laugh. The hairs on Joe's neck prickled.

"As usual," Howie said, smiling, "Lenny lacks nuance. Yes, there might be an urn or seven with some ashes, but mostly, as I said, just a few keepsakes, as well as our favorite old dance outfits and some crafting supplies."

"Nice euphemism," Lenny said.

"Shh," Howie spat. "Now isn't the time." He turned to Joe and smiled. "The one thing we ask here is that we all respect one another's private spaces. I'm sure you understand . . ."

"Of course." Joe stepped away from the crawl space. "I promise not to be nosy." To change the subject, he gestured to a desk that had been set up on the other side of the attic. "That wasn't there before."

"We figured you could use it." Lenny crossed to the old oak executive desk with pride. "This way you can do your studying to get into medical school."

The blood in Joe's veins grew cold. "How do you know about that?" he asked, trying not to sound as disturbed as he was. "I never told you anything about med school."

"Don't get your jockeys into a knot." Lenny groaned as he fiddled with a vase of fresh African daisies on the desk. "Parfait Bob over at the liquor store gave us the skinny."

"I don't know any Parfait Bob," Joe said, confused.

Howie sat on the alpaca bedspread and sighed. "You know how it is: tell-a-gay, tel-e-phone. I suspect your friend Ronnie must've lovingly bragged to someone who told somebody who told Parfait Bob. Don't worry. We aren't stalkers, and we certainly can't read minds."

"Speak for yourself," Lenny muttered.

"What Lenny means is, on this island the hagiographies of handsome men spread faster than chlamydia. But I will say, my instincts say you will make a fantastic doctor."

"Damn right," Lenny added. "You'll look swell in green scrubs with all that chest hair and swarthy coloring—a gay Doctor Kildare."

Joe smiled, though he still felt out of sorts with the idea of strangers talking about him.

"Don't hold your breath," he said. "The doctor thing is just a pipe dream. I got drunk one night and told Ronnie about it. Now he's decided I just need to 'positive think' my way into med school. He even recites daily affirmations for both of us. It's a little woo-woo nuts."

"It's not the worst approach." Lenny was back to fiddling with the daisies. "Though the efficacy rate is low, it's not zero."

"*Anyway . . .*" Howie stood up. "We should let you unpack before your interview."

"Yeah, I probably should." Joe dropped his duffel on the bureau. Looking around, he noticed there were several prominent discolored blank spots on the wall where photos had been removed—including the Anne Boleyn decapitation photo. "Why did you take those old photos down?" he asked. "They were pretty boss."

"Oh, right," Howie said. "We wanted to make space for you to put up your own photos."

The only photo Joe had with him was one of him and Elliot together on the beach at Ocean City. It was, in fact, the only clear photo he had of Elliot at all. All the others had been smudged or destroyed in the basement flood. In the snapshot, Elliot wears his favorite white-and-yellow rugby shirt and is playing the guitar—the slash of the dimple, the jut of his lower lip—while Joe lies on his side, facing him, his back to the camera. It was taken shortly after they first fell in love, before Elliot got sick, before everything.

"I don't have any photos," Joe lied.

"Then you must take some this summer!" Howie said. "Trust an old queen, Joe. We *are* what we remember. You'll understand one day. Anyway, we're off to go clean a house on Bay Walk. But first I have something for you." He handed Joe a tiny, handsewn, saffron-colored pouch. "It's a little good luck charm I whipped up—a mix of protective and relaxing herbs. It might be useful. You never know."

"Thanks." Joe sniffed the little packet, which smelled mostly of lavender and jasmine, but with darker undertones—mold and camphor. "Smells interesting."

"Come on," Lenny whined. "We got crap to do!"

Joe shoved the charm into his back pocket and listened for the screen door slamming, followed by the rattle of their cleaning cart rolling down the walk. As he unpacked, his eyes kept wandering to the empty spaces on the walls and the locked crawl space.

They were definitely hiding something.

7.

The Interview

"You will know the Great Balance has arrived when all fighting ceases, when love, sex, and joy reign supreme."
—*Disco Witch Manifesto #8*

At 4:17 PM Joe went into the bathroom to tame his wavy thicket of black hair with some of Howie's emerald-green Dippity-do. It was always a balancing act between trying to look more like Richard Gere and less like Elvis. He shaved the stubbly connecting patch of what would have been a pronounced unibrow. (While Elliot had loved Joe's unibrow, Ronnie had declared it a definite no-go.) Looking at himself in the mirror, he imitated Ronnie's seductive swagger: "Time to seduce Dory the Boozehound."

As directed by Howie, the bar was just a short hop down Picketty Ruff and up a flight of stairs over one of the two clothing boutiques that sold mostly Speedos, go-go shorts, and mesh tank tops. When Joe arrived at the door of Asylum Harbor, his heart sank. It was a one-story, gray clapboard structure with two darkened portico windows and a deck outside—more like a large storage shed than a proper bar. Its only exterior decoration was a white, circular life preserver placed next to the door with "Asylum Harbor" sloppily painted around the ring.

After taking a deep breath, he walked in. At first he could barely make out anything in the dim bar except for the silhouettes of two women, one short, the other tall, sitting at opposite ends of the long wooden counter.

"Mrs. Lieberman-Delagrange?" he said.

"Yes, Joe, come in!" The older woman's voice was warm and friendly, as if Joe had just offered her a piece of coffee cake. "But please call me Dory."

When Joe's eyes adjusted to the light, he could see that Dory, a Black woman, looked far younger than Howie had said, more sixty-something than eighty. She was elegantly dressed in a white skirt and a navy-and-white-striped blouse. Her short lavender-gray Afro was topped with a jaunty little sailor's cap. She definitely didn't resemble anyone nicknamed "the Boozehound." In fact, her twinkling dark eyes made Joe instantly feel calmer. The younger woman sitting at the end of the bar wore an oversized sweatshirt that said "Click Models." Rather than greeting Joe, she just sat there, sipping her can of Tab and reading a paperback version of *Anna Karenina* held in the light of a small red lamp. Despite her disheveled appearance and no makeup, she was strikingly beautiful, with flawless caramel skin and golden-brown curls.

"Come, Joe! Please sit!" Dory gestured to a barstool next to her. "That lovely though taciturn young woman at the end of the bar is my granddaughter, Elena. So, dear, you've bartended before?"

"Um . . . a little," Joe said. "Like at parties at my parents' house. Oh, right—I was also kind of a busboy at a restaurant during college, and . . . well . . . I *watched* the bartenders *a lot* . . . and . . . um . . ." Joe's face grew red at how lame he sounded.

"Doesn't matter," Dory said. "The vast majority of our customers drink beer or simple stuff like vodka cranberries. Maybe a martini once in a while. My drink is gin and tonic. Two slices of lime. Very clean. My father was a bootlegger on the island. Kept his still out where the Meat Rack is."

Meat Rack? Joe thought, gathering it must be either another gay bar or perhaps a butcher shop.

Dory continued, "His gin running is why I'm here . . . it's why we're all here, I must say. If it weren't for him getting rich off the hooch, then buying and selling property out here on the island, there might never have been a Pines nor a me nor an Elena nor ... I'm sorry, I can ramble. Just tell me to shut up."

"It's okay," Joe said. "I love hearing old stories like that."

"You're very sweet." Dory smiled and stroked his cheek. "Anyway, any of the more complicated cocktails you can learn from a book behind the bar, isn't that right, Elena?"

Elena finally, but briefly, looked up at Joe with an expression somewhere between disdain and deadpan. "Sure. Why not," she mumbled before looking back down at her Tolstoy.

Joe couldn't believe her rudeness. She could have just said something pleasant, even if she didn't mean it—just as a sign of respect for her grandmother.

"I'm a pretty fast learner," Joe said. "I was great in chemistry in high school."

"Marvelous!" Dory gave one definitive clap of her hands. "I like your spirit. Howie was right as usual. You're absolutely adorable! You'll just have to meet Vince, the bar manager, but I'm almost certain he'll love you."

"Does that mean I have the job?" Joe asked, excitement bubbling around his heart.

"You do," Dory said with a smile, "at least conditionally. Let me give Vince a call ..."

Just then the front door pushed open, and a burst of bright light slapped the dim bar awake. There, standing in the door, was a man in his thirties, with a skinhead crew cut, black Fred Perry polo, and taut arms, mapped with rivers of veins and dozens of tattoos.

"Dory?" the man said with an Irish accent. "What are you doing here this time of day?"

"Well, look who it is." Dory's face lit up. "I was just about to call you. I've found our perfect *hot* bartender. This is Joe."

Dory's designation of Joe as a "hot" bartender made his cheeks and ears grow warm. Elena, looking up from her book, giggled at Joe's embarrassment. Vince, however, did not look happy.

"*You* found our new bartender, is it?" The pique in Vince's voice rose. "I thought we talked about this, Dor. As manager, I should be the one who decides on the second bartender."

All of Joe's excitement from a moment before bled out onto the dirty barroom floor. Once again he felt the chill of impending joblessness.

"I know you're the manager, Vince," Dory said, "but you've been interviewing for weeks, and I have this gut feeling about Joe—"

"Look, Dor, if you're not going to trust my expertise, why in the bollox did you hire me in the first place?"

Joe saw that Elena had stopped reading her book and was now watching the tense exchange between Dory and the Irishman. She appeared not to like the disrespectful tone Vince was using with her grandmother.

"Vince, you don't need to be so dramatic," Dory said. "I do trust you, but the bar opens this weekend, and you can't be bartending alone—"

"We can't be feckin' around, Dor, hiring any shitehawk piece of chicken that falls off the ferry."

Joe felt Elena's eyes skirt over to him. He tried to mask the wound of Vince's comment, but his face, unfortunately, showed everything, so he looked down at the floor.

"Vincent," Dory reprimanded. "Don't be rude."

"Apologies," he mumbled. "Look, we have a limited amount of time to start making a profit before Scotty Black finally has a reason to—"

"Cork it, Lucky Charms!" Dory slapped her ring-covered hand on the counter as her eyes turned to black ice. Gone was the sweet, elegant grandmother. *Here* was Dory the Boozehound, daughter of a bootlegger. "I'm well aware of the situation. And yes, you're the manager, but *I* pay the checks. I'd suggest you remember that." Vince's tight lips softened, making him look more like a chastised son then an irate employee. Dory's fierce black eyes melted into a cajoling twinkle. "Now, are we done with our little tantrum, Vincent?"

Vince rolled his eyes as a small smile battled its way onto his lips. Joe breathed a sigh of relief. That Dory and Vince clearly liked each other gave him some hope, but then he wondered, *What exactly do they mean by "the situation"? Is the bar in trouble?*

"I'm sorry, Dory," Vince finally said. "I'm just a bit tense with the opening. You know how much I care about this bar."

"I do, Vince," Dory said. "That's why I hired you: because we both care about this bar far more than we should. And you're right, I should have consulted you before implying it was a done deal. It's just when Howie Fishbein recommended Joe—"

"Howie recommended him?" For the first time Vince looked at Joe longer than for a few seconds.

"Exactly," she said with a raised eyebrow. "So, does that mean you'd like to interview him or not?"

Vince nodded a thank-you before turning to Joe. "Fishbein recommended you, huh?"

"Yeah . . . yes," Joe stammered.

"So, lad, tell me about your bartending experience."

"I . . . um . . . don't really have any."

Vince ran a hand over his pained face. "Isn't that precious." He walked a step closer. "So how do you make a Harvey Wallbanger?"

"I'd have to remind myself with . . . um . . . that book behind the bar." Joe thought fast. "But I bet it has Harvey's Bristol Creme in it. Besides . . . um . . . nobody in this place is gonna drink anything more than beer, gin and tonics, and vodka cranberries . . ."

"Is that so . . . ? Vince turned to Dory. "You want my official bartender interview, right?"

"Yes," Dory said. "Act like we're not even here. Be thorough."

"Okay, then." He turned back to Joe and commanded, "Take off your shirt."

Joe's face flushed as he checked to see if Vince was serious. He was. Elena, who had been sitting silently watching the whole thing, suddenly slammed her book down on the bar. "No, he won't! That's demeaning! Grandma, tell him he doesn't have to!"

"Look, we want customers, right?" Vince said to both Dory and Elena. Then he yanked off his Fred Perry polo, exposing his own ripped chest. "It's a shirtless bar—for all the staff."

Joe stared in awe. Almost every inch of Vince was covered in tattoos, including Celtic crosses and footballers' insignias. Circling his belly button was a cobra with fangs out toward the viewer. A tiny, copper-colored treasure trail beneath his belly button (the only hair on his torso) collided with a tattoo of red and orange flames erupting from his crotch. Standing next to all of Vince's tall, smooth muscle made Joe feel like a *Star Wars* Ewok.

"You don't need to do it, Joe," Elena whispered.

Joe, who had written off Elena as stuck-up and unfriendly only minutes before, felt grateful that she had become his out-of-nowhere champion.

"This is business, Elena, darling," Dory said. "I'm sorry, Joe, dear, but the shirt . . . lose it."

"It's okay." Joe nodded to Elena before squeezing out of the tight T-shirt, getting his Swatch caught on the arm hole for a split second.

Elena shook her head, appalled, before walking to Joe's side, her eyes warning Vince not to touch.

"Turn around," Vince commanded. "Rear view is good. Turn back. Chest hair pattern has its merits. Flex."

Joe obeyed. Vince's expressionless eyes assessed his physique as if he were the third runner-up at the Westminster Dog Show. Before he met Elliot, Joe had always considered himself "end-of-the-night handsome"—believing that he was the kind of guy you'd only go home with given no other options. Elliot falling in love with him made Joe feel truly attractive for the first time in his life. *Stop thinking about him,* Joe berated himself. *Now is not the time. Remember what Ronnie taught you. Look sexy!*

"Well," Vince sighed. "At least the two of us won't be in competition with each other, which is good. And we can corner two markets the Promethean lacks. I'll lure the customers that go for sexy, fit, football hooligans, and the lad here will attract those who prefer cuddly, cartoon-eyed, lost-boy types."

While Joe was trying to wrap his head around Vince's ability to simultaneously compliment and insult him, Dory smiled. "So are we hearing your approval, Vince? Was Howie right?"

"He's rarely wrong," Vince said with a surrendering chuckle.

"I'm glad I hired you, Vince." Dory's elegant grandma energy had returned. "Elena has agreed to help with the decor. She's got quite the eye."

Vince nodded his head at Elena. "Let's keep it nautical and sleazy, if that's okay."

Elena smiled. "Sure," she said. "Like a bordello at the bottom of the sea." She put her arm around Joe's shoulder. "Though we know who they'll really be looking at—cartoon eyes and all."

Joe did all he could not to start jumping up and down. He not only had a bartending job, but he also had both the owner and her granddaughter in his corner.

"Now, if you wouldn't mind"—Vince stepped behind the bar—"I'd like to get this bar opened by Friday afternoon. So if you fine ladies could leave wee Joe and me alone for a bit, he and I have some things to discuss."

As they were leaving, Dory stopped to pat Joe's cheek. "Come over to my house any time to talk, okay, my dear?"

After the door shut behind them, the bar was noticeably silent except for gurgling from the beer fridge. Vince took out a shot glass and poured himself a Jack Daniels, keeping his eyes on Joe as he drank—saying nothing. Joe's cheeks grew hot. He looked up at an old novelty clock hanging over the bar. It featured a muscular little merman figure with a black beard and a teeny trident. The trident ticked off the minutes while his pearlescent fishtail indicated the hour. The merman reminded Joe of someone. Was it that mysterious Gladiator Man he had seen in the harbor earlier that day? No, it actually looked more like that deckhand from the ferry.

"I've always loved that old merman clock," Vince said, having finished a second shot. "Sit closer, lad. I'm not gonna bite your head off."

Joe walked over to the stool nearer to Vince. "Okay to put my shirt back on?"

"Not yet," Vince said, leaning his tatted forearms onto the bar. His face came so close that his hot whiskey and Marlboros breath blew up Joe's nose.

Why is this asshole so sexy? As soon as the thought popped into Joe's mind, Vince grabbed him by the back of his head and crushed his mouth onto his. Vince's lips and tongue, like two small fists, beat Joe's mouth into submission, sucking and biting his lips. For an anxious moment Joe worried that he had tasted blood, and squirmed, his mind sifting through all he had read or heard about whether one could or couldn't contract the virus from an open wound in the mouth. *Stop him!* his brain shouted. But the erection in Joe's pants didn't want Vince to stop.

Then, trying to approximate the sexy, whispery growl of the Irishman, Joe pulled away slightly and whispered, "You want me to do that bite thing to your lips now?" And just like that, Vince released Joe's head and gently but firmly pushed him back down onto the customer's side of the bar. "Wait . . . did I do something wrong?" Joe asked.

"Not at all." Vince wiped his mouth with the back of his hand like he had just eaten something rotten. "I needed to get any sexual tension out of the way, lad. It can cause problems between bartenders. Let me be crystal clear: as cute as you are, I have no interest in fucking people with whom I work. Are we understood?"

"Um . . . of course," Joe said, though he didn't fully.

"Also, I need you to follow some other rules. While you work at this bar, I expect you to flirt your ass off with customers, but no going home with any. If you do, they'll lose interest and stop coming. Hear me? And drill this into your squishy, wee pate: no matter how much they seem to be in love with you, *they will never date you.* They'll take you to bed and then talk about you like you're nothing more than a red-faced Sunday morning brag. Got it?"

Joe nodded.

"And another thing—no cruising the Meat Rack."

"What *is* the Meat Rack exactly?" Joe asked. "Dory mentioned it."

Vince shook his head. "How wet behind the ears are you, lad? Have you not been to the Grove yet?"

Joe knew "the Grove" meant Cherry Grove, the original gay community on Fire Island, which had its own ferry from Sayville. Ronnie had told him the Grove was cheaper and more "artsy" than the Pines, with way more lesbians per square foot. He also said since that demographic "didn't fit the agenda" (meaning Ronnie's quest for a hot, rich husband), it made the most sense for Joe and him to stick to the Pines.

"Not yet. Is the Meat Rack in the Grove?" Joe asked.

"No. The Meat Rack is the beach forest between the Pines and the Grove. It's this giant maze of trees, rolling dunes, and swamp that makes it a pain in the arse to get from one town to the other—much to the satisfaction of both, I'd say. They call it the Meat Rack since it's filled with all sorts of hiding spots where all the lads and pensioners go to get their rocks off al fresco."

"No way," Joe said, smiling at the thought. "Out in the open? Daytime too?"

"Whenever. Used to be even more of a scene before this feckin' plague that's killing everybody. And while doing the dirty in the Rack sounds grand, as soon as an island bartender sets foot in there, all the gay hens will be on the phone clucking their heads off. Best for us bartenders to keep ourselves a mystery. Are we clear?"

"Um . . . yeah. I guess," Joe said. "Now, can I put my shirt on?"

"I don't give a rat's ass, but here, take this."

Ronnie tossed a small red and black book at Joe, which he caught.

"*Mr. Boston Official Bartender's Guide*," Joe read out loud. "Great. This will be helpful."

"Helpful?" Vince scoffed. "You're to have it memorized by your first shift Friday night. I'll also need ya that morning for load-in."

Joe flipped through the hundreds of drinks in the book. "When you say 'memorize,' what do you *really* mean?"

"*Memorize* the damned thing! Every blasted drink. If we're to get this bar in shape, it's no playing around. And join the gym next door. I want us both sporting cantaloupe biceps by the Invasion."

Joe nodded his head enthusiastically but then stammered. "Um . . . what exactly are we invading?"

"Nothing, Attila the Hun. That's just the name of one of the big weekends out here. The point is, you need to become a first-class bartender so we can keep this bar open. Got me?"

A thousand anxious bumblebees swarmed Joe's brain. He took a deep breath and then shook Vince's hand. "You can count on me."

8.
The Long-Distance Mini-Boogie

"To get home, Disco Witches often go in the completely wrong direction."
　　　　　　　　　—*Disco Witch Manifesto #26*

Howie and Lenny were standing in the dining room at the end of the long, lemon-yellow, twirly kitchen telephone cord. While Howie held the receiver slightly away from his ear, Lenny leaned in close to hear the weak, rattling voice of their beloved friend and mentor, Max De Laguna.

"So you haven't noticed anything?" Howie asked Max, who had finally returned Howie's phone call from his bed at Saint Vincent's Hospital. "No dreams at all? Not even some foggy images before waking?"

"Nada, mi amor," Max whispered, the rattle in his chest lingering long after the words were over.

Howie desperately needed Max to decipher the many ill omens he had witnessed over the previous weeks, the most foreboding being that poor dead whale that had washed up on the beach, the strange flock of magpies flying from left to right over the bay, and the great horned owl that he had heard screeching her warning of death all around the Meat Rack. But Max, still seriously ill and stuck in Manhattan, had been struggling to see much of anything at all, be it natural or supernatural. In a long-shot experiment, Howie had arranged a party-line call the night before with Max and the other surviving members of their coven—Lenny, Dory, and Saint D'Norman—in order to perform what Howie was calling a long-distance, clarifying, in-bed boogie spell, something they had never attempted before.

It had also been Howie's first attempt at designing a spell totally by himself. Typically, their entire repertoire of dance magic would first be formulated and tested by Max—or at least had him leading the construction and choreography. But with Max being unable, Howie had thought he'd give it a try on his own. It was the most basic design, set to "Dance, Dance, Dance (Yowsah, Yowsah, Yowsah)" by Chic. While focusing deeply on the ill omens Howie had reported, all five coven members had done an abbreviated hustle-like dance step in their separate spaces while remaining energetically connected via their telephones. Max performed his dance moves while lying down in his hospital bed since he was not well enough to stand. While "boogying," they chanted the sacred questions together: Knuf annaw uoy OD? Em htiw Knuf annaw uoy OD? Then they'd all taken valerian root tea to sleep, with promises to report back in the morning. Thus, the next day's follow-up call.

And the news was not good. "Absolutely *nothing*?" The disappointment dripped from Howie's voice.

Even over the phone, Howie could envision Max with his gigantic black eyes—even bigger since he had gotten ill—staring up at Howie with that kind but firm look that meant Howie had missed the mark. He knew Max had doubted Howie's idea for any spell where the witches were not on the same dance floor, but he appreciated that his great mentor had humored him and given it a try.

"Nothing. You too, Howie?" Max asked, his voice weak, pronouncing Howie's name like "Hooey" as he always had. "Did you have the clarity?"

"As foggy as June in San Francisco," Howie said glumly.

"The others?" As soon as he spoke the words, Max started coughing violently, which made Howie and Lenny look at each other with worried eyes. Since learning he had the virus seven years ago, Max's health had remained miraculously stable—until the previous year. Since then, it had been one opportunistic infection after another. "Que paso con Dory and Saint D'Norman? Did they see anything in their dreams?"

Howie sighed. "Worse. Saint D'Norman, who usually dreams every night, said it had been his first dreamless night in months. It seems my first solo attempt at designing a spell was one tremendous turd."

"It could have been the connection," Lenny hollered so Max would hear. "I heard AT&T was doing some work on the lines over in Babylon."

Howie could practically hear the smile on Max's face. Lenny had always made him laugh, even in the worst of times.

"You have the gift, mi corazón," Max said to Howie. "But as our Great Goddess Mother has shown us, there always needs to be el quorum de los cinco." He gasped another deep, rattling breath. "A quorum of five, blessed with the gift and within ten paces of one another. The sacred energy cannot take the Belt Parkway for the holy connection. I have taught you this before, queridas."

"Of course, Max," Howie said. "I know the distance rule. I just had hoped the Great Goddess Mother might show some pity considering our diminished circumstances. I thought why not give it a shot, in case."

He and Lenny waited for more of Max's words of wisdom or for him to offer his usual positive spin on things or to simply say, *"Let's wait and see what the Great Goddess Mother will show us."* But instead, Max said nothing at all for close to a minute. All they could hear was their beloved high priest's shallow breathing. Their brief conversation had exhausted him.

"Are you okay, Max?" Howie whispered.

"Si, mi corazón," Max finally said. "As you know, all I have taught you is in the manifesto and spell book. I will bring them out with me when I come. Promise me you will memorize them, mi amor. It's time." Again Max was overcome by violent coughing, and Howie imagined Max's jolting lungs, his bleeding throat, his eyes pressed shut as he bore the pain.

When the coughing spell subsided, Howie said, "We should let you get some rest now, Max. But one more thing before you go. Our new boarder in the attic, the adorable young man we told you about—he's not quite the right age to be the you-know-what, but occasionally, when I'm attempting a read on him, my large intestine starts bucking like Mae West during Fleet Week. And he was a little too interested in some of our vintage photos, which I'm pretty sure were taken when you-know-what was lurking, so we hid them in the crawl space."

"Sí, sí, sí," Max said in that way of his that let Howie know he was listening deeply.

"And his aura," Howie continued. "Great goddess, it's like one of those spinning-wheel splatter paintings of divinity, delusion, and despair. I know you'd need to see him in person to check the sacred rubric, but is there any way you could give us a hint as to any significant red flags—"

Max gasped and, using what seemed like his last breath, said a word that sounded like *no* but also could have been *yes*. Then, with great effort he pushed out the words. "Trust yourself. (cough) You have the power. (cough) Must look for the . . ." Max then fell into an even more violent coughing fit. This time, Heshy, Max's boyfriend and caretaker (not a member of their fellowship, and in fact a doubter of their magic) got on the phone to let Howie and Lenny know that Max needed peace and quiet and not to call again until Heshy gave them the okay.

"But he was going to tell us something very important," Howie pleaded into the phone. "Heshy, can you wait until he stops coughing and just ask him what is it we need to look for?"

Heshy muttered an obscenity before hanging up angrily.

Howie held the phone to his ear as the dial tone of disconnection whined. Once more he whispered into the deadened mouthpiece, "What do we need to look for, Max?"

9.
The Hook

"Seek not only the beautiful youth nor the Olympian in his prime, but explore also the filthy and profane, the aged, the unusually formed, the destitute and unmuscular, for the Great Balance requires a cornucopia of sensual and sentient beings."
—*Disco Witch Manifesto #15*

"Tom Collins?" Ronnie asked, fanning himself with Joe's *Mr. Boston Official Bartender's Guide*. He had been quizzing Joe about cocktail recipes for over an hour as the two sat at the end of Harbor Walk, which jutted out into the Great South Bay—the spot known as "the hook."

"Gin!" Joe called out proudly. "Two parts fresh lemon juice, one part sugar syrup . . . four parts Coke?"

"No," Ronnie growled. "Come on, Joey, we went over this already. Not Coke—soda water. Think! Why would you need sugar syrup if you were already using Coke?"

"Right, right, soda water!" Joe punched himself in his thigh. "There is no way I'm gonna know all these cocktails by tomorrow. How would I pass an organic chemistry class if I can't even memorize a fucking drink recipe?"

"Easy, Joey Bear. To be honest, if someone orders a Tom Collins at a gay cruise bar, they're a dick."

"I can't fuck this up." Joe pressed the heels of his hands into his eyes. "I can't lose this job."

"Look," Ronnie said, "if you get stuck, just hide the *Mr. Boston* under the sink so your boss and the customers don't see." He demonstrated. "First, flash a flirty smile and say you ran out of something. Then bend over like you're looking for it, but give 'em a little show." He pulled his shorts down enough to expose the tops of his cheeks. "See? While everybody's fixated on your butt crack, you scan the recipe! No one will be the wiser!"

Joe jokingly covered his eyes and groaned. "No way am I doing that." He grabbed back the *Mr. Boston*.

"Stop being so negative, Joey!"

"Quiz me some more."

"Let's take a breath." Ronnie lay back on the warm wood of the dock. "So, how's it going with your weirdo roommates?"

"I like them a lot," Joe said. "Lenny can be a little crabby, but he's really a sweetheart. He taught me the difference between a Prince Albert and a freedom ladder and made me this hoagie." He held up the torpedo-like sandwich that he was halfway through eating. "Although he called it a 'hero.' Wanna try?"

"Nah. I'm trying to shred. What about that other one?"

"Howie? He's really cool, like an eccentric old aunt. You won't believe how they fixed up that attic room for me. Totally rad." He chewed the next bite of his hoagie more slowly. "There's just this one weird thing . . ." He shook his head. "Never mind. It's stupid. Anyway, I really lucked out."

Ronnie's bullshit meter went off. Joe was holding something back. Having been best friends with him for six months, he knew Joe was oblivious to the harsher realities of the gay world. But who the hell moves into the attic of two creepy old strangers he'd met in the harbor? "Okay, spill it," he said. "Have they 'accidentally' walked in on you when you were showering?"

"No," Joe said. "They aren't like that. It's just . . ." He put down his hoagie. "When they fixed up the attic they purposely hid some of their old photos from me and padlocked this crawlspace and . . ." He groaned. "I'm being an idiot. Just forget I said anything. Not a big deal. The important thing is, I really want you to like them. Howie knows a ton of interesting stuff."

"Whatever you say." Ronnie stomach gurgled with discomfort at the thought of the two strange older men. He wouldn't let anyone hurt his best friend. "New topic! Tell me more about that hot Irish bar manager of yours? Was he a good kisser?"

"Ugh," Joe groaned. "Fuck that guy."

"I mean he sounds like a major ass wipe, that's for sure." Ronnie squirmed out of his T-shirt to show off his tanned and swollen torso. "But I saw him wearing a tank top and carrying a case of beer yesterday. Fuckin' A! That body . . . woof!"

"Whatever," Joe said. "I thought you were looking for a rich guy?"

"I am. But I'm up for a little fun in the meantime."

"You know Vince told me the rich guys who summer out here never date any of the workers. He says they'll fuck us, but that's it. Says they think we're all trash."

"He said that?" Ronnie's eyes narrowed. "Hot or not, that brainless Irish douche don't know shit."

"Well, he's worked out here for almost ten years, so—"

"Doesn't mean squat!" Ronnie sat up. "Maybe the A-listers won't date losers like Vince whose only goal in life is to work on the island forever. You and me are different. This place is just a means to an end to us. One summer and done. I'm gonna be a rich motivational speaker and you're gonna be a friggin' doctor!"

"About that," Joe said. "Please stop telling people I'm going to medical school. Because it's just not true—"

"I've made my mind up!" Ronnie blurted. "Now I have to sleep with him!"

"What? Who?"

"Your boss, Vince."

"But you just said he's a brainless douchebag."

"That's exactly why I'm going to give him the lay of his life and then watch him beg for more while I ignore him. That'll show that overgrown leprechaun he can't go around spreading bullshit about who we can date and treating my little buddy like a cheap piece of kissable meat."

"Whatever floats your boat." Joe did his "Ronnie-you're-ridiculous" head shake. "Can we get back to work? Quiz me again about—"

Joe's face suddenly brightened as he appeared to catch sight of something over Ronnie's shoulder. "Wait a minute—that's them!"

Ronnie turned to see two ridiculously dressed older men heading toward Bay Walk, pushing a cleaning caddie. The short one resembled a Neapolitan lawn ornament in chaps, while the tall one wore flowers in his baseball cap and was waving a massive feather duster.

"Hey there, Joe!" the tall one called out.

Joe jumped up and waved them over. "Howie! Lenny! C'mere a minute. I want you to meet Ronnie!"

"I see you two found the hook," Howie said as Lenny parked their caddie. "The most perfect spot. And now we get to make the acquaintance of the famous Ronnie! Joe has told us wonderful things. I'm Howie Fishbein and this is Lenny D'Amico."

As Ronnie shook Lenny's and Howie's hands, he felt an uneasy tingling in the lower part of his stomach, just above his appendix scar. "Yeah, 'sup," he said, lowering his voice and glowering. Something about the bigger guy instantly bothered him.

"Such a strong handshake," Howie said. "Joe mentioned you have bartending skills. I sometimes arrange parties out here for my customers, and they're always looking for handsome bartenders—generally shirtless, though. These men have no imagination. If you like, I can put you on my list."

"Sure, thanks," Ronnie said, distracted by how intently Howie was staring at him. It wasn't the leer of other men, undressing him with their eyes. Howie's eyes were scalpels dissecting his soul. "Is something on my face?" Ronnie snapped.

"You're eyeballing him," Lenny snarled. "How many times I gotta tell you not to—"

"You're right," Howie said. "Sorry. It's just you look so . . . have we met before?"

"Nope," Ronnie said. "Never."

"Strange. I could have sworn we . . . well, in case I ever insulted you in this life or a previous one, I sincerely apologize."

"I'll keep that in mind." Ronnie sniffed, ignoring Joe's eyes warning him to be nice.

"Oh, hey," Joe said brightly. "Ronnie, you should see Howie and Lenny's album and cassette collection. It's seriously gargantuan."

"Do you like dance music, Ronnie?" Howie asked. "We're big fans."

Ronnie shrugged. "New stuff is cool. Madonna, The B-52s... disco sucks, though."

Howie and Lenny gasped as if they were silent movie actors. Joe just looked pissed.

"You don't like any disco?" Lenny asked. "Not even Gloria? Donna? Vicki Sue?"

"Gag me." Ronnie mockingly stomped his feet in a four-on-the-floor rhythm singing a Gibb-worthy ah-ah-ah tremolo. "It's all the same song—"

"Ronnie's being a dick today," Joe said while giving Ronnie the side-eye. "And I've seen him dancing the Hustle at Kurt's in Philly dozens of times."

"I went to disco nights because I like to fuck hot, rich guys in their forties," Ronnie sneered. "The music itself was painful as hell. I had to go home and listen to Kiss and AC/DC just to clear my head of that monotonous shit."

"Monotonous shit, huh?" Lenny looked ready to fight.

"Perhaps you don't yet fully comprehend its beauty," Howie said gently. "The disco aesthetic is highly misunderstood. You know it all started in Manhattan's Black and gay dance clubs? That's why white straight men attacked it. Perhaps you can let us try and change your mind."

Ronnie rolled his eyes despite Joe glaring at him.

"By the way"—Howie squinted at Ronnie—"has anyone ever told you that you have a very interesting aura? It's all over the place, but with some striking flourishes of indigo—which represents insight." A flash of pity passed over Howie's face. "A very difficult time growing up, I suspect. But you're a survivor."

"You can tell all that, huh?" Ronnie scoffed, distancing himself from the fact that Howie's obvious guess had landed a bull's-eye.

"I believe so." Howie did another disturbingly deep stare into Ronnie's eyes.

"So I guess you think you're psychic or something?" Ronnie bulged his eyes mockingly. "What else can you tell me about myself?"

While he believed in creative visualization and the power of positive thinking, Ronnie drew a hard line at bullshit like crystals, auras, and palm reading. Not that he hadn't tried them—but ever since he'd wasted an entire week's paycheck on a bus ticket out to New Mexico to witness the "Harmonic Convergence"—a huge cosmic turd—he had developed a deep disdain for the mumbo-jumbo branch of the New Age business.

"Not psychic at all." Howie laughed. "Trust me, we've known some excellent clairvoyants. Our beloved friend Max reads souls like they're *Reader's Digest*."

"Doesn't even use tea leaves or runes," Lenny added.

"The best I can do," Howie said, "besides my prescient indigestion, is see auras, but my eyes have gotten cloudy over the last few years. Although, for some odd reason, they're extremely bright today. Probably sunspots." He narrowed his eyes, his brow puzzled, before waving a hand through the air as if to wipe away the awkward conversation. "But enough of all this silly metaphysical talk. Look at you two handsome young men, working on Fire Island for your first summer. So exciting! If I *did* have the ability to see the future, I'd predict you two falling hopelessly in love with Fire Island and never leaving."

The thought gave Ronnie the shudders. "Ugh, I'd rather chew glass."

"Ronnie!" Joe snapped, not even hiding his anger anymore.

"I mean, no thanks." Ronnie tried to leave it at that, but something inside of him refused. "This place is pretty 'n' all, but me and Joey have big goals that do not include getting stuck spending the rest of our lives cleaning other people's houses on fucking Fire Island."

A large sandbag of silence landed smack into the middle of the four men. Joe, looking humiliated, started busying himself with wrapping up what was left of his sandwich. Lenny and Howie simply shot glances at each other. Hot fingers of embarrassment crawled across Ronnie's face. He hated losing control like that. Why did he dislike these two men so much—especially Howie? Was it that he was old? No. He liked older men. Was it because Howie dressed androgynously? No again. Ronnie was friendly with plenty of drag queens—at least casually. Yet the worms of disdain squirmed in his gut.

"I better go check on the Bolognese on the stove," Lenny finally said.

"Good idea," Howie agreed. "I think I'm gonna go back to Jerry's house. I left some towels in the dryer."

"Wait," Joe said. "I'm sure Ronnie didn't mean that to come out the way it did."

Ronnie couldn't even look up as he shrugged. "Sorry."

"It's okay." Howie smiled at him. "You're not wrong about how some of us get stuck here. If I had my druthers, I'd have preferred to get stuck in P-town or Key West. But I do believe the universe puts us where we're most needed. Sometimes it ends up being wonderful—and other times we must patiently wait for the 'wonderful' to arrive. And sometimes that waiting takes a very long time. But it's good to trust life, Ronnie. I hope you will someday."

Fuck this guy, Ronnie thought. *How dare he say something like that to me?* Of course Ronnie trusted life. Pathetic old gay guys like Howie were just jealous of his good looks and positive energy, so they tried to crush his spirit. He definitely needed to watch out for Joe with these guys.

"Gotcha," Ronnie said bitterly.

"Fine, then," Howie said, pushing pass the awkwardness. "We'll leave you two to your day off." He took hold of the cleaning caddy. "Lenny, shall we?"

As soon as they were out of earshot, Joe pounced. "What the fuck was that?"

"You don't think that was a nasty comment he just made about me not trusting life?" Ronnie's voice leaped an octave. "He basically called me stupid and trashy."

"He didn't call you trashy *or* stupid. He's totally on your side, and you just told them their whole lives were wasted! What the hell?"

"That's not how I heard it! And by the way, I know you told him stuff about me . . . like how I grew up?"

"How you grew up?" Joe looked puzzled. "I barely know anything about how you grew up. I just told them that you were a nice guy. Thanks for proving me wrong."

Ronnie looked out toward the bay. Two black swans were fighting over a fish. The smaller of the two refused to relent and was able to swallow down the fish in a gulp. The larger one, irate at the loss, opened his bill and screamed, then nipped at the smaller one's tail feathers before turning and paddling away.

"I'm sorry," Ronnie finally said. "It's just guys like him, dressing like that, smiling all the time, making vague wacko comments—they bug the shit out of me. Also they were looking at both of us weird. Totally creeped me out. If you want my opinion, I think you should start looking for a new place to live as soon as possible."

"But I like their place." Joe was adamant. "And I'd prefer you didn't act like a dick and ruin this situation for me, okay?"

"Yeah, sure, whatever." Ronnie huffed a big, bored sigh. "I promise I won't cause problems for you. Can we talk about something else now?"

Ronnie went back to quizzing Joe on the cocktail recipes, but he felt no joy in it. He hated how he'd let Howie get to him. Why would the older man think Ronnie didn't trust life? Life was great. Life was a pearl-filled oyster. Fuck those two weird old house cleaners. Fuck them to the end of the world.

10.
The Sad, Sad Beauty of Howard Fishbein

"Disco Witches get older. Fear not. Keep boogying. The Great Goddess Mother has a DJ set just for you."
—*Disco Witch Manifesto #73*

Howie awoke from another bad dream, which he couldn't remember. Even though Lenny was only two rooms away, and Joe was asleep above his head in the attic, he felt so alone and frightened. He couldn't stop thinking about Max's terrible coughing and the last words he'd heard him speak: *"Must look for the . . ."*

"What did you want us to look for, Max?" Howie whispered to the giant black-and-white photo facing his bed. It was of Max dressed as his most famous drag-queen prophetess character, Eartha Delights and Her Ominous Bush. "You need to get better and call me back, Max. I need you."

Howie got up from the bed and tiptoed into the living room. He drew down from the top shelf his favorite photo of Max and himself from that first summer they spent together in Provincetown. It was 1960, and they were both working as barbacks at the A-House, both so young and beautiful. Max had emigrated from Guatemala as a teenager and still spoke slightly accented English.

The photo had been taken at the top of Pilgrim Monument, the two-hundred-and-fifty-two-foot memorial that defines the center of Provincetown. It was Max's idea to climb the tourist monument—and that's where he and Howie had kissed for the first time.

Howie spent so many hours that summer stretched out naked in the dunes, listening to Max recount stories of his mystical youth among the volcanos of Lake Atitlan or, more recently, as a love rebel in the communes of Lavender Hill. It was Max who would teach Howie his rightful place in the world and unlock his magical gifts.

"We're in our first Saturn Returns, mi amor," Max had told him during that metamorphic night of dancing, his beautiful brown skin gleaming with sweat, his eyes lit up from magic mushrooms. "The significance of us is limitless!"

Howie was so desperately in love with him, but by the end of August, despite a summer of discovering and increasing their magical collaboration, Max told Howie the actual limits of their limitlessness. "Come come, don't cry, mi corazón," he said. "Neither of us is made for just one love. We are amantes sagrados, the children of Dionysius and Diana—we are fire! We must burn, mi amor! We must burn and love and burn and love! We will change the world!"

Young Howie's heart broke for the first time that day. But he knew he would rather be proximate to Max's brilliant light than to search for some lesser, consistent affection. From that point on, he and Max maintained their non-romantic, but passionate, mentor-mentee relationship and eventually, as with the other members of their coven, became family. Howie couldn't (didn't want to) imagine his life without Max.

More mental fireflies of Max flashed across Howie's brain: the night they cast that first spell on the dance floor of the A-House, the discovering of the other blessed ones in their midst, the foundation of their dance coven, their inaugural sacred gathering in the salt marsh at the end of Commercial Street, Max's nine tortured nights in the dunes composing the sacred Disco Witch Manifesto, all their struggles and triumphs in the wild sixties, and the move to Fire Island in the seventies, where they became island protectors, moving into 44 and ¼ Picketty Ruff. So many years of love, sex, and magic until that darkest of days seven years prior when Max broke down sobbing as he showed Howie the crimson lesion on his stomach.

"I have so much yet to do, mi amor, so much," he'd said. "How will the earth ever forgive me for leaving it too soon?"

Max had been holding on, but how different he looked from the photo the last time Howie had seen him at the autumn equinox. The bittersweet irony of their chosen dance track: "I Will Survive." But would he? Would anyone? Howie felt those prescient eels of impending doom slither around his gut again. Did the omens indeed foretell something devastating was in the works? If Max could not rally and get out to the island, then they would have an impossible task ahead of them. *Without Max we are nothing.*

Howie kissed the photo and returned it to the shelf. He then went into the bathroom, flipped on the light, and began to stare at his all-too-human face in the mirror. There they still were, the sagging jowls, those thinning lips, and the eye bags bulging like little worn-out pocketbooks. That he would still be vain at such a moment made him shake his head. *The young heart thinks youth will last forever. They believe old farts just appear out of thin air full of wrinkles and regret.*

Was that why Joe's friend Ronnie resented Howie so much? Did he blame their generation for this plague? Did he mistake them for the Darkness? Or was Howie just an awful reminder of the winters yet to come?

Didn't Ronnie understand? The more one fights the inevitable, the more painful it is. Howie knew that all too well.

"Are we just wasting our time," he asked his reflection in the mirror, "pretending we will ever be able to make magic again?"

After one long, deep sigh, he switched off the light.

11.
Opening Night

"Disco Witches always have their dancing shoes ready—just in case."

—*Disco Witch Manifesto #5*

"We got just two hours until this bar opens," Vince said, stepping out of the liquor closet with two bottles of Johnny Walker Black. "I need to run over to Mulligan's Grocery to pay our tab and grab more limes. Elena, darlin', would it bother your decorating if I borrowed wee Joe for a bit?"

Elena's eyebrows raised in amused disbelief as they often did around Vince. "Aye-aye, Captain . . . darlin'."

"Much thanks. Now, Joseph, I hope you're clear on the order of the speed rack like I taught you. Left to right: rum, vodka, gin, brandy, whiskey, bourbon, tequila, triple sec, vermouth! Got it?"

"Yeah, Vince," Joe muttered.

"You better. I'm testing you when I'm back."

As soon as Vince had left, Joe's body slid down the wall into a head-buried crouch. "He's going to kill me."

"No he's not," Elena said as she affixed a large, desiccated starfish to the old-fashioned fishnet on the back wall.

"He will," Joe said. "I was gonna stay up all night cramming the *Mr. Boston*, but I fell asleep in the middle of the Gin Rickey.

Nothing stuck. The only cocktails I have memorized are the martini and Sex on the Beach. That takes rum, right?"

"Vodka with peach schnapps," she corrected.

"Figures I'd screw up anything to do with sex. He's going to fire me."

Elena offered Joe a sympathetic pouty face. "It's okay, hon. It'll work out fine. Dory loves you, and that's the only important thing."

"Thanks for saying that." Joe took in Elena's decorations. The plain walls were now draped with old netting, green glass balls, and artificial fish. Vintage photos of whales and naked sailors hung under each fixture. "By the way, you did a kick-ass job with this place. You've got a great eye."

Elena sighed and readjusted the space between a plastic lobster and a giant seahorse. "This bar is immune to a makeover. It's like trying to make Anita Bryant look like Cyndi Lauper."

"That's not true. It really looks great." Joe thought how much Elena had changed in only a few days. Her hardness had been replaced with a sweetness and vulnerability. Every so often he'd see her stop what she was doing and stare into the air with a melancholy look on her face. Did Elena have an Elliot somewhere too? Or some other kind of heartbreak? He was about to broach the topic, when Vince burst through the door with the small crate of limes.

"Have you been practicing," Vince shouted, "or yabbering like a lazy gobshite?"

Before Joe could respond, Elena interrupted. "You lucked out with this one, Vince. He's like the Boris Becker of bartending." She winked at Joe. "I will let you two *gobshites*—whatever the hell that means—get to whatever you're doing next."

"Hold on there," Vince said. "Joe and I want to buy you a drink for the great job you did with the redecoration. Place looks pure class. Joe, get the lady a drink!"

"That's okay," Elena said. "I'm good—"

"Come on!" Joe said, not wanting to be left alone with Vince. "Let us buy you a beer at least!" He pulled their three most expensive beers from the cooler and set them on the bar. "We got Heineken, Corona, Amstel even! What'll it be? Have all three if you want."

Elena stared at the three icy, sweaty bottles for what seemed to Joe an unusually long time. "I really... um... can't," she said, anxiously throwing her decorating materials in a bag. "But that's really sweet of you. I have to go to a meet—to meet some friends. But that beer looks really good... I mean wet and all. Okay, I'll check in later. Good luck tonight. Bye!" She blew a kiss to Joe and bolted out the door.

"Well, she was certainly in a hurry," Vince said, puzzling his brow.

"Yeah," Joe said. "I hope she's okay, and nothing bad is going on."

"Not really our business." Vince slammed the limes on the counter. "What *is* our business is this bar, which is opening"—he looked at the merman clock—"in exactly one hour and forty-three minutes. Now, Joseph, do you think you can relieve at least some of my terror by showing me you've memorized the order of the speed rack?"

"Um, I think so..."

"Don't *think*, Joseph. *Know!* Now let's see it!"

Joe stared at the bottles on the bar top as if they were nine brawny Irish thugs about to shove his head down a toilet. "Is it... rum, vodka, brandy...?"

Vince pinched his eyes like he was in pain. "What in Christ's name am I going to do with you? Memory is a bartender's most important skill." His voice ached with frustration. "You need to remember customers' names, what they regularly drink, whether or not they paid their tab, whether they earned a shot after their third drink—and you need to remember all that while you're making two drinks and serving a third and setting up the goddamn speed rack like I taught you!" He slammed his fist on the bar top, causing Joe to jump.

"For Chrissake, Vince!" Joe snapped. "I swear to God I'm trying my best, but you've been running me like crazy and acting like a dick, and I've barely had any sleep in the last week, and I'm..." He stopped himself. No way did he want to cry in front of Vince.

"Okay, okay. You're right." Vince sighed and softened. "I'm being an ass. I'm sorry. The thing is, we just have to make sure we're offering, hands down, the best bar service in the Pines."

Exasperated, Joe looked around at the shabby bar. Even with Elena's Herculean decoration efforts, she was right; the bar couldn't be made into anything more than what it was: a booze-serving, sleazy shoebox.

"Why? Will it really matter that much?"

"It will, Joseph, it will. You see, Scotty Black—that same shoibag who made us do the load-in from the other side of the harbor this morning, the same putrid turd who lied about giving you a job out here—has been scheming to shut down Asylum Harbor for good."

That must've been the "situation" he and Dory had been talking about. "But doesn't he earn money from Dory renting the space?"

"He does, plus a percentage of the till. But he claims having an unpopular bar in the harbor hurts his other businesses. And there's a clause in their agreement that says Scotty can cancel Dory's lease if Asylum Harbor doesn't turn a profit for at least two of the four months we're open. So, my point is, it'll take all our charm, looks, and outstanding service to convince these early season lads to stick with us through the summer. If we don't, then Asylum Harbor closes, Dory's heart breaks, and you and I will be out on the boardwalk begging for our supper. Now do you understand?"

Joe nodded.

"Good, good. That's grand. But in order to provide top-quality service so we can stay open, you're going to need to start remembering things, starting with"—he slammed a bottle from the speed rack back onto the counter—"how to set up the feckin' speed rack like a bartender and not a bloody eejit!"

"Why you calling my buddy an idiot?" Ronnie called out from the doorway. He wore a sleeveless denim shirt unbuttoned to his belly button, *Playgirl* model style.

"I can't talk now, Ronnie," Joe called from the bar, not wanting to piss Vince off again. "We're in the middle of something—"

"Just a quick flyby." Ronnie tossed Vince one of his top-shelf seductive smiles. "Hey, Sid McVicious, you better be nice to my Joey."

Joe watched as the Irishman narrowed his eyes to cold green slits, a wolf ready to devour a wounded deer. *This is it*, Joe thought. *He's gonna explode.*

"Who the feck are you?" Vince's voice turned into a low leonine rumble.

"The name's Ronnie Kaminsky. I'm Joe's happiness mentor and bodyguard. Who the *feck* are you?" The Irish brogue attempt made Vince smile—something Joe barely ever saw.

"You can call me Vince, but what in Saint Agnes's tit is a *happiness mentor*?"

"It just means I guide people to become their best selves." Ronnie sauntered into the center of the bar. "Really my main job is being Joe's best friend."

"Are ya now? I will say I'm surprised wee Joseph here has any friends other than the sparrows and bunnies singing circles around him in the meadows."

"Don't take my buddy for granted," Ronnie said. "He may look like an adorable, furry Disney character, but he's got a killer's instinct."

Vince and Ronnie briefly held their deadpan stare before bursting into laughter. When the laughter subsided, they shook hands, scanning each other's faces, sniffing each other's scent, their muscular fingers exploring the skin and veins on the other man's wrists. Joe might as well have disappeared into the rubber sludge mat.

Vince finally released Ronnie's hand. "You're working over at the Flotel, right?"

"Really I'm just killing time there until the Promethean opens," Ronnie lied. "But I should be head bartender at High Tea by mid-June at the latest."

Joe was astounded by Ronnie's blatant dishonesty. Although, it was unlikely he and Vince would still be talking after Ronnie accomplished his pump-and-dump revenge plan—something about which Joe was feeling worse and worse.

"Careful Scotty Black doesn't make you do anything you'll regret," Vince said.

"Trust me." Ronnie lifted his upper torso over the bar closer to Vince, then said in a husky whisper, "I'm a very big boy, and I never do anything I regret."

The men were back staring into each other's eyes. Joe wondered what it would be like to be them at that moment, two muscle studs in their prime, both confident and hungry for each other. He knew it was just a game for Ronnie, and probably for Vince as well, but still, the sight of their mutually rapacious longing highlighted all that was missing in his life—all that he doubted he'd ever have again.

"I'm afraid your wee friend and I have to get back to work," Vince purred. "I'd ask you to stop by at the end of my shift, but we don't close until four in the morning."

"I don't mind. I rise very, very early." Ronnie let his torso slide off the bar and turned to leave. Just before he walked out the door, he looked back at Vince (as Joe knew he would) and tossed his chin upward like he was an extra-sexy Humphrey Bogart in *Casablanca*.

As soon as he was gone, Vince's smile vanished. "If you think pimping out your hot friend is gonna make me go soft on you, think again. Now start prepping the limes! We've only a little over an hour left, so I don't have time to quiz you. But if I hear you're messing up the drink orders later tonight, I'm nipping off your fingers with my teeth."

12.

The Canoodlers

> *"The Disco Witches do not by nature disdain the overlords or their minions. We welcome the allies who give us space to dance, make love, and build our temples. But when the overlords set their weapons and laws against the holy lovers, then we fight and dance for their defeat."*
> —Disco Witch Manifesto #88

With only twenty minutes left before Asylum Harbor was to open for the season, Joe was on his third run to Mulligan's grocery to grab something the bar was missing. This time, Vince had sent him back for a quart of heavy cream in case customers started ordering brandy Alexanders or white Russians, two more drinks Joe hadn't a clue how to make.

As he was half walking, half jogging back to the bar with the cream, a familiar face stopped him in his tracks. It was that deckhand from the ferry, the better-looking one who had laughed at Joe the day of his arrival. Only this time he didn't have his teenage coworker with him—he was sitting with a cute blonde girl on the steps near the liquor store. The last thing Joe wanted to do was to walk by and subject himself to the deckhand's homophobic tittering again. He suddenly felt like he was back in junior high and needed to avoid the bullies in the hallways.

For a moment Joe studied the young couple from a distance, recognizing the girl as one of the many Mulligan cousins who worked the cash registers at the grocery store. The two lovebirds were sitting close together, with their knees touching, her hand taking his hand at one point, massaging it as they talked about something that appeared serious. At one point the deckhand reached up and tenderly moved a lock of the girl's short blonde hair behind her ear with his hand. Even from this distance Joe could tell they were damned nice-looking hands—strong and probably rough from pulling and tying up the ferry ropes all day. And then there were his forearms and those long, hairy legs . . .

Ugh! Joe hated when he found straight guys attractive. *What a waste of time.*

The deckhand and the girl looked so smitten with each other, like leads in one of those sixties beach movies, *Beach Blanket Bingo* or *Where the Boys Are*. Where better to fly their horny, heterosexual flag than in one of the only gay-friendly communities on Earth? *The hell with them,* Joe thought. *Get a fucking room!*

Joe realized Vince would be tossing a fit if he didn't get back immediately; he didn't have time to detour all the way around Ocean Boulevard and back just to avoid passing the deckhand and his date. So he decided to quickly pass by with his head down, hoping the deckhand didn't notice. But just as he stepped in front of them, the deckhand coughed, causing Joe to look up and find himself staring straight into those insanely blue eyes. *They are not just blue. They are the bluest blue I've ever seen.*

Realizing he had been staring at least two seconds longer than he should, Joe abruptly looked away, acting like it hadn't happened. The expression on his face must've looked ridiculous, since it caused the deckhand and his girlfriend to snort with laughter.

A wave of humiliation crash inside Joe's stomach. He sped around the corner and up the steps to the bar. When he hit the doorway, Vince was staring switchblades at him. "Where the feck have you been?" Vince snapped. "And why's your face all lobster red like that?"

13.
Cranberry 'n' Vodka

"Disco Witches dance to save the world, and because the rhythm compels them."
—*Disco Witch Manifesto #2*

By seven PM Asylum Harbor was doing steady business. Like Dory had promised, customers were only ordering beers, vodka cranberries, martinis, and the most basic mixed drinks. But just in case he needed to employ Ronnie's cheating trick, Joe hid the *Mr. Boston Official Bartender's Guide* in the crack between the beer cooler and the sink, for easy access.

"What'll it be?" Joe said to the next customer, copying Vince's cool, causal demeanor.

"A vodka cranberry please, but only a light splash of the juice, if you don't mind."

"Gotcha," Joe said.

The first wave of customers was mostly male and older, wearing Ralph Lauren and smelling of Cartier cologne and cigarettes. But when the merman's tail hit eight PM, a more varied crowd paraded in, including several younger men and a handful of women. Joe kept hoping the Gladiator Man (or someone who looked like him) might walk through the door, but no dice. And he kept thinking about the annoying deckhand in the harbor, and how stupid he'd felt staring at him the way he had, and then them laughing at him. It was the same way the deckhand had laughed at Joe that first morning on the ferry. *What is that guy's problem with me?*

"What're you daydreaming about?" Vince asked.

"Nothing. I didn't realize there were so many people out here yet," Joe said.

"Mostly owners. You won't see half of 'em again until October, when they close up for the winter. The preseason young ones are mostly workin' fellas like us, out here for the long haul. House boys, rent boys, pool boys."

"That's a lot of boys," Joe said. "What about her?" He pointed to a voluptuous blonde standing at the bar, with yellow bangs sweeping her eyelashes and a smile so big it was like she had enough teeth for two women.

"That's Chrissy Bluebird. A legend. Got famous doing that seventies porn *Holly Humps Houston*. Has her own cable access show. Hey, Chrissy! Meet Joe, our new bartender!"

Rather than shake Joe's hand, Chrissy reached over and tousled his chest hair. "Hey, handsome, you be safe out there, you hear me? Maybe I'll have you on my show one day!" She then applied an additional layer of lip gloss on her already glistening lips and was quickly overtaken by another gaggle of middle-aged gay men.

Joe smiled, watching her work the crowd like she was a porn star Princess Diana. "That's pretty cool, we have celebrities coming into the bar."

"This island is crawling with that kind of famous shite." Vince tossed his head, indicating several more customers arriving. "Back to work!"

Joe scooted over to his end of the bar and started popping off beer caps like they were candy dots off paper. He was mastering the double pour, one hand vodka, one hand gin. It soon felt like he had been bartending all his life, and the manageable but steady stream of customers showed their appreciation—with cold, clean dollar bills left on the counter with a wink and a smile.

"Nice to meet ya, Joe!"

"You must come visit our place on Pine Walk!"

"We're having a party in two weeks. We'll put you on the list!"

During the next lull Vince walked over to a beaming Joe. "Don't let all this attention go to your head," Vince teased. "The sludge mat gives you an extra two inches of height. Also, a bag of oats would be popular if the customer thought it stood between him and his booze."

Joe didn't care why he was getting the attention. He liked being liked, and he liked being really good at something for once. Maybe this bartending thing was his true calling in life. But then, just after ten, a deluge of nearly fifty new customers flooded the bar. "What the hell?" he shouted over to Vince. "Where'd all these guys come from?"

"I told ya," Vince said, shaking two tumblers simultaneously. "We're the only game in town right now. Remember, we need these lads coming back! So look sharp!"

Joe moved as fast as he could, slamming cocktails on the counter with one hand and collecting money with the other, the whole time trying to remember Ronnie's hints on the gay game and how to flirt for better tips. But the line of customers grew restless, hollering for Bud Lites, Heinekens, vodka cranberry, vodka cranberry, vodka cranberry. Sweat dripped from Joe's pits. His hands shook. A vodka cran spilled all over his chest, garnering a glare from Vince. Joe didn't dare stop to wipe it off for fear he'd get further behind on serving. Just when he thought he was catching up, a man in his thirties with bulging muscles and a radiant smile approached the bar. "I'll take a Grey Goose and cranberry for me, handsome!" he chirped. "And three Absolut and tonics for my friends. His twinkling eyes lingered on Joe's nipples, which peeked from his furry, vodka-and-cranberry-stained chest.

As Joe grabbed the Grey Goose, Vince trotted over and whispered, "Psst! That's Frankie Fabulous you're serving."

"Is he famous?" Joe asked.

"Pines royalty. Gets invited to every party since he's always smiling and brings his own entourage. We need him to become a regular, so don't screw this up."

Joe returned with the Grey Goose, but Frankie Fabulous was wiggling his fingers at him.

"We've changed our minds," Frankie said with twinkling eyes. "We'd like one Manhattan for my fuddy-duddy friend here, and three Long Island iced teas for the rest of us. We're celebrating the new bar decorations . . . a sexy one in particular."

"A Manhattan?" Joe tried to smile as his stomach did an anxious somersault. "And three Long Island iced teas? Gotcha." *Fuck, fuck fuck!* He couldn't remember a single ingredient in a Manhattan other than a cherry. Nor did he recall seeing a jug of ice tea (Long Island or regular) anywhere during setup. He hated to do it, but he'd need to employ Ronnie's cheating trick for the Manhattan without Vince noticing.

"Hey, Frankie!" Joe shouted, deciding to figure out the cocktail first. "I'll be right with you, just need to grab some special cherries." He winked. "That's a million-dollar smile ya got!" Then, as Ronnie taught him, he shimmied his jeans down and bent over to show a slice of his butt crack while he reached between the cooler and the sink for the *Mr. Boston*. It wasn't there. His stomach knotted. Frankie Fabulous was whispering to his friends, giggling, as were several other customers who had approached the bar to order drinks and catch a peek. Joe just knew they could see he was a fraud. Having no other choice, he bolted over to Vince's side of the bar. "Um . . . hey," he said. "Frankie Fabulous asked for a Manhattan, but I can't remember how to make it and I can't find the *Mr. Boston* anywhere. Also, he wants three iced teas . . . the Long Island kind, but I can't find iced tea anywhere either."

"Ya didn't memorize the book like I told you, did ya, Cheater Peter?" Vince pulled the *Mr. Boston* from his back pocket and tossed it at Joe's cranberry-stained chest. "We'll be having a talk later. Meanwhile, a Long Island iced tea is a cocktail. It's the five white liquors, with a splash of Coke. Now hurry up and get those men their drinks, 'cause I'm in the weeds! And pull up your feckin' pants!"

Joe rushed back to his station with the *Mr. Boston*. The line for drinks had grown to three deep, and Frankie Fabulous's smile was starting to look less genuine.

"Those drinks are seconds away, handsome!" Joe smiled extra hard, bent over, and found the drinks in the Mr. Boston. His brain couldn't hold onto anything. More men were shouting their orders. *Concentrate. Concentrate.* He felt a weird, warm sensation in his right back pocket. Howie's good luck charm? He fished it from his pocket and huffed in its weird scent. A sudden sense of calmness and surrender came over him. "Fuck it," he muttered, shoving the charm back in his pocket and turning toward the choir loft of booze bottles. Five white liquors? Vodka, gin, and . . . triple sec! That was it. What else? Rum. Yes. But that was only four.

His eyes raked the bottom of the back shelf for another white liquor—any white liquor. What exactly was Everclear? Didn't matter! He poured a hefty dose into the ice-filled tumbler and topped it off with a splash of Coke. After shaking the tumbler, he filled three tall glasses. They sure looked like iced teas. For the Manhattan, he only remembered the whiskey and cherry and faked the rest.

"Here ya go, hot stuff!" He placed the counterfeit cocktails in front of Frankie Fabulous, and sexily licked the excess booze off his fingers—something he'd seen Ronnie do. "You and your handsome friends suck these up. Who's next?" he called out, wanting to be in the middle of another order before shit hit the fan. Fear and adrenaline pumped through his veins. If he was gonna go down, he was going down in a flaming cocktail of glory. "You got two holes, gentlemen! Let's fill 'em!" he called out (another Ronnie-ism).

The crowd laughed and catcalled. Vince gave Joe a "what-the-feck-are-you-doing?" look. Joe had no time to engage. A dozen more orders came in, including three more perplexing cocktails. He felt almost fearless. He patted Howie's good luck charm in his pocket, then did as he had done before: briefly bent over, showed some crack, glanced at the mixology book, remembered maybe two of God knows how many ingredients, and pretended to make the drink like he was Tom Cruise in *Cocktail*. He was sure he'd be fired at any moment, but five minutes passed, ten minutes, thirty minutes—and not one complaint. But then, just before midnight, Frankie Fabulous beelined for Vince. He was not smiling. *This is it,* Joe thought. *I'm going home.*

"Vince!" Frankie Fabulous slurred loud enough for Joe to hear. "Vincent, my Irish person, I must talk to you about your new man! He's . . . he's . . . just so adorable, and such a poo . . . I mean a probe . . . I mean professionalism. Those Long Island iced teas he made were the bestest Long Island iced teas I've ever had in my lifetimes! It put your cocksnails to shame! Shame! Shame! Keep this going and maybe this old bucket of blood might not die when the Promethean opens." He belched. "I think I'm gonna be sick..." Frankie Fabulous stumbled out the door to barf off the side of the deck, showering the walk below.

A huge smile erupted across Joe's face. Vince would be compelled to praise him after Frankie's compliment. But instead, Vince looked straight past Joe and turned pale. Standing inside the entryway was a tall, older man with a carefully coifed shock of white hair, wearing an untucked Oxford shirt and designer jeans. As he walked to the center of the bar, customers parted like the Red Sea.

"Hey there, Scotty!"

"When's the Promethean open, Scotty?"

"Looking really fit there, Scotty!"

When the man and Vince finally locked eyes, Joe could sense the air between them turn to dry ice.

"That's Scotty Black, isn't it?" Joe whispered.

"Yeah," Vince said. "Look at his face. He's worried sick we're doing better than he thought."

"Why?" Joe asked. "I thought you said his agreement with Dory says we have to stay busy?"

"It does. But the chiseler *wants* a reason to kick Dory out," Vince said, barely moving his lips. "He's been telling everyone he wants this to be Asylum Harbor's last season."

Scotty Black's icy eyes slowly rolled from Vince to Joe, whom he looked up and down. A faint smile dented his cheek, and a moment later he left.

"So that's what he's after, is it," Vince muttered to himself, then said to Joe, "Don't be surprised if that slimy bastard tries to pilfer you from the bar."

"Me?" Joe asked. "He'd want me for the Promethean? But he told Ronnie he wasn't looking for any other bartenders—"

Vince grabbed a loop on Joe's jeans and yanked him like a disobedient child. "I'm tellin' you now, if you dare go with that bastard, I'll cut your hairy little throat."

How strange, Joe thought. Just forty-eight hours before, he hadn't had a job, and now he had a bar manager and the most powerful club owner in the Pines fighting over him.

"Don't worry," Joe said. "I would never bail on Dory or you."

"Remember that." Vince released Joe from his grasp. "Take your dinner break now. We'll be slammed again in about twenty minutes. Howie left you some food in the *Charlie's Angels* lunchbox at the end of the bar."

"When?" Joe said, surprised. "I haven't seen Howie all night."

"It's not my job to be your feckin' secretary!" Vince snapped. "Now go eat somewhere where customers can't see ya chew. And memorize that goddamn book!"

14.
One Night Only

"Romantic love is the fourth holy sacrament. Disco Witches always choose passion over caution—sometimes to our detriment. Luckily, broken hearts can be as powerful as magic wands."
— *Disco Witch Manifesto #11*

Ronnie and Vince were walking west on Bay Walk. Moonlight through trees cast lace carpets at their feet. In less than three hours it would be another day of scrubbing toilets and making beds for Ronnie, but before that . . . "So where's your place again?"

"It's all the way on Beach Hill at the dead end," Vince said. "I warn you, it's just a rinky-dink pool house I'm renting. Price is right, though."

"All we need is a place to lie down." Ronnie's cock strained against his zipper. "Hold a sec." He quickly shoved his hand down his 501s to rearrange himself.

"The old knob needs to breathe, eh?" Vince chuckled. "It's a wonder you don't get gangrene with as snug as those jeans are. Wouldn't want anything to fall off."

"I'm cool." Ronnie smiled, his junk now comfortably lying left.

"C'mere." Vince pushed Ronnie against a wooden trash shed and kissed him.

It was not the kind of violent kiss Joe had reported. Vince kissed Ronnie with the right amount of push and pull by the lips and tongue, a good balance of wet and dry, hard and soft, with the perfect number of rest stops and a hungry tension, like a roller coaster climbing to a drop. Vince somehow understood exactly what Ronnie wanted, as if there was a set of instructions written in Braille right on the surface of his lips. But what was that thing Ronnie felt in the base of his stomach? *Butterflies?*

No, no, no, no, no! Get control of yourself. This is supposed to be a revenge fuck.

"Let's just do it here," Ronnie growled, grabbing Vince's crotch as if they were two strangers in a sex club.

Vince jumped back and laughed. "You always come on so hard, lad?"

"No," Ronnie stammered. "I'm just horned up." It was the lamest thing he could have said, and he knew it. Why was he so nervous? Okay, Vince was hot—big deal. He was also an asshole and not much different from any Saturday night fuck Ronnie could score back in Philly. Okay, most Philly guys weren't as hot as Vince. But they also weren't as arrogant. And they sure didn't have an accent like some shamrock-mouthed mafioso (which, he had to admit, was *fucking* adorable). But when Ronnie thought about his well-planned ladder to power and success, Vince was barely a rung up from, well, Ronnie himself. Vince had spent his whole life working in bars and now managed the worst bar in Fire Island Pines. He had no future. None. That was why this was gonna be just one fuck and done, and then Ronnie could get back to his plan to find Mr. Right. "Sorry I came on so strong." Ronnie slid up to Vince and caressed his neck. "I just really want to be inside you."

Vince rolled his eyes. "Jesus, Mary, and Joseph. Are you feckin' serious, lad?"

"I don't understand . . ." Ronnie's voice leaped an octave.

"Just cut it with all that fake sexy-talk shite. And another thing, you're making some grave assumptions. If anyone is going *inside* anyone, it's me going into you. And before any of that squishy stuff happens, I wanna know your game."

Game? Ronnie thought. *My game? Why is this guy trying to make a hookup so complicated? And why does he have to be such a goddamned good kisser? Focus! Eyes on the prize, Ron, eyes on the prize!*

"I don't have any game." Ronnie shrugged. "I'm a pretty simple guy."

"Simple guy, are ya?" Vince mocked. "We'll see about that. But here's the thing—I'm too old for shagging strangers, so tell me why I should want to fuck you."

"Um . . ." Ronnie hesitated. "Well . . . I mean, I'm pretty hot?"

Vince yawned. "If that's all ya got, I might as well just shove my mickey in a melon and get some good sleep. Surely there's something more complex about ya. Your wee friend Joe says you grew up in Philly?"

Ugh, Ronnie thought. Joe blabbered too much. How was he to play the cold, calculated sex god if Joe had already humanized him?

"Yeah," Ronnie said. "Northeast Philly."

"You were the youngest I take it?"

Ronnie looked at him. "How did you know that?"

"I'm a bartender. It's not hard to recognize a baby brother when I see one."

"Yeah?" Ronnie raised a brow. "What else does your bartender experience tell you about me?"

Vince stopped and scanned Ronnie's face. "Well, besides being needy and constantly craving validation, I'd say you had a bit of a rough time at home. Is that it?"

Ronnie suddenly felt as if he were standing there on the walkway completely naked—and not in a good way. "Did Joe say something? That little weasel needs to keep his mouth shut."

"Nobody said anything." Vince placed his warm hand on Ronnie's shoulder. "The reason I know the score is, I had a rotten upbringing myself. I recognize the shite mindset. My da was a drunk—cliché it is, but true. Could barely keep his job digging graves in Drogheda."

"Drug o' what?" Ronnie asked.

"Drogheda. It's the town where I grew up. My ma, though, she was pure class. Worked like a terrier to keep us fed. The cancer took her about five years ago now."

"I'm really sorry." Ronnie noticed how the moonlight reflected off the wetness in Vince's eyes and how his body smelled a little sweaty but nice. When Vince started to walk again, Ronnie sped up to catch him. "I get it, though," he said, letting his shoulder bump up against Vince's. "My mom died a few years ago too. Emphysema. I hadn't seen her in years. She sort of ran out on us."

"That's lousy for sure." Vince slapped a leaf off a lilac bush. "Were you still young when she left?"

"I was ten. She didn't get along with my dad or older brothers. They were Philly trash, drug dealers and petty criminals. She was different. I still can't figure out why she ditched me."

"No idea at all?" There was an ache in Vince's voice, as if he yearned to figure out a way to help the young boy Ronnie had been.

Ronnie shook his head. "None. Totally didn't make sense. I was her favorite. When I was little, she'd always tell me how we'd both become movie stars one day. I promised her if that happened, I'd buy her a big mansion down the Jersey shore, and we wouldn't let my brothers or father visit." He stopped and turned his face toward a thick rhododendron. Why was he telling him this? *Rule number one for a good anonymous hookup: don't ruin it with talking too much.* But still he continued. "Then one day I got home from school, and I was all excited to show her this macaroni mosaic I made in art class, and she was gone. I bawled my eyes out. Nobody explained anything to me. I eventually found out she drove off to Hollywood with our Charlie Chips delivery man. She told my dad she'd send for me once she got settled doing hair on movie sets. But she never did."

"That's a rotten thing to do to a kid." Vince slipped his hand into Ronnie's.

"Yeah. It was." Ronnie felt disarmed by the warmth of Vince's fingers. "The worst part was, I got stuck with my dickhead dad. He practically wanted me committed."

"What do you mean?"

Ronnie shook his head. "Let's talk about something else." He stopped walking and pulled Vince's hand to his nose and sniffed it, trying to steer sexy back into the conversation. "I like the way you smell."

"Look, lad," Vince said. "I don't want to force ya into talking about your private life if it makes ya uncomfortable, but I'm curious why you're changing the subject."

Ronnie laughed nervously. "Well, I *was* kind of weird as a kid . . ."

Vince smiled. "And . . . ?"

"Okay, okay. Well, it's like this—I thought I could fly."

"Aw, that's cute for sure," Vince said. "Kids have terrific imaginations."

"This was more than that." Ronnie's brow dipped. "It felt completely real, like you and me standing here right now. Every night for almost a year I dreamed that I could wiggle my fingers like this and I could float off my bed, out the window and all over Philly and parts of New Jersey. Sometimes I'd wake up on the floor in the morning, with bruises from falling off my bed. My mom would say my dreams were one of the things that made me special. But my father would call me 'Unlucky Lindy' or 'Butterfly Boy,' and he worried I might have some mental issues since I insisted it was really happening. I finally got sent to the school shrink, and eventually the dreams stopped."

Without warning, Vince pulled Ronnie into a tight hug. *That's a strange reaction*, Ronnie thought. But it was also perfect. Too perfect. It was the kind of hug he would have loved to have gotten from the rich older lover he intended to meet that summer—but not from Vince. Worse was that look in Vince's eyes, as well as those damn butterflies fluttering around Ronnie's stomach again. Where was a can of Raid when you needed one?

"Hey, Vince, I need to be honest with you about something, okay?"

"Sure," Vince said.

"I like you a lot . . . but I'm not interested in dating you."

And there it was, just like Ronnie thought, that look of disappointment in Vince's eyes.

"Is that so?" Vince released Ronnie from his arms. "And who says I was interested in dating *you*?"

"I didn't mean that." His voice wavered. "Just making sure we're on the same page."

"Well, isn't that simply precious of you." The Irish skinhead scowl was back. "Pretty feckin' arrogant to assume I'd be interested in anything more than a shag with the likes of you."

"No it's just . . ." Desperation tore through Ronnie's voice. "I wanted to explain—"

"I'm only codding ya, boyo." Vince's sexy smile returned. "We are definitely on the same page. Haven't the slightest interest in dating anyone at this point, especially not some flyby summer worker—no matter how shiny a penny he may be."

"Great. Then we understand each other." Ronnie wanted to feel relieved, but he didn't. He needed to be more clear—for himself. "So here's the deal—tonight is gonna be a one-night stand, okay? But the good kind. What I mean is, we'll make it count. One great night of sex—every dirty fantasy we have. Then we'll say goodbye forever. No mess, no stress. Okay?"

Without responding, Vince looked off down Bay Walk. It was unclear to Ronnie whether he would agree or bolt . . . until Vince pulled him in close, squeezed one hand down the back of Ronnie's jeans and clutched the meaty globe of his ass.

"Okay then, lad," he said. "But if it's only for tonight, this is mine." His finger hit the bull's-eye between Ronnie's cheeks, causing him to gasp in both shock and pleasure. When Ronnie reached around for randy reciprocity, Vince grabbed his wrists and flipped him into a bent-over hold. "Your muscles might be bigger, lad, but mine actually work. Do we have a deal?" He kissed Ronnie's neck.

"Yeah," Ronnie said, way too turned on to remember his initial pump-and-dump plan. Would it be so bad to let the butterflies flutter around his ribcage for one lousy night? By morning they'd all have flown away. It was Fire Island, after all. "We definitely have a deal."

15.
Sunrise Surprise

"The Great Balance is our eternal aim, but we can never stop dancing—even if the Great Darkness is spinning in the DJ booth."
—*Disco Witch Manifesto #13*

At 5:03 AM Joe had finished mopping the floor and hosing down the sludge mat. All in all, his end-of-the-night bar-cleaning duties took one entire side of Elliot's *Love Songs 1*. His pulse wouldn't stop buzzing from the first night's excitement, not to mention the Devil Dog–sized roll of bills in his pocket. In order to blow off steam before bed, he decided to watch the sunrise on the beach while finishing the leftovers in his *Charlie's Angels* lunchbox.

Barely a seventy-foot walk from the bar door, stepping onto the beach at dawn was like arriving in a temporary paradise, with its miles of empty sand, raging ocean, cawing gulls, and spectacular awakening sky.

"*Red sky at night, sailor's delight. Red sky in the morning, sailors heed warning,*" he whispered out loud. How to identify a coming storm was one of the few things his late father, a former navy man, had taught him. Although, beyond a few wisps of red, that morning's sky was mostly orange, yellow, and a little purple. What did that foretell?

Elliot had been obsessed with sunrises. Once, they'd spent a week together in Ocean City, New Jersey, and he'd insisted they depart Philly at three in the morning so they could catch the sunrise over the ocean together. When they reached the Great Egg Harbor Bridge, Elliot had shouted, "I spy the bay!" with glee. It had been his family's tradition that whoever was first to see their watery destination shouted it out as if they had won something. Joe loved how Elliot was able to mix his powerful, grown-man self with a child's sense of wonder.

As the sun's blazing head tipped over the horizon, a strong breeze blew salty-sweet air up Joe's nose. He opened the *Charlie's Angels* lunchbox and pulled out Lenny's homemade chocolate chip cookie. Just then, from the corner of his eye, Joe noticed a tall, brawny man in a gray sweatshirt and jeans, walking along the edge of the water a hundred yards down the beach. He squinted and stopped chewing. It was *him*, the Gladiator Man! Remembering Ronnie's advice to never miss opportunities, Joe dropped his lunchbox and darted onto the sand, waving his arms wildly. "Hey you! Can you talk for a minute?" he screamed. "Stay right there for a second!"

The Gladiator Man stopped walking, adjusted his stance so the rising sun illuminated his perfection, and then waved back. Joe's heart kicked like a rabbit. It was going to happen—he was finally going to meet the Gladiator Man. Joe planned to ask where he lived, talk about how he was new to Fire Island, let him know he was single. He would *not* talk about Elliot.

He hoped he wasn't appearing too enthusiastic. Ronnie had once told him that after you know a guy likes you, it was necessary to play it cool for a while. "Guys without barriers look broken," he had warned. "Like a cracked ashtray you find in a bargain basement." When Ronnie hit on a guy in a bar, he'd keep looking at his watch and checking the door like he was expecting someone else. "Eighty percent indifference, twenty percent flirting and he's all yours." Joe had tried it himself once, but the guy had looked creeped out and bolted. Ronnie said it was because Joe's abrupt switch between flirting and indifference looked more like he had a deranged twitch.

But that morning on the beach, there wasn't an indifferent cell in Joe's body as he charged across the beach like a desperate soldier at Iwo Jima. The closer he got, the more handsome Gladiator Man appeared. His heavy eyebrows hung low over dark brown eyes that, even at fifty feet, sliced into Joe's soul. His salt-and-pepper beard was darker around the mouth and had a dollop of gray in the middle of the chin. His massive pectorals and shoulders pushed against the fabric of the gray sweatshirt. His two hairy forearms, muscular and foreboding, hung by his sides, with hands thick and powerful, like two leashed pit bulls ready to either embrace or kill. He was all that Joe had ever desired—sexually speaking. Of course, Joe would have to be careful. Being older, the man was more likely to have the virus. Joe couldn't bear losing someone else. But it wasn't the time to worry about that. He hadn't even met the man yet.

"Hey! I saw you the other day!" Joe huffed and puffed, a cramp in his side, the soft sand shackling his legs. "I wanted to say hi, but you left before I could."

Closer, closer. He was just fifteen yards from Gladiator Man when another voice called out from behind him. "Hey, buddy! Yo, buddy! Where you running? You forgot something!"

Joe turned. There, shouting from the top of the steps, was that blue-eyed deckhand again—the one with the girlfriend in the harbor. He started down the steps and across the sand toward Joe. He appeared to be soaking wet under his Pines Ferry sweatshirt.

"What do you want?" Joe asked quietly, annoyed, hoping the Gladiator Man wouldn't hear.

"I was just letting you know you forgot your *Charlie's Angels* lunchbox on the steps," the deckhand teased with a friendlier than expected smile as he dangled the campy lunchbox. His low voice bore the scars of too much drinking and yelling at televised sporting events. "You wouldn't want to lose something as nice as this."

What? Joe wondered. *He interrupted me to laugh at me again?* Couldn't this straight idiot see Joe was in the middle of something important? And who went swimming in the ocean alone at five in the morning?

"I left it there on purpose," Joe said, not adding that he hadn't wanted the Gladiator Man to see him with the kitschy lunchbox.

"So, if you wouldn't mind putting it back on your way home, okay? Thanks!" He turned back toward the Gladiator Man, who had begun walking away. Did he think Joe and the deckhand were together? "Hey!" Joe shouted. "Wait a minute!"

"Which is it?" the deckhand said from behind him, sounding irritated now. "You want me to stay or go?"

"I wasn't talking to you," Joe snapped.

"Right," the deckhand said, sounding a little confused. "So what are you doing on the beach this time of the morning anyway? Taking a run?"

"Look," Joe said sharply, "I can't talk right now." He then readied himself again for the chase. But when he looked for the Gladiator Man, he was gone. Joe fell to his knees and punched the sand. "Fuck!"

The deckhand stepped back. "Jesus. What's wrong? Did something bad happen?"

"Yes . . . no. It's just . . ." Joe groaned in frustration and brushed himself off. "I was trying to catch up to someone. Sorry. I didn't mean to snap at you before."

"Ah, no worries." The deckhand pulled a mini-bottle of Johnny Walker from his board shorts, took a swig, and then offered it to Joe.

"No thanks." Looking closely, Joe noticed the deckhand's eyes again. Even while bloodshot and glassy, they were an even more stunning blue than before. For some reason, near the ocean and in the morning light, his eyes appeared almost cobalt blue—or was that ultramarine?—and framed by long black eyelashes flecked with wet salt and sand— much like the rest of him. "You know it's not safe to go swimming drunk," Joe said. "Especially when no one's around to save you if something happens."

"I didn't swim drunk," the deckhand said, taking another sip. "I swam *hungover*."

"You woke up hungover and decided it was a good time to swim?"

"Never went to bed. I took a swim to wake up. I live over in Sayville. A passenger gave the crew a couple of bottles of Jose Cuervo yesterday, so we had a little party after work on the beach. I guess my boys ditched me when I fell asleep. Wouldn't be the first time."

"They sound like real class acts," Joe muttered.

"Don't be so judgy." The deckhand yawned. "I have to work the first boat out, which means I'll need to hitch a water taxi back to Sayville. Might need another dip first. By the way, you said you were trying to catch up to someone? Who?"

"Who do you think?" Joe said, annoyed. "That big muscular dude? The one you scared away?"

"Muscular dude?" The deckhand smiled and gestured to the completely empty beach. "Nobody on this beach but us and the gulls. You sure I'm the only one who's been drinking?"

"For Chrissake," Joe said. "How hungover are you? You didn't see that huge guy with a beard literally standing just over there?" He pointed to the spot where he'd last seen the Gladiator Man.

"Chill out, shortstop. Don't get your skirts all bunched up."

The deckhand's smirk and gay-baiting comment were the last straw. Joe mustered his most threatening glare (which wasn't very threatening) and wondered if he'd remember any of his wrestling moves from middle school. "You always act like such an ass?"

"Just joking with ya." The deckhand made the peace sign. "It's weird that I'd miss seeing another human being that close by, but then again I wasn't really focused over there." His eyes momentarily latched onto Joe, but then he quickly looked away like he was embarrassed. "Or maybe I am still a little drunk. I better get back in the ocean and make myself right!" He yanked off his sweatshirt. His lean torso was more muscular than Joe had imagined, with a perfect little patch of hair at the top, and a small treasure trail between his belly button and board shorts. When he turned and jogged toward the water, Joe noticed he had an almost comical gait. There didn't seem to be anything wrong with his legs, though—still long and hairy, and too sexy for a straight guy. Then Joe noticed something odd. The deckhand had huge, paddle-like feet—with toes ever so slightly webbed. Thus, the reason for the funny jog. Any awkwardness disappeared, though, as soon as he dove into the waves. His arms, like twin porpoises, sliced through the water while his legs kicked fountains. When he was twenty-five feet from the shore, he dove under and disappeared. Ten seconds passed, twenty, thirty, sixty. At ninety seconds, Joe walked to the water's edge, and recounted the CPR class he had been forced to take at his old job. *Tilt the head, make sure nothing is in the passageway, then press your lips . . .*

At that very moment, the deckhand, like a deranged seal, exploded from the water, enrobed in a spray of iridescent water droplets. *He was gasping and laughing.*

That guy's nuts, Joe thought, before looking back at the stretch of beach where he had last seen the Gladiator Man. Sand, bushes, trees, and nothing else.

16.
Breakfast Revelations

"A Disco Witch must be on high alert at all times—even in their dreams."
—*Disco Witch Manifesto #39*

Joe awoke at two PM with an unusually painful hard-on. He vaguely remembered having another Elliot dream—something that had happened regularly in the twenty-two months since his death. When he tried to recall the details of the dream, he realized the man in the dream wasn't Elliot at all. It was Gladiator Man, wearing Elliot's favorite long-sleeve rugby shirt. It was three sizes too small on him, and the seams were ripping, slowly exposing his muscles and skin. The dream Gladiator Man, like some puppet master of lust, had the power to simply look at Joe with his angry-sexy stare and instantly cause an overwhelming and unquenchable longing in Joe—a longing that could make him do anything.

"Joseph!" Howie's voice called up from downstairs. "Breakfast is on the table!"

"Coming," Joe shouted, waiting a moment for his hard-on to deflate. Then he scrambled down the ladder to find a plate of eggs with a side of brisket on the table. Howie was cooking something else on the stove. "Where's Lenny?" Joe asked.

"Out back in the yard, exercising." Howie pulled down several little jars from the floor-to-ceiling spice rack next to the stove. Each shelf was crowded with dozens of small jars containing dried leaves and powders, as well as others that appeared to hold small twigs, roots, and other organic materials. The lowest shelf had corked test tubes filled with liquids, mostly brownish and yellow, but a few with more vibrant blues and greens.

"Whatcha cooking?" Joe grimaced at what smelled like potpourri and rancid tuna.

"Just putting a little infusion together for Chrissy Bluebird. She's in the middle of selling her late mother's house and has lots of inner turmoil. She tried carrying around my cleansing green tourmaline for a week, but it didn't work. So I'm preparing an old radical faerie remedy I learned from a sous chef up at the Moosewood Kitchen in Ithaca."

"Gotcha," Joe said, suppressing about a dozen questions. As he dove into his breakfast, he looked out the window and saw Lenny twirling around in a circle in the middle of the herb garden. He held one arm up toward the sky, the other toward the earth, his eyelids half closed. Joe expected him to stop any second, but the man kept spinning, first slowly, then faster, à la Stevie Nicks's "Stand Back" music video. "I thought you said Lenny was exercising?"

"He is." Howie stirred the various pungent ingredients into a doll-sized saucepan.

"Looks more like some sort of dancing to me," Joe said, crunching off a bite of toast.

"Well, dancing is exercise—especially twirling. It's also fantastic for the brain and an important tool for restoring the Great Balance." Howie stuck his head out the open window. "Take it easy, Lenny! Remember your stent! Also finish up and eat lunch! I need you to drop off this infusion to Chrissy before you go to your meeting!"

"Be right there!" Lenny hollered back, gasping heavily, having stumbled out of his spin. "Let me just do a minute on the left so I'm not lopsided!" Five minutes later, still sweating, Lenny sat at the dining room table, eating a brisket sandwich and flipping through the personals in the *New York Native*.

"Oh, by the way, Joe," Howie said. "*Everyone* has been gushing about your bartending debut."

"Seriously?" Joe said, feeling a little giddy that people might actually be talking positively about his bartending skills.

"Absolutely," Howie continued. "You are a huge sensation."

"*Really* huge, it seems," Lenny said. "You know they've already nicknamed you Falafel Crotch, right?"

"Falafel crotch?" Joe squinched his eyebrows. "What does that even mean?"

"Lenny, stop it." Howie looked annoyed. "Why'd you mention that?"

"What's the big deal?" Lenny slapped the air with his sandwich. "It's 'cause you got a big package—if it's real. Also, because you're Armenian, which is the Middle East. Besides, everybody gets a nickname around here. Really, it's a compliment. The guys think you're aces."

Joe sighed. "I guess it's better to hear what people are saying. Still, that nickname's bullshit. Falafel isn't even Armenian. And Armenia is in Central Asia, not the Middle East."

"I'm happy to spread a new nickname around if you want," Lenny said. "What's an Armenian food that sounds good next to the word *crotch*?"

"Let's just forget it," Joe said. "Anyway, I totally had a blast last night. I even invented my own version of a Long Island iced tea and took home over two hundred bucks in tips. Oh, and I think Vince went home with Ronnie."

"Do tell." Lenny salaciously sipped his coffee.

"How nice!" Howie effused earnestly—clearly, he wasn't holding a grudge about Ronnie's rudeness from the previous day. "I sense those two would be good for each other."

"Oh, it's just a sex thing," Joe said. "Remember the whole point of Ronnie being out here is to find a rich guy to marry. He's pretty focused."

Howie nodded his head over his now steaming saucepan. "Like I said, Fire Island summers rarely turn out the way you plan. It's all up to the Great Goddess Mother, after all."

Great Goddess Mother? Why did he keep saying that? His housemates' obscure and unexplained allusions were starting to frustrate Joe, as well as give him the heebie-jeebies again.

"What do you mean exactly?" Joe asked.

"I mean that at her best, Fire Island has a way of giving you what you need, not necessarily what you want. But at other times . . ." He looked into his saucepan, as if the strange concoction had reminded him of a sad memory. "At other times it can tear your heart out—"

"Hey, let's keep it light," Lenny interrupted, his mouth full of brisket. "So, Joe, what time did you finish work?"

"Five AM.," he muttered, still absorbing Howie's puzzling comments.

"And you just went to bed after?" Howie asked.

"Not exactly," Joe said. "I went to chill on the beach and ended up seeing this guy . . ."

Joe caught himself. Did he really want to tell Lenny and Howie about the Gladiator Man? They knew almost everyone on the island, it seemed. But then again, what would they think of him practically stalking a complete stranger? A stranger he was so obsessed with that he was now haunting Joe's dreams. They'd think he had lost his mind . . . and maybe he had.

"I knew it." Lenny said. "You met someone! Do tell."

"Nothing happened," Joe said. "It was just some random hottie. Unfortunately, he left before I could say anything, and I ended up talking to some asshole deckhand who was out swimming at five in the morning."

Lenny's and Howie's eyes lit up with a newfound eagerness.

"A deckhand from the ferry?" Howie asked, giving a side-glance toward Lenny. "Swimming that early? Which one?"

"Be specific," Lenny added. "What did he look like?"

"I dunno," Joe said. "Like any hungover straight guy, I guess. Around my age, tall, arrogant, and annoying."

"Dark brown hair?" Lenny asked Joe for confirmation. "A little scruffy but adorable, with stunning blue eyes?"

"Yeah, his eyes were kinda blue," Joe said, not wanting to go overboard with praising the looks of a cock-blocking straight man.

"I wouldn't call him 'adorable,' but he's good-looking enough. Oh, and he had huge feet, and I swear his toes were webbed."

"I knew it was him." Lenny laughed and clapped his hands. "That's our boy!"

Joe let his fork clack down on the plate. *They really do know everyone.* "Your boy?"

"All you had to say was webbed toes." Howie smiled broadly. "That's our Fergal!"

"Fergal?" Joe wrinkled his nose at the funny name.

"We call him Fergal the Ferryman," Lenny declared.

"Such a cutie patootie." Howie faux swooned. "He's worked on the ferry since he could crawl. Always such a sensitive soul. As a child, we'd watch him comb the shoreline for any beached sea life he came across: horseshoe crabs, octopi, baby sharks. He started swimming before he could walk. Max, Lenny, and I would babysit sometimes, and we'd all spend hours splashing and diving. Such a wonderful, curious child."

"His uncle, Captain Harve, became my—" Lenny stopped himself. "Became one of my best straight friends, very open minded. I call him hetero-savant."

Joe smiled and shrugged. "So, I guess Fergal's not homophobic like I thought . . ."

Howie and Lenny looked at each other and chuckled.

"Homophobic?" Lenny said. "Someone's not paying attention."

"Just between us," Howie said with a wink to Joe, "while it's said that in the past our young ferryman has dabbled with girls quite successfully, he's definitely not straight."

"But I saw him talking to a girl the other day in the harbor," Joe countered.

"Talk schmalk." Lenny waved his hand. "According to my own hypersensitive, cosmically powered gaydar, I'd say our boy's at a sixty–forty split these days, with the percentages having shifted in our direction."

Joe's brain skidded to a stop, recalculating all its previous assumptions. "Fergal is bi?"

"More like gun-shy gay," Howie added.

"Then why did he act like such a dick around me before?"

"Usually, people act like dicks because they're nervous or insecure," Howie said. Then his eyes glazed a bit, seeming to watch a more intriguing idea flit across his brain. "Very interesting, Fergal swimming at dawn. I'll look closer next time. It's been all very hazy."

"*What* exactly was hazy?" Joe threw up his hands, making his frustration evident. "Can you please just say what you mean?"

"Oh, pish!" Howie laughed and tipped the pot of his rancid potpourri into a very small tincture bottle. "We're as clear as a cataract." He sniffed the greenish-brown liquid in the bottle and scowled as if Joe hadn't said anything. "Lenny, I'm not sure if I did this right. I think it needs more elder knot and some maidenhair. If you're in the Meat Rack later, could you keep an eye out?"

As Howie and Lenny began cleaning up while discussing where to find the plants, Joe was forced to surrender once again to the strangeness of his housemates with their mysterious and obscure slogans; their healing potions; their spinning in circles; the omnipresent disco music playing; and the strange, flamboyant way they dressed. Of course, while they sometimes tied his mental wiring into knots, he had to admit he enjoyed how different they were from the middle-class gays of Philly, with their limited ideas of gay identity. Most just wanted to be able to pass as straight, get into a monogamous relationship with someone equally "straight acting" who worked in a law firm, and own a Society Hill townhouse and maybe a weekend place in Bucks County. For Joe, Howie and Lenny's weirdness was a bit like being awakened with a bucket of multicolored ice water being poured over his head. Despite what Ronnie always said, there wasn't just one way of being gay. Joe liked how Howie and Lenny made him feel a little less self-conscious. Maybe they wouldn't judge him if he admitted to stalking the Gladiator Man—and they, of all people, might actually know who the man was.

"Hey," Joe interrupted. "I wanted to ask you about this other guy . . ."

"Uh-oh, here we go," Lenny said, giving a wink.

"Was it the other man you met at the beach?" Howie started wiping off the condiment bottles.

"I haven't really met him," Joe said. "But he's probably the hottest man I've ever seen in my life."

Howie and Lenny cast their rags aside, sat down at the table with their chins on their fists, and stared at Joe with enraptured faces.

"Go on," Howie insisted. "We love stories about beautiful men."

"I'm sure you know him," Joe said. "He's really built, about six four or six five, salt-and-pepper beard?" Both his housemates nodded their heads in approval. "He looks like a cross between a *Colt Magazine* model and an actor in one of those old Italian gladiator movies? About thirty-five or forty—maybe older, maybe younger, hard to say."

"Not ringing a bell," Lenny said, looking at Howie, who appeared to agree. "But sounds delicious."

"Come on," Joe practically begged. "You had to have at least seen the man I'm talking about. He was in the harbor the day I met you guys—he was wearing a Titans sweatshirt? I keep trying to talk to him, but he keeps disappearing. He has these really dark, intense, angry eyes that feel like they're ripping you open—"

At the exact same moment, Howie's and Lenny's expressions changed to something a lot like... dread? No, that couldn't be right. But there was no doubt their eyes showed recognition. "So you *do* know him?"

"No," Howie muttered. "We have absolutely no idea who you could be talking about."

After Joe had pressed Howie and Lenny two more times about the Gladiator Man, he surrendered and headed into the bathroom to shower. Once he was out of earshot, Howie whispered to Lenny anxiously, "This must be what Max was trying to tell us to look out for."

"You're jumping to conclusions again," Lenny insisted. "Remember, he's nowhere near the age of the others."

"Yes, but did you see how mesmerized he was when he talked about that Gladiator person? The hottest man he'd ever seen? Couldn't look away? Kept disappearing? Angry, dark eyes ripping him apart? That's nearly the identical language all the others used. What if a chosen one can be a few years younger? People mature at different ages. I can't believe it's happening again at the worst possible time—"

"Basta! You're being paranoid! It was just some random hot guy. Joe's on Fire Island for the first time, for Chrissake."

"Oh come on, Lenny! Someone who looked like his Gladiator Man would be the talk of the town this early in the season. You know that!"

Lenny shook his head adamantly. "I'm not buying it. Joe seems too levelheaded. The others were all in very bad places in their lives."

"Then why are my intestines all balled up like this?" Howie's eyes lowered to the table as if he were searching the swirls in the wood pattern for possible disasters.

Lenny took his old friend's hand sweetly. "Let's just take a breath, okay? The world is a mess, and our heads aren't in the right place. Let's not start comparing Joe with . . ." Lenny stopped himself from saying the name, but Howie knew exactly who he meant.

A dark memory—an event that was considered one of their coven's worst failures—flashed simultaneously before their eyes. It had happened during their final summer as the holy guardians of Provincetown, Massachusetts. The young man's name was Lucho, an adorable carpenter who did repair work on the artists shacks in the dunes. Half Portuguese, half Nauset Indian, Lucho had been born on the Cape and had beautiful, sad black eyes, a beard, and a traditional azulejo design tattooed onto his shapely right pectoral. So sexy yet so pure, and prone to falling desperately in love with the worst men who visited P-town. His dream was to become a writer and to compose stories that would change the world.

Max, consulting his sacred rubric, had concluded without a doubt that Lucho was one of the chosen ones—a holy lover, blessed by the Great Goddess Mother, destined for greatness, a warrior for the restoration of the Great Balance. Because of this he would be marked for death by the Great Darkness, and require protection and guidance by the Disco Witches in order to survive his dark summer of the soul.

It had been the Monday after Labor Day. Max, fearing Lucho's most recent man obsession had been sent by the Great Darkness to lure Lucho toward annihilation, asked Lenny to stand sentinel over the boy while the others attended a midsummer "cleansing boogie" at the A-House. Lucho, a master trickster, managed to slip away under Lenny's nose. A local drag queen reported seeing Lucho stumbling in a stupor across the stone jetty to Long Point, "as if he was chasing something."

A dozen Disco Witches piled onto the dance floor in a last-ditch effort to boogie out some protective magic to save Lucho from his dark fate, but it was too late. Rumors spread that Lucho had left town without telling anyone. The regular folk assumed the disappearance was simply another instance of a worker who couldn't bear the pressure of another Provincetown summer and fled on the midnight bus. The Disco Witches knew differently. Lucho's tank top and shorts were found in a tidal pool behind Herring Cove beach. They never found his body.

"To be quite honest," Lenny said, having shaken off the awful memory and averting his eyes from Howie's, "I'm not sure I believe in all that crapola anymore. We did a lot of drugs back then . . ."

"Just stop, Lenny," Howie spat. "It's not time for your periodic agnosticism again. Think of that anxious look in Joe's eyes. Think of how he was transfixed by those photos in the attic—the ones we know were taken on the days when you-know-what was afoot."

"Okay, fine." Lenny threw up his hands. "Maybe it's not just us being delusional together. But until Max gets out here and gives Joe the once-over, there's no way to know for sure. Of course, there's another way."

"What is it?" Howie said excitedly, hoping Lenny had remembered something.

"If Max doesn't get back in touch soon, we could just send someone to get the sacred texts from him. We might as well face it: it's time you took over—"

"I don't want to hear it!" Howie slapped his hand on the table. "Max is going to get better."

"Sweetie." Lenny gently reached for Howie's arm. "It's time."

"Don't," Howie snapped, pulling himself away. "I'm not ready for him to be gone. Please, just give him a little more time to get better. Meanwhile, let's just focus on keeping Joe out of any harm's way. We can't risk losing another. We just can't."

17.

The Great Darkness

"The Great Darkness is everywhere. It is the doubt within love, the oil that turns rancid. It is that moment in a perfect night of dancing when the electricity goes out, the amplifiers die, your ecstasy stops working, and your beloved looks at you with disgust in his eyes. At its most triumphant, it is AIDS and the hatred toward those who are infected."
—Disco Witch Manifesto #149

"So, that's it?" Dory said. "You think these omens you've been seeing have been indicating that our Joe might be one of the chosen ones?"

Dory and Howie had been sitting on the large white sofa in Dory's huge living room, sipping cups of wormwood tea. Her walls were painted a very pale lavender, matching the color of her short afro, while three huge oil paintings splashed bloodred hibiscus flowers across them like a floral crime scene.

Howie nodded ominously. "I do. I've been getting this strange feeling ever since I first saw him in the harbor."

"Hmm," Dory hummed, closing her eyes and picturing the young bartender. "He *does* have something about him—a sensitivity that clearly comes from having experienced something difficult."

Her mind flashed to all those vulnerable young people sent to them in years past. Beautiful lost souls with such promise, hunted by the Great Darkness but (mostly) protected and instructed by Max and his disco witch coven. This was the Disco Witches' most sacred purpose, to ensure these *chosen ones* made it through their darkest nights of the soul and did not die in the process. How many sacred dances had the Disco Witches performed, hoping to save some bewildered, holy innocent from the claws of a dire fate brought upon them by their destructive predilections? How many of these chosen ones had they taken under their wings, teaching them to honor the gifts that the Great Goddess Mother had bestowed on them? Convincing them to wait for her miracle? Dory glanced at the cold gray Atlantic looming outside her massive picture window as if it were waiting to crash through at any minute. "But without Max or his rubric, there's no way for us to know for sure?"

"Exactly," Howie said. "Though without a quorum, I'm not sure how much use we'd be anyway if Joe did end up being in danger."

"What else makes you think it might be Joe?" Dory asked. "I vaguely remember Max saying something about a similar aura."

Howie took a deep breath. "Well, that was one of the first things I noticed, of course. Joe's aura fluctuates with a predominance of violet, purple, gold, and silver, all streaked with tormented bands of black and green—just like the others. Also, like you said, he wears that look of someone who has suffered a deep and recent wound, though that hasn't been confirmed."

Dory raised her one eyebrow. "I'd bet a thousand dollars on that one. What about his gift?"

"Oh, that definitely could be another indicator." Howie lowered his voice again, but this time there was a smidge of excitement in his tone. "Don't say anything, but we found out Joe is toying with the idea of going into medicine."

For a brief second Dory's heart swelled with hope. "Are you saying Joe could be instrumental in finding the—?"

"Shh!" Howie cut off Dory from saying the word *cure*. Then he made spitting sounds three times, a protection against tempting fate. "Let's not get ahead of ourselves. I will say, I've been getting these auric flares and gastric nudges that he very well could play a role, or at least accomplish something important." Howie's expression grew grim. "If he survives, that is."

A wildfire of gooseflesh rushed up and down Dory's arms. "What haven't you told me?"

Howie closed his eyes and shook his head. "I didn't want to say anything, but just this morning, Joe told us he saw a mysterious, beautiful man—once in the harbor upon arrival and once on the beach early this morning. A man who, he says, was the most handsome man he'd ever seen, resembling a gladiator. He said he looked at Joe in a way that was both desirous and disdainful. Those are my words, but that's what he meant."

"Please tell me you don't mean—" Dory quickly covered her mouth, fearful she might summon evil by saying the full name in its original tongue. (Of course, to pronounce the name properly, complete with audible and inaudible inflections, one needed to be intoxicated on ayahuasca and sucking on the skull of lizard.) "The egregore?" she finished with a whisper.

She recalled how Max first explained it to her. These "men" were not men at all, but rather nefarious presences born of the holy lovers' self-hatred. These dark spirits walked the shadows of Fire Island, periodically taking over the bodies of lonely, shame-filled outcasts, transforming them into the young men's darkest and most desirable fantasies. Max called them irresistible, false prophets of passion who would lure the most blessed youths toward self-destruction and—if the Disco Witches did not intervene—death. Max had told her, "The egregore is one of the Great Darkness's most potent weapons in prolonging its reign—kill the brightest lights before they reach their full potential and destroy all hope of restoring the Great Balance."

Howie nodded fearfully. "Of course, Lenny thinks I'm way off base. None of us have seen anyone gorgeously suspicious. But then, with all the losses to our powers, would we even have the ability to register a nefarious and deadly presence sent by the Great Darkness? Lenny thinks Joe just saw the first really hot man of his life. I didn't mention it before, but Joe's from the suburbs of Philadelphia."

"Ah, I see," she said. "So, Lenny doesn't believe Joe is in danger?"

Howie sighed. "Lenny doesn't know what he believes."

"Is he doing his denial thing again?"

"Lately, he's even been questioning our past accomplishments. Implying that a lot of the magic might have been our imagination.

Max told me last autumn that he thinks Lenny's suffering the results of trauma from having lost so many of our friends."

"Aren't we all?" Dory cast her eyes to the ocean, thinking of all the dying men and women who had gazed out on the same ocean for the last time.

"Yes, but he knows damn well what happened on those dance floors and what didn't happen." Howie bristled before his shoulders surrendered. "To be honest, sometimes I wonder if Lenny's right. Could we have imagined it, Dor? Was it the drugs? Could it all have been one giant mass delusion, like Our Lady of Fátima or trickle-down economics?"

"You're being silly," Dory said. "When Max gets out here, he'll be able to clarify what is what. And then we'll have our quorum and the sacred documents, and we'll sort all this out." She took Howie's hand. "Meanwhile, we need to keep our heads on and our eyes open. We haven't lost that power yet."

18.
The Graveyard Girls

"When not dancing, practice your twirling, make love, read books, nap, have your best friend over to bake cookies and try on outfits."
—Disco Witch Manifesto #79

The Fire Island Pines Muscle-Up Gym was set on the large outdoor patio between the Flotel Motel and the back of the Promethean dance club. Half-rusted exercise equipment lay jumbled across the concrete as if it was the detritus from Jack LaLanne's flooded basement. Joe lay on a bench finishing a second set of grueling chest presses while Ronnie stood over him like a drill sergeant.

"Okay, let's go—one more set!" Ronnie barked. "No pain! No gain!"

"Come on!" Joe said, huffing and puffing. "Just give me a break for, like, five minutes."

"No way. I'll give you forty-five seconds."

"Okay. Great," Joe said, figuring how he might stretch the break longer. "By the way, I wanted to ask you how your plan to get revenge on Vince is going. What did you say a couple of weeks ago? Oh, right, you said, 'I'm going to give him the lay of his life and then ignore him.' If I'm not mistaken, you two have been sleeping together almost every night since."

"Yo, keep it down." Ronnie lowered his voice. "You're the only one who knows about us, and I'd like to keep it that way."

"Why? You seem to really like each other. And he's been in a heck of a better mood since you two started dating." Joe thought about how Vince had stopped yelling at Joe every time he hadn't cut up enough lemons, and how Joe had even heard Vince humming a Lionel Richie song while wiping down the speed rack.

"We're *not* dating," Ronnie spat. "I already told you. Yes, Vince is *way* hot. But, face it: he's gonna spend the rest of his life on this fucking island, scraping together some half-assed existence like the rest of the poor working slobs out here. That's not who I'm looking for." He then sped through his list of creative visualization on the topic of *man of his dreams*, including his age, height, penis size, and minimum annual income. "He'll also inspire me and finance my motivational speaker business, and we will live together happily until he dies peacefully in my arms, after which I'll meet someone else wonderful." Ronnie gasped for air. "One thing is certain—come September I'll have a deluxe one-way ticket off this island with a hot, rich daddy. If and when I set foot in the Pines again, it's gonna be because I'll be owning a house, not cleaning one."

Joe scrunched his brow. "But what about Vince? Is he cool with keeping it casual?"

"Yes. We agreed—great sex, no emotional connection, and . . ." Ronnie trailed off, narrowing his eyes. "Wait a minute. I see what you're doing. Think you're so smart, huh?" He put on his drill sergeant voice again. "Back to work, wimp! Time to muscle up! Last set! Let's go! One! Two!"

Joe rolled his eyes, grunted, and struggled the bar up and down six times until he let it slam back down into the rack with a groan. "That's it. I'm done. This shit is too hard."

"Come on!" Ronnie shouted. "Are you serious about this or not, Joe? Jesus Christ!"

"Did someone call my name?" a nasally voice droned loudly.

Looking over, Joe saw three men in dark sunglasses and dark club wear (clearly from the night before), standing at the gym entrance. One, the source of the voice, was a tall, large-boned man in his thirties, with dark curly hair and a cigarette clenched between his fingers, like an old-timey movie star. All three had grayish skin and were sweating profusely and chewing gum maniacally. The cigarette-smoking man gestured to his two companions, who followed him across the gym floor like zombie handmaids.

"Your day can get started now!" the chubby tall man announced. "The Graveyard Girls have arrived!"

Ronnie threw his bulging arms around the man and his silent companions. "Joe! This is Thursty, he manages all the bars for Scotty Black, and these two handsome gents here are his boys, they do everything at the Promethean, from bartending to running the lights and sound. They call them the Graveyard Girls because they work harder than anyone out here."

"Something like that," Thursty mumbled.

Joe offered his hand to shake, but the men appeared not to notice. He surmised the Graveyard Girls' moniker might owe to the fact that the three men, completely clad in black, were the sort who stayed up all night getting high on coke and Special K and looked more like corpses than the staff of a beach resort.

"Man, oh man, these guys live the life, Joey," Ronnie effused. "Every winter they work in South Beach or Key West and then spend summers up here working for Scotty Black. They save beaucoup cash since they never need to pay for a permanent place to live, and get to party for free!"

"Wow. That's great," Joe said, trying to fake excitement at what, in actuality, sounded a bit like drug-induced indentured servitude.

"We're just a tribe of wandering gay Bedouins," Thursty droned before dragging on his cigarette. "Although our caftans—when we wear them—are far more colorful." The other two Graveyard Girls started to laugh, but no sound emerged from their gaping mouths, as if they were sealed behind an invisible pane of glass, which Joe found very unsettling.

Thursty removed his sunglasses, revealing disturbingly bugged-out eyes that raked across Joe's body. "Mmm. Where did Scotty find this swarthy little sausage? Rounds? The Townhouse?"

"Huh?" Joe had never been to those notorious Manhattan hustler bars but still understood Thursty's intimation. "Nobody *found* me anywhere. And I don't work for Scotty Black. I work for Dory and Vince over at Asylum Harbor."

"Oh, so *you're* Falafel Crotch." He and the other Graveyard Girls did another round of their creepy silent laughter while gawking at the front of Joe's shorts.

"The name is Joe," he said firmly, grabbing his towel as if to wipe his sweat, but letting it fall so the Graveyard Girls would stop staring at his bottom half.

"Whatever," Thursty said. "I know Asylum Harbor doesn't provide housing, so where are you living on those shitty tips? You should talk to Scotty and see if he has any work. It's cold at night, sleeping on the beach."

Joe clenched his jaw, but before he could snap out a response, Ronnie gave him a cautionary eyebrow raise. "Joe's found a temporary place to stay for cheap. Unfortunately, it's with these weird old house cleaners over on Picketty Ruff."

Thursty's already buggy eyes bulged from his head so far that he resembled a rubber novelty toy. "Howie, Lenny, and Max are your housemates?"

Joe was taken aback at how he instantly knew who they were talking about. "Yeah," he said. "I moved in two and half weeks ago. Although I haven't met Max yet. I might have to find a new place when he does move back in, but right now I'm staying in their attic."

"The kid lives in the Picketty Ruff boys' attic," Thursty emphasized to the other two Graveyard Girls, who lowered their sunglasses, exposing their own buggy eyes.

"I keep telling him it's a mistake," Ronnie said with obvious disdain. "He needs to find a cooler place to live than with those geriatric housemaids, right?"

"Shh!" Thursty's dime-sized pupils grew to fearful nickels. The sight unnerved Joe and made him wonder why Thursty would have such a reaction. "I wouldn't be calling the Picketty Ruff boys *maids*," Thursty said. "Not if you're smart. There are stories, but . . . never mind."

All three Graveyard Girls exchanged anxious glances with one another.

"What kind of stories?" Joe finally asked.

After looking toward the back fence, Thursty walked a step closer to Joe. "Well . . ." He huffed his dead-cat-smelling breath into Joe's face. "Unpleasant stories."

Joe shook his head. "No way. Howie and Lenny are the nicest guys I've ever met."

"Or that's what they want you to believe," Thursty whispered darkly. "Have you noticed how Howie is constantly offering people little potions or spooky voodoo charms?"

"Wait, seriously?" Ronnie exclaimed.

"Cork it!" Thursty hissed and gestured toward the Picketty Ruff side of the fence. "Sound travels like a bullet around here."

"So, what's wrong with Howie giving people good luck charms?" Joe said. "It's not like they're hurting anyone."

"You think so, huh?" Thursty said.

"Tell 'em about Rehoboth," the mid-sized Graveyard Girl mumbled through the keyhole of his K-hole.

"I don't really want to hear any more," Joe fumed. "Let's get back to our workout, Ronnie."

"Hold on a minute, Joe," Ronnie said. "You should know the truth about those guys. So what exactly happened in Rehoboth?"

"If you must know . . ." Thursty lowered his voice again, but this time adding a Vincent Price–like pacing to his tale. "Several years ago, back in the late seventies—"

"I think it was the mid-seventies," the shortest Graveyard Girl offered.

"Pipe down!" Thursty snapped. "I'm telling the story!" Then, sotto voce: "So, back in the mid-seventies, their little 'gang' was down in Rehoboth for the weekend and showed up at the Pink Alligator disco."

"The Pink Alligator?" Ronnie said. "Never heard of it, and I've been to Rehoboth a dozen times."

An angry whine trumpeted through Thursty's nose. "If people would stop interrupting, they might find out why." He took a breath. "Anyway, Max, Howie, Lenny, and the rest of their group go into the club all dressed in their wild outfits and start dancing in a little circle. Then one of them—I think it was Howie, but it might have been Max—hits on this cute little hunk of rough trade. But the rough trade isn't having it. He calls him and his group a bunch of disgusting sissies or something. They complain to the manager. But the manager tells him, 'This ain't no drag club.' Kicks *them* all out. They're furious and an hour later they return. But this time they're dressed in these weird robes, so the doorman doesn't recognize them. Then they start doing one of their hocus-pocus, disco witch dances, spinning and flagging and chanting some weird shit—like an incantation."

While Thursty yammered on, Joe shook his head to show his disbelief in the story. *Disco Witches?* Absurd. But at the same his head flashed to the image of Lenny doing his "exercise spinning" in the backyard. Gooseflesh crawled up Joe's arms.

"So after about an hour, Howie and company leave again. Next thing ya know, people start smelling smoke. Sparks start bursting in the wiring over the dance floor. Suddenly, the entire club starts flaming harder than a croquet match between Paul Lynde and Charles Nelson Reilly! In just two hours the Pink Alligator is a pile of ash. A dozen queens were charred beyond recognition—including the rough trade who rejected Howie.

"They were accused of starting the fire?" Joe asked.

"Of course not." Thursty pulled down his pruny eye bag with his pointer finger. "I'm just saying it seems a very big coincidence how that all lined up." He suddenly looked at his companions. "Fuck, this conversation is completely killing my high."

"Mine too," the mid-size Graveyard Girl added.

"It's like I've been saying," Ronnie said to Joe. "Something's not right with those guys—especially that Howie."

"Stop it, Ronnie!" Joe bristled, lowering his voice. "That's a bullshit story from an obvious drug mess."

Thursty glared at Joe, but his flash of fury quickly converted into a cowering smile. "The little furball's probably right." An anxious quaver filled his voice, as he looked back toward Picketty Ruff. "I'm sure that story is just gossipy bullshit. We adore the Picketty Ruff boys, right, guys?" The other Graveyard Girls nodded their drug-addled bobbleheads. "Do send our regards to the boys for us." Thursty put on his sunglasses and indicated for his friends to do the same. "We better go take our energy vitamins and get ready to work a triple today. Let's go, girls. We'll sleep next week." Thursty turned the Graveyard Girls around one by one and gave them a stumbling shove toward the gym's exit.

Once they were gone, Joe could no longer contain his anger. "How can you suck up to guys like that?"

"Look, I know," Ronnie said with a shrug. "They're total douchebags. But I'm trying to make friends—for *both* our benefits. If you wanna be on Scotty Black's good side, you gotta be on the Graveyard Girls' good side."

"But all that bullshit about Howie burning down that club? That's some first-rate defamation shit, if you ask me."

"Whatever." Ronnie raised his eyebrows and pointed to the back fence. "But it proves my gut reaction about Howie and Lenny wasn't totally wrong. Something is off with those guys."

19.
The First High Holy Day

"A good night of dancing is not measured in hearts stolen, but in how many lives have been made larger. (Of course, one can do both with the perfect outfit.)"
—Disco Witch Manifesto #27

By the Friday afternoon of Memorial Day weekend, every inch of the Pines hummed with young holiday revelers, all shamelessly attired in the tightest go-go shorts or Speedos, and little else. Howie had told Joe that Memorial Day was the first of Fire Island's four high holy days, the second being the "invasion" on July Fourth; the third being the Morning Party, a fundraiser for Gay Men's Health Crisis in mid-August; and the last being Labor Day, the official end of the summer season.

In the weeks since his encounter with the Graveyard Girls, Joe had neither seen nor heard anything to worry him further about Howie and Lenny. Mostly, people spoke fondly of his housemates. Ronnie was the only one who talked smack about them—at least to Joe's face. Sure, Howie and Lenny were quirky as hell, but they were also very kind and were always feeding Joe and trying to teach him things. These older, overly caring oddballs were a nice balance to all the young hot guys on the island who could be snooty, especially when they found out Joe was a bartender.

Meanwhile, the bar was doing far better in the early season than both Dory and Vince had predicted. If things kept up reasonably well, they thought they could keep Scotty Black from trying to take the bar over—at least anytime soon. And the cherry on top of everything was Vince had told Joe he could end his Saturday shift early and attend the Promethean's opening party. "The bar will be slow anyway that night," Vince said. "You go, have a night out dancing, and, please Jesus, get laid for once, would ya?"

Joe was thrilled. Beyond it being his first weekend night off on Fire Island, he thought he might maybe—just maybe—run into that Gladiator Man. For the first time in a long time, everything seemed to be looking up. That is, until he returned to 44 and ¼ Picketty Ruff and found Howie out on the back deck at the other end of the twenty-foot spiral telephone cord, looking very upset.

"Oh no," Howie moaned to whomever he was speaking with. "Are they sure?"

Joe strained to decipher the one-sided conversation, which mostly consisted of sighs, head shakes, and grunts of disappointment. Something was really wrong.

"Sure. Sure. Right," Howie said as the call edged toward an ending. "Thanks, Heshy. I know. I know. I know. I guess right now all we can do is burn some sage and offer it up. Keep us posted, dear." He slowly walked back into the kitchen, hung up the phone, and stared at it hanging in its cradle as if it were a dying kitten.

"What happened?" Joe asked gently.

"That was Max's boyfriend." Howie's eyes welled. "They found a lesion on Max's brain."

Howie's huge body collapsed into a kitchen chair as his face filled with a look of hopelessness. Seeing him that way caused Joe's mind to flash onto dark memories he longed to forget—the day Elliot had been diagnosed with thrush, then Kaposi sarcoma, then the lymphoma scare. The incessant doctors' appointments, the obsessive scouring of newspapers and medical journals for any scintilla of hope. How foolish Joe had been to think that by coming out to Fire Island he'd be able to forget. How could he? Almost every day, he'd hear people talk of friends who were sick or dying. Every day, men with AIDS would sit at his bar, nursing their drinks, with clothes hanging off their bodies like scrawny kids playing dress up. Seeing their gaunt gray faces, powdery lips, and sunken scared eyes, Joe would tell himself, *Elliot never looked that sick toward the end. Elliot never suffered like that.* But the longer he lived on the island and the more he saw the anguished faces of men like Howie, the harder it was to believe all the lies Joe was telling himself. This disease was not gentle, nor straightforward, nor did it allow some handsome, noble death. It was out there, aiming for you and all those you would or could love.

"I'm so sorry," Joe said. It was all he could say.

"Thank you." Howie wiped his eyes with the hem of his robe. "But I do have some good news to sprinkle on this misery pie. In a moment of lucidity, Max spoke to Heshy. He agreed that you can stay in the attic the whole summer if you like. Heshy says Max is beside himself to meet you. Of course, that could be the lesions talking . . ." Howie feigned a laugh. "No. Of course, he really wants you here. We all do."

A surge of warmth hugged Joe's heart. "Thank you, and please thank Max for me too."

"I'm still hoping you'll be able to thank him yourself. Either way, you're a Picketty Ruff boy now." Howie rustled Joe's wavy hair, but a second later, Howie's smile vanished, and like he had several times over the previous weeks, he looked at Joe in that odd way, with his eyelids almost squeezed shut.

"Is something up?" Joe asked. "You keep looking at me funny."

Howie opened his eyes back to normal. "Just be careful this weekend, okay? The high holy days can be tricky, no matter who you are."

Joe squinched his nose. "What's that mean?"

"It's just things may tempt you out there—delicious and dangerous things. You can always talk to me and Lenny about it. We won't judge. Okay?"

"I'll be careful," Joe said, assuming Howie was talking about safer sex.

"And if you wouldn't mind, please keep us posted of your whereabouts. I know that sounds like I'm a silly old worrywart, but, well, I am." He smiled sadly. "I'd better go find Lenny and tell him the news about Max."

Howie trudged out the screen door, a look of grave concern on his face.

"*A Picketty Ruff boy now.*" The hairs on Joe's neck stiffened. Those had been the Graveyard Girls' words just before they told him about that bar in Rehoboth burning down.

Saturday afternoon, Joe awoke with his head still swimming with faint images of a dream. He couldn't remember the details except for it having to do with people running from a spreading fire. Like most dreams, Joe was left with more of a feeling—in this case a dire desperation, a longing to save people, and a fear of being consumed by flames himself. The Graveyard Girls had gotten back into his head about Howie and Lenny.

Joe pulled on a T-shirt and gym shorts, but as he was headed downstairs, he stopped at the padlocked crawl space and got on his knees to peek through the crack in the door. He saw nothing but shadows and a glint of light on the floor. He pressed his nose against the space under the door and sniffed. Beyond the usual scents of cedarwood, dust, and cardboard boxes, he detected a faint, familiar, smoky odor. If only he could get inside.

"What are you doing?" Howie's voice cried out. Joe's body jolted. He then realized Howie was yelling at Lenny downstairs, from the base of the ladder. "We don't have a lot of time!"

Joe jumped up and quickly clambered downstairs. Howie was indeed in more of a dither than usual, scribbling a list on the back of an envelope and wearing his shockingly "hetero" "ready-to-go-over-to-the-mainland" Mets cap and jacket. "Breeder drag," Lenny had once called it.

"Good morning, gorgeous," Howie said to Joe. "How was the bar last night?"

"Great." Joe grabbed the bagel that Lenny had obviously left out for him. "It was packed. Vince even sounded optimistic about us staying open. What's going on? Did something happen?"

"I'm afraid Lenny and I have to scoot over to Sayville to do some shopping for a last-minute soirée Dusty Jacobson decided to throw Monday night."

"On Memorial Day?" Joe asked. "One of your high holy days?"

"Indeed it is," Howie said glumly. "Alas, there's an even higher and holier day that we call *payday*. The gig will cover expenses for a month. Stores are closed Sundays, so we have to head over today. The Great Goddess Mother will understand. We need last minute decorations for a sexy merman theme. Which means nets, glass balls, and a mermaid costume that can fit a two-hundred-and-thirty-pound Bulgarian stripper—I'll need to whip that up myself of course. Oy! Johnny Weissmuller meets Esther Williams madness! We'll be back in about three hours, so hold the fort down—"

"Howie, enough with the blabbing!" Lenny said, rushing from his room. "We don't want to miss the boat!" He turned off the stereo and carefully returned the cassette to the shelf. "Joey, I left you some meatballs and gravy in the fridge for your dinner. But like I keep saying, now that we're stuck with you for the summer you gotta learn to cook for yourself. Capeesh?"

"Got it," Joe said.

"Good," Lenny said, rushing out the door. "But don't cook anything until Wednesday, 'cause I'm gonna roast a leg of lamb—"

"Lenny!" Howie screamed at the screen door. "The boat!"

A moment later the house was deathly quiet. Joe suddenly realized it was the first time he'd be completely alone in the house for that long—no disco music, no housemates watching his every move, no threat of a surprise return. Joe's limbs began to tremble with excitement. If he was going to find out what was inside the crawl space, that three-hour window was the time.

"The one thing we ask here is that we all respect one another's private spaces," Howie had told him the first day he had moved in. If they discovered him prying, he might be kicked out. But he needed to find out what they were hiding in there. Was it proof that could confirm or deny the Graveyard Girls' horrific accusations? And if Joe was going to be called a Picketty Ruff boy, wasn't it only fair he knew the truth?

The only thing was, to get into the crawl space, he'd need a key.

20.
Saint D'Norman

"All that we are is within the twirl, all that we see is within the twirl, all connection is within the twirl. Praise the Great Goddess Mother! The sacred twirl will open your eyes, but only if you're looking inward. If you look outward, you will fall."

—*Disco Witch Manifesto #7*

The last time Saint D'Norman had visited the clinic about a sick stomach, his new doctor, a young, straight GI resident, was not very friendly and seemed uncomfortable seeing a patient with AIDS. Then, without even touching him, he offered some rote advice about avoiding coffee, alcohol, spicy foods, and any strenuous activity. When Saint D'Norman asked if that included dancing, the doctor said, "Yes. Why would someone your age and condition be out dancing anyway? It's time you stayed home and rested." Then he showed him the door.

On his way out, Saint D'Norman flashed his smile at the young resident, and said, "No dancing, huh? Kiss my ass, you arrogant, know-nothing, latex-loving motherfucker. You're fired."

As a flamboyant child raised in the less than accepting neighborhood of 1960s South Central Los Angeles, dancing was little Donny Norman's way of mentally escaping from a world in which he just didn't fit. When he was seventeen, he'd finally escaped for real, with a cross-country bus ticket, all the way to Greenwich Village and the dance floors of Manhattan. There he met his true family and turned into the fabulous Saint D'Norman, the snapping, popping, bumping, twirling disco witch sensation.

Off the dance floor, he became a registered nurse. He had always had a gift for healing, inherited from his West African great-grandmother, and Cherokee great-great-grandfather. The most vital thing he learned during his decades of nursing was that losing hope was one of the worst things that could happen to a patient. No way was he going to let any doctor (or Miss AIDS herself) make him lose hope—or the chance to dance.

When the crisis first started, the ravaged bodies of three of Saint D'Norman's former lovers walked into the hospital where he was working. Seeing them there, looking like that, told him all he needed to know—he had the virus too. He vowed to do his darnedest not to get sick himself, and for the next five years he kept that promise. Dance, he believed, was one of the practices that kept him strong.

But just being infected with the virus still took its toll, even before he got any of the opportunistic infections. First, he lost his job at the hospital, then his beloved West Village apartment, and finally even his ability to afford a summer share in the Pines. Without a place on the island, he couldn't help with the coven's most important summer work, and with so many sick or dying, they needed him desperately. Lucky for everyone, Dory had been more than happy to offer Saint D'Norman a free place at her house on Ocean Walk. Not wanting to feel like a parasite, Saint D'Norman "volunteered" (with pay) to work as Dory's off-the-books major domo. He loved feeling useful again, and the more than decent pay allowed him to venture into the city to buy sparkly new dance outfits, although the opportunities to wear them had grown fewer. But like Max always told him, a disco witch always needed to be prepared. This was why Saint D'Norman decided to wear a shimmering turquoise caftan for that afternoon's twirling practice.

"Well, let's get this show on the road," he said to the empty deck as he pressed "Play" on the high-end boombox Dory had given him. A moment later "Boogie Wonderland" by Earth, Wind & Fire started to fill the warm air with pure bliss. Then, as he had been taught so long ago, Saint D'Norman crossed his arms over his upper chest and slowly began to spin in a counterclockwise direction, gradually raising his arms, his right palm lifted toward the heavens, his left palm downward toward the earth. Besides reinvigorating his attitude and getting exercise (fuck that doctor!), Saint D'Norman was using the sacred twirl to see if he could hook up a connection to the Great Goddess Mother. He was hoping to gain the clarity Howie had been seeking with that lame-ass, long-distance-boogie spell he'd tried over the phone. *Howie-girl needs to do some spinning herself and clear that too-busy-for-her-own-good head of hers.*

After a few minutes of spinning, some flickers began behind his eyelids. A memory was trying to push through. He put his twirl into high gear, spinning like a dreidel on the ball of his left foot. Bit by bit, word by word, the memory started to grow brighter until it was like a billboard in front of his face. *Max's rubric. There it is, clear as day.*

Saint D'Norman stumbled out of his spin. He knew Howie and Lenny were about to head over to Sayville on the 1:55 PM ferry. He had just enough time to catch them and tell them everything. *Just wait until those queens hear this!*

21.
Howie's Room

"Disco Witches respect the private spheres of their brothers and sisters. Unless granted permission, no one wants someone else's dirty fingers on their magic wands."
—*Disco Witch Manifesto #86*

So, where exactly *were* they hiding the crawl space key? Joe looked back and forth between the doors of the three downstairs bedrooms. Lenny's was the smaller room at the back of the cottage, next to the laundry machines, allowing for maximum privacy in case the randy little leatherman coaxed some hot bottom into his sling. You could tell when Lenny was using the contraption because he'd put an old pair of sneakers in the dryer and run it for an hour to silence the sounds. The center room off the dining room, the largest, was Max's, which hadn't been occupied since the previous summer. And finally, Howie's room, at the front of the house, next to the screen door, allowing him to oversee the comings and goings of 44 and ¼ Picketty Ruff all year long. The key would obviously be kept there.

After double-checking that no one was out front, Joe pushed Howie's door open. Other than a few glimpses, he had never stepped inside. When he did, his eyes were bombarded by a rainbow fantasia of feathers, sequins, glass beads, and wall-to-wall camp. A Disneyland fantasy boudoir by way of a whorish Glinda the Good Witch. *How am I going to find anything in this mess?*

There were shelves of ornate hats ringing the ceiling, jewelry trees dripping like Spanish moss with silver necklaces, two mannequins draped in lavender organza. The bedspread was an intricately handmade quilt of pinks, greens, and yellows, featuring a pattern of winged phalluses, all erect and ejaculating daisies. Joe felt a strong urge to laugh—almost like the room demanded it. How could someone with a room like this burn down a disco? But then again, hadn't that serial killer John Wayne Gacy worked as a clown at children's parties?

He continued his search, crossing to the bedside table, thinking if Howie had an important key, he'd want it close to him when he slept. On top of the table were two books worn thin by repeated readings. The first was an old mimeographed manuscript titled *Faggots & Their Friends Between Revolutions*. The second sent a burst of ice water through Joe's veins: *Witchcraft and the Gay Counterculture* by Arthur Evans. A quick perusal proved the book was more of an anthropology textbook rather than a black magic how-to. Joe wondered if Howie's taste in literature had ignited the rumors. Perhaps an old hookup had glanced at his bedside reading and told everyone Howie was a witch.

Mustn't get distracted. Focus! The key, the key—where is the key?

He slowly pulled open the little table drawer. It was filled with the usual gay bachelor accoutrement (condoms, lube, poppers) as well as a small stash of magazines: *After Dark*, *The Advocate*, *Latin Inches*, and *Good Housekeeping Needlecraft*. Still no key. He looked in enamel jewelry boxes on the bureau. Alas, they were only filled with rings and brooches, coins from around the world, old postage stamps, rubber bands, and a staggering number of nail clippers.

Feeling frustrated and guilty, Joe sat on the flying penis comforter and sighed. He was being ridiculous. He felt Howie's good luck charm in his pocket and thought about how the boys had taken him in and found him a job. Lying back on the bed, Joe stared at the ceiling painted with the constellations of the night sky. As he searched for Orion's belt, he suddenly felt an overwhelming sense that someone was watching him. But the door was shut tight. He gazed out the window and around the room twice before he saw it.

In the very middle of the wall facing the bed was a very large, ornately framed Hollywood glamor shot of a woman with giant black eyes. On closer inspection Joe saw that the subject wasn't a woman at all, but a Hispanic-looking drag queen dressed in a blonde wig, with thick layers of makeup and giant fake eyelashes. She had strong Indigenous features, like a Mayan Mae West. The photo was signed, *To Howard Fishbein, mi alma gemela. Your love forever, Eartha Delights and Her Ominous Bush. Release and trust the power! XXOO Max.* The gaudy frame was its own handmade work of folk art, decorated with so much gold paint, jewels, and pearls.

Inspecting closer, he saw that under and between all the fake glass jewels were gilded souvenirs of the drag queen's life: theater tickets, cocktail umbrellas, a large glass-ruby cocktail ring, a mascara brush, a cock ring, two horse-sized false eyelashes, plastic red lacquered fingernails, Central American worry dolls, and membership cards to the Paradise Garage, the Saint, and Flamingo East. At the very bottom of the frame was a small brass plaque with words etched in elegant calligraphy: *On this Earth she danced with passion, Maximon Javier Ramon De La Laguna, 1934–*

Then, just above the frame, was a small shelf with a lotus-topped metal vase. On a closer look, Joe realized it was most likely the urn that would hold Max's ashes when he died. The frame, it appeared, was meant to honor Max in perpetuity. Had Max and Howie worked on it together? Had they already known, when they made it, that Max was going to die soon? What was it like to know you're dying and to partake in the building of your own memorial?

Joe's heart grew heavy as he thought about how much Howie must care for his friend to build such a work of art. He wondered if perhaps they were more than friends. Did Howie love Max as much as Joe had loved Elliot? Did he love him more? Joe gazed into the drag queen's dark eyes and grew dizzy. Suddenly, he heard the sound of disco music. Had the stereo started on its own? Or was it coming from the neighbors? Sensing an odor emanating from the photograph, he stepped closer and sniffed. The smell of acetate, jasmine, and musk filled his nostrils. As he looked deeply into the drag queen's eyes, her lips appeared to whisper, *"We aren't dead yet,*

Joe. We love you. You're in danger, Joe. Dance with us, Joselito, dance with us."

Joe's body started to quake uncontrollably. What was *wrong* with him? Was he going crazy? It took him several seconds to recognize his own weeping. He felt so foolish. He had never even met the dying drag queen. He needn't be heartbroken over her too. Wasn't mourning Elliot enough? He had to stop staring at the photo, but he couldn't. It was as if the drag queen wouldn't let him go, wouldn't let him forget.

"Stop lying, Joe," she whispered. *"You must stop lying about Elliot! Danger, Joselito, danger!"*

Joe gasped for air. "Fuck you!" he shouted. "Leave me alone! It's *your* fault this disease even started! It's your fault Elliot's dead! Now, where is that goddamned key?" Rage filling his chest, Joe tore himself from the photo and returned to his hunt for the key. He scoured the top shelf of the closet, felt along the windowsill, and searched the pockets of Howie's maroon bathrobe. Finally, as if being led by some odd intuition, his eyes fell on the bronze lotus flower at the top of Max's empty urn. He leaped to his tiptoes, reached inside the lotus flower, and there it was. A key.

He glanced at his watch; it seemed impossible, but two hours had passed since he'd entered Howie's room. He had to hurry. After putting the room back in order, he rushed up to the attic and stared at the little locked door. Was it the right key? Of course it was. The padlock opened on the first try. Joe's body vibrated with both excitement and fear. What would be inside? Cages? A trapped door leading to a secret space where they imprisoned young bartenders from seasons past? Cast iron pots and yards of black velvet draping the walls? He pushed the small door open. The heat from the cramped, unventilated storage space whooshed out at him. He finally pinpointed the other smell—frankincense! It was a smell Joe equated with the Armenian Apostolic Church he'd attended as a child. Priests swinging large brass incense burners. Aunt Vartu lying in the coffin, lips and cheeks too rouged.

The lightbulb string hanging from the eaves tickled his neck. Heart pounding wildly, he held his breath and yanked. The small room lit up, and a flood of disappointment hit him. There were no dead bodies hanging from the rafters. Nor was there a giant cauldron or jars filled with baby's hearts. Not even empty cans of gasoline. Instead, the interior of the crawl space was filled with what had been moved for his comfort—sealed boxes of craft supplies, racks of clothes, and coffee cans filled with decorative buttons, trims, and glass eyeballs.

The Graveyard Girls' gossip had clearly been the hazing of the island's new bartender, nothing more. Such a bullshit waste of time.

Just as he was about to pull the lightbulb string, he noticed a cardboard box opened and haphazardly shoved right next to the door as if it had been placed in a hurry. Every other box in the room was sealed and neatly stacked. He was overcome by the same madness he had felt while standing in front of the drag queen's photo, that voiceless voice propelling him toward the box, the faint sound of disco music, the scent of the jasmine-musk perfume. He slowly moved the flap to look inside, as if it might contain the smallest dead body. By the shapes and sizes of the frames, Joe instantly recognized the photographs that had been removed from the walls of his attic room. He pulled one from the box and saw it was exactly like all the others he had seen already, vintage shots of the boys and their friends enjoying themselves at various events going back decades—nothing that seemed worthy of hiding.

Joe laughed at his own foolishness. Maybe he'd secretly *wanted* Howie, Max, and Lenny to be pyromaniacal dancing witches. He picked up another of the frames, a black and white photo that showed a much younger Howie, Max, and Lenny. Lenny with his full head of black hair cut in a severe crew cut; Max, an androgynous, Guatemalan hippie with his arm around Howie's slim waist. He also spotted a glamorous, younger-looking Dory along with her friend Saint D'Norman in the photo. Both were dressed in white elephant bell bottoms and crop tops, with religious icons around their necks, similar to what Joe had seen on Howie. The entire group stood by a Provincetown Inn sign, holding American flags like it was the Fourth of July. Joe examined the other retro-looking men standing nearby. Most had mustaches and long hair; some were handsome, others not. His eyes wandered to the upper corner of the photo, and chills suddenly ricocheted across his flesh.

Looming there in the background was a man who looked uncannily like the Gladiator Man.

No. It wasn't that he looked like a younger version of Gladiator Man, but rather he looked almost exactly like the man Joe had seen both in the harbor and on the beach. But it couldn't be him—the photo was from the late 1960s, and the man in the photo, like Gladiator Man today, appeared to be in his late thirties or early forties. Yet it was the same beard, the same build, the same square jaw, the same gray sweatshirt with the word "Titans" on it. Even the way the man folded his thick furry forearms looked exactly like Joe's Gladiator Man.

Joe pulled the next frame from the box. This photo, in gilded Kodachrome, was labeled *Bicentennial Party at Big Bill Missellwick's House, July 1976*. Everyone was dressed in kitschy, patriotic, fetish outfits—sexy Ben Franklins, slutty Betsy Rosses. Searching all the faces, Joe couldn't find him at first, but then he noticed a blurry form of a muscular man leaning against a tree in the background. He couldn't make out the man's face exactly, but he was the only person at the party not in a costume. He had the beard, the posture, the gray sweatshirt (though Joe could only make out the letters A and N). It could be him. But it *couldn't* be him.

Joe thrust his fists into the box and pulled out another, then another and another. One, circa 1970, showed Bette Midler singing to a crowd at Christopher Street Liberation Day in Washington Square Park. Another was titled *1979 Island House Party, Key West*. And then he pulled out the Anne Boleyn decapitation hat photo. In each one Joe found a similar-looking muscle man who very well could be Gladiator Man, standing in the background, rounding a corner or riding a bike, always staring into the camera—staring directly at Joe. "*Here I am,*" the figure seemed to say. "*I've been waiting for you. Come find me.*" Joe closed his eyes, hoping for an end to what had to be a hallucination.

A loud banging on the downstairs screen door shot a bullet of panic through every nerve in his body. What would Howie and Lenny do if they caught him in there? He shoved the framed photographs back into the box and yanked the lightbulb cord. He had to lock up and get the key back into its hiding place. As he jammed himself through the small door, he felt the most shocking pain, as if a very small assassin had jabbed a mini dagger into his leg. Looking down, he saw the bloody nail sticking out of the door frame. It had sliced a two-inch gash into his calf muscle. After fumbling with the padlock, he bolted down the ladder.

"Joe! Hey! Joe!" the gravelly deep voice yelled from the screen door.

Joe's heart pounded. He limped across the living room, hoping the shadowy figure behind the door didn't see him as he rushed back into Howie's room. He quickly dropped the key into the lid of the lotus urn. The drag queen's voice echoed in his head, *"They're going to find out, Joselito, they're going to find out! Danger, Joe! You're in danger!"*

"Shh!" Joe hissed before hobbling to the front door and opening it. There, staring at him through the wire mesh, was Fergal the Ferryman.

"What do you want?" Joe snapped, far meaner than he'd intended.

"What's wrong? You okay?" Fergal asked, his brow worried.

"No! I mean yes. I mean, come back later. Howard and Lenny aren't here."

"I know they aren't," Fergal said. "They asked me to tell you they'll need your help getting some stuff up to the house—holy shit, dude, what the fuck happened to your leg?"

Looking down, Joe saw that the lower half of his leg was covered in blood. He felt the hot pulse of the gushing wound and grew dizzy. The last thing he saw before fainting was the ferryman's terrified expression and how his blue-blue eyes were almost glowing.

22.

Warning Signs

"The eyes of the watcher must be keen. Drink coffee or other noncorrosive stimulants. Carry eyedrops."
—*Disco Witch Manifesto #67*

"Injured men always look a little hotter," Howie joked as he finished retaping the bandage on Joe's calf.

The wound would heal nicely thanks to the herbal poultice Dory had suggested. Howie had most of the ingredients in his back garden, while Lenny was sent to the Meat Rack to hunt for a necessary medicinal mushroom.

"It took me forever to find that motherfucker," Lenny groused. "You try foraging for a fungus that looks like a used condom in the Meat Rack."

Howie gave Lenny the side-eye of disbelief as he secured the last of the white medical tape and patted Joe's leg. "Dory has always been an absolute miracle worker with some of these old folk remedies. Hopefully this will stay stuck this time. It's like bandaging a satyr with those hairy legs of yours. And I know that of which I speak."

"You've taped up satyrs?" Joe asked without even a smile, which Howie found curious.

"Well, the back room of the Mineshaft could get a little wild on Wednesdays," he joked, clutching invisible pearls at his throat.

There! He saw it again, that look on Joe's face, an emotional cocktail of fear and suspicion. Howie first noticed it just a few hours before when Joe awoke after having passed out at the sight of his own blood. Howie could practically hear the mental gavel of Joe's judgment pounding the air as he dissected every word that fluttered out of Howie's or Lenny's mouths. *Guilty! Guilty! Guilty!* At the same time, Joe barely seemed to register the outrageousness of Lenny's Saturday night outfit, which included a full leather harness with metal studs, and a front strap that (Lenny reported) led down to an entire junkyard of cock rings, Prince Alberts, and so many shiny scrotal gewgaws that at least one previous trick had likened it to going down on the Tin Man. About all that, Joe remained mum, yet he kept staring out of the corner of his eye at Howie, as if he were afraid the man was going to pull out an ax.

Howie squinted his eyes. Joe's post-injury aura had changed to a dark muddled blue and a sickly green, undulating and pushing outward. The boy was definitely lying. How had he *really* hurt himself—and why was he blaming Howie and Lenny for it?

At least they didn't need to worry about him being in mortal danger any longer. Saint D'Norman had rushed to the docks to catch Howie and Lenny before they boarded that afternoon's ferry. While practicing his twirling, he'd experienced a vivid recall of Max, in a bout of mushroom-induced intimacy, having shown him the secret rubric years before. The spinning and Great Goddess Mother had jiggled the memory loose, and Saint D'Norman recited it to Howie in its entirety.

A chosen one would need to meet all five main prerequisites, including having an aura that frequently depicted both transcendence as well as severe blockage (Goddess, yes! Joe had that in spades!); having been born into a family of historical tragedy (check—his Armenian heritage); having experienced a recent, soul-crushing heartbreak (undetermined, but from what Howie's gut said, probable); being in his first Saturn Returns, aka between the ages of twenty-eight and thirty (no check, thank the Goddess); and most importantly, bearing a winged, heart-shaped mole (and/or freckle) on his back or the back of his neck. (Lenny vaguely remembered Lucho having a mole on his back, but he'd thought it looked more like a sausage sandwich.) So, while bandaging Joe's leg the first time, just after the accident, Howie feigned a scream worthy of a schlocky Vincent Price horror film.

"What's wrong?" Joe asked, startled.

"Oh dear!" Howie cried to the others. "I think I saw a tick, climbing down Joe's neck."

"We better check it out in case," Lenny said, playing along.

"I didn't feel anything," Joe said.

"We can't be too careful," Dory added. "Deer ticks carry just awful diseases. Take your shirt off." All four then scoured Joe's head, neck, and back, which showed no sign of any winged-heart-shaped mole—or really any mole whatsoever.

"Clean as a whistle," Saint D'Norman said, sighing. "Could be a skin cream model."

"Hallelujah." Dory clapped her hands.

"Indeed," Howie said, realizing that Joe, having failed at least two (possibly three) of the sacred rubric's criteria, couldn't be one of the chosen ones. So why, two hours later, was Howie's gut still jack-knifing like there was still some danger afoot?

"Hey, Joe," Lenny said, adjusting his harness in the living room mirror, "maybe with a wounded leg you'll be easier to catch." He sniggered. "I tell ya, you'd have to be a dickless cockroach not to get laid on Memorial Day weekend . . . unless somebody put a hex on you."

There it was again! Howie saw it even more clearly. Joe had flinched at Lenny's little joke about the hex. *Is that it?* Had some gossipy queen said something to Joe? Max always chastised him about assuming everyone would be so welcoming to their metaphysical-spiritual unconventionality. "Remember, mi cariño," Max had once warned, "there are a thousand different ways to burn us at the stake. Don't make it easy for them." It was always best to listen to Max. But would Joe be so prejudiced? Howie knew so little about him other than that he couldn't be the chosen one and that he was lying about something . . . or several things. Lenny had already deduced the lie about the injury. Joe said he had just arrived home after slipping off the boardwalk when Fergal found him. Yet Lenny, being experienced with BDSM techniques, including flogging, impact play, and some light body mortification, had practically a forensic scientist's knack for understanding wound patterns. The gash in the leg, Lenny said, had to be made by a metal spike sticking out the side of some immovable structure. Joe would have needed to be rushing in a horizontal trajectory, not vertical as would have happened with a slip off the side of the walkway. But rushing from what or whom? And where had it happened? There had been blood down the ladder, across the living room, at the front door . . . and in Howie's room.

Why had the boy gone into a forbidden space? Howie wished he or Lenny had the ability to read minds. Saint D'Norman and Max, of course, dabbled in mentally connecting with the dead, but Joe was very much alive. In time Joe might eventually open up and reveal what he was hiding—or that's what Howie hoped. He deeply wanted to be a true friend to the boy, but they'd need to fully trust each other. And that meant Howie would need to confess the whole sordid—and magical—truth about their unusual collective, something he was not yet ready to do.

"I better get back to the bar," Joe said. "Vince shouldn't be left alone so long."

"You try and have fun tonight." Lenny winked. "It's your first big night out!"

"But do be extra careful," Howie warned, closing the first aid kit. "The Promethean is insane on opening night, and the dance floor gets slippery from all the sweat. If you need a bandage replacement, just call and I'll run over and set you up."

"Just call him Florence Night 'n' Gay," Lenny quipped.

"Thanks." Joe tested the bandage on his leg, as if he didn't trust it.

"By the way," Howie asked, "was there anyone special you were planning to meet out dancing tonight?"

Lenny clicked his tongue and winked. "Like that bearded hunk you told us about?"

"No," Joe said flatly, then got up from the table and deposited his breakfast dish in the sink, never once looking directly at the men. "I'm just going alone."

Howie shook his head at Lenny and shrugged. Even if Joe wasn't the chosen one, there were so many other dangers young men like him might still face on Fire Island. It was a disco witch's obligation to watch out for all the innocents, not just those who had been singled out by the Great Goddess Mother.

"You know, Joseph," Howie said, "I suspect you must be very overwhelmed. I mean, with the new bartending job and summer exploding, like some adolescent Mormon seeing his first JC Penny underwear ad. What I'm trying to say is, it's not surprising that you're acting a little strangely."

"*Me* acting strangely?" Joe scoffed petulantly, his voice rising with anger. "If you ask me, I'm the least strange person in this room right now." Howie glanced at Lenny with a "what-the-hell-is-going on?" expression. Remorse filled Joe's face. "I'm sorry. I shouldn't have snapped. It's just my leg hurts and . . . and it's like you think you know things . . . I mean, when things aren't what you think they are . . . that people are hiding things—never mind. I'm just a little tired with all the work, I guess."

Lenny gave a mild harrumph, while Howie was befuddled by the shear breadth of Joe's emotional muddle. It was like a swirling spiritual milkshake made of fear, anger, heartbreak, dishonesty, longing, confusion, and the sour milk of regret.

"Joseph . . ." Howie touched Joe gently on his shoulder. "I want you to know you can always talk to Lenny and me about anything. We have a lot of experience out here. And not everyone is cut out to deal with the strange passions and . . . um . . . dynamic personalities that fill this island. If there is anyone or anything that confuses or scares you, please come to us. There was a time when—"

"I'm late." The chill had returned to Joe's voice. "I might not be home tonight. Don't wait up." A moment later, the screen door slammed.

Howie looked at Lenny's face, which reflected his own deep concern. "Something's definitely up. He must have gotten into the crawl space."

"Thanks a lot, Ophelia Obvious," Lenny droned. "You got anything more specific?"

Howie sighed. "Nothing. At least we don't need to worry about any friggin' egregore anymore—at least for him. But let's still keep an extra careful watch tonight."

23.
Saturday Night

"There's a time to watch and a time to dance!"
—*Disco Witch Manifesto #58*

Thanks to Dory's poultice, the wound on Joe's leg didn't hurt at all despite him having been on his feet bartending for over five hours. By ten pm the bulk of the customers at Asylum Harbor started to head out to eat a late dinner, shower, maybe douche, don their sexiest butch drag, and return to the harbor for a night out dancing at the Promethean. It would be the start of a pattern for most of the summer people that would repeat like clockwork until September: beach, low tea, high tea, hopefully Asylum Harbor, dinner, Promethean, hook up or hit the Meat Rack, bed. Rinse, wash, repeat. Fun, fun, fun, and . . . more fun. Or that's what it looked like on the outside.

Joe wished he had their same ability to access so much casual joy. But he was stymied by the specter of his great sadness, his fear of the virus, and his more recent rumination on what he had seen (or thought he had seen) in the crawl space and in Howie's room. And what about that thing Lenny had said about a hex? And the way Howie was always staring at him like he did? And the potions and the club in Rehoboth? And had all three of them really needed to check him for ticks? He should have just confronted them. But what exactly would he have said? That he suspected that they were members of a potentially murderous coven of gay psychopathic witches? Confess that he'd broken into their crawl space and found photos of the hunk whom he'd been obsessing about, who might be a latter-day Dorian Gray on steroids? Or a ghost? Or a gay vampire?

Have you completely lost your mind? Joe thought to himself. *You don't even believe in horoscopes!* There had to be some logical explanation. He just needed to find someone to talk to about it without sounding like a crazy man.

"Hey, Joe!" Ronnie's voice called out from the edge of the bar. "You daydreaming or something?"

Joe's body jolted at sound of his name being called, and he quickly smiled to cover his reaction. "Wow, look at you," he said, noting how dressed-up Ronnie was. "Did someone beat you with an LL Bean catalog? Where's your usual 'muscle jock' clubbing outfit?"

As long as Joe had known Ronnie, he'd always worn the same outfit when they went out dancing: a Phillies T-shirt with the sleeves and midriff cut off and extra short shorts to emphasize his massive quadriceps. His lion's mane of blonde hair would always be unleashed to his shoulders, in case he wanted to whip it on some unsuspecting daddy bear to start a conversation. But that night Ronnie had slicked back his hair into a more conservative ponytail and wore his black Fred Perry polo shirt tucked into his dress-up Levi's 501s like some born-again preppy.

"Not tonight," Ronnie whispered. He furtively glanced over at Vince who was busy moving the empty cases of beer out to the back landing. "Look, Joey, I'm sorry, but there's been a change of plans. I can't do the Promethean with you tonight."

"Are you serious?" Joe groaned. "Why?"

"Hey." Ronnie widened his eyes. "Keep it down, okay? It's just I got a last-minute invite to a fancy dinner party. It's a great opportunity, and I don't wanna miss it."

"What about after?" Joe lowered his voice. "It's just I need to talk to you. I saw something at Howie and Lenny's. It's pretty hard to believe, and I know it doesn't make sense but—"

"Look, buddy, I really want to hear all about your housemates' newest weirdness, but"—Ronnie leaned in and curled his lips like he was trying to prevent an even bigger smile from tearing his cheeks apart—"I just gotta tell you something."

"Go ahead," Joe said, not having seen Ronnie this excited since he first convinced Joe to go out to Fire Island.

"I think I met *him*," Ronnie whispered.

"Who?"

"Him! The whole reason I came out here? The life partner I've been creatively envisioning every day for the last two years? His real name is Hogarth Miles Winkle the Third. Did you hear that?! The third! He's a third generation of something! He goes by the name Trey. Trey Winkle! He's perfect! He's got salt-and-pepper hair and only comes to about here on me." Ronnie indicated a height just below his ear. "Perfect size! Perfect age, like ten years older than me. He's class from head to toe. We're talking Ralph Lauren, Hermès cologne, a Cartier watch. Not to mention Gucci loafers I know were going for at least three hundred and fifty bucks at Wanamaker's."

Joe asked Ronnie to hold up while he made a round of kamikazes for a group of guys from Staten Island who were celebrating a friend's recent breakup, and then he had to serve about five more customers before he could turn his ear back to Ronnie.

"Okay, expensive shoes," Joe finally said. "So what?"

"The point is, he likes me. I think it could be something serious."

"Where'd you meet him?" Joe said as he washed the stainless-steel tumbler on the scrubber brush that stuck out of the sink.

"The Meat Rack. But he didn't even ask me to fuck him right away. Just mutual sucking and a quick rim job. He says he wants to get to know me first before we go further. That's gold, right? We also have a ton in common. He's read, like, all the New Age books I've read, and even *finishes them*. Also, get this: he owns an apartment on the Upper East Side of Manhattan, has a place in South Beach, and is building this nutso-ritzy beach house out here—right on Ocean Boulevard. It's massive. Everyone is talking about it. It's gonna be finished in about two weeks. He's the real deal, Joey. The real fucking deal!"

Joe's hope of getting Ronnie's attention long enough to discuss what he'd seen in the crawl space was completely gone. His friend was lost in the glittering swamp of romantic fantasy. And the more he thought about it, the more he knew Ronnie wouldn't be the one to talk him down. Ronnie had already made up his mind to hate Howie and Lenny and might just agree with anything Joe said just to get him to move out. And then, if it all turned out to be a big crazy mistake, he might never get Ronnie and the boys to become friends. No, it was best to let Ronnie follow his most recent romantic infatuation to its conclusion and for Joe to dig a little deeper until he was one hundred percent certain about what he had seen.

"If he's what you really want. But"—he tossed his head toward Vince, who could be seen through the glass door, collecting beer bottles on the deck—"what about him?"

Ronnie's elation fizzled like a wet firecracker. "You had to bring that up."

"Look," Joe said. "Vince can be a dick, but he's also a decent guy."

"I know that," Ronnie bristled. "But like I told you before, Vince and I have no obligation to each other. It's just sex. He and I talked about it."

Joe raised an eyebrow. "You told him about this new guy?"

"Of course not. I'm not gonna rub his nose in it. I intend to have a conversation with him soon, but I wanna do it right. That's why I need you to back me up."

"What do you mean?" Joe asked warily.

"I'm telling Vince I'll be cleaning up after a late-night catering gig at Jerry Herman's place so I won't be able to meet him after the bar closes. So, if he asks—"

"Fuck you, Ronnie," Joe hissed under his breath. "I'm not lying for you."

"You don't need to lie. Just don't say anything yet, okay? And remember why we both came out here. I'm just keeping to my plan, right?"

"Yeah, I guess. But still, don't play Vince for a fool, okay? Can you at least tell him tomorrow?"

Ronnie crossed his heart. Joe nodded but did not smile.

"Hey, I got about two minutes before I gotta bolt," Ronnie said. "So what's that weird shit you said you saw at Howie and Lenny's?"

"Nah, it was nothing. Forget it."

"If you say so. You're still going out dancing, right? Remember, you have a purpose out here too—starting with having a good time."

24.

Fun on the Outside

"It's at night when the gods and demons boogie most freely with our hearts. Dance with them, but beware."
—*Disco Witch Manifesto #32*

The air outside the Promethean throbbed with dance music. Rivers of men in tight shorts, combat boots, and tank tops poured into the club from every direction. Despite having done two shots of Jägermeister before leaving work, all of Joe's excitement about his first big night out had been replaced by anxious thoughts. Was it the right time to go out and let loose? He was living on an island filled with dying gay men; a possible hot, muscled-up, Gladiator ghost; and what may or may not be a coven of gay pyromaniac Disco Witches—and he was supposed to just forget all of that (and Elliot) and go have fun?

As Joe turned to head home to 44 and ¼ Picketty Ruff, a voice called out from the edge of Fire Island Boulevard.

"Hey, Joe!

It was Elena, dressed in a sweatshirt and shorts, stunningly beautiful as always, calmly sitting, like an oasis on the edge of the boardwalk, with a thermos of tea. Next to her sat that same blonde cashier from Mulligan's grocery—the pretty one Joe had assumed was Fergal's girlfriend that day he had seem them sitting together. He sure had misjudged Fergal there.

Elena waved him over. "Come meet my new friend, Cleigh,"

Joe crossed and shook Cleigh's hand. "Hey," he said.

"Hey," Cleigh said, in one of those great raspy voices of a girl who drank a lot of beer. "Elena's told me a lot about you. She's a big fan." She narrowed her eyes. "I think I've seen you before, right?"

"You know how it is," Joe said, hoping she didn't remember. "Small island." He leaned on one of the wooden columns as he felt a slight swoony buzz from the Jägermeister.

"You okay?" Elena asked, scrunching her eyebrows as her golden-brown eyes seemed to dig into Joe's brain. Did everyone on this island worry about him?

"Yeah. I'm cool," Joe said. "I was gonna go out dancing, but I'm not sure I'm feeling it."

"Come sit with me for a few minutes." Elena patted the edge of the boardwalk. "Cleigh was just taking a water taxi back to Sayville."

"I'll catch you tomorrow at the . . ." Cleigh suspiciously stumbled on what she was going to say. "You know, *that thing* we're going to."

"Right," Elena said with a smirk. "See you tomorrow at *the thing*." Then they hugged in a way that was both awkward but also seemed to hold a secret meaning. Joe wondered if Cleigh had already said something to Elena about that day she had seen him, and maybe why she and Fergal had laughed at him. Or maybe it was just the embrace of two straight female comrades stranded amid the hordes of homosexual men.

"What are you doing out so late?" he asked, plopping down next to her.

"Couldn't sleep. That's why Cleigh came out to meet me. My mind was spinning."

"Join the club. What was it spinning about?"

She looked over her shoulder back toward the harbor. "Well, that's kind of the crazy part. It was spinning about Cleigh."

Oops, Joe thought. Maybe it wasn't only Fergal he had misjudged. "You mean you like her? And she likes you . . . *that way*?"

"Maybe. I just think she's really cute and smart and looks like Kristy McNichol. And, well, I think, under different circumstances, there would be potential for something to happen between us. But I'm just not in a place for that sort of thing."

"I didn't even know you were gay."

"I'm not. I mean, I worked in fashion, so I've dabbled, but this is different. I really, really like this girl. But I just ended a seriously destructive relationship back in the city with this guy I used to party with, and I'm not supposed to even consider dating anyone right now or make any big changes in my life." She grunted in frustration. "And turning into a lesbian sounds pretty big, right?" She sighed and then, all of a sudden, closed her eyes and tilted her head like she was entering a trance. It went on for at least forty seconds, which concerned Joe.

"Is something wrong?" Joe asked.

"No," she whispered, her eyes still closed. "It's just the music. Hear that bass?" Joe could hear the distant *thump thump thump*. "It was the sound of my heartbreak back in the old days."

"Old days? You're still in your twenties, right?"

"I meant before I got sober."

Joe recalled having offered her a beer the day the bar opened, and her reaction. "I'm sorry, I didn't know. I shouldn't have offered you that beer—"

"Don't worry about it." She laughed. "You were being nice. I should have just said something. I guess I'm still new to it . . . though it feels like a lifetime ago at the moment. It's why Dory brought me out here, so I could get away from the mess I made back in Manhattan."

"I guess we all have some kind of mess in our past." Joe suddenly groaned, holding his stomach.

"Are you sure you're feeling okay?" Elena reached over and felt Joe's forehead.

"My stomach's a little wobbly. I did some Jäger shots." Then, without thinking, he said, "Unless Lenny put something in the Bolognese he cooked for me tonight."

"You might be right," she said darkly—or that's how Joe heard it. "Those boys are always offing some young bartender with poison pasta."

Joe's eyes widened and he lowered his voice. "Elena? Have you heard something?"

She looked at him puzzled. "What are you talking about?"

"Shh." Joe looked around at the blue and gray silhouettes of men roaming the shadows. Any of them might have been Lenny or Howie or one of their devotees. He scooched closer to Elena. His Jäger buzz was giving him courage. "Look, I heard some really crazy stuff about Howie, Lenny, and Max. Your grandmother and Saint D'Norman too."

Elena looked at Joe suspiciously. "What did you hear?"

Joe took a deep breath. "I heard that all of them are involved in this secret club—they go to discos and dress up in wild outfits and act like they can cast spells on people and . . . and maybe, at least once, they've burned a dance club down. I know that sounds nuts, but—"

Elena burst into laughter, hugging Joe like he was a slightly drunk twelve-year-old. When he realized she didn't believe him, his heart sank, and once again he felt totally alone.

"Joe, who told you that? Those four old queens and my grandmother are the nicest people this side of *Mr. Rogers's Neighborhood*. Someone actually said they burned down a club?" Again, Elena covered her mouth to hold in her guffaws.

Joe's face flushed. "But have you seen how they used to dress? There are pictures—"

Elena patted Joe's hand. "Shh. Honey, I've looked at Dory's shelves of photo albums ever since I was a baby. Everybody used to dress up like that to go to the disco dancing back in the day. It was like church for them. They aren't actual witches." She sputtered into another round of giggles. "Oh my God, baby, island fever has gotten you."

Elena's words made some sense, but they didn't explain what he'd heard in Howie's room and what he had seen in the crawl space.

"But you don't understand, I heard things, saw things . . ." Again he looked around for any hint of his roommates. "I snuck into this locked storage space in the attic. It's where they keep all their supplies and . . . it doesn't matter. There're these photos in there; they were on the walls when I first saw the attic, and then, for some reason, Howie and Lenny hid them in the crawl space. I swear!"

"Hid them?" Elena tilted her head. "Okay, so, what was in the photos?"

Should he really tell her everything? She might call 911 or refer him to a psychiatrist. But who else could he tell?

"Well, when I looked at them—I mean looked really closely—I recognized this guy I've been seeing out here. He's in the background of at least five of the photos they've hidden, but—here's the thing—the photos are really old, and he hasn't aged at all. I mean he looks exactly the same after ten, twenty, thirty years."

Elena's smile dropped. She looked concerned. "You think they're hiding photos of a guy whose appearance didn't change over thirty years?"

"Yes!" Joe said.

"Describe him to me."

"Well, he's about six four with short, dark hair and this sexy, salt-and-pepper beard . . . crazy handsome and built huge, like one of those guys in those old gladiator movies. You know the dubbed ones where everyone talks with a British accent, but they're supposed to be Romans?"

"Mm-hmm. So, you saw this gladiator guy's face up close in photos and in real life?"

Joe thought about it. No. He hadn't seen his face closer than thirty feet. And except for the one clear photo, the Gladiator Man was always in the background, with his face partially obscured . . .

Joe's memory started to blur. His face felt hot and sweaty. "It really looked like him, I swear."

"Joey, baby," Elena said kindly, "I hate to say this, but all gay guys look alike."

"No they don't!" Joe protested.

"They do. You just can't see it, honey."

Joe gestured to a smooth blond body builder, in a spaghetti-strap tank top, walking next to a short, thin Latin guy in biker shorts. "You're telling me they look alike to you?"

"Of course they don't look alike," she said. "I'm not comparing the bears with the twinks or leather clones." Elena impressed Joe with her knowledge of the taxonomical variations in gay male archetypes. "I'm saying just look within those categories—the guys look so much alike they could form their own sixties girl group. What's that expression? Oh, right: 'There are only six gay men in Manhattan, and the rest are done with mirrors.'" She pointed to the stream of men heading into the club. "Just use your eyes."

When Joe actually looked over at the specific brands of gay men standing in line, the similarity became starkly evident. Bears, twinks, muscleheads, silver foxes, lumberjacks, trolls, clones, wolves, chickens . . . it was like an illustrated gay *Grimms' Fairy Tales*. Even the "regular-guy" gays were all *regular* in exactly the same way.

"I guess we do all look alike," Joe admitted.

"If you get up close and add a personality, everyone is unique," Elena said. "But from a distance, it's like looking at dozens of G.I. Joe dolls on the shelf at F.A.O. Schwartz. It's the same with fashion models. Just squint and, other than our race and hair color, we're basically carbon copies. It makes sense that you thought you saw the same guy in all those old photos. Sounds like this guy you saw is one of those Tom of Finland muscle clones."

"Ugh," Joe said, realizing the impact of the insanity of his early summer—the move from Philly, the sadness, the unrelenting schedule, the heat of his attic room. "I feel like such an idiot."

Elena hugged him tightly. "You are not an idiot. This island will do that to you. It makes everyone go a little nutso. I'll be honest with you, I had something similar happen to me out here when I was a kid. Dory had me come out here the summer after my mother died—kind of like she had me come out here this summer—to heal. She thinks the island has special powers."

"She does?"

"She does indeed. And it's infectious." Elena started to laugh at a memory.

"What is it?" he asked, reflecting her laugh. "Come on, tell me."

"It's so stupid." She shook her head. "Once, when I was a kid, I thought I saw her group of friends elevating a few inches off her living room floor while they were having a dance party. I also remember thinking I heard strange voices."

Joe stopped laughing. "Are you serious?"

"Yeah," she said, still giggling until she registered Joe wasn't laughing too. "I mean no, Joe, it didn't really happen. It was just a weird window reflection, my mind playing tricks on me. That summer I just needed to believe in something magical, like Dory did. If magic was real, than maybe my mother's death wasn't an ending. You know what I mean?"

Joe thought about it, and there he was, like always: Elliot. If Gladiator Man was a ghost, then Elliot might be able to return as well. If a dying man's photograph could talk, then maybe Elliot could send him a message. If there was such a thing as Disco Witches, then maybe there would be some meaning to the awfulness of the world and the AIDS epidemic. "I think I get it now," he said. He lowered his voice even more. "I need to tell you something else." He took a breath, ready, finally, to talk. "About two years ago the only guy I ever loved died, and I've been struggling to get over it. That's one of the reasons I had to get out of Philly."

"I didn't know," Elena said. "I'm so sorry. Was it . . . ?"

She didn't finish the sentence, but instead looked down at the ground, worried. Joe wondered if she was assuming he was infected too.

He nodded. "Don't worry," he said. "I'm not positive. I got tested nine months ago. And I never have unsafe sex, so I should be okay."

"Well, that's good," Elena said, looking up.

"Elliot and I were always safe too. Sometimes I wish we weren't. I know I shouldn't say that, but that's how I feel. I loved him so much. Watching him at the end . . . I just wished I could leave too." Joe swallowed hard. The alcohol was making it even harder not to break down into tears when he told her about Elliot.

"It's good he cared enough to be careful for you," Elena said. "Not everyone is that lucky." Something had shifted inside her. The closeness Joe had felt toward Elena just moments before had fallen away. Her warmness had chilled.

But he kept going. For the first time he thought he might be able to tell someone the complete truth. "What really happened was . . ." He scooted a little closer, lowering his voice. "We weren't exactly . . . *together* when he died. I mean, I wasn't there, because—" His voice caught in his throat.

Elena gently touched his leg as she bit her lower lip and scrunched her eyes sympathetically. The warmth was back. "I'm so sorry," she said. "Was it his family? They tried to stop you from seeing him, didn't they?"

"No, you don't understand," Joe snapped, annoyed she couldn't read his mind. He took a deep breath, hoping to stem the tears, but the Jäger shots were making it impossible to control himself. "I wasn't there because—" He gasped for air as his shoulders shook and the tears began to fall. He couldn't do it. He couldn't tell her.

Elena pulled him to her shoulder and stroked his hair. "Oh, baby," she said. "It's okay. It makes total sense you'd think your roommates were witches. We all need magic to heal this shit."

Joe wiped his face with the bottom of his T-shirt and sat up. "I am so not gonna get laid looking like a fucking crybaby," he said. "I definitely need more cocktails."

Elena smiled, keeping her hand on his knee. "What about just heading to bed and trying again tomorrow? You'll have your pick of this island with those gorgeous eyebrows."

"Not so much. Also, if I don't try tonight, it might be weeks before I get the time off again." Joe stood up and swayed a little.

"But you'll be okay, right?" Elena sounded like a stern but caring field hockey coach.

Joe nodded. "Hey, you'll keep all that stuff secret, right?"

"Sure," Elena said. "You have my word. We'll keep each other's secrets."

Joe nodded in agreement. After he hugged her goodbye, he headed toward the Promethean, feeling her eyes follow him the whole way.

25.

Sentinels

"Disco Witches must stay open to the wisdom of the Great Goddess Mother from wherever and whomever it comes."
—*Disco Witch Manifesto #56*

The line forming outside the Promethean vibrated with a primordial energy. The staid and sober had gone to bed hours before. At one AM the hard-core partiers had only just awakened from their disco naps. Howie Fishbein sat on a nearby bench, his eyes fixed so intently on the club that it appeared as if he were waiting for it to lift off its foundation and fly across the bay.

His mind, however, drifted back to thoughts of poor Lucho and the tragedy that had befallen him. Despite Max's assurance to Lenny that what had happened wasn't his fault, he'd never fully forgiven himself. Howie knew Lucho's death had contributed to Lenny's periodic agnosticism. Couldn't he remember how they'd had far more successes than failures over the years? How they had guided so many innocent lives—both the chosen and unchosen—to safety through danger-filled summers?

There was that beautiful young Spaniard, Alberto, whom they had saved just in time before his motorbike drove off the end of the Provincetown pier. It was in the middle of the night, and Alberto, drugged-out on horse tranquilizer, had been told by a devastatingly handsome egregore that it was a special motorbike that could ride across the waves. "We shall escape together, and you no longer will be in pain," the egregore had whispered. "If you love me, you'll trust me."

If it hadn't been for the Disco Witches' sacred boogie, they never would have been able to control the tides that evening, causing them to ebb nearly thirty minutes early, and fast enough that Alberto's motorbike landed safely in the wet sand, and at the perfect spot for the Disco Witches to find him and guide him through the rest of his summer. How strange were their Goddess-given powers. The Disco Witches didn't always know how or why their dances worked to save these young men's lives, but Max always said when faced with a new challenge, "Just direct your mind toward the heart of the holy lover as you dance, and the Great Goddess Mother will take care of the way." When things worked, he'd write it down in the spell book. When it didn't, they'd try something else.

Alberto went on to great success as a fine artist, as well as founding a wonderful pet adoption service for animals left behind by those who had died from AIDS. And what about all the others they had helped in big and small ways? Had Lenny forgotten them? Of course, when the plague years began, it had made their work harder in identifying those under mortal threat. So many young people with hearts full of sadness, living on the brink.

But what of Joe? Was he in some other kind of mortal danger? Howie couldn't stop thinking of how Joe first described seeing the Gladiator Man. Was there any way, despite the rubric, that they could be missing something? Would they fail Joe like they'd failed Lucho? Or was there another chosen one they had totally overlooked? And if there was, what power would the witches have to help anyway? With barely a quorum of their kind left alive, what would the remaining Disco Witches become? Simply a useless handful of nostalgic costume queens weighed down by mourning and false magic?

"Oh, please, Great Goddess Mother," Howie whispered to the stars, "please, give us some clarity—"

"Hey, Howie!" a voice called out.

Howie turned toward the voice from the shadows and squinted. "Fergal? Is that you? What are you doing on the island so late? Don't you have to work the first ferry?"

"I usually do," Fergal said. "But I took the morning off. Thought I'd go out and have some fun."

Howie saw the young ferryman's face twitch. His aura's murky indigo spoke of deep intuition and feeling, but it gave way to an underlying violet, which meant that he too might have at least an inkling of psychic power. Though whether Fergal knew this or not, Howie couldn't tell. Very few magic folk are aware of their powers.

He squinted; there was some other dark force weighing on the young man. Flecks of dirty gray . . . getting over a cold perhaps? But again that prescient violet kept bursting through, so hungry to be seen. *He wrestles something inside his heart.* But what? Having known the young ferryman since he was a child, Howie had always suspected the boy might turn out to be one of those tormented, beautiful half-humans fathered by some profligate deity but completely clueless as to their origins. He had the haunting gaze, those otherworldly blue eyes, the underlying sadness that came with being only half of this world. Not to mention the hard drinking, his being prone to risk taking and extremes, his uncanny and precocious swimming abilities and those toes—ever so slightly webbed.

Yes, yes, Howie thought. Fergal might very well be a demigod, a bastard child of Poseidon perhaps, lost and longing to be set free or to find some purpose that would fill the god-shaped hole that sat in the middle of his heart. Of course, Howie also knew it could be his own wishful thinking again. *Oh, how the queer and magical, so lonely in their journey to maturity, all long for everyone they love to be queer and magical too!*

"Is that new asshole roommate of yours giving you more trouble?" Fergal asked.

"Are you worried about Joe?" Howie again squinted his eyes.

"Fuck no," Fergal said bitterly, though his lie was as transparent as Chrissy Bluebird's mesh bikini top. "I don't give two fucks about that stuck-up little asshole. You shoulda heard how he acted the other day before he fainted, or when I saw him on the beach. He thinks he's God's gift."

"I see," Howie said calmly. "But remember, he's brand new to the island. And I'm not sure if you've noticed, but he's carrying sadness inside him, which sometimes expresses itself as attitude or irritability. Too much sadness can be dangerous when confronted with Fire Island's high-pressure homosexuality. Certainly, you've seen what can happen?"

Fergal looked to the Promethean and then out over the harbor. It was so apparent to Howie that the anger the ferryman wanted to hold onto was confused by a salmagundi of conflicting emotions, primarily hurt pride and . . . desire? Brilliant fireflies of realization swarmed Howie's brain. That was it! Fergal was attracted to Joe. That was why he felt like he hated him so. Ugh, how complex and layered affection could be. But Fergal needed to protect himself. Young men like him—if he was, indeed, of mixed heritage as Howie suspected—were prone to falling in love too quickly and too passionately. No one suffered a broken heart worse than someone who was half god.

"Look, if you want my advice," Fergal said, clearly changing the subject, "you and Lenny have been through a lot lately and are always worrying about someone else. The old-timers are always blabbing about how great it was when you guys used to get all dressed up and go out dancing. Maybe this summer, try to get out there and have some fun."

"You're a very wise young man," Howie said. "One can't stay in mourning forever, I suppose. You never know; perhaps we'll test out our dancing shoes one night."

"Good. Now, I'm gonna go take a walk around the club myself and then probably crash at my buddy's house or catch a water taxi back home."

"Wonderful. Do a twirl for me as well. And, if you wouldn't mind, if you see Joe get into any trouble, do let me know. He's not as selfish and rude as you may think."

"Sure, Howie. 'Night."

Howie watched Fergal walk toward the club. Trailing after him was the glow of that fearless violet, as well as gold, silver, that dirty gray, and finally one of the most passionate shades of red Howie had ever seen.

26.

The Wawa Outside of Which I Wept

"Heterosexual overlords are not the only architects of the Great Darkness. Be wary of those holy lovers who have not grown past their self-hatred. Their hearts will be impenetrable to all but evil. Their kiss brings poison."
—*Disco Witch Manifesto #101*

When Joe opened the door of the Promethean, the one hundred and ten decibels of sound shook the fillings in his back teeth. A giant blow dryer's worth of humid air blasted his face, filling his nostrils with the scent of booze, poppers, and man sweat. The packed bar area was so dark it was impossible to make out anyone's face, but all the silhouettes looked like those of muscle gods in the prime of life. When the strobe lights went on, though, he suddenly saw the hollowed cheeks and cavernous eyes of those who were sick.

He pushed his way to another spot. That time, when the strobe lights exploded, he swore that for a split second he saw the face of Elliot in the crowd. He fixed his eyes on the spot, held his breath, and waited for the next clarifying flash of light. As he often did, he played a mind game: What if Elliot hadn't died? What if Elliot was actually here in the club, dancing? What if Elliot had faked his death just to get away from Joe? At the next strobe blitzkrieg, Joe saw that the man didn't look like Elliot at all.

The Jäger was really fucking with him now, but it wasn't enough that he could forget all the bullshit swarming in his head. He elbowed his way to the front of the bar, where he saw the medium-sized Graveyard Girl working the beer tap. He didn't appear to be high on K this time, and looked pretty good wearing a pair of butt-less chaps exposing his round and smooth cheeks like two kickballs.

"Hey!" Joe screamed above the boom-boom-boom. "I met you the other week with Ronnie and Thursty at the gym. I'm Joe from—"

"You're wearing too many clothes!" Without warning, the Graveyard Girl reached over the bar and yanked Joe's T-shirt up and off his back. "That's better!" He rubbed Joe's chest. "Mmm ... like Sean Connery and John Stamos had a baby. What'll it be?"

"Something strong," Joe said. "Maybe tequila?"

"Looking to get fucked up, huh?" the Graveyard Girl said.

"Yeah," Joe said. "A little."

"Got just the thing. It's called a Knockout punch. It'll help you feel all warm and sexy!"

"Sounds perfect!" Joe shouted over a remix of "All She Wants Is" by Duran Duran. "Give me an extra-large!"

About fifty seconds later, the Graveyard Girl held up a huge tumbler glass of punch. "It might sting a little at first," he said. "Best to take a big gulp to numb the throat."

Joe did as he was told. The Knockout—which Joe could now recognize as an extra-strong variation of a planter's punch—carpet-bombed everything in its path—tongue, gums, and back teeth. Joe's face scrunched in agony. "Holy shit, that's strong. How much do I owe you?"

"Always on the house for a fellow bartender. When you need a refill, just say the word!"

"Thanks," Joe said as he pounded down another gulp of the Knockout and made his way to the jam-packed dance floor. He could feel the alcohol pinballing around his synapses. He took another gulp, which no longer burned, but felt warm against his numb cheeks and throat. As Jody Watley's "Real Love" blasted over the sound system, his body begin to sway, and all the dark and anxious thoughts that constantly swirled around his brain began to slip away. He took another gulp, then another.

After fifteen minutes he was feeling pretty good. He took in the whole dance floor. It was exactly as Ronnie had promised back in

Philly—shirtless young muscle studs everywhere, the potential for copious amounts of sex, a feeling of freedom. He returned to the bar, and before he could even ask, the Graveyard Girl pushed another Knockout into his hand. Locked and loaded, Joe was finally ready to shoehorn his hot Armenian American body into that sweating fortress of heaving flesh.

Drinking is miraculous! The Graveyard Girls are miraculous! Fire island is miraculous! For the first time in forever, he wasn't thinking about Elliot or HIV or lying to everybody. He felt okay. Better than okay. Everyone around him was staring and smiling at him. Several men tousled his chest hair. A few grabbed his butt, and one unseen hand fondled his crotch. After politely moving the hand away, he crossed back to the dance floor's edge and set down the remainder of his second Knockout on a cleanup tray. He'd rarely been that drunk and knew he needed to pace himself.

"Bad drink?" a man to his right asked loudly.

Joe felt the air and spit of the words more than he could hear them. He couldn't make out the man's face since he was backlit by lasers and strobe lights. His most defining attributes were his height and that, unlike almost every other man in the club, he wore a shirt.

"Do I know you?" Joe asked.

The towering man adjusted his position so that his face was given a demonic glow by a red work light. It was Scotty Black. His perfectly coifed white hair, glowing pink, was frozen in a 1970s *GQ* middle part. "Don't my bartenders know how to make a good cocktail?"

"It's probably the best cocktail I've ever had!" As proof, Joe took another huge sip of the Knockout. His throat squeezed shut in protest, causing him to spit some out. Feeling guilty, he took another gulp, even bigger than the last. One of his eyelids closed more than the other. Scotty Black, like the first time he had seen him, raked his satanic eyes up and down Joe's shirtless body.

"You've been working out." Scotty let his lips touch Joe's ear. "You almost look Promethean-good. You sure I can't steal you away from Asylum Harbor? My guys make at least five hundred dollars on a night like this."

Joe had never made five hundred dollars in one night anywhere. His mind flashed to all the things he might do with that sort of money. But then he thought about Vince and Dory and the little merman clock over the bar. Fuck Scotty Black and his money. Fuck him for trying to shut down Asylum Harbor. Fuck him for not giving Ronnie the bartending job like he'd promised. "You know what? You're a full-on dickwad," he drunkenly mumbled.

"Pardon?" Scotty Black leaned his ear down to Joe's mouth. "I didn't hear that. Have you been overserved?"

"Are you kidding?" Joe shouted louder that time. "I'm absolutely sober! I just said, thanks for the offer, but I like working at Asylum Harbor. We're doing great."

"You think?" Scotty snorted. "Dory needs to face facts. I'm not in the charity business. That shitty little bar won't make it through August. If you reconsider my offer, call me."

Scotty slipped his card into Joe's front pocket, letting his hand linger before he slowly removed it. It took Joe's last sober brain cells to stop himself from tossing the remains of his Knockout into Scotty's face. "Sorry, Mr. Black!" he shouted over the music, "I'm feeling a little fucked up! I also have to go meet a friend . . . upstairs. Thanks for the offer. I'll think about it!"

Joe shook his head and stumbled up to the balcony. He wanted to find a spot where he could be alone. His happy buzz that had been climbing higher and higher on the roller coaster of inebriation abruptly tipped over and began its morose descent. Glassy-eyed, he gazed over the roiling dance floor, desperately searching for anything that might lead him back to the previous happy feeling. Those last few gulps and running into Scotty Black had ruined everything. The recurring darkness that had slipped away earlier came roaring back along with its rum-soaked forbidden memories.

Two years before in Philadelphia.
   The middle of a Sunday night.
   The last conversation he would ever have with Elliot.
   Joe had been drunk that night too. He was blabbering into a pay phone in front of the twenty-four-hour Wawa market on Walnut

Street, chomping on pork rinds—his go-to food when he was sad and drunk. He was just around the corner from Woody's Bar, the place where he had first fallen in love with Elliot.

"Hello?" Elliot's low and sleepy voice answered the phone. "Who's this?"

Crunch, crunch, crunch.

"Joe?" Elliot said. "Joe, is that you? Are you crying?"

"No," Joe said, sniffling.

Crunch, crunch, crunch.

"Are you eating something?" Elliot asked.

"No," Joe lied. He simply wanted to tell Elliot that he missed him. It had been only three days since they had taken a relationship break—their third such break in a month to be exact. Between his mouthful of fried pig skin, drunkenness, and weeping, it came out, "I (snuffle) m- m- miss (snuffle) y- y- you." Crunch, crunch, crunch.

"Joe, you're not supposed to be calling me, remember?" Elliot said matter-of-factly, as his therapist had probably instructed him. "We agreed we shouldn't talk for a while."

"How long of a 'while'?" Joe pleaded. "I feel like I'm going to *die* from being so sad. My heart hurts, Elliot. People die from broken hearts too, you know!"

"Joe, come on—"

"You're the only person I've ever loved, Elliot. I *still* love you."

"That's not the point."

"I don't want anything to happen to you, Elliot. What if something happens while we take this break? What if you get, ya know, sick again or something, and—"

Joe couldn't finish the sentence. Was it that he wanted Elliot to love him again or just to absolve him of the mantel of being the worst lover any dying man had ever had? Joe's shoulders shook, bits of pork rinds flying out of his mouth and onto the mouthpiece of the pay phone and his tear-covered hands. Homeless folks walking by looked at him with pity.

"Jesus Christ, Joe." Elliot's cold voice echoed through the receiver. "We've talked about this over and over. I don't know how long I have left on this planet, and I don't want to waste it constantly arguing with some muddle-headed boy who can't get his life together, can't control his emotions, and always has one foot out the door of this relationship!"

"That's not true!"

"It *is* true! You know it. I loved you, Joe, but it was just too hard."

Elliot's use of *love* in the past tense sent Joe into another bout of uncontrollable crying. Elliot waited until Joe's deluge had settled into mere snotty hiccups of weeping. "I'm sorry, Joe," he said. "I can't take your periodic rages at me for being sick. That constant expression of worry on your face. You look at me, and all you think about is me dying."

"That's not—"

"And you're always trying to control my every move, what I eat, how much I sleep, how long I stay out at night."

"I'm just trying to take care of you!"

"It's not helping, Joe! It's crushing me! I don't want to think about it—don't you get that? And meanwhile, you've done nothing about your own life. You clean bedpans in a mental hospital. Focus on yourself, Joe. Grow the fuck up. Please don't call me again."

"Okay. But we . . ." He gulped air, trying not to sob. "We're still together, right?"

"I . . . I'm not sure. I'll call you in a few weeks."

The click of the hang-up. The ghostly whine of the dial tone. The crunch of the pork rind. The odor of the barbecue mixed with spit, tears, and the plastic of the pay-phone mouthpiece. Joe shivered as the cold Philadelphia wind blew through the giant hole in his stomach.

The DJ was spinning "Good Life" by Inner City when Joe realized he must have blacked out leaning over the edge of the Promethean balcony. He could have died, and his last memory would have been that final conversation with Elliot—a memory he had come to Fire Island to escape. He needed to shake the sadness from his head. He took one last long, painful gulp of the Knockout, hoping it would work like turpentine, melting away the blue and black paint of awful memories. Below him a thousand shirtless men's bodies rose and fell like a bubbling cauldron. The disco lights swooped, the strobes exploded, the red laser beams stabbed the darkness. Joe tried to spot anyone he might know who could rescue him, but between the lights and his blurry eyes, everyone looked the same.

Except for . . .

He squinted his eyes to make sure he wasn't imagining anything. He wasn't. It was *him*. Gladiator Man. Every hair on Joe's body leaped to attention. A bullet of desire blasted away the previous moment's darkness.

"Hey! You! Hey!" Joe screamed.

Being several inches taller than anyone around him, the Gladiator Man towered over the center of the dance floor like a colossus, his massive shoulders spanning those of two men. A perfect dusting of fur spread across his bowling ball pectorals, and a treasure trail traipsed downward through the granite landscape of his ripped abdomen. His tight white jeans glowed in the black light, making him even more of a beacon. It was as if he *wanted* Joe to find him.

"Is this really happening?" Joe's drunken guts ached with sexual hunger as he closed and opened his eyes. When he looked back down, the Gladiator Man gazed directly back at him. This time, there was no mistake. *He sees me.* Abandoning any attempt at Ronnie's lesson on seductive disinterest, Joe frantically waved his arms. The beautiful man smiled and waved back, the underside of his hairy forearms mapped with veins. He pointed up to Joe, and then back at himself, as if to say, *"You and me—us, together."* Then he tossed his head toward the front door. The meaning was obvious.

Joe vigorously gestured that he would be right down. "Wait for me!" he shouted over the din of Frankie Knuckles's dance mix of "The Real Thing" before he bolted down the stairway, climbing over a man who had passed out on the steps. Joe's heart was trying to sledgehammer its way out of his chest. When he arrived at the edge of the dance floor, he elbowed and jammed his way through the crowd. Most of the dancing revelers were too wasted to care. Several thought he was trying to play with them and proceeded to grab his ass while a gaggle of older Asylum Harbor regulars, rolling on ecstasy, encircled him in a group dance hug.

"Falafel Crotch! Our favorite little bartender on the whole island," one of the men spit into Joe's ear. "We love you!"

"Lemme go!" Joe wiggled from their clutches and dove deeper into the crush of the dance floor. A burst of multiple strobe lights briefly blinded him, but he was able to discern he was close to the middle. "Where is he?" he cried out. "Fuuuuuuck! I cannah looze you again!"

"Who are you talking about?" a sardonic voice yelled. "I'm right here!"

It was Thursty and the shorter Graveyard Girl, holding a Diet Coke can in his hand, meaning he was probably high on something. Thursty, however, was clearly drinking one of those Knockout punches.

"Having fun tonight?" Thursty shouted, patting the fanny pack around his thick waist. "I got C, K, T, E, X—the whole fuckin' alphabet. I also have a package deal tonight on E, K, G—the cardiologist's special! What do you want? Thirty percent off for island employees!"

"I don't do drugs!" Joe shouted back.

Thursty rolled his eyes. "Oh puh-lease, Sandra Dee! You're gonna end up begging me for something by the end of July. Might as well start now and not waste time!"

Joe shook his head. "Did you see a huge muscle guy with a beard? Sexy, slightly hairy chest? About five inches taller than you, but crazy handsome?"

Thursty gestured to the room. "We're in an ocean of *crazy* handsome men, Baby Falafel Crotch! Dig in!"

"No! And don't call me that! I'm talking bigger, better than them! He's perfect. He looks like a gladiator! He likes me!"

Thursty yawned and gestured over by the door. "All gladiators have gone to the Colosseum."

"What's that?" Joe shouted.

The two Graveyard Girls looked at each other and rolled their eyes.

"The Meat Rack!" the short Graveyard Girl shouted into Joe's ear. "Gladiators are in the Meat Rack tonight! Don't forget your armor!"

The Graveyard Girls returned to dancing. Joe's chest tightened with excitement. A drunken smile burst onto his face. He wasn't supposed to go into the Meat Rack, but he also didn't want to miss his chance. He wiped the gunk from the edges of his very dry mouth. The last thing he wanted was his first kiss with the Gladiator Man to taste like dirty socks. But he had no time to go to the bar for another drink.

"Hey, I need to wet my mouth!" he shouted to Thursty, who was now bobbing up and down to Madonna's "Holiday." Not wanting to waste any more time, Joe grabbed the Knockout from Thursty's hand, drinking half in one long swig.

"Hey!" Thursty yelled, grabbing his drink back. "You know, you are a very rude little boy!"

"Thanks!" Joe shouted as he began pushing his way through the bodies until he was finally outside and the cool air burst against his body. He felt substantially drunker than he had only moments before. Looking down Fire Island Boulevard both ways, he could only see blackness in the distance. He wanted to cry out in frustration, but at the same time his body began to tingle with an insatiable sexual hunger, as if some invisible energy was tickling its fingers across his skin, tweaking his nipples, then reaching down his pants and diddling his balls. He rubbed his hands across his own chest, trying to satisfy his urge to be touched, but it was no use. There was only one man who could satisfy the urge. There was only one man who could take all the pain away.

"Joe!" a familiar voice called from behind him. It was Howie, dressed in his usual maroon bathrobe and baseball cap. "I've been looking for you! How was it inside?"

"Is incruminable," Joe slurred, staring at Howie's blurry face. "But I . . . I canna talk . . . I have ta meet someone."

"Joe," Howie begged with tinge of panic in his voice, "you look a little funny. Have you been imbibing?"

"I had jus' a few sips. I'm okay. I feel very sessy, though. It's weird."

"Well, how about you and I go back inside? I haven't danced in over a year—we can take a spin around the floor! Michael is about to play his Grace Jones set."

As Howie blabbered on about a long-ago night at some Manhattan dance club, Joe looked westward and spied Gladiator Man's white pants heading into the darkness. "Is him!" he cried.

"Him?" Howie asked. "Who?"

"I have ta go! Issa 'mergency! See ya later!"

"Emergency?" Howard shouted after Joe. "What are you talking—"

Oblivious to Howie's shouts, Joe clumsily ran down the boardwalk, the agonizing hunger in his belly spurring him onward and his full-on erection pointing toward the Meat Rack.

27.
The Longest Journey

"Love is not the cause of happiness—it's a symptom of it."
—*Disco Witch Manifesto #29*

At a casual pace it would take a sober-ish man approximately ten minutes to walk from the Promethean to the Meat Rack. Joe, drunker than he'd ever been and drawn by the most intense erotic desire he'd ever had, stumbled and swerved down the dark boardwalk for at least twenty-five minutes. In his mind he had been running, but he just couldn't catch up to the mountainous muscle butt in the tight white pants. It was as if the boardwalk had turned into a conveyer belt going in the opposite direction. Sometimes he'd lose sight of the pants when they walked into the darkest shadows. Joe's heart would sink, but then seconds (minutes? hours?) later the pants would reappear like magic. Twice, he dozed off while standing only to be awakened by his trumpeting erection beckoning him to follow. *What the hell was in those Knockouts?*

After five more minutes of stumbling after the white pants, he saw them stop. The Gladiator Man had reached the end of the boardwalk and the beginning of the Meat Rack. It was the perfect moment for Joe to catch up. But even as he tried to run, his lasagna noodle legs kept tripping while his erection grew more turgid. He readjusted himself so his penis pointed straight up in his pants, thinking it made him look less trashy. The next thing he knew, he was standing just ten feet away from Gladiator Man, a monument of masculine perfection, with intense dark eyes, a long Roman nose, and a small mole on his cheek, just above the beard line, like a punctuation mark on his sexiest of smiles—a smile clearly meant for Joe. Joe attempted to say something, but the words got caught somewhere between his uvula and Adam's apple.

"I . . . um . . . I . . . um . . ." Frustrated by his inability to form words, he gestured to his heart and then grabbed his crotch in a sloppy dumbshow of lust.

The Gladiator Man grinned and tossed his massive head toward the Meat Rack. "Follow me," he said in a low rumbling voice that literally caused Joe's testicles to vibrate. He stumbled closer, his hunger and fear inextricable.

"I wanna . . ." Joe said, finally able to speak in words that felt as if they were being pulled from him. "I . . . so lonely. So empty. I need you." The Gladiator Man moved closer. Joe felt his dragon hot breath on his cheeks. Were the man's eyes glowing? His body odor was a mix of Aramis cologne and . . . horse sweat? Joe's cock punched at the teeth of his zipper. "Kiss me!" he begged. "Please kiss me before I . . . oh, fuck." His guts began to heave. He bent over and Lenny's Bolognese came gushing out à la Linda Blair in *The Exorcist*—once, twice, three times. When the urge to expel subsided, he fell to his knees, wiped his mouth on his wrist, and gazed up at the Gladiator Man's face, which had grown as tall as the treetops. "Do you still want me?" Joe asked feebly before his eyes grew so heavy and everything went black.

It seemed like only a moment later when he felt the warm calloused hands stroking his aching head. A faint glow from the dark blue and orange sky crept through his crusted eyes. The island birds were singing their sunrise chorus. *Morning? How long was I asleep?* Joe felt so comfortable on the cool wood of the walk, his head nestled in the strong but soft lap. Had Gladiator Man stayed with him at the edge of the Meat Rack the entire night? The man's touch felt so warm and kind, so unlike what he had thought his sexy scary touch would feel like. He nuzzled his head deeper into the man's lap and considered the possibility of living there forever. But then a wave of humiliation gushed through his veins. The Gladiator Man had seen him vomit his guts out. Instead of fucking him royally, Gladiator Man was cradling him like a sick infant. "Ugh, I'm so embarrassed," Joe groaned.

"You okay?" the man asked. "You were out for a while. It's almost five."

Joe rubbed the muck from his eyes and mouth. The man's voice was different from earlier—still deep but now with a thick Long Island accent. Joe's eyelids opened, and he noticed the material of the man's pants. The jeans were blue, not white like Gladiator Man's, more baggy, not tight. The hair on the man's arms was a different texture. It wasn't Gladiator Man at all who was stroking his hair.

"What the hell, Fergal?" Joe pushed himself from the ferryman's lap and floundered up to his feet.

Fergal, wearing a wrinkled but new Pines Ferry T-shirt, quietly got up from the ground and brushed the sand from his jeans. He too looked like he hadn't slept the entire night. His thick, asymmetrical eyebrows twisted in a confused puppy-dog look.

"It's a good thing you tossed your cookies," he said. "You could've been a lot worse off. Here, drink this. You're probably dehydrated." He picked up a bottle of Frostie Blue Cream soda from the ground and handed it to Joe who downed almost half the bottle in one gulp. Then he took another quick sip, gargled, and spit the remaining foul taste from his mouth. Remembering he was still shirtless, he brushed off the bits of sick and sand sticking to his chest hair. "How long have you been sitting here with me?"

"A long time," Fergal said. "Howie and Lenny were freaked out. Word is you drank one too many Knockouts. Those things can kill ya, by the way. They sent me looking for you. I found you stumbling down the boardwalk."

Fucking Fergal, Joe thought. *Chasing the Gladiator Man away again. But when?* How long had Joe been blacked out? Could it have been Fergal's hot breath he felt last night? Did he smell like Aramis and horse sweat? He leaned over and sniffed Fergal's T-shirt. It smelled like beer, Old Spice aftershave, and something else. He took another whiff. The ocean?

"Why are you sniffing me?" Fergal laughed and stuck his nose into his own armpit. "Not so bad. I showered last night before I went out."

"It's . . ." Joe sputtered, his thoughts all muddled in his head. "Nothing. One of the Graveyard Girls said those Knockouts would make me feel warm and sexy."

Fergal smirked. "You feel warm and sexy last night when you were spewing chunks all over the boardwalk? By the way, here." He offered Joe a stick of Wrigley's Spearmint gum. "For your breath."

Joe grabbed the gum and shoved it into his mouth, chewing furiously. His best opportunity to hook up with Gladiator Man had been wasted by him getting sick in front of some arrogant, closet-case ferryman whose eyes, he realized, were the same color as the Frostie Blue Cream soda he was drinking. In the middle of his gulping, he felt another wave of nausea and promptly sat back down.

"Maybe I should get you home," Fergal said, offering his hand.

Joe glared at the hand, which Fergal lowered as he continued to gaze down at Joe expectantly. "Why are you looking at me like that?" Joe bristled.

Fergal curled his wayward eyebrows until they angled toward the middle. That was when Joe noticed the ferryman's Frostie Blue Cream eyes had fallen into shadow, darkening until they had become more of a navy blue, the color of the deep, deep sea.

"Well," Fergal said, "I'm just wondering if you're ever gonna thank me. I probably saved your life last night."

"That's a little dramatic. I was basically fine. Just a little too buzzed."

"A little buzzed? You almost fell off the boardwalk, like, ten times, and you passed out three times. I tried to get you back to Howie and Lenny's, but you insisted on going to the Meat Rack. I had to take care of you the whole night—you think that was fun? Everybody was worried sick about you. Some guy croaked last

August from drinking too many of those Knockout punches—and you're half his size. I almost had to call 911. Instead, I stuck my fingers down your throat and made you vomit."

"No, you didn't," Joe stammered. "You're making that up."

"You really are an ungrateful little sonofabitch." Fergal pointed to his foot. "See that? You fucking puked all over my new boat shoes. Know how much these cost me?"

Joe stared at the crusty ochre splotch on the leather. He couldn't believe he had lost his grasp on reality that much. "Tell me something," he snapped. "Before you shoved your fingers down my throat—uninvited—did you happen to see me talking with some big hot guy in white pants?"

Fergal, mouth agape, shook his head. "Shoved my fingers down your throat 'uninvited'? Fuck you, Joe. Get yourself home. I'm done." He turned and began heading toward the harbor.

A confused anger surged through Joe's veins. "Hey!" he growled, stumbling to his feet, and clumsily jogging up to Fergal. "I still have questions."

"What?" Fergal spat and turned to face him.

A dark presence suddenly overtook Joe's body, and without knowing why, he shoved Fergal's shoulder, causing the taller man to lose his balance, stumbling a step backward.

"What the hell?" Fergal looked more puzzled than angry. "Why'd you do that?"

Joe, in fact, had no idea why he'd done it. He didn't want to hurt the ferryman—quite the contrary. He longed to feel Fergal's warm hands gently stroking his head again. He wanted to crawl inside the ferryman's long lean arms, wanted to kiss him even. But the more he wanted it, the more the dark muddle inside grew stronger. "Are you going to fight me or not?"

"No." Fergal scoffed, turning to walk away again.

A panic filled Joe's chest. "Hey! Wait!" he shouted, wanting to apologize for his confusion.

Fergal turned back toward Joe with a look on his face that said, *"What the fuck do you want?"*

Again, not knowing what strange force was moving him, Joe aggressively grabbed the front of Fergal's Pines Ferry T-shirt to pull him in for a kiss, but instead tore a gaping hole that showed the entirety of the ferryman's chest.

Fergal, clearly unaware of Joe's intentions, twisted his eyebrows in fury. "This is my new work shirt!" He yanked back the remnants of his torn shirt, causing Joe to stumble off the low boardwalk and fall onto his butt in the soft sand. "Why the hell are you trying to attack me?"

Looking up at Fergal with the ripped shirt dangling around his neck, his bare chest, and the tree branches behind him forming a halo around head, Joe thought how much the man really did resemble the little figure on the merman clock. "I wasn't!" he blurted, his head still in a hungover muddle. "That time, anyway. I was just trying to . . ." he began, trying to stifle his tears. "I don't know."

Fergal shook his head and again began to walk away. Joe dropped his head to his knees, and a huge sob heaved from his lungs. Seconds later, he heard the crunching of Top-Siders in the sand. He looked up. There, staring down at him, was Fergal's sweaty, stubble-covered face inlaid with those glowing blue-blue eyes, looking simultaneously angry and sad.

"What?" Joe snuffled, feeling tears roll down his cheeks. "I'm sorry. I really wanted—"

Fergal dropped to his knees and hugged him, tucking Joe's head against the warmth of his chest. For the first time since he could remember, Joe felt completely safe and protected. But still there was something more he wanted, but he was too frightened to ask for fear Fergal would stop holding him. Then, as if the ferryman was reading Joe's mind, he took him by the shoulders and gently kissed him on his quivering lips. All the unsatisfied sexual hunger from the previous night rushed back through Joe's body, and with a simple parting of his lips, the two men began hungrily going at it. The taste of Fergal's mouth was sweet and unusually salty, causing Joe to plunge his tongue deeper like some sodium-deprived forest creature. But it wasn't enough. He yanked Fergal's torn shirt over his head and ran his hands across his tight abdomen, then up through the small patch of chest hair that formed a diamond just below his clavicle. He lifted Fergal's arm and pressed his nose to the tuft of black hair in his armpit, then began lapping at the musty saltiness there. He wanted more.

"Kiss me again," Joe demanded.

Fergal complied. Joe drank him in. Still not enough. It could never be enough. He desperately needed Fergal's body even closer—he wanted him inside him. Again, like he knew exactly what Joe wanted, Fergal flipped him onto his stomach, and began to grind his crotch into the back of Joe's jeans. He wrapped his forearm around Joe's neck and used his free hand to yank Joe's pants and underwear down, exposing his ass. Fergal dug into his pocket for a condom.

"Never mind that!" Joe arched his butt. "Fuck me now! *Please*, Elliot."

Everything stopped. "Elliot?" Fergal repeated with disgust, and then lifted himself off Joe's body. The chilly morning air blew across Joe's naked back. He was confused at first, but then he realized what he had said.

"I'm really sorry," he stammered. "It's not like I didn't know who you are. It's just that Elliot was... he was..." No, no, he couldn't tell Fergal, a stranger. He couldn't. "Look, I just forgot your name for a second. It's not a big deal. Who can remember everyone's name on Fire Island, right?" He laughed nervously. "Hey, we can still do this..."

Fergal silently lifted Joe from the sand, pulling up his underwear and jeans as if he were someone else's disobedient child. All the previous passion in his eyes had vanished behind a wall of blue ice. Joe wished Fergal would just say something, but instead the ferryman turned and started walking back toward the harbor.

"Come on!" Joe called out. "It was just a dumb mistake! Come on! Don't be that way!"

Fergal's body, like a study in perspective, grew smaller and smaller as it moved down Fire Island Boulevard toward some distant vanishing point.

Joe's entire viscera felt as if it had been scooped out with a shovel. Sand and wind blew through the gaping hole. *You are alone. You will always be alone. You deserve to be alone. Forever.*

28.

Mourning Doves

"The overlords, trapped in their armor of fixed identity, try to decimate the holy lovers with fists and laws, but Disco Witches always fight back—not only for the holy lovers, but for the overlords themselves. When the holy lovers are finally free, all will be free."
—Disco Witch Manifesto #20

The mourning doves that nested in the trees and eaves of 44 and ¼ Picketty Ruff were especially prolific and quite musical. Their songs often reminded Howie of Broadway show tunes, inspiring him, as they did that morning, to begin spontaneously humming while watering the riots of salmon-colored impatiens on the back deck.

"Now what's that song again?" he asked of the chirping doves. "Oh, right, that's it. Thank you, ladies."

It was that most optimistic Broadway gem "Put on Your Sunday Clothes" from the Jerry Herman musical *Hello, Dolly!* The song was perfect for starting his day off, which, like for most island workers, was Monday and not Sunday. "Put on your Monday clothes lalala-lalala . . ." he sang. When the doves switched to one of Herman's most heart-wrenching ballads from his lesser known musical *Mack and Mabel*, Howie shouted through the kitchen window. "Lenny! Get out here! You gotta hear the doves! They're doing four-part harmony on 'Time Heals Everything'!"

"It's that new bird feed from Mulligan's!" Lenny hollered from the kitchen, where he was preparing his double-meat, three-cheese lasagna. "Twenty percent more sunflower seeds!"

"Well, it's working!" Howie shouted. "I don't understand it! I'm feeling such a sense of bliss this morning! The psychic cilia inside my intestines are wiggling with joy for a change!"

"Holy shit!" Lenny called out. "That's the most positive thing you've said in years!"

"I didn't say I'm not still worried. We still have that blood moon coming Morning Party weekend. And let's not forget the Great Darkness is still out there. Remember the omens? We'll still have to be on alert for other confused young people who might be in danger. At least we're certain Joe is safe."

"Like I said all along!" Lenny shouted through the kitchen window, with an emphasized "Ha!"

"When you're right, you're right." A slight twinge pierced Howie's gastrointestinal bliss. "I trust Saint D'Norman's twirling visions," he shouted back. "Like the rubric says, if a holy lover misses just one of the five sacred criteria, he's out of the running." He knew he didn't need to say it, but something compelled him. "Nope. We don't need to even worry. Joe is missing . . . what was it? Three out of the five, including the all-important flying-heart-mole-thing on his back." He scoffed. "I checked, you checked, Dory checked. So we're all good. Triple-checked."

Lenny stuck his finger out the window and flicked it like he was ticking a box. "You mean quadruple-checked. You forget that Saint D'Norman checked too—and he's an R-friggin'-N. That kid's skin is so perfect, he shoulda been a Noxzema model!"

"Exactly," Howie said. "The age, the recent traumatic heartbreak, and the mole. Three strikes! He's out. Oh, and he hasn't mentioned anything about seeing that Gladiator Man in weeks, which is also a relief. If I remember correctly, poor Lucho had seen the egregore at least seven times by midsummer." There was that gut stab again, and suddenly a shadow fell across the back garden. "So why, on the day I'm the happiest I've been in months, am I still getting worry knots in my gut?"

"You wouldn't be who you are if you didn't worry," Lenny said through the window. "It's like your connective tissue. You'd fall apart without it." A moment later Lenny emerged from the kitchen door with a cigarette between his lips, a dish rag over his arm, and a Jackson Pollack's worth of red sauce spatter all over his shirtless chest and belly.

"Great Goddess Mother, what the fuck happened to you?" Howie exclaimed.

"I was cooking," Lenny said.

"Who's your sous chef? Jack the Ripper?"

"Whatcha talkin'?"

"You got tomato gravy all over yourself, for goodness' sake. And why are you smoking those cancer sticks on such a stunning day?"

"Basta!" Lenny took a deeper drag from his Marlboro and wiped the sauce from his gut with the dish rag. "It's not like I'm smoking three packs a day anymore. Besides, I'm celebrating. I shouldn't say anything of course—anonymity and all—but my sponsee's got ninety days clean and sober today."

Despite Lenny never saying it outright, Howie knew he was talking about Dory's granddaughter, Elena, and he was thrilled.

"That's marvelous," Howie said, dramatically fanning away Lenny's cigarette smoke. "Leave it to an addict to celebrate someone's sobriety with another addiction."

"Small steps. Small steps." Lenny chuckled. "Now do I need to make plates of lasagna for two or three? Is our wayward Armenian American foster child up yet?"

Howie looked up past the mourning doves in the eaves by the attic vent. "Not yet. I heard him go to bed about five thirty this morning. Alone, as usual."

Lenny looked to Heaven and shook his head. "Seriously? What a waste. If I looked as good as him, I'd be shish-kebabbing so many bottoms I could open a Greek food truck."

"How vivid," Howie droned à la Bea Arthur before growing serious. "Have you noticed how Joe seems even more out of sorts since Memorial Day? I can't figure it out. I just wish he'd open up to one of us. I almost got him talking yesterday, but he made up some excuse about needing to buy deodorant before work, when I know he has two sticks of Right Guard in the medicine cabinet." Howie chewed on his right thumbnail. "I just know something bad must've happened that weekend. That's why my gut is like this. Whatever it was, I sense it's earthbound—"

"Basta!" Lenny barked. "Why not just friggin' ask him?"

"How can I ask him? He's never around. He inhales his meals and then he's off to bartend or work out or lock himself up in the attic like Rochester's wife in *Jane Eyre*—"

The wire of the back door sprung open, and Joe, his hair still mangled from sleep, stepped out onto the deck with a blue flier in his hands. Howie hoped he hadn't heard them talking.

"Well, look at that!" Howie waved his watering can. "Sleeping Beauty awakens!"

"Morning," Joe mumbled, his crusty eyes looking intently at the blue mimeograph paper.

"Do you like my flier?" Howie asked. "Dory asked me to design it. She's throwing a benefit for ACT UP at Asylum Harbor in a couple of weeks."

"What's ACT UP?" Joe asked.

"It's this new AIDS protest group in the city," Howie said. "Remember Larry, the guy I introduced you to at the bar a few weeks ago? The one who wrote that delicious Liv Ullmann movie musical *Lost Horizon*? He and some other folks formed a group to try and get the government to do more about the AIDS crisis. You know, demonstrations, sit-ins, die-ins, things like that. They call themselves ACT UP, which stands for the AIDS Coalition to Unleash Power."

"A bunch of hophead radicals if you ask me," Lenny grumbled as he plucked fresh basil from the garden.

"Do not start with me, Lenny!" Howie snapped. "Do you expect us to just accept government inaction about AIDS, lying down?"

"Easy there, Jane Fonda." Lenny raised his voice to match Howie's, then turned to Joe. "I'm not saying do nothing. It's just the way they do it—being disrespectful to the police and mayor, causing more straights to hate us. Basta! It's an embarrassment!"

"An embarrassment?" Howie repeated, seething. "You know what's an embarrassment, Leonardo Gennaro Vincenzo D'Amico?" He poked a finger into the air. "That in 1976, when twenty-nine *white heterosexual men* died in Philadelphia from Legionnaire's disease, the country went mad to find a cure. And now ninety thousand mostly gay men are dead from AIDS, and what is the government doing? Bupkis! They want us dead. Being good, quiet gay boys doesn't fucking work!"

The emanations from Howie's own angry aura created a haze over the entire garden. A cluster of mourning doves, their song silenced, scattered to the highest branches of the birch tree. Howie knew arguing with Lenny was a waste of time. More importantly, he didn't want to be in a bad mood, in case Joe was finally ready to talk.

"Lenny," Howie said, looking at his watch, "don't you have to set up your little meeting at the fire house?"

"Shit!" Lenny yipped. "Put the lasagna in the fridge when you're done making yourselves a plate."

After Lenny scurried back into the house, a quiet settled over the back deck. Howie noticed how Joe looked both intrigued and disturbed as he studied the ACT UP flyer.

"Do you like it?" Howie asked. "I did my best to be lighthearted but also serious."

"Do you think any of that protest stuff could make any difference?" Joe said.

"I do. We need to stay angry but also remain hopeful. It's difficult." Howie lowered his voice. "Don't tell Lenny, but Dory and I have been to a few ACT UP actions."

Joe smiled. "You carried picket signs and everything?"

"Yes," Howie whispered. "We even got arrested at City Hall."

Joe scrunched his thick eyebrows. "No way. You and Dory went to jail?"

"Only for about eight hours. It was fabulous! Screaming my lungs out for Mayor Koch to come out of the closet and do something about AIDS. It was the most therapeutic thing I've done in ages. If I weren't stuck out here, I'd do more, but I do what I can. Don't mention anything about me going to jail. It wouldn't be good for Lenny's heart."

"No worries." Joe looked again at the blue flier. "Why's he so against it?"

"His Roman Catholic internalized homophobia mostly. He thinks we need to be martyrs to get anywhere. Funny thing is, he used to be a total radical back in the day."

"Lenny? You're kidding."

Howie shook his head. "Both of us were at the second night of the Stonewall riots. He threw beer cans at the cops. Ever since he passed fifty, he's become his mother." Howie sighed. "The thing is you have to make a ruckus if you want change. No, there isn't a cure yet, but there never will be if we don't demand they look for one. As that Irish poet who drank himself to death at the White Horse Tavern said, 'Rage, rage against the dying of the light.'" Joe's eyes remained fixed on the flier. "Haven't you ever wanted to just go into a rage about AIDS?"

Joe pulled a birch leaf from a low-hanging branch. "Sometimes . . . no—always. But it doesn't do any good in the end."

Howie squinted. The brownish green in Joe's aura was a signifier that he was unable to release something acutely painful—a psychic bramble stuck to his soul.

"Joe," he said softly. "What is it?"

"I just don't like to think about that stuff. It makes me sad."

Of course. Howie saw it so clearly now. "AIDS has taken someone from you, hasn't it? Someone very important?"

Joe looked down at the tray of impatiens and flicked at the soft, tooth-edged leaves. His murky aura became streaked with shimmers of blackness. Inside those shimmers Howie saw windowless walls, devastation, lies, yearning, loss, loss, loss.

How awful that someone so young should have lost such a love. No wonder his aura had looked the way it had. But then another realization—with the loss of his love, that meant it wasn't actually three strikes against the rubric. It was only two. Thankfully, two was plenty to disqualify Joe from being the chosen one.

"I'm so sorry," Howie said. "I foolishly assumed since you were so young, you might have been spared. I didn't know."

"His name was Elliot." Joe's voice cracked. He turned his eyes from Howie's as if he were embarrassed by his grief. "It's been close to two years. I should be over it by now, but . . ."

A breeze tousled the trees. Two mulberries dropped to the deck. A mourning dove chirped. Howie had to be careful to avoid any sort of interrogation that might slam the door to Joe's heart. "Healing isn't on a fixed schedule," he said. "It comes when it comes."

"I know," Joe said, turning back. "But at some point you have to get the fuck over it, right?"

"Sometimes that's true. But is forcing yourself to forget working? For me, mending a broken heart requires going on all sorts of emotional detours—ruminating on what might have been, hoping for the impossible, and lots of raging and crying, crying and raging. Stopping the process too early can, well, prolong the suffering or even leave thick scars on our souls that affect all our future relationships. Or that's the way I look at it, anyway."

Joe appeared even more lost than before. Howie worried that he had said too much. But then Joe looked straight into Howie's eyes in a way he had never done before.

"I'm just so lonely," he said. "Elliot was the only guy I ever dated. I mean . . . other than one-night stands and all. I never was able to love anyone else, before or since. Ronnie says I'm emotionally stuck. He says I need to get out there and date other guys—just let myself have some fun."

"That's definitely part of the process," Howie agreed. "I'm a great believer in taking action at the source of one's despair. But only when you're ready. If you stay open, the Great Goddess Mother will reveal pathways to healing. But in the meantime, go easy on yourself."

"Yeah, Ronnie says the same thing—but without the Goddess Mother stuff." A brief smile before the muddled expression returned. "I've been trying to *stay open* and hook up, but something always gets in the way. I don't know what's wrong with me."

"I wasn't talking about hooking up," Howie said, smiling. "I'm talking about sharing about it with people who understand. Like a support group or . . . maybe, if you'd like, you could check out an ACT UP meeting with Dory and me sometime. There's not a person in that room who hasn't had their hearts ripped open by this disease one way or another."

"Maybe. I dunno," Joe said. "It sucked not being able to talk about it when Elliot got sick. I guess we were both afraid how people would react."

"But you have to talk about it—scream about it. 'Silence equals death,' as they say." Howie's heart thrummed excitedly. "I have a brilliant idea. Why don't you volunteer to bartend at the ACT UP benefit? We're having a meeting later this afternoon at Dory's house. Join us?"

Joe shrugged and put the blue flier down on the picnic table. His aura began to flicker like a broken neon sign proclaiming blockage and heartbreak. He was hiding so much more inside about Elliot's death. It didn't take any superpower of prescience to see that. But what?

"I can't," Joe said. "Ronnie and I are going to a housewarming party on Ocean Walk. He's been dating this rich guy who built some fancy new beach house. Folks are calling it the Taj Ma Homo."

"I've heard," Howie said, half-heartedly. "Everybody's been talking about it. I didn't know Ronnie was seeing someone new. What happened to Vince?"

"It was just a fuck-buddy thing—according to Ronnie anyway. He's been hot-and-heavy with the new guy for weeks. Says it's his affirmations paying off." Joe rolled his eyes. "His name is Trey something. Know him?"

"I can't say that I do," Howie said.

For a moment it looked like Joe wanted to say something else, but then he stopped himself, just like all the other times. *If he doesn't share whatever he's hiding, it will eventually consume him,* Howie thought. *Holding things in can make anyone prey to the Great Darkness, whether they are the chosen one or not.*

"What?" Joe said. "Why are you staring at me like that?"

"No reason," Howie said. "It's just, did something happen on Memorial Day weekend?"

Joe's eyebrows bunched suspiciously. "Why'd you ask that?"

"You've seemed out of sorts ever since."

"Nothing happened," Joe insisted a little too forcefully. "I've just been bored. Ronnie's off dating Trey, which has also put Vince in a bad mood. Elena's been all wrapped up with AA and that girl

Cleigh from the grocery store. I've been trying to meet guys out here, but no one I like seems interested."

"I doubt that, with the way men talk about you on this island. You're very attractive, Joe."

"No, I'm not," Joe said. "The only people who hit on me are old men or guys who just want to say they fucked the bartender—you know how it is out here. The only time I came close to hooking up was after I got obliterated on those damned Knockout punches. It was with that asshole Fergal of all godforsaken people."

"You and Fergal the ferryman almost hooked up?" Howie's belly gurgled with glee at the idea. "Impressive. He's very picky as well as adorable. I was starting to worry we had jumped the gun on our estimation of his shifting sexual proclivities."

"You didn't jump the gun. He's definitely into dudes. But it doesn't matter. I screwed it up big time."

"Hmm," Howie said, mostly to himself. "So, Fergal is the reason you've been in such a state the past few weeks?"

"No, I'm not in a state about Fergal," Joe snapped. "Fuck that guy. I'm in a state about this bullshit island. It's not the right place for me. Also, working out here doesn't make it easy to date or even have fun. I don't get out until five in the morning, and none of the stuck-up renters have any interest in dating a bartender.

Howie shook his head as he put the watering can down and proceeded to pull out any dead leaves from between the impatiens blossoms. "Let me tell you something, Joseph. If you're not connecting with other young men, it's not because you're a bartender. Like I said, you may just not be ready. No one can predict when the Great Goddess Mother will bestow either sex or love on us. She has her reasons."

Joe huffed a big exasperated breath. "Who exactly is the Great Goddess Mother, anyway?"

Howie smiled at the sight of Joe's sweet, frustrated eyebrows. He wished he could tell him everything, but it still wasn't time. "That's just the name we use for our favorite deity—like the good that's in most people. It really doesn't matter. My point is, it's best not to aim too hard for love or you'll miss it. It's not a fixed target, after all. Your job is to heal, then just wait and see what the universe puts in your path—love and sex will come. Do you understand what I'm saying?"

"I guess the Great Goddess Mother loves Ronnie more," Joe said sarcastically. "He sure hasn't had any problems hooking up."

"Well, Ronnie's got confidence, and despite whatever hardship he's suffered in his life, there is something fearless about him. That's why he's having more experiences. To be quite honest, in many ways—and don't tell Ronnie I said this—you're far more attractive."

"Oh, come on." A sudden vulnerability flushed Joe's cheeks. "If I'm so great, then why did Fergal practically run away from me?"

"Well, what happened exactly?"

"We made out and it was really, really hot, and I suggested we, ya know, take it a little further. But then I said something totally stupid, and I apologized and all, but he got this disgusted look on his face and left, like I was dirt or something. Wouldn't even let me explain."

"Hmm," Howie said. "I've known Fergal most of his life. He's not the type who would just walk away for no reason. Unfortunately, when people like him feel strongly for someone, it can be overwhelming."

"Trust me," Joe snorted. "The only feeling he was having for me was repulsion."

Howie smiled. "There's also the possibility he knew you weren't ready."

"I don't think someone could be as ready as me." Joe sighed, looking up into the mulberry tree. Its leaves painted lace shadows across his face. "You know what I really hate about AIDS? I mean, besides it killing people?" He looked back at Howie. "It makes love almost impossible."

"I'm not sure I agree," Howie said. "Quite the opposite. I think the crisis has shown us what loving really is." Joe looked ready to speak, and Howie's hopes rose, but once again Joe appeared to silence himself. Finally fed up, Howie exploded. "Stop that, Joseph! The Gnostic Gospels say, 'Bring forth what is within you and it will save you. If you do not bring it forth it will destroy you.' So, enough with your avoiding me—tell me what's going on!"

"Fine," Joe said, meeting Howie's level of frustration. "You want me to *bring it forth*? How do I fall in love again when they say fifty percent of gay men out here are probably infected with HIV? If I fall in love with a positive guy again, then I'm back to where I was with Elliot—always worrying about losing him or getting infected myself. And if I fall in love with someone HIV negative, then I'd worry I was just loving him because he's negative; or, more likely, I'll feel guilty as hell that I'm having a life when Elliot had to die." Howie reached for Joe, but Joe stepped back as if the touch might turn off the spigot gushing from his soul. "Then there's my other dirty little secret," he continued, his voice clawing through the ache. "Maybe I was only able to love Elliot *because* he was dying. Maybe I need a giant exit sign in any relationship because I'm actually incapable of real love." Joe pressed the heels of his hands into his eyes. "Fuck! I just want my head to be quiet!"

"It's all right, Joe," Howie whispered, longing to hug the boy. "I understand."

Joe pulled his hands from his face and looked directly into Howie's eyes. "Can I ask you something? Even if it upsets you?"

"Sure. I'm an open-ish book." A whirlpool of nerves swooped through Howie's digestive tract.

"That day I injured my leg? I know I wasn't supposed to, but I went into your room."

"We know," Howie said. "The blood spatter was like a subway map."

"Well . . ." Joe hesitated. "There's that big photo of Max dressed in drag on your wall—her ominous something?"

"Yes. Eartha Delights and Her Ominous Bush. It's Max's alter ego—his elevated spiritual, drag-queen self. When he dresses up as her, he believes he has special powers." Howie swallowed hard, not yet wanting to reveal that he too had "special powers"—or at least *used to*. "Why are you asking?"

"Max is important to you, isn't he?" Joe widened his eyes at Howie. "I mean, really important?"

Howie pulled his robe around himself, as if he felt a draft. What exactly was Joe trying to get at? How much had he seen in the house? Was this the reason for Joe's distance these past weeks? If their friendship was to progress, perhaps it was time to have the discussion. "What do you want to know, Joe?"

Joe bit his lip. "That photo of Eartha Delights... when I looked in her eyes. It was like she made me so angry and sad and... I heard things. Voices and music and..." Joe took a deep breath, seemingly unable to articulate more but clearly wanting an answer.

What had Joe experienced? Was it possible Max, even in his delirium, had been able to connect with Joe via some sort of telepathy? It made no sense, since Joe wasn't in the coven. Still, Howie would need to check with Max (as soon as he was well enough) to see if he had experienced anything unusual that day. But for now, Howie would need to be very careful in his explanation so as not to scare Joe. As much as he hated doing it. Howie would need to lie.

"What you experienced is totally understandable," Howie began gently. "You've been through such a great tragedy at far too young an age. Plus, you've been uprooted and flung onto this incredibly insane and intense gay island. Now take all of that and combine it with the adrenaline from, well, knowingly sneaking into our private space. That's like a hurricane in your head. It's natural you'd think you heard voices when you looked at Max's future reliquary. We created it so it would evoke profound feelings, and you're a very empathetic young man, Joe. I'd be more troubled if you *didn't* hear voices and music. Frankly, that photo of Eartha inspires so many people to experience outrageous things. You should see how many of my tricks look up at her in the middle of the night and run screaming from my room." Howie chuckled. "At least that's what they tell me is the reason." He placed his hand warmly on Joe's shoulder. "You didn't see or hear ghosts, Joe, and you're not going crazy."

Joe sniffled. "Thanks. By the way, that photo and frame are beautiful... what did you call it?"

"It's a reliquary," Howie said. "A place where we'll keep Max's ashes when he's gone. He and I have been working on it ever since he found out he had AIDS. He wanted to be part of creating it, leaving those he loved something to visit and celebrate his glorious life."

"I notice how you look at him in some of the photos," Joe said. "Did you used to date?"

"A long time ago," Howie said, relieved that Joe seemed to buy his explanation. "Though not in the usual hetero-Hollywood misrepresentation of love. The physical part of our love was brief, but we love each other in a much more expansive way. We've both had lots of other lovers since, of course. He and Heshy have been together for nearly twenty years. And Lenny and I are... well... whatever we are. But Max remains the most important person in my life—in all our lives, really. He was the linchpin in our entire friend group when everyone was still alive. He's the one who brought us all together and called us 'an army of lovers'—battling to spread joy and love on every dance floor. That was back in the sixties in P-town. Later, Lenny and I followed him here to 44 and ¼ Picketty Ruff. He taught us everything that made our lives most valuable. Of course, there were many more of us back in the day—all collected from dance floors or one-night stands." Howie smiled, thinking of the coven at its most populated and fertile. But then he remembered, and darkness filled his eyes. "Over the last eight years, AIDS has taken eighty-two of us."

"Lenny mentioned that," Joe said, his eyes softening as he looked down. "I can't imagine. I'm so sorry."

Howie nodded. "Max's army of lovers has dwindled to just five. If he dies..." Howie felt his tear ducts itch. He squeezed his eyes shut so he could finish his sentence. "So much of what gave my life meaning will be gone. I am who I am because of him." Howie could no longer hold it in. He placed the watering can down and clasped his hand across his face.

A moment later he felt Joe's arms around him, hugging him long and hard. "I get it now," Joe said. "I'm really sorry about Max. And I'm sorry I went into your room. I shouldn't have, and it won't happen again."

"It's all right, Joe. That's how we become better friends. We fail, we forgive. There is no real friendship without failure. Are we okay now?"

"Definitely." Joe released the hug and picked up the blue flier from the table. "Count me in to bartend at the ACT UP benefit. I'll be happy to donate my tips too."

"Wonderful," Howie said, wiping his nose with the hem of his robe. "I'm sure Dory will very much appreciate it."

For a split second it appeared like Joe might have had something more he wanted to say, but then he folded up the flier and put it in his back pocket. "I gotta go get ready for this party. Later, Howie. Thanks for the talk." And he was gone.

"Finally," Howie whispered to himself. Joe was opening up. But still, all the joy that had previously filled Howie's gut had vanished, and so had all the show tune-singing mourning doves. He stood alone on the back deck. The only sound he heard was the whispering of the mulberry tree, and then, as if it had been waiting for his attention, one long, foreboding hoot of a great horned owl—the same one he had heard haunting the Meat Rack earlier in the season. An omen of death had returned.

29.

Trey Winkle

"Disco Witches are terrible at discerning good dicks from bad dicks. Our hearts, while large, can be stupid about love."

—Disco Witch Manifesto #9

Ronnie and Joe walked east along Fire Island Boulevard to get to Trey Winkle's brand-new, ridiculously expensive beach house on Ocean and Sky. It was the invite-only, cocktail-party event of the season that everyone was dying to attend. This was why Ronnie and Joe had just purchased brand new clothes from one of the exorbitantly overpriced Pines boutiques. On top of their identical pairs of Guess acid-wash jeans, Joe wore a mint-blue Ralph Lauren polo, while Ronnie's just-pumped pectorals threatened to rip the seams of a pastel-pink Izod. From a distance the two men resembled a pair of muscular blueberry and strawberry acid-washed ice-cream cones.

"Trey better like this new outfit," Joe grumbled. "It cost me a week's tips."

Despite his complaints, Joe liked how the new expensive clothes felt, and appreciated that Ronnie had invited him to the ritzy party. Being a worker on Fire Island had been making him feel like a second-class citizen. It was fun to pretend he was just one of the wealthy summer people, able to walk into a fancy store and not think about the price of a shirt or shoes and just buy them because, hey, he liked them. But then the next moment, he felt annoyed again about buying something he really couldn't afford.

"Why was your rich boyfriend so adamant about pastel colors again?" Joe asked. "I hate light-colored shirts. I never make it a month before they're stained. Navy blue is way safer."

"Trey says it's all about pastels this year. If you wanna be a successful gay, you gotta look the part. Oh, and by the way, don't use the *boyfriend* word in front of Trey. Too soon. I'm in phase one: playing distant. Yesterday he called me at ten in the morning, and I didn't return his call until two. I didn't even apologize. He was totally pouty. It was so cute!"

"Hard to believe someone who owns the Taj MaHomo is shy."

"Don't call it that," Ronnie warned. "I don't think Trey would like it."

Joe was growing weary of how Ronnie was behaving about this Trey guy. "Howie says everyone is calling it that."

"Figures a low-class queen would say that. It's so *common*."

"Howie isn't common," Joe said. "Please stop saying stuff like that."

"Sorry. I don't mean to insult your disco witch housemaid freaks."

That did it. Joe had had enough. "Why are you being such a dick about them, Ronnie? Sure, Howie and Lenny are a little weird with all their magical woo-woo crap, but it's just their way of coping with loss. They have good hearts. I had a really good talk with Howie today. He's helping me a lot. I bet if you took a little time and got to know them, you might like them."

"No thanks. We become who we hang out with. And I, for one, do *not* want to become like them. That's why I'm taking you to this party. You'll meet the very top of the rich, gay food chain."

Ronnie went on to list the famous fashion designers and record executive billionaires that would be in attendance. None of whom impressed Joe all that much. He, of course, was hoping Gladiator Man might be among the A-list guests. He hadn't seen him since that awful night of the Knockout punch delirium.

"I heard Madonna might show up at the party," Joe offered enthusiastically, trying to get his mind back into a more positive mood.

"I don't know about that," Ronnie said, "but one of Trey's friends is Lorna Luft's accountant, so she might be there. The important thing is we need to differentiate ourselves from the rest of the working trash on this island. That's why you need to study the guys you meet today. These fellas want to date class acts. So, copy their behavior, but don't say anything too brainiac—it's not hot. Just nod your head and give half smiles. Full-on smiles make you look desperate. Just do it like this." Ronnie stopped walking and pretended he was listening to some classy guy talking to him. He nodded his head, his eyes half squinting, and gently lifted the corners of his mouth.

"It looks like the sun is hurting your eyes," Joe said.

"No it doesn't. It's my sexy and slightly disinterested look. It makes me look hot but mysterious. You try!"

Joe tried it himself, the squint, the partial smile.

"You look like you're taking a shit," Ronnie said.

"I'm trying," Joe said, frustrated with his willful facial muscles and with himself for caring so much about Ronnie's sometimes nonsensical flirting techniques. But still, Ronnie was the expert in the hookup department.

"Try harder," Ronnie commanded, "but make it look easy."

Joe made another attempt, but whatever he did made Ronnie groan.

"Not to be mean, but your smile is way too working-class friendly. Rich guys want a hunk who's quiet, elegant, and someone they can take anywhere. Your goal is to become the human equivalent of a Gucci loafer. It goes with everything, looks valuable, and doesn't distract. Be a crazy-expensive loafer, Joe."

Just as Joe considered what it meant to be a loafer, expensive or otherwise, a tall, shirtless runner turned the corner onto Fire Island Boulevard and ran smack into Joe.

"Hey!" Joe shouted as he stumbled back.

With the agility of Bruce Lee, the runner quickly grabbed Joe's arms so he wouldn't fall. It was only then that Joe registered the shirtless runner was Fergal the ferryman, looking agonizingly sexy with sweat pouring down his face and chest. The sight of his blue-blue eyes, the smell of his musky odor, and the warm touch of his rope-callused hands reminded Joe of everything he had felt that morning they'd kissed—the morning when Joe had ruined everything. For a quick second the two young men silently and awkwardly looked at each other while Fergal's hands remained wrapped around Joe's biceps. Then, as if he'd only just realized who he had been touching, Fergal abruptly released his grip and stepped back. Joe swore he saw repulsion in the ferryman's eyes, so he scowled in return. Fergal gave a small, annoyed click of his tongue, then shuffled around the two men and jogged away.

"Hey," Ronnie said to Joe, "wasn't that the bi deckhand who almost fucked you Memorial Day weekend?"

"Shh!" Joe whispered angrily. "He might hear you."

"Only if he has superman hearing." Ronnie chuckled. "Boy oh boy, that one clearly has some strong feelings toward you."

Joe felt his face redden. "No, he doesn't."

"I didn't say they were necessarily *good* feelings," Ronnie said.

"I don't want to talk about it," Joe mumbled.

"Mm-kay. Well, no great loss. Sure, he's got those knockout eyes, a pretty sweet bod, and that hot Long Island blue-collar thing going for him. But trust me, it won't age well. He'll hit his forties, get bloated from beer, and start hitting the piano bars, ruining all his macho value. Forget him."

"I already have!" Joe snapped. "So can we just stop talking about him!"

"Sure, sure," Ronnie said. "Take a chill pill."

As they continued down the Boulevard, Joe couldn't stop thinking about how lame he had acted with Fergal. *I should have just pretended like I barely remembered him. Or maybe I should have said something like, "Hey there, Fergal. What's up? Good to see ya. Nice day for a jog. Me? Well, I'm just headed to another swanky party, and I haven't even noticed how much you hate me, or that you're not wearing a shirt and you look so goddamn cute in those jogging shorts with those sexy, sweaty hairy legs, while I'm standing here barely able to speak in this douchebag mint-blue polo that I nearly bankrupted myself to buy and . . ."* Ugh! Joe wished he hadn't ever agreed to go to the stupid party. Then he never would've run into Fergal. He should have just stayed up his attic room and slept. But five minutes later, when they arrived at the massive gateway to the Taj MaHomo, his attitude shifted.

"Holy shit," Joe said, his eyes widening at the sheer size of it.

"Not bad, huh?" Ronnie said proudly. "Remember, class acts say things like, 'You did a lovely job' or 'I saw a chaise like that at Bloomingdale's.'"

The huge property was surrounded by extremely tall bamboo trees and a twelve-foot-high wooden fence, creating a lush and mysterious barrier. The only hint of a house seen from the boardwalk was the Japanese-style wooden shingles atop a widow's walk that towered over the other surrounding houses.

Ronnie announced himself through an intercom. A moment later the door opened automatically. The verdant bamboo garden surrounded a massive, three-story beach mansion, most of which was made entirely of glass, with a central core created from (according to Ronnie) aged koa wood from the Big Island of Hawaii. It was the most beautiful and elegant house Joe had ever seen. Wooden walkways through the trees crossed a series of artificial waterfalls and small ponds roiling with hundreds of koi, their bodies speckled orange, white, and black.

"Wow!" Joe said. "This is incredible. Or, should I say, um, he did a lovely job."

"Yeah," Ronnie said, the color draining from his face.

"Are you okay?" Joe realized that since Trey had been staying at a friend's condo during construction, Ronnie hadn't fully understood until then just how opulent the house would be or just how rich of a "rich boyfriend" Trey actually was. But now, he did. Trey was really, really, *really* rich.

"Yeah... I mean it's a nice place," Ronnie said, his voice catching nervously. Then, back to his old bravado. "I've seen bigger."

"I haven't," Joe whispered.

They followed the little wooden path around the house to the sprawling back deck that featured an elegant, cerulean-tiled pool. Although he saw no sign of recognizable celebrities (unless Frankie Fabulous qualified, since he was everywhere) there were plenty of pastel-wearing, Rolex-sporting men in their forties and fifties who looked like they might have starred in aftershave commercials in their youth. He and Ronnie were the only working stiffs at the party—minus the guys actually working, who all had been shipped in from Manhattan. Then Joe noticed something strange.

"Ronnie?" Joe whispered. "Everyone is staring at us and whispering." He glared at his friend. "We were actually invited, right?"

"Yes, we *were* invited," Ronnie said. "Geez. We're just younger and good-looking. They're older and richer. Just act like you don't notice and be cool. That's it." A minute later he elbowed Joe's arm. "Don't look, but that guy by the giant fern works for the mayor of New York City. I *said* don't look. The guy talking to him is this big artist out in the Hamptons, and the one over by the punch bowl is . . ."

As Ronnie kept pointing out the bigwigs, Joe did his best to both look and not look. "What about him?" Joe tossed his chin toward a shorter man holding court with a bevy of men surrounding him. "Who's that guy?"

"Are you serious? He's that record producer who's, like, best friends with Tom Cruise and John Travolta. Worth millions. We flirted once. But he was dating this hot Olympic diver."

Ronnie explained that the men at the party were the sort who spent their summers visiting each other's newly renovated beach houses for supper parties, or pool lounging, rarely rubbing elbows with the less affluent renters—certainly no bartenders or hotel porters. Catching himself staring too much, Joe looked over at the catering table piled high with shrimp cocktails, caviar, giant wheels of cheese, salamis, quiches, olives (with and without pimentos), and tropical fruits. Nothing had been touched. It seemed to Joe as if everyone was waiting for some elegant bell to ring so they could dig in.

"Jesus!" Joe whispered to Ronnie. "Look at that spread. I'm starving."

"Don't you dare." Ronnie grabbed Joe's wrist. "We can't eat until everyone is eating."

"Can't we grab just one shrimp or something—"

"Trey!" Ronnie cried out, waving his arm to someone several feet behind Joe.

"Ronnie!" the man called back, with a jovial New England drawl. "There you are!"

"Remember," Ronnie hissed at Joe, "don't gush and don't touch the food."

Trey Winkle bore little physical resemblance to Ronnie's description. Sure, Joe conceded, he was handsome enough, with perfect, Vitalis-slick, salt-and-pepper hair, blindingly white teeth like sculpted Chiclets, and a surgically perfect nose, but there was an uncanny quality to him. While Trey was reportedly in his mid-forties, he looked to Joe like some high school class president done up in old-age makeup for the Spring production of *Arsenic and Old Lace*.

"There they are!" Trey greeted Ronnie with a firm handshake and lingering kiss on the cheek. It was as if he wanted to demonstrate possession but didn't want to be tawdry about it.

"Trey, this is my best buddy I told you about." Ronnie slapped Joe on the back as if they were football players in a Catalina porn video. "Joe Agabian."

"I certainly have heard a ton about you!" Trey gushed, shaking Joe's hand firmly. "But Ronnie didn't do you justice. Look at that sexy smile—and those eyebrows! He says you're from Philadelphia?"

"Well, really I grew up just outside Philly," Joe said.

"You don't say!" Trey said. "The Main Line?"

"Langhorne," Joe said. "It's in Bucks County—"

"I know the area well! My cousins went to George School, and we summered once in New Hope. I'm not sure Ronnie told you, but I went to Wharton for my MBA. Awful neighborhood of course. But I had a place in Society Hill. We'd play lacrosse in Fairmount Park on weekends. Play any sports out there?"

"Not really," Joe said, but then, sensing Trey didn't like that answer, he quickly added, "I mean not team sports. I did some intramural gymnastics my first semester at Temple. I lived in Northern Liberties with my boyfriend before he—" Ronnie started coughing loudly. Joe got the message: *No dead boyfriend stories.*

"Before I broke up with him and moved back to Bucks county," Joe finished.

"His bad luck!" Trey interrupted. "Look, I'm dying for you to meet someone." He waved beyond Joe's head. "Ace! Ace, you handsome old bastard! Come over here!"

Joe turned and saw an older man approaching the group, holding two freshly poured cocktails that had been dyed a deep, deep grenadine red. The man was tall and lean, in his late sixties, with slicked back, silver hair. He wore a yellow button-down, tan slacks, and a pricey-looking gold wristwatch that glinted in the sun.

"Ace." Trey put his arm around Joe's shoulder and shoved him toward the man. "This is Joe. He went to George School in Bucks County! It's a very prestigious Quaker school."

"No I didn't—" Joe attempted to clarify, but it was no use.

"I just adore a literate Quaker!" Ace's thick, syrupy accent sounded like he was a character from *Gone with the Wind*—one who'd drunk one too many mint juleps. He looked Joe up and down. "And, my dear, you look extremely literate."

Joe blushed as all the surrounding men sniggered.

"Gentlemen," Trey said to Ronnie and Joe, "this is my dearest friend Ace Dandridge, who happens to be a painfully successful entrepreneur back in Atlanta, and an even more painfully successful sodomite everywhere else!"

This set the group to laughing again. Joe joined in, grateful the focus was off him.

"Oh, stop, Trey Winkle, you honey-mouthed Yankee!" Ace cooed. "I might take offense if that comment hadn't come from a man whose derrière has been exploited by more stock brokers than a Morgan Stanley expense account!" More guffaws.

Trey grabbed Joe's hand and pulled him closer to Ace, almost like he was the guest of honor, which seemed odd to him since Ronnie, after all, was Trey's new boyfriend.

"So, Ace," Trey said, his hands sliding onto Joe's shoulders, "Joe here works at . . . what's the name of that bar again?"

"Asylum Harb—" Joe started to say.

"That's right! That quaint little bar no one ever goes to behind the Promethean."

"Is that foul-smelling petri dish still open?" Ace asked with an exaggerated gasp. "I believe the last time I was there was back in '78, when I lost my William and Mary class ring up the backside of this hot little Puerto Rican."

"That's the place," Trey sniggered. "It was a different bar back then. Less petri, more dish. But Joe wouldn't know about that since he's only *twenty-four*!"

A smirk from Ace. Knowing giggles from the crowd. Joe so wished he hadn't told the lie about his age. He realized that if he did meet someone he really liked that summer, he'd have to eventually tell them the truth. And why had Trey mentioned his age anyway? The whole ceremony felt like a hazing, like he and Ronnie were being put under the microscope of a group of elderly frat boys.

"This is Joe's first summer in the Pines," Trey continued. "Can you imagine?"

"It appears the stock price of *chicken* will be going way up this year," Ace joked.

This caused yet another eruption of laughter, including from Ronnie. Joe attempted one of his non-smiling smiles, which was even more difficult because he didn't fully get the joke. Then, from the corner of his eye, Joe noticed guests filling up plates from the food table. He didn't want to miss his chance. He figured he'd eat enough shrimp cocktail to offset the cost of the expensive outfit. He just needed to make his move.

"You look thirsty, Joseph!" Ace cried. "Would you like one of my fancy Alabama slammers? I asked that Brazilian bartender to mix in extra grenadine with his muscular finger! It's so red, isn't it? I like to pretend I'm drinking his blood!" He made a ridiculous face, lapping at his deep red drink like a vampire bat.

The entire crowd around Ace erupted into groans and guffaws. Ace laughed as well, doubling over, causing his two Alabama slammers to splash their grenadine bloodbath all over Joe's brand-new mint-blue polo.

"Hey! My shirt!" Joe cried.

"Oh, shoot! I am so very sorry there, Joseph! Let me get that for you!" Ace started exaggeratedly rubbing at Joe's chest and groping his crotch with a cocktail napkin, expanding the crimson stain to his new jeans. Furious, Joe grabbed the napkins from Ace to try and clean himself. All the A-listers laughed. Joe knew that each of them could have bought two, or even ten of those polo shirts, and it wouldn't have meant a thing to them. But there he was exposing just how big of a deal it was to him.

"No biggie." Joe tried to stem a desire to cry or scream. "I'll just go rinse off. I have to take a leak anyway."

"I'm sure Ace would love to help you!" Trey roared.

More hysterical laughter from a dozen men, including Ronnie. Joe forced a smile, suppressing his rage as he trudged into the house. Once inside the museum-like living room, a shirtless waiter pointed him toward the guest bathroom. It was huge, decorated in slate and glass, with three sinks and a glass shower stall big enough for a small football team. He pulled off his stained polo shirt and jeans, spritzed them with expensive-smelling verbena hand soap, and rinsed them under cold water. The stain got lighter on the jeans, but the polo was clearly ruined. All those bar tips wasted. Joe squeezed the sopping clothes in a gray bath towel, and then pulled them back on. It was then that he heard two men's voices, just outside a high bathroom window.

"His name is Ronnie, right?"

"Does you-know-who know about him?"

Joe lifted himself on his tip toes, pointing his ear toward the open window.

"I doubt it," the first man replied. "Trey and Bill have one of those suburban DC don't ask, don't tell policies. The only rule is Trey can't fuck any disease carriers. But with all the rough-trade he's fucking, like that Ronnie trash, they should have built a private AIDS testing facility rather than that second jacuzzi."

The two men laughed while reprimanding themselves for being "terrible." Joe's face grew hot with anger. These men were just like all the other bigots he had met in his life—the straight people who told AIDS jokes or the gay guys in Philly who would warn each other about who "had it" and who didn't. On top of all of that, Joe now knew Trey was lying to Ronnie. He had to warn him. As he was about to head back out, the men outside the window said something else.

"But what about that hot little Italian number he brought?" the first man enthused.

"I know! Mamma mia! I'd like him to deliver *my* pizza."

"They say he bartends at that horrible little bar behind the Promethean—"

"You mean the Asylum Troll bar? Gross! Is he a gift for someone?"

"Well, my understanding is that Trey is trying to get Ace to invest in some South Beach property. So he asked that muscly hotel maid to provide some hot trade to put Ace in a good mood."

"My goodness. All I get are dinners at the 21 Club. Next time he wants me to invest, I'm holding out for a free night with a wop rent-boy."

Joe stepped away from the window and stared at his furious reflection in the huge bathroom mirror. The deep red splotch just beneath the logo of the polo made it look like he had been shot in the heart. Was what they'd said true? Had Ronnie brought him to the party as a gift for Ace? Joe stormed back out to the deck and grabbed Ronnie by the wrist.

"Hey, Ronnie, I need to talk to you," Joe whispered more loudly then he'd intended.

"What is it, Joey baby?" Ronnie said, suddenly bug-eyed and chewing gum like a madman. "Pretty sweet digs, huh?" The words started machine-gunning from his mouth. "Was the bathroom nice? It has a huge shower, right? All these rich gays have huge showers. The fish ponds are my favorite. I love fish. Did I ever tell you that before? I love giant ten-man showers and fish ponds! I like anything in water, I guess. And to think, this is practically mine. All of it. Am I talking too much? I feel like I'm talking too much! I hope you're not talking too much, I told you that's not sexy—"

"What the hell," Joe whispered. "Are you on coke?"

"Maybe just a little!" Ronnie giggled. "You want some? Hey, Trey!"

"No!" Joe growled through his teeth. "You know I don't do that shit. I want us to get out of here. Now."

"Are you fucking kidding me, Joey?" Ronnie rubbed his pointer finger on his gums, then licked the back of his hand to get any remnants of powder.

"I'm not kidding, Ronnie. I just heard some guys say really mean shit about people with AIDS. I'm wet and my shirt is ruined, and all these people are a bunch of assholes."

"Keep your voice down," Ronnie hissed before pulling Joe away from the crowd. "You're being ridiculous."

Joe felt trapped and angry, while ten feet away Ace and several other of the men were staring at him, pruriently sniggering. "Damn it, Ronnie, I want to go."

"No!" Ronnie's body twitched as he laughed bitterly through his clenched jaw. "When have you even been to a party like this? I'll answer that—you haven't. Ever. You need to see your opportunities, baby Joey. Take that fucking wet shirt off, already!"

Ronnie pulled up the hem of Joe's ruined polo. Joe yanked it back down.

"No, Ronnie."

"These guys won't mind."

"Ronnie, listen. I heard a couple of guys talking outside the bathroom. They said mean things about you—"

"So what? Old fags talk. That's all they got. You know that."

"No, I don't, Ronnie," Joe's face felt hot, and his head swirled with hurt rage. "And look at my shirt and pants. Over a hundred bucks down the toilet!"

Ronnie laughed. "Joey, Joey, Joey. You need to stop being so cheap!"

Joe waited for Ronnie's crazed eyeballs to make contact, but they didn't—they couldn't. Did Joe even know his best friend anymore? Were they even friends at all if what he had heard was true? Was this entire summer the biggest mistake of Joe's entire life?

"Ronnie, I need to ask you something. Did you bring me to this party to pimp me out to Ace what's-his-name?"

Ronnie's coke mania briefly paused as he forced a nervous laugh. He took another shaky gulp of his drink. "I'm gonna need a refresher." He waved at a shirtless waiter. "Hey, Hercules!"

"Just tell me you didn't," Joe begged, feeling his anger melting rapidly into heartbreak.

"Oh, for Chrissake, Joey, I didn't 'pimp' you. Yes, Trey asked me to bring someone attractive for Ace. How is flirting with some rich old queen gonna hurt? You do it all the time at your bar. And so what if maybe you let him kiss you or something? If you stopped playing the poor widow Pollyanna you wouldn't need to worry about getting your fucking polo shirt dirty! Grow the fuck up—this is how this world works. It's what you got inside your pocket or inside your pants. Every fucking man at this party, if he wasn't born into money like Trey, had to sell his fucking ass one way or another to get here. You're just pissed because I accomplished what I came out to Fire Island to do, and you didn't."

Joe looked out onto the ocean and the sky turning orange. A flock of seagulls swooped into the surf. Beachcombers gawked at the ritzy party to which they had not been invited. Joe was doing everything in his power to hold back what he really wanted to say. "You're acting like such a dick, Ronnie. I'm just saying, this Trey thing isn't what you think it is."

"I don't wanna hear it!" Ronnie shouted, the cocaine revving his voice an octave higher than usual. Party guests moved closer, excited to see a scene between the two young working-class hotties. "I did you a favor bringing you here. I tried to help you be something better than you are—meet people that could help you. But what's the point? Look at yourself! You're cute, sure, but you're not all that."

Seeing everyone listening, Joe's face grew hot. He wanted nothing more than to be a million miles away. "What the hell happened to you, Ronnie?" he said, his voice low. "Doing coke? Hanging with shitheads like these? This island has changed you. You've always been a little full of it with all your bullshit affirmations, but you used to have some sort of integrity."

"Bullshit affirmations, huh?" Ronnie's voice grew louder. "You think this house is a bullshit affirmation? You think Trey is a bullshit affirmation? Maybe you should look at yourself, Joe. What do you have, with your negative thinking? You're fucking miserable! You're twenty-four, short, all alone, and working in the shittiest bar in all of Fire Island. Figures, the only person who ever considered dating you was fucking desperate and dying of AIDS."

Every voice on the back deck fell silent, while Ronnie's words ricocheted like bullets inside Joe's brain. Or were they his own words?

He took a deep breath and pushed his face right up into Ronnie's. "You're a piece of shit." He took sharp breaths in between his words to stop himself from crying. "Know what else I overheard? Seems your little rich boyfriend isn't even single, and he plans to dump your selfish, steroid-pumped, hotel-maid ass any day now. He calls you trash behind your back. They all do. So you're not only a whore, Ronnie, you're like the *shittiest* whore on the whole island."

Ronnie's eyes darted to Trey and then back to Joe. "You're just making that up because I finally told you the truth." His voice cracked with a murky mix of anger and tears.

"Oh yeah?" Joe's lip quivered. "Go ask Trey about someone named Bill down in DC. Go on, ask him."

Ronnie's face, already pale, went blank. He tightened the rubber band around his blond ponytail and with a cold, steady voice he said, "Get out of my party."

30.

Invasion Deflation

> *"The Great Darkness has reigned for one hundred thousand DJ sets and will reign for at least one hundred thousand more. Do not despair. Put on your dancing shoes and continue to work toward the Great Balance."*
> —*Disco Witch Manifesto #42*

Before Joe knew it, the summer of '89 was headed toward its muggy, monochromatic middle. It had been weeks since Ronnie had kicked him out of Trey Winkle's party, and although he caught occasional glimpses of him working at the Flotel, they'd had no interaction whatsoever. Elena, meanwhile, had been just too busy to hang out, since she was always going to one of her AA meetings or spending time with Cleigh. Vince, heartbroken that Ronnie had ditched him for Trey, reverted to his old miserable self, summoning countless Irish synonyms for calling Joe a "lazy eejit."

And then there was Fergal the ferryman. Every time Joe'd pass him on the dock, the ferryman not only averted his eyes, he acted like there was nothing but rotten fish in the space where Joe was walking. As for the Gladiator Man, Joe hadn't seen him since that night he drunkenly stumbled after him down Fire Island Boulevard. It was as if he'd never existed. Or maybe he did, and he just was avoiding Joe. Without any friends around or mysterious obsessions, Joe spent most of his free time alone in the hot, stuffy attic, listening to *Love Songs 1*, looking at his one photo of Elliot, and ruminating over the mess he had made. The only bright spot in that part of the summer was how Howie and Lenny were getting all excited about something called the Invasion.

The history of the Fourth of July "Invasion" (the second high holy day in Howie's calendar) was burned into most Fire Island old timers' heads. As legend had it, back in the summer of 1976, during the nation's bicentennial, some of the funky denizens of Cherry Grove, including one dressed in drag, ventured over to Fire Island Pines to eat at a restaurant. The restaurant staff refused to serve the man in drag, since the Pines was much more conservative than the free-spirited Cherry Grove. Infuriated, the rejected Grove patrons decided to take action. On the Fourth of July they gathered their friends, all dressed in the most lurid and flamboyant drag; rented a water taxi; and, like good patriotic libertines, *invaded* the Pines. Everyone had a blast, including the snooty Pines homos. From that day forward, every July Fourth, a boatload of drag queens—in the hundreds—recreated the invasion of the Pines.

Joe was hopeful that year's Invasion might bring the possibility of new customers to Asylum Harbor, new friends for him, and the possibility he'd run into the Gladiator Man again or any cute fellow who might wake him from his stupor.

Unfortunately, none of that happened. The Fourth of July came and went, and like most invasions it left a disaster in its wake. Instead of discarded weapons and dead bodies, Asylum Harbor was strewn with lost nylon wigs, feather boas, false eyelashes, and so many Lee Press-Ons that the floor crackled beneath Joe's feet. There were no new friends, no new regular customers, and Joe's record as "the best-looking bartender to never hook up on Fire Island" was on track for a Guinness World Record. While the day of the invasion brought the biggest crowd yet into the bar, the following week saw a return to the sparse pre-Invasion levels.

Adding to Joe's misery, one of the Graveyard Girls spilled the beans to Vince that Trey had given Ronnie an eighteen-karat gold, tricolor Tiffany ring. Vince went mental, demanding that Joe join him in a thorough and complete housecleaning of the bar to get rid of all the bad energy of the first half of the summer.

"We may be the most unpopular bar in Fire Island Pines," Vince announced with his arms full of industrial cleaning supplies, "but feck it, we're gonna be the cleanest."

At least being angry at Vince felt better than being depressed. Joe dove into the work with a vengeance. Soon, Asylum Harbor's stink of stale beer and vomit was overlayed with the scent of lemony wood polish and the sweat of one exhausted Armenian American bartender.

"All done." Joe flopped onto a stool and dropped his head on the counter while Vince inspected his work.

"You call that wood shiny?" Vince snarled. "Feckin' hell! My Aunt Siobhan could polish a bar better than you. And she didn't have any hands! Do it again, ya lazy lug!"

"I've had it!" Joe threw his rag at Vince—though it sadly curved and landed at least six feet off its mark. "It's not my fault that Ronnie isn't banging you anymore. Clean the fucking bar yourself."

Vince's icy eyes glared at Joe. "For one thing, you ungrateful sod, it was I who was doing the banging. And two, what gives you the idea I give three roasted fucks about that two-faced, disloyal, gold-digging, bastard best friend of yours?"

Hearing Vince refer to Ronnie as his best friend felt like a punch to Joe's solar plexus. "You know damn well Ronnie and I aren't best friends anymore. We aren't even mediocre friends. And besides, you two agreed at the beginning not to be boyfriends."

"That's not true!" Vince's voice nearly squeaked in protest. "I mean, okay, maybe we said something of the sort. But still, how could a lad be all lovey-dovey one day, saying shite like 'Vince, darlin', I've never felt so comfortable with somebody in my life,' and then, not a week later, he's off playing the Leona Helmsley of homos with some rich poof. The worst part is, he didn't even tell me himself. I had to hear it on the street."

"I'm really sorry, Vince," Joe said, softening his tone too. "I get it."

"You know something? I don't even care anymore. And I have you to thank for it—this bar cleaning really helped. Clean bar, clean head." Vince forced a laugh. "I'm so over that bastard, I wouldn't touch him again for all the dick in Drogheda. No, ma'am!" He held his smile a moment longer before he caught sight of his own reflection in the counter and his eyes glazed over. "Maybe we should also clean out the storage closet and line the top shelves with some doilies. Might look snappy, huh?"

Nope, poor Vince wasn't anywhere near being over Ronnie. Joe knew the signs; he'd already spent two long years staring at his own heartbreak in a mirror. The stern forehead, the tight jaw, and the eyes—oh, the eyes—darting around as if the very air in front of him might hold an answer to the riddle *Where do you put the love for someone who is no longer there?*

Joe grew even more resentful at his ex–best friend for what he had done to his brokenhearted bar manager. What an idiot Ronnie was. Not just an idiot—ungrateful as well. In Vince he had a decent man, someone who truly loved him. Someone who wasn't sick or dying. Someone with whom he could have a future. Did Ronnie not get how few gay men had an opportunity like that anymore? It was so unfair. How dare he throw that all away on some rich, cheating douchebag?

"Vince, face it," he began, attempting to copy Ronnie's self-help-guru style of talking. "Men suck. Straight men, gay men. We all suck. And in my opinion, you may be the meanest manager in the history of food and beverage, but you're a damn handsome fella, and you could do way better than that two-faced, gold-digging Ronnie Kaminski. He's just a—"

"Cork it, Dear Abby," Vince growled. "I'll have none of that bad-mouthing."

"But you just said—"

"I know what I said, but I don't need your swaddling and burping, thank you very much. Just get back to work. Those Cuervo bottles better be so shiny I'm blinded!"

At that moment Dory Lieberman-Delagrange walked into the bar, holding Howie's arm, the two deep in conversation. Howie held a clipboard with a checklist. Joe sighed in relief, not just because he hoped their visit would interrupt Vince's demonic cleaning purge but also because he always felt lighter and safer in their presence for some reason, especially since he had gotten beyond all that silly disco witch gossip.

"Yes, that's perfect." Dory exclaimed to Howie. "We'll have the finger food up against the wall on the deck with four of the tall round cocktail tables set out there, and seven or eight more in here."

Howie nodded and then threw his arms open toward Joe and Vince. "And look at these visions! How are the handsomest bartenders on all of Fire Island? Wait until you see Dory's plans for the ACT UP benefit—it's going to be phenomenal. We were out all day yesterday, postering every flat surface and telephone pole from here to the Grove."

"Saw 'em last night," Vince said. "You can't swing a dead cat without hitting one of your fliers. I'm thinking we might need a couple of bruisers to manage the crowd."

"As long as they're shirtless and have admirers with checkbooks," Dory said. "By the way, Vince, how is the bar doing in general? Saint D'Norman suggested receipts are still down?"

"He's not wrong about receipts, I'm afraid." Vince sucked air through his teeth. "The Invasion didn't have any follow-through. Low Tea and High Tea have taken a worse toll than we expected. All the gay sheep wanna follow the crowd. If it gets much worse..." Vince didn't need to finish his sentence.

"Well, I'm not counting this bar out yet," Howie chimed in. "What you've done with this place is nothing less than miraculous. This time last year this place was a morgue—and not in a good way. It's alive again!"

"Still not anywhere near where we need to be to stop Scotty Black from exercising his option to close us down," Vince said.

"But there's still a healthy crowd coming in just before dancing," Howie said. "It's not exactly wall to wall, but it's a big improvement. Scotty just needs to give it more time."

Vince couldn't even force a fake smile. He merely downed the rest of a shot while Dory took a huge gulp off her Beefeaters and tonic. Even Howie sighed with a tone of surrender.

Joe slapped his hand on the counter. "Howie's right," he barked, trying to blow air into Howie's deflated rallying cry. "Maybe this ACT UP benefit will get some younger guys in here."

Howie beamed. "Exactly. If you can get some of those hot, white T-shirt and black combat boot boys in here, you never know. It could become the hip new thing."

"Not a bad idea," Vince said. "Maybe put up some of those Silence Equals Death posters."

Just as all four started to look on the bright side, the sound of someone running up the wooden steps caused them all to turn toward the door. There, Lenny stood, huffing and puffing, with an enraged look on his face.

"What is it, Lenny?" Howie begged in a panic. "Are you okay?"

Lenny nodded and waved, taking deep breaths, unable to form words. Joe ran over to him with a glass of water. Lenny drank, then sat on a stool.

"Thanks, Joseph. I'm fine. It's . . ." *Deep breath.* "It's . . ." *Deep breath.* "The benefit posters. They've been . . . torn down."

"What?" Dory said, alarmed. "How many?"

"All of 'em!" Lenny barked. "There's not a trace anywhere on the island. I even called Babs over in the Grove. There too. Gone. Someone doesn't want this benefit to happen."

'Who would do something like that?" Dory said. "We're just trying to help end the AIDS crisis."

"We all know who's behind it," Joe blurted, his body tense with rage. "Why don't we just say his name? Scotty Bl—"

"Easy, lad!" Vince checked the door, then lowered his voice. "Keep your head. Island politics is no joke out here. We're still in business with him."

"He's also not the only one that doesn't want the word *AIDS* associated with the Pines," Howie added, shaking his head.

"Exactly," Vince said. "So, you see, lad, we can't go accusing people without absolute proof. It's not only our livelihoods at stake." His eyes pointed over to Howie and Lenny. "Some folks here have to keep in good with you-know-who."

Joe nodded, still furious but comprehending how Howie and Lenny's housecleaning business also depended on Scotty Black and all his rich friends.

"But you're not wrong," Vince said. "Scotty knows the benefit might help Asylum Harbor make its nut, which would dump a cold bucket of ice water on that gombeen's plans to shutter us."

"I'm not giving up," Dory announced. "I'll just have to see if the printer can send more posters over by tomorrow. Hopefully they'll stay up long enough this time to get the word out. "

"Lenny and I won't have time to put them up again, I'm afraid," Howie said. "We have back-to-back gigs until the benefit next week."

"If I start my shift late, I can do it," Joe offered.

Dory patted Joe's cheek. "Thank you, darling. You're a wonderful young man. I'll see if Elena can help you. We'll try our best."

"It's all we can do," Howie added. "Though I'll also put in a request to the Great Goddess Mother to send a Chesapeake Bay's worth of crabs straight into Scotty Black's boxers."

Howie, Dory, and Lenny tried to laugh, but they couldn't. Joe knew how important this ACT UP benefit had been to them, especially to Dory. Of course, it had also become important to him. Joe desperately wanted the benefit to be a success in honor of Elliot, as well as all the friends Howie, Dory, Lenny, and Saint D'Norman had lost or were losing. Joe's eyes narrowed as he slammed his fist on the bar counter. "No *way* are we letting Scotty Black get away with this."

31.
Fresca and Secrets

"When we've packed our dancing shoes, our magic tools, our snacks, and our favorite disco outfits, we think we are ready for any challenge. But without our brother and sister Disco Witches, we have nothing."
—*Disco Witch Manifesto #102*

When the very last benefit poster was affixed to a telephone pole, the large spool of tape screeched with joy. Joe and Elena had not only successfully replaced all the torn-down posters, they'd increased the coverage by twenty percent. Every legal surface in the Pines and the Grove proclaimed that Dory Lieberman-Delagrange and a raft of celebrities would be hosting the *"ACT UP NY Benefit at Asylum Harbor Bar, July 20, 1989, 2 PM to 6 PM. $25 donation. FREE DRINKS. Act Up! Fight Back! Fight AIDS!"*

It seemed the perfect time for the two to celebrate by relaxing with a couple cans of Fresca. As it was past five, the beach was empty except for two Cherry Grove nudists, their jiggly bits splayed for roasting by the last wink of the sun.

"God, I'm tired." Elena yawned, stretching out on the still-warm sand. "Hopefully the posters stay up long enough for people to see them this time."

"They better." Joe lifted his face to the salty breeze. Despite the circumstances, it felt great hanging out with Elena for an entire day. He looked over at her lying there with her golden-brown curls gilded

Kodachrome by the setting sun. Women like Elena could be so much easier to talk to than men. There wasn't the constant obsession to hook up with "the hottest daddy," like there was with Ronnie. Nor was there (usually) any worry that one might be sexually attracted to the other. Elena was a complete respite from all that.

An array of squawking drew Joe's eyes from Elena to the waves. A group of seagulls and cormorants were dodging down for sand crabs in the shiny part of the sand, their reflections making it seem as if some other bird was right under their feet, racing them to their catch.

"How can this island be so beautiful," Joe said, "and yet at the same time inspire evil dickheads like Scotty Black and Trey Winkle?"

"It's just the way it is." Elena kept her eyes closed. "There are monsters and angels crawling all over this bloated sandbar. Let me tell you, Dory's got stories. Remember the goldfish pond that the homeowners' association put up in the harbor?"

"Oh, right," Joe said. "Back in May. Where the wooden bench is now. It had a little fountain with plants and, like, five fish. It was cute. Why'd they replace it?"

"Classic Pines politics. The owners spent months arguing about it. This one thought it was classy, that one thought it was a waste of money, and another was angry he didn't get to design it. Blah blah blah. You'd think they were negotiating a nuclear arms deal. Next thing you know, someone poured a gallon of detergent in it, killing all the fish and plants. Thus, the bench."

Joe grimaced. "They actually murdered goldfish over a grudge?"

"Yep. They *feel things* just a little too deeply out here. It's the same thing in fashion. At nearly every runway show, everyone's freaking out, screaming like someone just ate a baby."

Joe laughed.

"I mean, Jesus, it's just a fucking dress! The homeowners out here are the same. One moment they're Auntie Mame, and the next they're Anthony Perkins in *Psycho*—especially if it's related to a water feature or the typeface on a signpost. Not everyone is evil. But if you want to fall in love with the island, you need to separate its beauty from all that nonsense."

Joe lay his body down next to Elena's. He listened to the fizzy sound the sand made when his head shifted back and forth. He dug his hands and toes deep through the toasty powder until they hit the cooler, damper grit. After a bit he sensed something in Elena's silence. "What are you thinking about?"

After a brief hesitation, she said, "Remember how you were worried that your roommates were witches?"

Joe bolted upright. "Did you hear something?"

She laughed, and without even looking, she gently pushed Joe back down. "Relax! No broomsticks seen over High Tea just yet. It's just . . ." She inhaled deeply. "Since coming out here, this place has been kind of magical for me. Remember I told you how I was having these conflicted feelings about Cleigh?"

Joe turned toward her with raised eyebrows. "Yeah?"

"Well . . ." She giggled. "It's not conflicted anymore. In fact, we're talking about dating for real once I get a year clean."

"I'm really happy for you," Joe said, and he meant it.

"But it's not just her—it's the fact that this is the longest I've been sober since I was like twelve. I'm actually excited about a future. That's a first for me." She smiled. "See what I mean? Magic. Of course, Lenny is a big part of the reason."

"Lenny? What does he have to do with it?"

"You didn't know Lenny's my AA sponsor?" Elena asked.

"What?" Joe took a second to absorb what Elena had said, but then gasped as he got it. "Holy crap, I thought all those 'meetings' he was setting up were euphemisms for kinky leather parties."

Elena grabbed at her hair in embarrassment. "I'm an ass. So much for anonymity. Forget I said that."

"Okay," he said. "I'll forget it." Although he knew he wouldn't. Then he wondered whether Lenny had been a drug addict like Elena or just a run-of-the-mill drunk, like the men who drank themselves into a stupor every day at Joe's bar. "You think you really know people," Joe mused out loud. "And the next thing you know, they surprise you . . . good and bad."

"That's what Dory says is the best thing about life: the surprises."

"She's the best," Joe said. "Know what I still can't figure out? How did a class act like her start hanging out with a pair of house cleaners like Howie and Lenny?"

"She met them out at a club after my grandfather died. That woman loves to disco dance. Or rather she did. I think she feels guilty experiencing joy while her friends are sick or dying."

Joe squeezed his eyes tight until the blood red glow through his eyelids turned black and the peaceful feeling drained from his body. "I wish you hadn't said that." He folded his arms across his eyes.

"What?" Elena said. "It's not like she can ignore it."

"I know," he said. "But I have to think about that shit all the time. I wake up, I think about AIDS; I go to bed, I think about AIDS. I came out here to forget, but each week I see these faces at my bar getting sicker. Some guys that had been regulars at the beginning of the summer have stopped coming. I just know they've either gotten sicker or died. I hate it."

Elena fell silent. Joe turned on his side to see why. Her eyes were closed.

"Are you mad?" he asked. "Did I say something wrong?"

After a few moments, she opened her eyes and told Joe her own sad secret—a secret she had been keeping the whole summer. She too was HIV positive, her infection the result of dirty needles she'd shared with her ex. Her words came out sharp and detached. As he listened, a sense of numbness swallowed him.

"I haven't gotten sick yet," she said, as if to soften the news. "The truth is, I wouldn't even have known I had it if my junkie ex hadn't gotten PCP pneumonia. Most women get misdiagnosed and don't get tested until they're really sick. I was lucky to find out early. It helped me sober up and start taking care of my health." She looked over at Joe, who was staring down at the sand. "Sorry I didn't tell you before. I wanted to that night you told me about losing your boyfriend, to let you know I understood. But I just wasn't ready for the pity. Know what I mean?"

Joe nodded and grabbed her hand, giving it a squeeze.

"There are so many people way worse off than me out here," she said. "By the way, you and Cleigh are the only ones who know. I haven't even told Dory."

Joe inhaled sharply. "You haven't told Dory?"

"I know, I know." Elena shook her head, more to herself than Joe. "I will—just not yet. But *not* telling *you* had become this block to our friendship, and I don't want that. I really care about you, Joe."

Joe felt as if he were sinking into quicksand while people all around him were stretching out their arms trying to save him. The only problem was, his saviors were drowning in their own quicksand. *Will everyone I love die of this fucking disease?* He remembered when Elliot had first told him. He wore that same expression Elena had right then—like a scared little child, staring at the sea, frightened that her friend might no longer love her. What was Joe supposed to say to someone who'd told him they had a disease that would probably kill them? That would cause the majority of the world to fear them?

"I care about you too," Joe said. "I hate that you have it. I'm sorry—I know it's selfish of me, but . . ." He screamed loudly out to the ocean: "I hate it!"

The two nudists in the distance sat up and looked over. A flock of seagulls down at the shore flew off, angrily squawking.

"Me too," Elena said, and looked at him, unsure. "Is this gonna make it hard for us to be friends?"

Joe's head felt heavy with conflicting thoughts, including the option to just start digging into the sand until he never had to see another human being who would break his heart. He scootched closer to Elena and gently tapped her sandy foot with his own. "No way," he said. "But I'm telling you now: I'm not going to let you get sick. You need to stay healthy until there's a cure. Promise?"

It was a pointless request, and Joe knew it. But he felt like he had to say it to Elena, to the beach, to the sea. He needed to say something to dampen the roar of his helplessness.

"I can't promise, but I'll try," Elena said. "I do have this feeling that if you, Cleigh, and Dory hold onto my soul tightly enough, then maybe I won't be able to die."

Joe leaned in and kissed Elena lightly on her forehead, her nose, her lips. "Remember that," he whispered.

32.

The Prodigal Stud

"And when the Great Balance is achieved, all our lost lovers and friends will return to us, joy will abound, and the dancing will last for days."
—*Disco Witch Manifesto #219*

It was four forty-five AM Sunday morning when Joe locked the door to the bar. It had been a slower night than usual, and tips were down significantly—most likely due to several prominent house parties on top of the usual competition. But he also worried his flirtatious bartender personality had been impaired by all the concerns piling one on top of another inside his head, especially Elena's recent revelation. He already felt himself wanting to take control of Elena's health, the same way he had tried to control Elliot's, berating him to get more sleep and not drink alcohol or stand too close to someone with a cold.

"You're suffocating me," Elliot had told Joe. "Every time you nag me about my health, it reminds me I have the disease. I can feel you staring at me in that sad, scared way you do. Stop it. I'm not dead yet."

Joe winced at the memory and wanted to avoid the same mistakes with Elena. It would be a struggle not to hover over her, not to worry, not to try and use his constant surveillance to keep her alive. How did Howie and Lenny do it? The vast majority of their friends still living either had AIDS or were HIV positive. They had lost eighty-two of their closest friends to the disease so far. *How do they breathe without crying?*

As he headed down the stairs from the bar, he noticed a shadowy figure stumbling around the corner of Picketty Ruff. Joe clenched his fists and stayed on high alert on the short walk home. When he opened the gate latch, he heard a huge crash behind him. The man had fallen off the walk and into the neighbor's trash cans. Joe ran over and called into the pile of disrupted garbage, "You okay?" Then he recognized the long blond hair, the gym shorts, the bloated muscles covered in old bits of lettuce. "Ronnie? What the fuck are you doing?"

"I'm fine," Ronnie stammered, staring up from his bed of trash, struggling with the simple maneuver of removing his left leg from the garbage can. "Lost my footing. They should really fix that boardwalk. Someone is gonna sue. I should sue. I mean if I was hurt I would, but I'm not." He attempted to kick off the trash can but only got his right foot stuck in a different one.

Joe considered walking away and leaving his inebriated ex-friend to his mess. But after a few more seconds of watching him pathetically wrestle with the cans, Joe jumped down and pulled Ronnie's legs from the mucky containers. "Jesus, Ronnie," he said, retching as he got them both back onto the walk, "where have you been? You smell worse than a bathhouse toilet."

"There's that judgmental Joe," Ronnie scoffed. "If you must know, Thursty gave me the weekend off, so I've been partying a little, that's all." He looked at his crotch. "Fuck, I think I tore my best sexy shorts!"

"Why were you sneaking around my house?" Joe asked.

"I wasn't!"

"Right." Joe shook his head. Ronnie's eyes were so alert he looked in a state of shock. An almost inhuman creaking noise came from his grinding teeth—the final telltale sign that Ronnie was most likely coked-out. "So why aren't you asleep in Trey's tennis court–sized bedroom?"

"I just needed some space this weekend." Ronnie crossed his arms—a feeble attempt at bravado. "But things are great—fucking spectacular! Just like I visualized. I've made so many great connections—rich guys, famous guys. One of Trey's friends got sucked off by Liberace in Vegas once. Yep, I'm living large ... I'm really living—" Ronnie suddenly gasped like someone had punched him in the stomach. His head toppled into his hands, sobbing.

It was one of the saddest things Joe had ever seen. Without thinking, he pulled the smelly, sweaty man into his arms. "Ronnie," he whispered, "it's gonna be okay. Now tell me what's going on."

Ronnie lifted his head from Joe's shoulder and went to wipe his face on the sleeve of his nonexistent shirt. "Fuck! What happened to my shirt?"

"I dunno," Joe said. "Where were you last?"

"Who the hell knows. It got kind of wild last night, I guess. Hey, it's Friday, right?"

"Nope. Sunday morning. You're telling me you've been doing coke since *Thursday*?"

"Who said I've been doing coke?" Again, Ronnie's head fell into his hands, shoulders shaking this time. "I miss you, Joey," he said between trilling gasps for air. "I'm really s-s-sorry about what ha-ha-happened."

"Ronnie, all right. C'mere." He pulled Ronnie's weeping head to his shoulder. "Just be careful not to get snot onto my shirt ... oops. Too late."

After about thirty more seconds of sobbing, Ronnie pulled himself somewhat together. The two men sat on the edge of the walk, overlooking the spilled rubbish.

"You were right, Joey. Trey Winkle was a snake. He *did* have a boyfriend named Bill—some older dude from Virginia who owns a bank or hedge fund or something. Trey barely has any money of his own. That's why he dates rich guys."

"You mean like you do?" Joe was surprised by his own candor.

"I hear ya, and I know you're still mad at me, but you have to understand, I really thought I could fall in love with him. I mean if he was the caring person I thought he was ... which it turns out he wasn't. He told me, 'You know, Ronnie, it's getting close to the last part of the summer, and I think I wanna be solo for the Morning Party and Labor Day, so it's time we said goodbye.'" Ronnie gulped air to stabilize himself again. "And then he handed me five hundred bucks and this shit." From his shorts pocket he pulled a sandwich bag filled with a half dozen brown glass vials inside and a tiny cellophane envelope with one blue pill. Most of the vials were empty, but three were full. "That's it. Two eight balls worth of coke, eight hits of X, and five hundred lousy bucks. You have no idea what things he made me do—and not just with him alone. It was fun when I thought he loved me. Now it disgusts me. *He* disgusts me. *I* disgust me."

Ronnie cried for another few rounds. Joe wanted to feel open enough to be of more help, but something was blocking him. "Ronnie, I'm sorry about what you're going through, and I want to figure us out, but what you said and did to me at Trey's party was really fucked up."

"I know!" Ronnie grimaced at the memory. "And I'm really, really sorry. You gotta believe me. When Trey asked me to bring you along for Ace, I told myself he just wanted to spruce up his party with another hot young guy. But I also guessed he wanted you to sleep with Ace to get him in a good mood. I just was so crazed with that shit and with trying to make Trey and me work. I rationalized it by telling myself if I ended up rich, then I could help you out too. But it was mostly me being selfish."

"What about what you yelled at me?" Joe's voice cracked with bitterness.

"I don't really remember what I said, but whatever it was—"

"You don't remember?" Joe scoffed. "You told me that the only people who could love me had to be desperate and dying with AIDS."

Ronnie squeezed his eyes as tears once again gushed down. "I said that? That is so messed up. It's also a fucked-up thing to say about people with AIDS. I was pretty drugged up, but that's not an excuse... I'm so, so sorry. You know I didn't mean it." He looked up at Joe through his wet lashes. "I think you're the best, Joe. You're handsome, smart, and got the biggest heart inside that furry little Armenian chest. Who wouldn't fall in love with you?"

Joe looked away for a moment and wondered about the depth of his rage toward Ronnie that day at Trey's. Was he really mad at Ronnie for saying what he had, or was he mad because it was what he still thought about himself deep down, that he was incapable of being loved by anyone who wasn't desperate? And then he recalled what he had said to Ronnie, and it made his heart ache. "We both said some pretty shitty things to each other. I'm sorry too."

"Please can we, you know, maybe try and be friends again?"

Joe looked at the fans of leafy shadows on Ronnie's wet, coked-out but open face. "Okay, but we've got to promise never to hurt each other like that ever again."

Ronnie crossed his heart. "I swear on the graves of my mother and Dale Carnegie. And if I ever hurt you again, I will apologize a lot faster next time."

Joe smiled and took Ronnie's hand. "Also, no more pimping me out." Then, à la Mae West: "If anyone is gonna pimp me out, it's gonna be me. Got it, my sexy Chippendales hobo best friend?"

Ronnie stifled another surge of tears—the happy kind this time. "You know something, Joey? Only a few weeks have gone by, but you seem different. More powerful or something."

"You think?" Joe thought about that. "Lenny and Howie say this island teaches you things. I'm not sure what I've learned, but I'm done playing the innocent little Joey. I'm not really innocent. I never have been."

Ronnie smiled, then suddenly tried blowing something out of his right nostril. "Fucking coke cakes up my nose so bad." He handed the bag of coke vials and the blue pill to Joe. "Can you ditch this for me? There's an X left." He tapped his head with his finger. "But I don't have any dopamine left upstairs for it to do any good."

Joe took the bag of drugs as if it held a dead rat inside. "I'll toss this shit in the bay or something. I think you've had enough for the summer."

"I've had enough for a lifetime." Ronnie again tried to dislodge blockage from his nasal cavities. "Fucks with my positive outlook something awful, not to mention my sinuses."

"By the way," Joe said, "any thoughts about what you're gonna do about Vince?"

Ronnie's face went sad again, but he simply shrugged. "Nothing to do."

"He's been completely miserable ever since you ditched him." Ronnie snuffled. "Miserable, huh?"

"Turns out the Irish have thirty different words for asshole, and Vince uses all of them whenever anyone mentions your name. It's pretty obvious he's in love with you."

Ronnie shook his head. "He's not in love with me."

"Yeah, he is. Howie says no one hates anyone like that unless they're in love with them. I think he's right. You should at least try."

"It's too late. I fucked up too bad." Ronnie's lower lip began to quiver again.

"Come here." Joe pulled Ronnie in close again and squeezed. While Ronnie's waterworks drained themselves out, Joe's mind flickered with plans of how he might get Ronnie and Vince in a room together at a time when Vince would need to be on his best behavior. "Hey," he said. "I have this dumb idea—hear me out."

33.
To Catch a Thief

"Life is like the best night of dancing—far too short. Do not waste time complaining about the music or how the drinks are not strong enough or how the pretty boy with red hair did not notice you. If you do, you'll miss your favorite song, and perhaps a more beautiful boy (with an adorable space between his front teeth), and suddenly the dance will be over without you ever dancing at all."
—*Disco Witch Manifesto #69*

Joe had just finished walking Ronnie home when he looked over at Fire Island Boulevard, and his stomach clenched. One of the new ACT UP benefit posters he and Elena had put up on the bulletin board was missing. He ran to check the nearest telephone pole. It too was barren. The same with the next three. All that remained were the poster's torn corners and bits of tape.

"Fuck!" he shouted. "Not again!" Just as he was assuming the worst, something caught his eye, far down the boulevard. It was the culprit, in the very act of tearing down another blue poster. "Hey! Stop it!" Joe sprinted down the boardwalk. "Don't touch that poster!"

When he was fifty feet away, he recognized the man. At first, he felt sadness and shock, but then a wave of fury crashed over him. "Fergal? What in the hell?" He steadily moved closer, clenching his fists. "You're the one who's been helping Scotty Black tear down the posters? How could you?"

Fergal dared to appear aghast at Joe's condemnation and mumbled a feeble "Look, stop making assumptions." His phony innocent act made Joe hate him even more. The evidence was right there in his hand, as well as in an entire bag filled with torn-down posters at his feet. *To think I had a crush on that asshole. To think I let him kiss me.* Joe lunged for Fergal, shoving him.

"What the fuck are you doing?" Fergal steadied himself.

"You knew how hard Elena and I worked to put these up again!" Joe screamed. "Don't you care about the AIDS crisis?"

"Could you pipe down?" Fergal whispered. "I didn't tear anything down."

"You fucking liar! You're holding the fucking evidence!"

"Could you just listen—"

"How could you do this to Dory?" Without thinking, Joe swung at Fergal.

Fergal quickly lifted the bag like a shield, blocking Joe's punch. "Would you just chill out?" When Joe took a second swing, Fergal dropped his bag and grabbed Joe's wrists, flipping him until he was bent over in front of him. He pressed his mouth to Joe's ear. "I said listen! I was *not* tearing down your posters. Look here—why would I have this if I was tearing shit down?" Fergal pointed to a massive roll of cellophane packing tape in his bag.

"Bullshit," Joe growled, confusion starting to overtake him. "Prove it."

Fergal grabbed his bag with one hand and Joe by the scruff of his T-shirt with the other and dragged him down the boardwalk until they reached the next utility pole. Stuck to the pole was a recently mended poster. "Open your fucking eyes," Fergal barked. "I just put that back up. I found the posters in the dumpster behind the Promethean. I spent the entire night, since one in the goddamned morning, replacing as many as I could! Look all down the boardwalk. I said look!"

Joe looked. And sure enough, the next pole had a repaired poster, and the next one farther down and the next one and the next. Each had clearly been torn down, carefully taped back together, and then wrapped on the pole with enough packing tape it would take a machete to get them down again. Fergal was telling the truth. Joe felt his face flush. "Okay. Fine," he grumbled through the fog of his humiliation and the remnants of his raging adrenaline. "Can you let go of my shirt?"

"Are you gonna promise not to swing at me again? Cause my arms are a lot longer than yours, shortstop, and I'd have no problem knocking your lights out."

"Okay," Joe said as Fergal released his T-shirt. "So, if you didn't do it, do you know who tore them down?"

"No friggin' idea," Fergal said. "One of Scotty Black's goons I guess. Maybe the Graveyard Girls or some other island wacko—I dunno. I got most of 'em back up." He walked a few paces away from Joe and started stretching and yawning while also muttering loud enough for Joe to hear. "I haven't slept *all fucking night*, and my thank-you is some fucking pint-sized muscle princess trying to lay me out—for the *second time* this summer, I might add—"

"Okay, already," Joe grumbled, so much confusion inside of him. "I'm sorry, all right? Stop acting like I actually hurt you. Jesus."

"I guess apologizing properly isn't really your style, huh? Can you at least put these last ten posters back up for me? I want to grab a water taxi and shower before I start work in an hour."

"Yeah . . . okay." Joe didn't move, immobilized by the breadth of his embarrassment and the preternatural power of Fergal's blue-blue eyes staring at him. "I guess I . . . you know . . . I misunderstood and . . . I'm sorry." He shrugged.

"Whatever. Just fix up any major damage. Then wrap the tape around the pole several times to make it harder to tear down. Here's a backup roll."

He handed him another thick cylinder of tape and started to gather his stuff. The thought of Fergal leaving on such a sour note sent a jolt of panic through Joe's heart.

"Wait a minute. You got five seconds more?"

Fergal groaned. "What do you want now?"

Joe's emotions were a mishmash as he found himself suddenly nervous, confused and overcome by the incredible generosity of Fergal's act and how he, Joe, had so terribly misjudged him—again. And underneath all that was a desperate sadness that he had missed out on something deeply important. "Seriously, that was a really decent thing to do, and . . ."

"Yeah, and?" Fergal raised his eyebrows indicating he was waiting for something more.

"Nothing," Joe said. "I just wanted to say thank you."

Fergal shook his head, snorted in disgust, and started to walk toward the harbor.

"Wait!" Joe called out.

"What the fuck do you want?" Fergal turned back and dropping his backpack to the boardwalk. "You sound like you want to say something, so fucking say it."

"Okay." Joe's voice shook with nerves. "That morning you kissed me when I was all fucked up. What's the real reason you didn't you want to, you know, go further?"

Fergal looked off toward the giant periwinkle pompoms of the hydrangea bush at the side of the walk. Joe couldn't help but notice how Fergal's ever-changing eye color was now the perfect shade to match the flowers in the early morning light.

"I don't fuck around with people so messed up they don't even know who I am," he began, his usually gruff voice knee-capped by emotion. "Not to mention, you thought I was someone named Elliot?"

"That wasn't it," Joe said, trying to control the emotion in his voice. "Elliot's my boyfriend."

"Oh great," Fergal groaned. "I get it now. Look, you swingers can do what you want. Hats off to you, but I'm not interested—"

"No!" Joe interrupted. "I mean he *was* my boyfriend. He passed away. Two years ago." He swallowed to clear his throat. "I knew who you were. Honest." Joe looked down at the bag of ripped and repaired posters.

The ferryman's eyebrows arched in a way that might have preceded a deep and long hug if they had been friends. "I'm really sorry about your partner."

"Yeah, well. Me too. It's the main reason I came out here—trying not to be so sad anymore.

"I didn't know that," Fergal said, any vestiges of his formerly sharp tone having been fully replaced with one of gentleness and true concern.

"So that's the whole reason you didn't have sex with me?" Joe's voice cracked. "Because I was messed up and called you the wrong name?"

"Yeah." Fergal looked over at a nearby doe, who appeared to be eavesdropping. "Actually no, that's not entirely true."

"Then why?" Joe asked.

Fergal sighed. "It's just summers on Fire Island can get very dramatic. I didn't want any trouble. I grew up out here, I've seen what guys go through every year. Watched them crying behind their Ray-Bans as they take the last ferry back. Hearts all busted. No thanks. Not for me."

"But it would've just been sex." Joe attempted a quick laugh, trying to approximate the cool sexiness Ronnie might muster in a moment like this.

Fergal shook his head. "No, it wouldn't. I can see it in your eyes. You're not that type. You wanna think you're just here to have a good time and fuck around. But I can see it—you'd want something more. You'd want to cuddle and all that bullshit and—"

"And what?" Joe suddenly felt even more exposed, even to himself.

"We're from different worlds," Fergal said way too earnestly.

"For real?" Joe laughed a little. "Did you steal that line from *One Life to Live* or something?"

"I'm serious." The blush was visible beneath Fergal's scruff.

"Long Island and suburban Philadelphia aren't that different."

"For one, you graduated from college. I didn't."

"So?" Joe scoffed. "Doesn't mean you're not smart."

"Also, I tend to go for older guys," Fergal countered. "You're only twenty-four, right?"

Joe looked up at the trees and then back at Fergal. His lie had even traveled the Fire Island gossip circuit. He felt smothered by a hot wet rag of embarrassment.

"Not really. I turned twenty-nine last March."

"But at least three people told me you were—"

"I lied. See, what happened was, when I first met my best friend, Ronnie, he took a guess that I was in my early twenties, and—well, I just let him believe it."

"Why?"

There it was. Joe had to decide whether to tell the truth, a half-truth, or another outright lie, or just keep quiet. But something about Fergal's expression made him not want to lie anymore. Not to Fergal. As he took a deep breath, he fingered Howie's good luck charm in his back pocket for courage. "The whole story is this: When I was *actually* twenty-four, Elliot and I fell in love. But he was sick. He had AIDS."

Fergal took a deep breath, and then gently said, "I'm really sorry."

"After he died, I wanted a redo of that part of my life."

Fergal nodded but then looked down to the ground like he was avoiding Joe's eyes. Joe had been through it a dozen times before. As soon as he told a guy that his partner had died of an AIDS-related opportunistic infection, they'd start asking themselves, *"Does that mean Joe has AIDS? Is he going around infecting other people? Is he going to die?"* He hated that they did this, but he knew he would probably do the same thing. "I'm not positive, if that's what you were wondering."

"I wasn't," Fergal responded curtly, looking Joe in the eyes again. "Why would you assume I'd think that?"

"I'm sorry. It's just . . . you know what I mean? Everyone thinks if you've been with someone positive for a long time, then you're . . ." Joe gestured to the air.

Fergal nodded again, and Joe was grateful for the lack of pity in Fergal's eyes. He would have liked to tell him everything, including the secret he had yet to tell anyone. But he couldn't; he had already exposed enough of himself for right now.

He studied Fergal's face. The shadow of his beard was even heavier than usual, and even though he looked dead tired, Joe couldn't help thinking how honestly and purely sexy he was. All of him, from his uncombed mop of hair to the scar above his lips, his hot-as-hell hairy legs and arms, down to those huge, webbed feet stuffed into Top-Siders—the ones Joe had vomited on that first night they'd kissed. Unlike all the pretty boys on the island, Fergal's good looks were misleadingly average—even a bit brutish—if you didn't look too closely. But when you took the time to really look at him, you couldn't miss the innocence and fire that made every inch of his face and body vibrate with an almost painful beauty. Sure, he was no Gladiator Man, nor was he an Elliot, handsome and academically brilliant, but the more Joe listened to Fergal's voice, looked at his adorably scruffy face, and watched the hair patch on his chest point up to his unusually large Adam's apple, the more Joe wanted to—

"So?" he blurted out.

"So what?" Fergal narrowed his eyes in a way that insisted Joe be clear.

Joe rubbed the good luck charm in his pocket again. "You wanna go out on a date with me or not?"

"You are really somethin'." Fergal shook his head, but the corner of his mouth twitched in an almost smile. "Can I be honest with you?"

"Sure." Joe's voice cracked, fearful that the honesty might hurt.

"I've actually never been on a real date with a guy—or a girl, for that matter. I mean I've fucked a lot of folks, obviously, but . . ." He looked like he was searching for something to say, but then just laughed like he was unable—or frightened?—to find the words. "What I mean is, I'm not sure it's a good idea—"

"I don't mean to cut you off," Joe said, playing with the newfound power that Ronnie had pointed out in him, "but I'm not gonna accept no for an answer. Look, I finish work early tonight. I know you didn't get any sleep, but it's gonna be a crazy week with getting ready for the benefit. My day off was even canceled." He cleared his throat. "What I'm trying to say is, we shouldn't waste time. Howie says wasting time is the worst sin in the world. And I know going on a date is way scarier than just fucking someone. I feel the same way. So, what I'm asking is—"

"Sure," Fergal interrupted, his face flushing while he attempted to maintain his gruff, matter-of-fact tone. "I guess I can get someone to cover for me after the seven PM ferry, and maybe I can catch a few naps on trips over."

"Great! I'm done with work at eight. Meet me at my house at 8:05, and I'll figure out a place we can go."

"Mmm-kay," Fergal said.

Joe didn't know what to say next, so he hemmed and hawed and bit his lower lip a few times. "I guess I'll catch you later," he finally said.

Then he walked a few tentative steps closer to Fergal, lifted himself up on his toes so their faces would be at equal height, and kissed him. Unlike the first time they'd kissed, this time was gentle. He was able to feel the softness of Fergal's lips set against the roughness of his beard. He pushed the kiss further. Fergal's mouth responded. They closed their eyes while their tongues grappled like two Turkish oil wrestlers who had fallen in love. When Joe swallowed the sweet but salty wetness of Fergal's mouth, he imagined a magnificent tsunami, the entirety of the ocean, sweeping him under.

34.

First Date

"Disco Witches should always carry snacks."
—*Disco Witch Manifesto #4*

"Careful what you're doing, lad!" Vince bristled at Joe, who had not been paying attention while filling the beer cooler. "You're feckin' mixing Bud Lites with the Heinekens!"

"Sorry, Vince," Joe said, waking from a daydream. He had been replaying his last kiss with Fergal and fantasizing about their upcoming first date—which would commence as soon as the merman hurried his fishtail to the number eight.

"I hope you're not getting your hopes up about that date." Vince slammed a vodka bottle into the well rack. "Not to be a downer, but statistically, romantic relationships on this feckin' island have the success rate equal to landing a man on Mars. And if you do, by some miracle, stay together through August, you'll for sure be signing the divorce papers before Christmas."

"I appreciate that useful and optimistic feedback, Vince," Joe said with a sarcastic smile. He knew Vince was only acting bitter because he was still heartbroken. Hopefully, Joe's plan for Vince and Ronnie to "accidentally run into each other" at the ACT UP benefit would work.

As Joe was reorganizing the beer cooler, the bar door pushed open, and in walked Fergal, wearing khaki pants and a long-sleeved blue button-down that made his eyes pop. He had also groomed his scruff and gelled his hair, looking JFK Jr. hot. Joe was speechless. Unfortunately, he was also shirtless and wearing his package-enhancing go-go shorts. Sensing the glaring contrast, he threw his bar rag over his shoulder to cover the little he could.

"Well, looky here!" Vince sang, sarcastically emphasizing his brogue. "Young Master Fergal all dressed up for his first communion! Or is it the wedding already?"

The few men at the bar all turned toward Fergal, who looked apologetically at Joe. "Did I wear the wrong thing?" he stammered.

"No," Joe said, his heart melting. "You look *choice*. Vince is just jealous because he hasn't worn a shirt since 1983 and forgot how buttons work."

Vince shook his head before petulantly polishing the rocks glasses.

"You actually had those fancy duds on the boat?" Joe asked.

"Nope," Fergal said. "I had my roommate drop them at the dock for me. I hope I didn't get here too early?"

"Nah, I was just going to leave in about ten minutes." Joe lowered his voice. "I'll need to go home first and throw on something a little more decent before we hit a restaurant. I don't wanna look like you're paying me."

"Good idea." Fergal laughed. "But I got a little surprise waiting for you over at your house."

"A surprise? For real?" Joe's heart did a little flip.

"Yep." Fergal leaned over the bar until he was touching distance from Joe.

"What is it?" Joe let the tip of his finger touch Fergal's, eliciting a smile.

"Then it wouldn't be a surprise."

Vince groaned like he had stabbed himself with broken glass. "Ah Jaysus feckin' Christ! Get the hell outta here already! The both of you! Please. Before I have to rip my ears off! Go! Now! Feck off! And use protection!"

As they walked back to 44 and ¼ Picketty Ruff, holding hands, the butterflies in Joe's stomach were dive-bombing one another as he absorbed the hugeness of what was happening—he was going on a date with someone he really, really liked for the first time since Elliot. But then he began to wonder why Fergal was being so quiet all of a sudden. Was he having second thoughts? Was he struggling to trust Joe? Joe *had* physically attacked Fergal—twice. *Stop thinking so negatively,* Joe told himself. *Do some of Ronnie's positive thinking.*

As they arrived in front of his house, Joe saw there was something different about it. For one thing, the lighting inside the windows looked dimmer than usual, like someone had unscrewed some of the lightbulbs. And instead of one of Howie's nonstop retro DJ mixtapes, he heard the strains of Cyndi Lauper's "Time After Time" being played.

"Something weird's going on," Joe said, unsure whether they should go inside.

"Um, this is your surprise," Fergal said like he was apologizing.

Joe turned to look at Fergal's face for more clues. "I don't understand."

The screen door swung open, and there were Howie and Lenny, smiling and wearing button-down shirts with clip-on bow ties, suit jackets, and aprons over their shorts, as if they were half-dressed waiters in a fancy restaurant.

"Welcome to Chateau Picketty Ruff!" Howie declared with a ridiculously thick French accent (by way of Far Rockaway, Queens).

"What is all this?" Joe said to Fergal.

Fergal cracked his knuckles and looked even more nervous. "I wanted to take you out for a really nice dinner—you know, something a little special. But I forgot I don't get paid until the end of the week. The Leviathan is nutso expensive, and I've heard the food isn't that good anyway. But I didn't want to cancel, so Howie and Lenny said they had a more affordable idea. I hope you're not disappointed." The tips of his ears had turned pink.

Joe smiled and squeezed Fergal's hand. "Not at all. This is amazing."

"Magnifique!" Howie proclaimed, deepening his accent. "C'est bon! I shall now go make Monsieur Fergal zee cocktail while Monsieur Joseph freshens up before zee din-nay?"

"What are you even saying?" Joe laughed.

Howie leaned into Joe's ear and whispered, sans accent, "Go shower up and clean all the important nooks and crannies, if you know what I mean." He winked.

"Gotcha," Joe said, feeling his cheeks grow warm. "I'll be back in about fifteen minutes."

While Howie and Lenny's did their French waiter routine with Fergal, Joe showered up and then headed to the attic to pull on his best pair of shorts and the expensive polo he had bought for Trey Winkle's awful party. The punch stain was still faintly there, but Lenny's secret laundry treatment had managed to render it almost invisible. This first date would be the perfect memory to rechristen it. Before heading back downstairs, he took a deep breath and looked in the mirror. "You're gonna be okay," he said to his reflection.

As soon as he stepped onto the back deck, he was hit with a blast of incandescence. Twinkling Christmas lights had been strung along the banisters and throughout the mulberry tree. White candles covered every surface, and a huge bouquet of white hydrangeas sat in the center of the picnic table, which was covered in a glowing white chintz tablecloth.

"Wow, Howie," Joe exclaimed. "This place looks . . ."

"Great, right?" Howie said. "I call it Chez Max. Max always makes us dine out here at least twice a week when the weather is nice."

"You know it's just a first date," Fergal said. "It's not like we're getting married."

"Yet!" Lenny yelled from the kitchen.

Fergal's face flushed again, which made Joe smile so hard his cheeks hurt.

"Now you two enjoy our evening's special cocktail." Howie handed them each a phosphorescent green beverage in a tall glass goblet with a silver stag horn stem.

"What are these?" Joe asked, sniffing like the pro mixologist he aspired to be. "A kind of mojito?"

"It's a secret." Howie winked. "Just a little fresh basil, some beach nettle, seaweed, tequila, and other thingamajigs I like to use. Old Guatemalan recipe of Max's. Trust me, you'll like it. Now, I'm making like magic ink and disappearing." Howie scuttled back through the kitchen door, leaving them alone.

Joe took a sip of the green cocktail and was instantly struck by its unusual deliciousness. He recognized some of the flavors, but there were other ingredients that were completely alien.

"Hey, this shit's incredible," Fergal said.

"It is!" Joe agreed, then laughed. "Although, knowing Howie, it's probably some sort of folk medicine aphrodisiac."

"Not really necessary," Fergal mumbled, letting his eyes linger on Joe.

Another huge wave rose and crested inside Joe's chest, swallowing his heart and swooshing it around with all sorts of sand, saltwater, and shells. It was the most overwhelming thing he had felt since he first met Elliot. It was both a joy and an agonizing fear that his soul's small vessel could not contain all his longing.

"So," Joe said, trying to make the moment normal, "have you heard any of those whacked-out rumors about the boys being Disco Witches? Freaked me out at first."

Fergal momentarily puzzled his eyebrows—most likely from Joe's sudden change of subject. "You have to take everything with a grain of salt out here. I will say, Howie, Lenny, and Max are pretty special. That's for sure. Anyone who's been out here long enough has heard some crazy stuff."

"Like what?" While Joe was curious, he was more grateful for the diversion from his desire.

"Just stupid stories. Like how when they used to go out clubbing, weird shit would happen. Really bad dance parties would suddenly become the best night of people's lives. Or they'd show up dressed in some nutso outfit and start dancing, and suddenly broken amplifiers or lighting systems would start working again—tons of crazy coincidences. Really, whenever they're around, the island always feels safer. Like someone is watching over us, protecting us. You know what I mean?"

"Yeah," Joe said. "As a matter of fact, I do. Dory and Saint D'Norman too. It's weird." He laughed. "There were times before I really knew them, I worried they might be psychotic arsonists, but even then I still got a warm feeling."

"Nothing like the warmth of a psychotic arsonist." Fergal laughed and then took Joe's hands into his. His calloused palms reminded Joe of the satin nubs of his favorite childhood blanket, which he'd rub for comfort. Between Fergal's fingers there was a slight webbing close to the palm, similar to what Joe had noticed between his toes.

"Weird, right?" Fergal said, stretching his long fingers to exaggerate the deformity.

"I kind of love it," Joe said, kissing Fergal's fingers, then the sun-bleached hairs on the back of his wrist.

Fergal pulled Joe to him and entwined his arms with his own, as if Joe were a small tree being consumed by a huge thick vine.

"How can this feel so good?" Joe said. "Just last week I hated your guts."

"That's summer on Fire Island for ya." Fergal wiggled his eyebrows. "One moment you wanna kill someone, the next you want them to have your butt-babies."

"Eww," Joe said, grimacing even though Fergal's comment made him hard again—like he had a direct mental connection to Joe's cock. Joe took another sip of the special cocktail. Again, the heady taste of the drink confounded him. He took several more sips, trying to decipher the mysterious mix of herbs and spices. Fergal drank as well. The whole time their unused forearms and hands remained entangled, unwilling to part.

"So, your name. *Fergal.* That's Irish, right?" Joe said, an attempt to regain his individuation and slow things down. "Is that your background?"

"Yep. Or half Irish anyway. My mom was Irish, but I never met my father. She said he was something like Italian or Greek."

"Did you ever try to find him?"

"Couldn't. My mom didn't know his name. I know that makes her sound kinda trashy, but she wasn't. She was working as a waitress out in Montauk, and one evening after her shift, she headed down to the beach to watch the sunset. She thought she saw a sea lion, but then realized it was a man playing in the surf. She said he was 'devastatingly handsome,' with long black hair and a beard. When he saw her, he stopped swimming and treaded water for a really long time, staring at her. Finally, he waved for her to come into the ocean with him. So, she did. After a bit they went up into the dunes and made love. When they finished, he gave her this."

Fergal pulled out the gold chain around his neck and showed Joe a small pearlescent shell decorated with tiny ornate carvings and what looked like some foreign language.

"It's really beautiful." Joe touched the shell, brushing his finger on Fergal's clavicle.

"After that, he split."

"What?" Joe said. "That was it? Just that one time? And she got pregnant with you?"

Fergal smirked. "They don't call them 'breeders' for nothing."

Joe laughed, but then his Armenian eyebrows signaled distress. "Hopefully you're not like your dad," he half mumbled, but then immediately wished he hadn't shown his hand so blatantly. "Sorry, that was a stupid thing to say."

"I'm not," Fergal said. "At least not in that way. I do like the ocean a whole lot, though. But I was raised by my Uncle Harve, who is a real gentleman. He taught me to be kind and respectful to all people, and to make sure that if someone is important to you, you show up for them. That's why I came out to him before I came out to my mother. Uncle Harve always stood by me. My mom, not so much."

"What do you mean?" Joe asked.

Fergal picked up the special green cocktail and gulped it as if it would give him the power to speak his mind. "So, Uncle Harve says something weird happened to my mother after she gave birth to me. She lost it and started disappearing for days, saying she was searching for my father. They'd find her sleeping on the beach. If it wasn't for Uncle Harve, I'm not sure what would have happened to me. I hate that I let him down sometimes."

"How?" Joe asked.

Fergal shrugged. "Nothing big. Sometimes I drink a little too much and stay out here on the beach, which probably reminds him of my mother. He worries I'll end up like her—or worse."

"You can't blame him," Joe said. "It's a pretty crazy time we're living in."

"It is," Fergal said. "That's why it's best to find a teammate to . . . you know." He blushed, letting the unfinished sentence fall into a moment of awkwardness.

"Hey, I wanted to say—" Fergal blurted.

"I wanted to ask you—" Joe overlapped.

"You go first." Fergal motioned with a wave of his hand.

"This seems really juvenile," Joe said, "but I need to know something. That first day I moved here in May, I saw you on the ferry, and you acted like a real asshole. You and the other deckhand laughed at me. And then you laughed at me again that day I saw you sitting with Cleigh in front of the liquor store. Why?"

"We weren't laughing at *you*." Fergal smiled. "I totally remember both those moments. Especially that time I first saw you. It was drizzling out and you were standing on the upper deck. I told Carl, the other deckhand, that if I was gonna go full-on homo, you'd be the kind of guy I'd want to be a full-on homo with."

Joe felt a flipping and buzzing in his chest, like his heart was doing gleeful somersaults. "For real? You told him that?"

"Yep. A similar thing happened when I was talking to Cleigh. We were talking about secret crushes we had, and then you walked up at that exact moment. It made me super nervous, because I knew Cleigh clocked that my crush was on you, and that's why I busted out laughing." Fergal looked down at Joe's hands and then back up into his eyes, and with a look of dead seriousness on his face, he said, "So, I guess this means I'm officially a full-on homo now."

Both men busted out laughing. Joe wanted to kiss Fergal so badly but wasn't sure if it was the right time. When their laughter subsided, there was another moment of awkwardness. They sipped from their green drinks, took deep breaths, looked at the fireflies playing hide-and-seek in Howie's garden. All of a sudden, Fergal leaned his tall torso across the table and gave Joe a deep kiss. Joe closed his eyes, once again astounded by the overwhelming taste and sensation of Fergal's beautiful mouth. When he opened his eyes, it seemed as if the entire back deck was aflutter with even more sparkling lights.

"Did that kiss make it brighter back here, or is it just me?" Joe asked.

"Um . . . you know, I think it did. Weird."

There was indeed more light. Before it had just been the mulberry tree and the deck that were lit up, but now the entire backyard was flooded with the little white lights, as if they were in the middle of a huge Macy's Christmas display.

"Hey!" Joe shouted toward the kitchen window. "Are you guys watching us?"

"Sorry!" Howie shouted from inside. "That's our last surprise before we serve dinner! We'll leave you two alone. I swear to the Great Goddess Mother!"

Joe shook his head and shrugged.

"Those guys are cheesier than a gay Hickory Farms," Fergal said.

"Yep, and I'm gonna have a talk with them about it later." Joe leaned over the table again. "But right now, I need you to kiss me again—"

Just as they were about to kiss, the stereo switched to Roberta Flack singing "Killing Me Softly With His Song" as Howie and Lenny emerged through the back door with the feast Lenny had prepared. He proceeded to explain each dish, emphasizing all their romance-enhancing ingredients, including a virility-boosting acorn-and-germanium-stuffed ravioli, with sides of rosemary potatoes, and broccoli rabe with feverfew flowers. Howie sprinkled rose petals on the table and poured them each a glass of red wine.

"I could definitely go for more of that green cocktail," Joe said.

"Me too," Fergal added. "That stuff was great."

"Unfortunately, that's all we had," Howie said apologetically. "You've had the appropriate amount, anyway. Don't wanna go crazy. Now, gentlemen, Lenny and I will be in the living room not paying any attention to what goes on out here—seriously this time. When you're finished, you can leave the dishes, okay?"

"By the way," Lenny added, "I left some lube and condoms out on the bottom rung of the attic ladder. Be safe!"

"Guys . . ." Joe squeezed his eyes closed, begging. "Come on!"

Howie and Lenny scooted through the back door, and Joe and Fergal were finally and completely alone. They devoured Lenny's feast, drank Howie's wine, and spent a lot of time laughing about all the ridiculousness that was Fire Island. Neither of them loved the whole party scene, and Joe shared his utter embarrassment at having to be shirtless and wear go-go shorts every day. But both agreed their summer gigs were better than waiting tables.

"So, you'll be here next summer?" Joe asked.

"Nope," Fergal said. "This is definitely my last summer on the boat. The ferry business is nice, but I got other plans. I've had this dream of moving out to Hawaii."

"Hawaii?" Joe said, surprised. "That's really, well, far."

"I know. But I can't live on Long Island forever. I met this guy a few summers ago. His name is Buck. He was the first guy I ever fooled around with."

"You mean you guys are . . ." Disappointment filled Joe's face.

"Oh, nothing like that," Fergal added quickly. "We just did it once. He's got a boyfriend, and is ancient—like forty or something—but still looks pretty sharp. Also, he's got platinum-blond hair and is my height, which is obviously not my thing. I've always had a thing for swarthy, shorty types like you. The sort you can cuddle and toss around like a teddy bear."

The mental image of being someone Fergal wanted to cuddle and toss around made Joe instantly have to camouflage his lap with a napkin. He loved knowing that merely by his Armenian genetics he was someone Fergal craved.

"Anyway," Fergal said, adjusting his own crotch, "this Buck guy is a waterdog, like me, and says I'd love it out in Honolulu. I can spend all day just staring at the ocean, like it's some big friendly blue-green monster."

"You ever get scared if the waves get too big?"

"Never," Fergal said, an intent, serious look on his face. "Duck diving under or riding a massive bomb is the only thing that makes me really feel like myself—like I'm free. You know when you're in the water and you see the entire ocean heave up like it's breathing? One second it's flat, and the next thing you know, you're facing a fuckin' mountain? It starts going higher, higher, higher, until it crests like it's reaching up for the sky, then it tips over and breaks, sending me rag-dolling in a big old sudsy washing machine."

Fergal laughed heartily at what he had just said, as if it was just the funniest story in the world. Joe laughed too, mostly because he wanted Fergal to keep talking. He loved Fergal's Long Island twang and never imagined he had all this beautiful weirdness in him. Being with him felt like some magic miraculous gift—the antidote to all the darkness.

"So anyway," Fergal continued, "Buck taught me how to surf on these rinky-dink waves out here, and I caught on just like that. He said that if I wanted to ride the real monsters, I had to check out this place called Waimea Bay in Hawaii. He said in the winter the swell can get as big as a building."

"For real?" Joe asked.

"Yep. Sometimes the waves are so massive you can't even get *close* to the water, or they'll yank you in, and bam! You're dead— just like that." Fergal snapped his fingers. "I gotta see that!"

Joe's eyes widened. He didn't like the dying part, but he'd be up to watching a wave the size of a mountain.

"When do you think you'll go?" he asked, hoping it wasn't anytime soon.

"Dunno yet. I'm close to saving enough money. Maybe I'll get my BA in marine biology from the University of Hawaii. You need a year of state residency, and then you can go for cheap. Can you imagine getting to surf and swim every day, all year long?"

Joe imagined what it might be like to watch Fergal swim in these theoretical giant waves, just like he'd seen him that first morning on the Fire Island beach. His lithe body, laughing and diving into the water like some handsome-as-hell dolphin. Joe wished he could give Fergal that kind of joy. He wished he could be Fergal's wave.

After that, they focused on finishing their meal, with small flirty looks at each other between mouthfuls. Their free hands playing with the other's, feeling the veins, the hairs on their wrists, the knobs of their knuckles. Neither wanting to interrupt the touching. But then Fergal looked at his watch.

"If I don't catch that last ferry, I'm gonna be stuck."

"You can stay with me, of course," Joe said casually, but then looked into Fergal's eyes. "I mean, I want you to stay with me. I really want you to."

Fergal looked down at his empty plate and then at Joe's hand, which he returned to holding. For a split-second Joe noticed that there was a brief look of sadness in Fergal's eyes.

"Okay, I'll stay," Fergal said. "But I don't want to have sex yet. Is that okay?"

Joe almost groaned in exaggerated fake agony. "You know what's going to happen, right? Neither of us will be able to sleep 'cause we'll be hard all night. I can't promise I won't try something."

Fergal smiled. "I got will power for both of us. But I'm serious. I want to know you better, and I want you to know me better. I'm not the kind that disappears like my father, but I also don't want to end up like my mother either."

"I don't think I'll get you pregnant, but you never know. Howie does keep saying this island is magical . . ."

"Very funny. But you got to promise—no trying anything or I'm swimming back to Sayville, and I've done it before, so don't think I can't. Okay?"

"Okay." Joe sensed that once they were in his attic bed, things would change.

But things didn't change, and while each man kept his underwear on, they couldn't help but kiss and snuggle. After three hours their mutual erections became painfully annoying.

"I'm gonna go sleep on the beach until the ferry gets here," Fergal finally said after another round of blue ball–inducing kissing. "Both of us have work tomorrow—I mean today. And I'm a little worried that if my dick doesn't go down, it might bust open."

"Just sleep downstairs on the couch, then," Joe begged, although his stomach sickened at the thought of Fergal leaving his bed.

"Nah. Twenty feet away from you isn't far enough to make my dick go to sleep. I'll call you tomorrow."

Joe grabbed Fergal and kissed him again. This led to another ten minutes of making out and groping through their clothes until both men were knotted-up in passionate agony. Fergal finally dragged himself down the ladder and out the door.

After hearing the gate slam, Joe listened through the attic vent for Fergal's departing footsteps, reminding him that what had happened hadn't been a dream. After Elliot, he'd thought any future love would feel inferior, like a slightly deflated balloon. But what Joe felt for Fergal wasn't second-rate at all. He closed his eyes and imagined Fergal lying naked on top of him. The heat of his breath. The smell of his body. Joe would run his fingers through the small patch of hair at the top of his chest, and Fergal would lift Joe's legs, pressing himself slowly inside. "Is that okay?" Fergal would ask. "Keep going!" Joe would beg. Fergal would press further inside and start to work his hips. Joe began to stroke himself, thinking of that pleasurable pain, thinking of Fergal's hairy thighs meeting his own, Fergal's balls hitting just below Joe's hole. Then, just as he was about to cum, Joe imagined looking up into Fergal's blue-blue eyes and saying "I think I'm in love with you."

But suddenly the person he saw in his mind's eye wasn't Fergal at all. It was the Gladiator Man atop him, his hand around Joe's throat, his massive cock thrusting painfully into Joe's ass, ejaculating fire into Joe's guts. Joe attempted to force his mind from the brutal fantasy back to Fergal, but it was too late. His cum shot across his chest, and in his mind he watched the Gladiator Man laugh.

35.

In the Bushes

"Sex is one of the holiest of all the divine ceremonies, second only to dancing."
—*Disco Witch Manifesto #16*

That morning Lenny got a call from Max's partner, Heshy. In addition to the lesions they'd found on Max's brain, he had contracted PCP pneumonia again. His health had declined to the point where they had to accept the fact that he wasn't going to make it out to the Pines that summer—or possibly ever again.

When Lenny told Howie, it sent him into one of his it's-the-end-of-the-world moods. It wasn't that Lenny wasn't distraught. He was. He loved Max as much as Howie—as much as anyone. But Lenny simply no longer trusted that maintaining the quorum would do much good anyway. He was still questioning whether their magic really had the power Max said it had. Sure, back in the day, when they were at full force, several unexplainably profound events occurred in the face of their twirling dance ceremonies. But had they really caused all of Manhattan to black out in '77? Did they really create and send transformative dreams to heal the psyches of the brokenhearted? Did they really protect "chosen ones" from succumbing to the Great Darkness? If the holy magic truly existed, would they have lost so many of their fellowship to AIDS? Would the remedial aphrodisiac 101 recipe Lenny himself had prepared for Joe and Fergal's date night have resulted in Fergal leaving Joe in bed alone? Would Lenny have lost Lucho, and would Max be days away from . . .

Pah! Lenny thought. *It's all a bunch of bushwa.*

All the confusion and bad news made Lenny's insides bunch up like a wad of overcooked emotional gnocchi. Since booze and cocaine were no longer tools for him to escape, he tended to fall back on the only spiritual salve left to him—sex.

Between the ages of eighteen and twenty-three, Lenny had been at his sexual peak. He had been adorable, with tanned smooth muscle, a head of hair like a shoe brush, and that alluring Dead End Kid edge. Manhattan's Midwest transplants ate him up. Wall Street closet cases would invite him to their suites at the Waldorf to act out *On the Waterfront* fantasies. They called him Chicken Parmigiana Lenny (a nickname he'd invented for himself).

Alas, on his twenty-fourth birthday those vengeful sisters, Gravity and Time, began their cruel makeover. His twenty-eight-inch waist widened into a giant wheel of Pecorino-Reggiano. His face grew puffy. And then his hair began to fall out—his worst nightmare. He tried endless diets, useless fitness machines, terrible hair loss interventions, and every skin-care product sold with the word *rejuvenation* on the label. Nothing worked—not even joining a coven of Disco Witches. With each fallen follicle "Chicken Parmigiana Lenny" was turning into "Leftover-Lasagna Lenny." He felt destined to become one of those creepy old perverts whose hands were always getting slapped away at sex parties.

However, Lenny's real problem was not getting older. As he'd once read in the Disco Witch Manifesto, their coven's illustrated bible of wisdom and snappy aphorisms: *"Desire among the holy lovers does not follow a simple downward trajectory from young to old, from fit to floppy. The same is true for a disco witch. Aging, of course, will alter the topography of love. To remain on the playground of Eros means knowing one's niche. Shift your strategy! YOU, exactly as you are at this moment, are desired!"* Disco Witch Manifesto #221

Lenny hadn't fully comprehended this particular nugget of disco witch wisdom until much later in life, when he had hit the bottom that is necessary for all great change. At the age of forty-nine, after years of increasingly numbing his self-hatred with various non-magically-approved substances, Lenny experienced a coke-induced heart attack that left him on the brink of death. Thanks to a spiritual intervention by Howie, Dory, Max, and Saint D'Norman, Lenny got sober and embarked on a new adventure of self-discovery as a proud, older, gay man. He made friends with his Pecorino-Reggiano belly, allowed his eyebrows to grow out, ditched his toupee, got into BDSM, and grew a mustache the color of the darkest night. While he still was rejected by many, an equal number of new play pals began knocking at the door of 44 and ¼ Picketty Ruff. Sexy men, young and old, craving an afternoon with the newly christened Leather Daddy Lenny.

From the moment he embraced his aging body, he saw sex, and the pursuit thereof, as pure cleansing joy—physically, intellectually, magically, and most important spiritually. Great sex soothed Lenny's soul. "Sex," the Disco Witch Manifesto proclaimed, *"is one of the holiest of all the divine ceremonies, second only to dancing."*

And that's why Lenny, feeling all arrabbiato y depresso, decided to head into the Meat Rack that July afternoon to get a booster shot of sexual healing. He didn't necessarily intend to have sex himself. (He was, after all, saving up for a rigorous sex date later that weekend with a very motivated power bottom named Calixto.) He was merely going to observe others having sex and make notes—something that also helped to clear his head and relax him. He had long kept detailed field notes of gay male mating practices in bathhouses, public toilets, and extemporaneous outdoor cruising venues. Lenny was, some said, the Margaret Meade of gay cruising.

Unfortunately, that afternoon there was very little going on among the trees and bushes in terms of actual sex. Mostly just a bunch of schlubs stumbling around the bushes with their peckers in their hands, hoping for someone else to make the first move. So much for Lenny's sexual healing. Since it appeared nothing noteworthy was going to transpire, he decided he probably should head back to work. Dying friends or not, toilets had to be scrubbed. On his way back to the path, he noticed a handful of homo hunters had become activated—someone new and/or hot must have entered the activity zone. Tracking their eyes and peckers, Lenny was able to locate the cause: Ronnie Kaminski, Joe's muscle-bound friend.

Lenny observed for a moment. Ronnie didn't appear to be looking for sex; rather, he was spreading out a blanket to sun himself on the dunes naked—a frequent habit of ultra-hot men to enjoy soaking in the sun's rays while also soaking in the validation that came with fifty lust-filled eyeballs. It was no surprise he'd grab a lot of attention, disrupting the natural migration patterns of the Meat Rack—although, Lenny mused, Ronnie's presence shouldn't be causing the level of emotional disturbance Lenny was witnessing in the energy of the forest and its inhabitants. Yes, some of the men were staring at Ronnie, but others looked agitated, wandering about erratically. Even more curious, every single man was featuring a boner harder than Manhattan schist, all pointing to the East. Even his own east-facing willy had become oddly turgid despite not feeling attracted to anything he could see. If he hadn't been so skeptical, this herd of hyper hard-ons would suggest an otherworldly catalyst was disturbing the sexual ecosystem.

Then Lenny felt something he hadn't experienced in years—something he'd thought had vanished with the power of his coven and his own belief in magic. His head began to spin, his eyes grew momentarily cloudy, and then his eyesight grew blisteringly sharp—so sharp he could see all the way to the eastern entrance to the Rack. There, pushing through the bushes, was a huge man, the height of a bull, with a beard and wearing a leather harness. No one else would have been able to see him at this distance, but Lenny did.

Despite his wavering beliefs, Lenny felt a surge of terror creep into his loins. His ears filled with banshee screams. His nostrils smelled the putrid scent of burning flesh. His mind's eye witnessed the countless beautiful young men throughout the centuries, wearing expressions of sacrificial agony at the final moments of their lives, pleading for help. The last of these young men was poor, poor Lucho. *Lenny,* the vision cried, *it's happening again! Do something!*

And suddenly Lenny knew with absolute certainty: this bull-sized god entering the Meat Rack was indeed the egregore sent by the Great Darkness on the hunt for the chosen one. But who? It couldn't be Ronnie, who was far too old. And Joe had failed the rubric.

Lenny needed to get out of the Rack as quickly as possible and let the others know that Howie's gut had not been lying to him after all.

36.
The ACT UP Benefit

"The disco witch does not sit idly by while her brothers and sisters suffer. Via spells, ceremonial dances, or direct action, the disco witch raises hell by any means necessary until the Great Balance is restored and all the holy lovers and their fellow Disco Witches are free."
—*Disco Witch Manifesto #65*

The Asylum Harbor ACT UP benefit was a raging success. A fire code–violating number of revelers, dressed in resort wear, stuffed themselves with donated bacon-wrapped shrimp, crab cakes, and drinks from the open bar. Chrissy Bluebird was there, and so were Frankie Fabulous, lots of hottie circuit boys, porn stars, and prophets, not to mention several of the Pines more notable celebrities (the Davids, the Calvins, the Barrys, the Tommys). No sign of the Gladiator Man, which was fine as far as Joe was concerned. Volunteering at the benefit was the first time he felt like he was truly doing something to fight the disease that had taken his Elliot away. How different their relationship might have been if he'd had something like ACT UP into which he could have channeled all his fear and rage. If only he had . . .

Stop! Don't think about it. Don't think about it.

"Hey, pretty great turnout, huh?" Elena said, stepping up to the bar with a big smile on her face and Cleigh's hand on her shoulder. Her year of refraining from "actual dating" was looking more and more in doubt.

"Yeah," Joe said, pulling himself out of his head. "Dory and Howie really can put on a show."

"They sure can," Elena said. "Anyway, we just wanted to say keep up the good work. Cleigh and I are off to schmooze a couple of rich lesbians."

"I'm sure we'll be able to get them to pony up a little more cashola for the cause," Cleigh added with her tough-girl twang. "I just need to gush about their handicaps in the last Dinah Shore Classic while Elena here flashes that sweet smile of hers."

Elena rolled her eyes, but Joe could tell she enjoyed Cleigh's flirting. Just as they were leaving, Fergal pulled up to the bar and casually grasped Joe's forearm affectionately before shyly pulling away. His smell, his touch, his voice made Joe's skin vibrate. Fergal had taken the day off from the ferry to volunteer as "sexy busboy," causing several ferry passengers to fork over the suggested donation just to get a glimpse of him wearing uncharacteristically short cut-off jeans and a tight-fitting ACT UP tank top.

"I don't recognize half these people," Joe said.

"A bunch are ACT UP members from the city." Fergal gestured to a small group in their twenties and thirties—mostly men, but some women, all dressed in the classic East Village boy outfit of white T-shirts, cutoffs, and black Doc Martens. "They came over this morning with that older guy Larry. He's one of the founders of ACT UP. Yells like a nut job when he's riled up but is a total sweetheart in private. He gets shit done."

Joe studied the activists' faces and bodies. Most looked healthy. Some of the men were extremely handsome, looking like those brooding male models in *Interview Magazine*. But a few had the familiar physical markers of the sickness—the hollowed eyes, the powdery lips, Band-Aids covering what might be skin cancers. If these particular ACT UP members were sick, they didn't seem self-conscious about it. Elliot had always been terrified of anyone knowing.

"How many do you think have HIV?" Joe whispered, his eyes locked on the group.

"Who knows." Fergal shrugged. "Dory and Howie don't have it, and they're ACT UP members. Besides, you can't know for sure. You have to protect yourself like everyone has it."

"You're right," Joe said. "That was a dick thing for me to ask. It just seems extra brave to be out there fighting when you don't know how long you have left."

"Yeah," Fergal said. "But maybe that's what keeps them going?"

"Maybe." Joe wondered if it was time to tell Fergal the whole truth about Elliot. But what if it frightened him away? He couldn't bear the thought of that.

"You okay?" Fergal asked. "You looked funky all of a sudden."

Before Joe could respond, three men, including the Broadway composer Jerry Herman, approached the bar. "We'd like three vodka cranberries, please, handsome," Jerry said, clapping his hands. "Oh, Joe, what a wonderful event you've all made!"

"Thanks, Jerry. Drinks coming right up." While Joe set up the highball glasses, he turned to Fergal. "Hey, babe, wanna go snag us some of those pigs in a blanket before they run out?"

"Babe?" Fergal repeated. Before Joe knew what was happening, Fergal had leaned over the bar and planted a quick but romantic kiss on Joe's lips. The entire bar stopped to watch. When the kiss ended, the buzzing reignited—only now it was about the sexy young couple. For once Joe didn't mind the gossip. He and Fergal were officially an item. Let them talk!

"Well done, Joe," Jerry Herman whispered, handing him a fifty-dollar bill. "This is for your great work on this benefit and for"—he winked—"finally getting laid, especially with sailor boy over there. You know, the whole island's been worried about you."

"Thanks." Joe tried hard not to let his face expose the truth, that he had yet to "get laid" by Fergal or anyone. "But today, Jerry, all my tips go to ACT UP."

Joe put the fifty into the donation beer pitcher. Soon, other men began offering more donations to ACT UP in honor of Joe losing his Fire Island cherry to the deckhand of their dreams. His ears reddened with guilt, which the men took as a sign of his charming shyness.

"Sorry about what just happened," Joe said to Vince, who looked annoyed. "I know that was against bar policy."

"Ach, who gives a flying feck," he said darkly. "This bar is probably doomed anyway. So I gather things are pure class with your fella, eh?"

"Yeah. I guess so. I mean . . ." He lowered his voice. "Here's the thing—and don't judge—but we still haven't . . . you know."

"Oh Jay-sus, Mary, and Joseph!" Vince shouted. "You're feckin' kiddin' me!"

"Shh!" Joe hushed him, horrified. "Vince, seriously?"

"Sorry," Vince whispered. "So not even knocking your knobs together?"

"I mean, we've gotten pretty hot and heavy. Like, we've stuck our hands down each other's pants and taken our shirts off. And kissed. Oh my god, he's the best kisser. I get chills every time. It's just when it looks like we're ready to finally go for it, he's suddenly says he's tired or that he has something to do that won't wait. I wondered if he thought we might not be, you know, compatible, so I hinted that I can do the whole versatile thing, but he just kinda laughed and said he wants to wait, because doing the 'big one'—he calls it the big one, which is cute as hell—makes a relationship more 'real' for him."

Vince groaned. "Real? What in Mary Magdalene's name does that even feckin' mean?"

"I guess he's just not ready. He likes me obviously—I mean that kiss and all?"

"I hate to say it . . ." Vince sighed nihilistically. "It's the homosexual rule of threes. If no sex by date three, you're sunk. And if you do end up having sex on date four, it will be so awkward you'll both lose your hard-ons. If I was you, I'd cut bait and run."

"But you're *not* me." Joe angrily shoved the metal scoop back into the ice. "Fergal is just different from other guys. Even Howie says so."

Vince shook his head bitterly and sniggered. "As if our man Howie even remembers a flea's turd about dating."

"Howie knows a helluva lot more than you do."

"Well, scarlet for your mother for havin' ya!"

"Vince, I literally have no idea what that means." A wave of men came up to the bar, sending both men scrambling to fill orders. When Joe finished his last vodka cran, he turned and noticed Vince, icy eyes toward the door, as if Charles Manson had just walked in.

"Look what the sewer rat dragged in," Vince whispered.

Joe looked over. It was none other than Trey Winkle along with two friends—WASPy Xerox copies of himself. All three were dressed in assorted pastel shades of polo-shirted pretension, smugly passing their eyes over the crowd.

"I don't think I've hated someone this much since junior high school," Joe said.

"Join the club." Vince sneered as he ripped open a Budweiser. "But ACT UP needs their money, so let's keep it pleasant. But go extra light on the pour."

Joe nodded, happy to cheat the man who had treated his best friend so terribly. But then, as those dramatic Fire Island fates would have it, Ronnie Kaminski—having taken Joe's suggestion to "run into" Vince at the benefit—walked into the bar dressed in his best Ocean Pacific board shorts and Phillies tank top. Oblivious to Trey, he tossed Vince a nervous smile.

"What fresh hell is this?" Vince coldly muttered. "Get him out of here."

Joe realized he had completely miscalculated Vince's reaction. "Wow," Joe said. "Lots of surprises today—"

"You set this up, didn't ya? Ya little bucket of snot." Vince threw his dirty bar rag into the sink, then stormed over to the far end of the bar.

Joe, seeing the hope drain from Ronnie's face, waved his friend over to the bar. "I think I made a mistake," he said. "I'm really sorry. Maybe you should come back another time."

"So he still hates me, huh?" Ronnie said. "I knew it."

"He doesn't hate you." Joe handed him a shot of tequila. "He just can't figure out how to stop feeling brokenhearted, I guess."

"Why does this summer suck so much?" Ronnie knocked back the drink as if his tonsils were on fire.

"Speaking of sucking." Joe made sure his lips were unreadable from across the room. "Your asshole ex is here too."

He pointed the soda gun toward where Trey Winkle and his friends had set up their judgment station. Having caught Ronnie looking at him, Trey smiled snarkily, then whispered something to his friends that ignited a round of sniggering.

"Fuck me!" Ronnie groaned. "First I get rejected by the man I love, and then that stuck-up jack-off laughs at me?"

"Ignore him," Joe said, mixing a tequila sunrise with one hand and knocking the heads off two draft beers with the other. "You probably should leave anyway. You don't want Scotty Black to find you here."

"That's true. I don't need to get fired on top of everything else."

"Do me one favor before you go," Joe whispered. "Maybe it's too soon for Vince, but on your way out just say a quick hello. I think maybe if he hears your voice—"

"Are you crazy? He hasn't even looked over since I walked in."

"I know. But what can it hurt? Just say one of your affirmation things first."

"That shit isn't working anymore. I keep chanting over and over, 'Vince is still in love with me. Vince is still in love with me.' But my subconscious keeps saying, a lot louder, *You blew it, douchebag. He hates you.*" He choked back tears. "Fuck this. I'm out of here."

As soon as Ronnie turned to make his escape, Trey Winkle and his friends walked directly over, blocking his exit.

"Look who's here," Trey said, turning to his clones. "Gentlemen, you remember Ron here? He used to hang out at my place?" He gestured to Joe. "This charming young bartender is his best friend, Joseph—you're part Iranian or something, right?"

"Armenian," Joe said flatly. "You ordering something or what? The bar is pretty busy."

"Of course," Trey said. "Three vodka martinis, if you would. Extra dirty. A bar like this wouldn't have Grey Goose, would it? Or is your top shelf just not *top* enough?"

Trey's pun caused his friends to snort.

"Yeah, we have Grey Goose." Joe's annoyance grew. "But with today's open bar your choices are Absolut, Absolut, or, um, Absolut. Of course you might find something you like on our *bottom* shelf, which happens to be Popov. You know Popov, right? It sorta rhymes with *jerk off*, which I'm sure you hear all the time." Ronnie's eyes warned Joe to cool it. "Anyway," Joe said, lightening up, "Grey Goose would be full price."

"That's fine." Trey tossed a hundred-dollar bill on the bar like it was a napkin.

Joe briefly considered blasting Trey with a stream of Coke from the soda gun, but then saw that Ronnie was on the brink of tears. Joe knew Trey would probably love to see Ronnie cry. He'd get to brag to his hideous friends how the muscle-head hotel porter was wandering the island bawling his eyes out over having been dumped by him.

"Hey, Ronnie," Joe said loudly, "you have to get back to work, right?"

"Yeah, yeah, I probably should." Ronnie's sad eyes were barely able to look up.

"Don't let us keep you," Trey said, still blocking Ronnie's way. "Those toilets won't clean themselves."

"Trey Winkle and the hot, sad hotel maid," one of his friends mumbled to the other with a smirk. "Very E. M. Forster. Well done!"

"Rough trade is delicious," the other friend slurred salaciously. "Then again, from what I've heard, Ron's moonlighting does make him a little more *Fanny Hill* than *Maurice*."

Ronnie didn't get the literary reference, but Joe did, having heard Howie mention the erotic novel about an eighteenth-century English prostitute. While Trey and his friends laughed, Ronnie tried to feebly join in, thinking he was saving face, which made the whole thing worse. That did it for Joe. He pulled down the Grey Goose and set it on the sink, out of view. He filled the tumbler instead with the cheap Popov, some vermouth, and then squeezed his dirty bar rag into the mixture. He shook the tumbler with a flourish and poured its contents into conical glasses.

"Here's your drinks, gentlemen," Joe said, adding the olives. "Extra dirty."

Then he handed Trey back only twenty dollars change from his hundred-dollar bill.

"Um," Trey said, looking at the twenty. "This is my change? For three drinks?"

"Ah." Joe quickly swiped the twenty back out of Trey's hand. "That's so nice of you to donate the rest to ACT UP," he shouted loudly. "Now, if you wouldn't mind giving me some space. I do have other customers. So, ya know, make like your love life and beat it."

Trey and his friends all looked as if a human-sized, brown-eyed Armenian pigeon had just shit on their heads.

"I'd watch yourself," Trey said through a gritted smile. "I have no problem speaking to the management of this shitty little bar. I'm a homeowner in this community, and my partner sits on the Pines Homeowners Association Board."

"Just forget about it, Trey," Ronnie interrupted, his voice thick with emotion. "Don't be a dick."

"A dick?" Trey snarled, his drunken eyes turning to rage, his voice rising to almost a shout. "That's rich coming from you! They aren't making hustlers as grateful as they used to ... or as honest! Do we want to talk about that bag of party supplies you stole from me?"

Ronnie's face turned the color of grenadine. Joe sensed that whatever Trey was saying was probably true. Still, he wanted to shove the lemon knife into his throat.

"That does it," Joe snapped. "Get out!"

"We'll go when we want, Falafel Crotch!" Trey snapped. "We paid a lot of money to be at this silly event. I'm sure Mr. Kaminski here got comped. Unless, of course, one of his hotel tricks paid his entrance fee in return for special service. Any deep cleaning duties lately, Ron?"

Before Joe could respond, a stainless-steel cocktail shaker full of white liquor and ice came rocketing across the bar, crashing on the countertop, and violently splashing its contents all over Trey and his friends. A second later, Vince reached across the counter with his flexed tattooed arm, grabbed Trey by the upturned collar of his lime-green Izod shirt, and held his face within an inch of his own.

"Look here, ya feckin' chiseler!" he yelled loud enough for everyone in the bar to hear. "I think you should be careful talking shite about anyone on this island, considering most of us know how you got that house and your money. And you better make the best of it because rumor is your meal ticket is planning to ditch your saggy arse. Now, leave this establishment before I test out my new Doc Martens on those pretty capped teeth of yours. Get me?"

"Let go of me," Trey hissed. "You have no right—"

"The hell I don't!" Vince shoved the man so hard he fell back into the crowd.

"Just wait until I talk to the owner of this bar!" Trey yelled as he stood back up.

"I'm the owner!" The crowd parted as Dory stepped calmly up to Trey, a hint of a smile on her face. "Vince here is the manager. Whatever he says goes. Joe, hand 'em a takeaway cup for their drinks." Joe did as she asked. "Now," she said, sharpening her sweet, shining black eyes into deadly daggers. "Like the man said, get the fuck out of *our* bar."

Trey Winkle and company, red-faced and fuming, shoved their way out of the bar and down the steps.

"Sorry about that, Dory," Vince said, finally cooling off.

"No apology necessary, honey. Those turncoat Reagan Republicans have always been trash. I've been fighting his racist partner on the homeowner's association board for years. Now, Joe, turn up the music, and let's keep this party going."

Joe stooped to adjust the stereo volume, and when he stood up, Vince and Ronnie were whispering to each other. He couldn't hear what they were saying, but fifteen minutes later, after arranging with Fergal to cover for him, Vince walked Ronnie out the back door with his arm around him like he might never let him go.

37.

The Truth

"In the time of the Great Darkness, we search for the truth. Upon finding it, we rejoice . . . except when we don't."
—Disco Witch Manifesto #17

Joe lay on his bed and stared at the moon through the slats of the attic vent. His body vibrated with the day's lingering excitement—Ronnie and Vince getting back together, the ACT UP benefit bringing in triple what they'd hoped, and Trey Winkle receiving the comeuppance he deserved. It was like Christmas, and every box under the tree was for him. The absolute best present, of course, was when Fergal kissed Joe in front of the entire bar, *claiming him* as his boyfriend. It was perfect.

Joe listened as the downstairs shower whooshed. He imagined Fergal's wet body, water dripping off his eyelashes, his lips, down his hairy legs. Joe's cock pushed against the cotton of his Fruit of the Looms. Fergal had kept him company the whole evening until he finished his shift. By eleven fifteen, Fergal had been so tipsy on Joe's strong cocktail inventions that he'd missed the last ferry. And this time it was Fergal who suggested spending the night together—with no warnings about hard-ons keeping them awake. And despite Vince's arbitrary superstition about fourth dates, their longing for each other appeared undiminished.

The sound of the shower stopped. Joe grabbed the phallic-shaped bottle of Pierre Cardin cologne and aimed it at his throat, then stopped. Getting a mouthful of perfume is never sexy. Was there a spot on his body he didn't want Fergal to kiss? No, no there was not. Joe returned the bottle to its spot, unused.

He considered how he should appear when Fergal first saw him lying there. Should he aim his ass toward the ladder, pretending to be asleep? *Way too obvious.* Should he pretend to read a book? No. That didn't feel right. Maybe he could say something nonchalant, like, *"What is it, Fergal? Sex, you say? Oops. I almost forgot."* That made Joe laugh. Finally, he lay on his back, arms behind his head, gently flexing his biceps. He sniffed his Irish Spring–scrubbed armpit, and then double-checked all private parts front and back. Spic and Span! He had never been more ready.

"Coming up!" Fergal hollered. "Need water or anything?"

"I'm good!" Joe called back and then stretched out his whole body, letting his toes and fingers release some of the tingly energy. He rearranged his chubby to be less conspicuous and reassumed his sexy (but not too sexy) pose. Seconds later, Fergal emerged from the floor hatch, shirtless and still damp. He wore a ridiculous pair of plaid boxers—the sort someone's dad might wear. Joe's eyes moved from Fergal's face to the sweet small patch of hair at the top of his chest, then down to his belly button and the perfect treasure trail that cascaded into his underwear, where something beneath was growing and begging to be set free.

"Wow," Fergal said, staring down at him. "You look . . . um . . . Wow."

Joe smiled. "You already saw me mostly naked that night I got messed up, remember?"

"That was different. You're not covered with vomit and snot now, which is a slight improvement."

"Hey, ferryman." Joe winked. "Get in my bed."

Fergal did a funny little leap and landed right next to Joe. Their limbs became like two jumper cables touching—the spark of the muscle and flesh, the electricity of their hairy arms and legs. Joe inhaled Fergal's soapy and musky smell. Both, still lightly inebriated, stared brazenly at each other.

"Crazy day, right?" Joe said. He needed to calm himself before he prematurely exploded. "This afternoon it hit me who you remind me of. You know that actor from that old TV show *Lost in Space*?"

"Who?"

"That guy who played Don—the co-astronaut? You know the hot, angry one? Judy's boyfriend? You look a little like him, but taller and less angry."

"You're the first person to tell me that." Fergal smiled and let his furry leg flop across Joe's.

"What was I saying?" Joe mentally swooned under the weight and warmth of Fergal's leg. "Oh right, well I used to jack off to the angry astronaut guy. That is, if I couldn't find the underwear section of the JC Penny catalog."

"Ha!" Fergal blurted. "I used to wank off to the *Batman* TV show."

"Batman or Robin?"

"*Robin* of course! He had that hot little body shoved into those cute green shorts. But there was this other TV character you remind me of that I used to be nuts about." Fergal started to laugh.

"Tell me," Joe playfully demanded, laughing too. "Come on, I told you my secret TV crush. You have to tell me! And please don't say Magilla Gorilla!"

"Nah, but it *was* a cartoon!" He snort-laughed. "You ever watch Yogi Bear?"

Joe scowled. "I remind you of Yogi Bear?"

"That's dumb!" Fergal said, faux insulted. "You don't remind me of Yogi at all." He wiggled his eyebrows and smiled. "You remind me of Boo-Boo Bear."

"*What?*"

"You know, Yogi's little buddy, Boo-Boo. I wanted him to be my boyfriend so bad."

"Oh, c'mon!" Joe protested. "I'm way more proportional than Boo-Boo!"

Joe playfully punched Fergal in his upper pec muscle, which led to them wrestling around. Fergal finally flipped Joe on his back, grabbed his wrists, and laid his entire body atop of Joe's, immobilizing him.

"Get off me!" Joe struggled, laughing, though he really wished Fergal would keep him pressed to the bed forever. After about fifteen seconds, Fergal rolled off, leaving a foot between them. He covered the crotch of his boxers with a pillow while Joe used the sheet to hide his own arousal.

"You know," he said. "Vince says that if gay guys don't have sex by the third date, they'll probably end up as just friends."

"He says that, huh?" Fergal's face was flushed and sweaty. His aquiline nose pointed toward the ceiling as his blue-blue eyes appeared to be staring at something above the bed. Suddenly he turned Joe onto his stomach, climbed on top of him and began to kiss his neck while rubbing his erection against the backside of Joe's briefs.

He loved the feeling of Fergal's cock pressing against his ass through the layers of underwear, and the way his chest was flush against his back, and how long, tanned forearms stacked on top of his, hands clutching Joe's. Unlike like Ronnie and his fellow gym bunnies, Fergal's flesh, while naturally muscular, still had a softness to it, so when he pressed it against Joe's, it was like they were melting into each other.

"Hey, what's this?" Fergal touched a sensitive spot on Joe's right shoulder blade. "You have a little scar here."

"Don't worry," Joe said quickly, knowing how any sort of unusual body marks might be cause for alarm. That was why he'd had it removed in the first place. He'd been worried guys might assume it was one of those dark purple Kaposi lesions—the skin cancer that affected so many with AIDS. "It was just this mole I had since birth. I had it cut out about a year and a half ago. It was ugly as hell."

"I doubt it," Fergal said. "Nothing that's part of you could ever be ugly." He then continued his pleasurable assault on the back of Joe's briefs, with intermittent kisses of Joe's neck and back, including the scar. After several minutes of getting to know Joe's rear side, Fergal sighed. "Okay, turn over." Joe flipped onto his back. Fergal then took him by the ankles and lifted his muscly legs into a bent position, then pressed down until Joe's knees were framing Fergal's face. "Limber, aren't you?"

"I took karate as a kid," Joe whispered. His nuts were ready to burst.

"Let's see how far you can go." Fergal pushed down until Joe's knees were by his ears, and his face was close enough to kiss him long and hard, the salty-sweet wetness pouring into Joe's mouth. He couldn't get enough, and neither, it appeared, could Fergal. It was as if they were both dying of thirst, and their mouths were the only potable water on Earth. After several minutes of making out, Fergal shoved off his boxers. His uncut cock sprang from a natural bush of black hair, its big head spitting and straining from the foreskin. It had to be one of the most beautiful dicks Joe had ever seen. However, he had underestimated its size. This inspired an excited tingling in the base of his stomach as well as a slight, anxious clenching in other areas.

Joe shimmied out of his briefs. His own cock, circumcised and as impressive as the rumors, thumped against his belly. Fergal fell upon him, licking Joe's hairy chest, exploring his nipples, his biceps, his belly, his thighs. Then he took Joe's dick into his mouth, and Joe let out a sigh at how warm, wet, and incredible it felt. Vince had been completely wrong. Joe was finally—*finally!*—having sex with Fergal the ferryman, and everything was working great. After making his way several times to the middle of Joe's meaty cock, Fergal tried to deep-throat him, which led to a brief choking fit.

Fergal didn't seem to mind, though. "Sorry about that," he said with a grin. "I'm not used to—"

"It's okay." Joe smiled. "My turn. Lie back."

Joe sat up and guided Fergal so that his head was resting on the pillow. Then, starting with another deep kiss, Joe worked his way down the ferryman's body, kissing the perfect hairy triangle at the top of his chest, then down to his small, smooth pink nipples, which he licked and then gently bit, gauging the intensity by listening to Fergal's groans. Then he moved on to his belly button and that sexy treasure trail, which Joe's lips rode all the way down until he landed face-first into that exquisite tangle of hair beneath. Unable to restrain himself any longer, Joe straddled Fergal, letting the wet tip of the ferryman's cock tease his hole. It felt so right that he was going to do this with him. It at last made sense why all the other men since Elliot hadn't worked. They just weren't right. *This is right. Fergal is right.* Joe stole another deep kiss before lifting Fergal's long muscular arms to dive into the thicket of black armpit hair.

"That tickles," Fergal barked with laughter. Then, less than a moment later, "Do it again."

So Joe did, and then he moved back down, running his tongue over Fergal's balls, then on to the shaft of his cock, then the tip of his foreskin, which, after spending some time with it, he gently pulled down to reveal the wet pink head. Finally, he took it into his mouth, causing Fergal to groan with pleasure. The sound poured warm honey throughout Joe's body. Wanting to hear what other sounds Fergal might make, Joe began testing out different spots on Fergal's cock, listening for which area or technique elicited the strongest reaction of pleasure. Finally, after a deep breath, Joe took the whole thing all the way down until it filled his throat, causing Fergal to growl like some waking monster as his entire body quivered. *Found it!* Joe loved knowing he could make Fergal's body react like that. It made him feel powerful—to be desired by someone whom he desired so completely. Joe pulled his mouth off for a moment to take a breath, but then Fergal lifted his hands to the top of Joe's head, encouraging him to go again. Joe happily did, going from the tip all the way to the base, up and down, over and over until Fergal's body began to buck.

"Stop, stop, stop," Fergal begged, pulling himself from Joe's mouth. "Getting too close." He took a few stabilizing inhales and exhales, then said, "Onto your stomach please."

Joe complied, figuring Fergal was ready to fuck him. Anal sex was a big deal for Joe since he rarely ever did it. Elliot had never fucked him despite how much Joe had wanted him to. As far as the handful of other men who had tried over the years, it usually ended badly. Joe just could never fully relax, his mind too consumed about worries over the virus. He'd always clench up, which made it painful. Could he ever be fully open? Could he ever have sex fearlessly? There was something about being with Fergal that felt different, that made him think it would be different with him. He trusted him—which was the hottest thing of all.

Joe's thoughts were suddenly interrupted by the feeling of Fergal's hands spreading his ass cheeks open. He squeezed his eyes shut and tried not to close up, but instead of feeling the painful poke of a cock, he felt the delicious scratch of Fergal's beard pushing into his ass crack. Now it was his own sighs of pleasure that filled the room as Fergal began to devour his hole in ways Joe had never felt before—in ways that seemed to defy physics. *Is that his tongue? His lips? His fingers and tongue together?* Joe wanted to ask him what he was specifically doing so he could one day return the favor, but, paralyzed by the sensation, he couldn't speak. In fact, something strange started to happen: He felt himself fall into a kind of trance. Flashes of ocean waves crashed inside his head as did images of Fergal naked, swimming in the deep, his weird webbed toes propelling him onward, his beautiful body undulating in an underwater world the exact color of his blue-blue eyes. The vision seemed to be inviting Joe to go deeper into the sea with him, guiding him.

Meanwhile, on land, *back there*, he could feel himself opening up as never before, and with each thrust of Fergal's tongue, Joe's body began twitching and begging for Fergal to go deeper. It was the most incredible thing he'd ever felt. Eventually Fergal lifted his damp beard and mouth and whispered, "Condoms?"

Joe almost wanted to cheer. He pointed to the side table, where a small Winnie the Pooh bowl sat filled to the brim with at least fifty various square packets and a small bottle of lube. "Howie and Lenny left that there this morning. I guess they sensed something."

Fergal picked one of the packets labeled Magnum and tore it open, sliding the rubber over his cock. He then lifted Joe's legs into position, rubbed some lube gently into the already wet hole for good measure, and pressed the tip of his cock against the opening. An electrical current shot directly from Joe's sphincter into his guts, making his toes curl with excitement. He longed for that moment when Fergal would painfully push past the rim until Joe's insides would suddenly relax and reshape to fit Fergal's cock perfectly. Pain would turn to pleasure—or that's what he hoped.

"Please," Joe begged. "I can't wait anymore."

He held his breath, but then Fergal stopped cold. After three labored breaths he pulled his body from Joe's and flopped onto his back. Then he snapped off the condom. Joe lay there, and a torrent of dark thoughts began swirling around his brain. Had Vince been right? Was good sex impossible after the third date? When he finally looked over at Fergal, he saw the tears in his eyes.

Joe sat up quickly. "Are you okay? We don't have to do anything. If you're not into it . . . it's no big deal. Really."

"Are you fucking crazy?" There was a thickness to Fergal's voice. "Not into it? I've wanted to be with you ever since that first day you came over on the ferry. And that morning at the Meat Rack when you were messed up? It took everything I had to leave. I wanted you so bad. He cleared his throat. "What I'm trying to say is . . ." Fergal squeezed his eyes closed, like the words he was seeking might be hidden behind his eyelids.

Joe was numb. His mind echoed with another *unfinished sentence* from years before, with Elliot. *No, please, no. This can't be happening again.*

"What?" Joe asked, hoping it wasn't what he already knew it was.

"I'm HIV positive," Fergal said. "I meant to tell you about it sooner, but then I got scared you'd reject me, and . . ." He stopped as if he ran out of air to inflate his words.

"When did you find out?" Joe whispered through his numbness.

"Last fall," Fergal said just as quietly. "Remember that Buck guy from Hawaii who taught me to surf? We got loaded and stupid one night. It was the first time anyone ever fucked me, and I didn't even like it. He didn't know he had it yet. The good news is my T cells are pretty high, but . . . you know." He used the corner of the bed sheet to wipe his nose and eyes.

For several minutes, the two men lay next to each other, staring at the shadows on the ceiling, not embracing, but not pulling away, their limbs simply waiting.

Joe listened to the old house settling. He listened for the crickets outside the attic vent. He listened for Fergal's breathing, the way he used to listen for Elliot's—an assurance that he was still alive. There it was, sitting inside his chest, the familiar grief for a man still healthy, a man he was certain he could fall in love with, a man who would die far too soon unless a miracle happened. He had thought his friendship with Elena, open talks with Howie, and the volunteering for the ACT UP benefit might make him less terrified of the disease, but it hadn't. Why was this happening? Didn't he deserve *some* respite from the constant fear that the man he wanted in his life might only have a matter of years or months left to live?

"Can I tell you something?" Joe asked.

"Yeah."

"I haven't been totally honest with you. I wasn't really lying... or maybe I was. But since we're coming clean about stuff... well, it's like this. When Elliot died, we weren't exactly *together* anymore."

Fergal shifted to look at him. "Why are you telling me this right now?"

"I just need to," Joe said simply. "You told me your truth, and now I need to tell you mine."

Fergal nodded. "Go ahead."

"So the whole truth is, he dumped me a year and a half before he died and had completely stopped speaking to me. I didn't even know he had passed away until former friends started leaving me condolence messages on my answering machine. They'd had no idea we'd even broken up. No one knew except our families. When Elliot started to get sick, he didn't want to be around the gay community. We started isolating ourselves from almost everyone. So when those old friends started to call, I should have told them the truth, but I said nothing. I guess I just wanted people to think we were still together at the end... *I* wanted to think it." Joe's breath sputtered as he tried not to cry.

"That must've been really hard." Fergal placed his hand on Joe's.

"No," Joe said, calmed by the touch of Fergal's hand and wishing he'd move it away at the same time. "I mean, it was, but that's not what I'm trying to say. When he and I first fell in love, I didn't know Elliot had HIV. It was weeks later that he told me, just after the first time we had sex. And I was so much in love with him I thought I could handle it. But then it was like... like I couldn't stop thinking about it, you know what I mean? Every other thought was about AIDS." Joe began talking fast, unable to look into Fergal's eyes. "He'd freeze up if I tried to talk to him about it. And every time he coughed or sneezed, I thought he was dying. When we made love, I'd spend half the time amazed at how lucky I was—and then the rest of the time wondering if I was going to get infected by what we were doing or wondering how and when HIV was going to steal Elliot away from me forever."

Fergal slowly moved his hand off Joe's. Despite the hot room, Joe felt a chill. He wanted to throw his arms around Fergal, but he knew he shouldn't. He had to say what he had to say first. Otherwise, it would all happen again, and he'd end up ruining Fergal's life too.

"Joe," Fergal said, barely any emotion to his voice, "what are you trying to say?"

"This thing, you and me together . . ." His dampening eyes focused on one of the vintage photos of Howie and Lenny on the beams. "I don't think I can do it again. I know I can't." Joe's voice cracked. "I'd be such a shitty boyfriend. I'm too selfish and too weak. I'd make it all about me—like I'm doing right now. You don't deserve that. You need someone better than me—someone stronger. You're the best person I've ever met, and I care about you so much, but . . . I can't." He took a stuttering gulp of air. "I'm so sorry. I still want to be here for you. I mean, as a friend. I can't imagine not having you in my life."

Joe reached over to take Fergal's hand, but Fergal pulled away. Rage had replaced the tears in his blue-blue eyes.

"I'm *not* Elliot," he said. "I'm *not* this disease."

"Fergal, please—" Joe reached for him again.

Fergal lifted his hands in warning. "Don't! I don't need your friendship or your damned pity. And guess what . . . Elliot didn't need it either!"

He leaped from the bed and pulled on his underwear, T-shirt, and jeans.

Joe got up and wanted to reach for Fergal but stopped himself. "Hold on—don't go yet. You're not being fair."

"Fair? Fuck you. I didn't ask to get infected. No one does. And guess what? I just might not die from this. You ever think of that? In fact, I don't plan to. And won't you be sorry then. This might have been your only other chance to fall in love with a decent guy, and you blew it."

"Wait," Joe begged, tears and snot dripping. "Don't leave like this. Stay a minute."

"It's too late. It's done. You know something? Elliot was right to leave you. What a fucking phony—you're so wrapped up in your own fears of what might be, you're turning into a very sad, stuck, and lonely little man. It's pathetic. I never want to see you again."

Fergal stormed to the ladder and descended.

Joe ran to the floor hatch to follow. "Fergal, can we please just talk?" By the time his foot touched the middle rung, he heard the screen door slam, then the gate. Fergal was gone.

38.

Disco Inferno

"When the fire started, we rang the alarms, but no one listened. It wasn't their fire, they said. They watched us burn and laughed."
— *Disco Witch Manifesto #201*

Less than a week after Joe and Fergal broke up, Howie was awakened by the siren blasting from the Pines Volunteer Fire Department. The smell of smoke indicated disaster was within a hundred feet of the house.

"Lenny! Joe! Fire!" he yelled, leaping out of bed and into his vintage lavender satin pajamas. He bounded into the living room and out the front door. When he looked down Picketty Ruff, his heart dropped into his stomach. A moment later, Lenny and Joe, half dressed, stood next to him, their terror-filled eyes watching the smoke and flames pour out the little windows of Asylum Harbor. The motley group of volunteer firefighters, having only gotten there minutes before, hoisted a hose up the steps. It appeared the fire was contained to the interior of the little bar. They had to be careful to drench the place, since the island's structures were mostly made of wood and built so closely together.

It took just forty minutes for the deluge of water to vanquish the conflagration, but not before it destroyed the entire inside of Asylum Harbor. Seeing how devastated Joe looked, Howie grew even more concerned. *For Chrissakes, First he loses Fergal, and now the bar? What the hell is going on?* Chills of foreboding swept up and down Howie's neck. Could this all be related to Lenny having seen the egregore in the Meat Rack? Even though Joe couldn't be the chosen one, it certainly appeared as if the Great Darkness or some other enemy of the light wanted to break the boy.

In the days that followed, the insurance investigators cleared Joe, who had gone to bed at least thirty minutes before the fire started. They determined it was most likely faulty wiring that had ignited some trash in the liquor closet. However, other rumors started to spread. This one saw a Graveyard Girl running down the boardwalk that night; that one swore there'd been a man in a polo shirt who pulled the alarm; another said it was a drunken daytripper, without a place to stay, who'd wandered in from the cold. None of the rumors led anywhere. The only certainty was that Asylum Harbor, as the island had known it for so many years, was gone.

Once the bar was cleared for safety, Joe, Dory, and Vince stepped into its charred remains, searching for anything salvageable. The oak bar top that Joe had spent so much of the previous two months polishing was one long piece of debris-covered wet charcoal. The storage room of beer and alcohol had combusted, leaving brown, green, and clear shards of glass. All of Elena's decorations were obliterated.

"Damn it!" Joe choked back tears when he saw the cindered remains of the old kitschy merman clock that hung over the bar. "I really loved that clock." The merman's bearded face, the one that had reminded him of Fergal, was blackened with soot. His trident was completely gone, and his plastic green tail had melted into something yellowish resembling a dried animal dropping.

Vince shook his head and punched the scorched wall. "That they can get away with this makes me want to scream!"

The light had vanished from Dory's eyes. "Is there any way we can possibly . . . ?" She was unable to say the words *go on*.

"It would take months," Vince said, calming himself. "And we might as well face facts, even if the fire didn't happen, we weren't likely to make the margins we needed to keep Scotty from exercising his right to kick us out. It's his property, and even if that old bucket of snot does use the insurance money to rebuild, there's no way he'll allow Asylum Harbor back in business. This is exactly what he wanted."

Joe kept recalling the rumors about the Disco Witches and the club fire in Rehoboth, but seeing Howie and Lenny's distraught faces now, he at least was certain they'd had nothing to do with *this* fire. "I just know Scotty Black did this," Joe said. "Think about it—the fire alarm gets rung by an unknown person at the exact right time, so it only destroys the interior of our bar but leaves the rest of Scotty's nearby properties unharmed. Isn't that suspicious to you? Why isn't *he* being investigated?"

"It wasn't Scotty," Dory said with that strange sense of mystery in her voice that reminded Joe of how Howie sounded sometimes. "At least not directly. There's some other darkness at play." Dory's eyes engaged again with the space around her. "It's my fault anyway. I've been too distracted. I was foolish to think . . ." She swallowed hard, stopping herself from crying. In his three months on the island, Joe had never seen Dory look so frail and old. He tended to forget she was eighty, but that morning she looked as if she were a hundred. She had told Joe the revived bar had been her dream of inserting some life back into the Pines after eight years of AIDS. Now it was all gone.

"Come now, Dory, darlin', let's go," Vince said, gently offering his arm to Dory. "I'll get some fellas to do the cleanup. That'll be my last job as manager I suppose. Joe, you come on too. You've had a hard week of it, lad."

"Just one more minute, and I'll be right there," Joe said.

As Dory and Vince stepped out of the charred doorway, Joe looked once more at the cindered refuse. He thought about how so much of what he had allowed himself to love in the world got destroyed one way or another—Elliot, Fergal, the bar. He pulled Howie's good luck charm from his pocket and tossed it into the ashes. Then he reached for the merman clock, snapped off the little partially burned head, and clenched it in his fist. This would be his reminder of a summer that would not stop breaking his already broken heart.

39.
What's the Buzz?

"When the world is falling apart, Disco Witches dance."
—*Disco Witch Manifesto #6*

The buzz about the 1989 Gay Men's Health Crisis Morning Party was as loud as a cornfield of gay locusts. Howie explained to Joe that the event—the third high holy day of that summer—had grown so popular the organizers decided to expand that year's event to a huge swath of the public beach at Ozone and Ocean. The dance floor would need to be built over the backyard swimming pools of two massive beach houses. Tickets would only be available via event "sponsors"—well-connected individuals who were certain to invite only the most beautiful, famous, infamous, and/or wealthy. But even quadrupling the size of the party still left many wannabe revelers bartering their virtue or vintage leather jackets to attend. Dory, as always, used her octogenarian strong-arming to convince as many vendors as possible to donate their services. This ensured the bulk of proceeds would go to GMHC.

"The party is happening the same day as the blood moon," a troubled-looking Howie told Joe. "These things can cause the cosmic environment to become frighteningly hospitable to otherworldly mischief."

Joe nodded, unsure of how to react to another of Howie's New Age panics. "Oh. Wow. Okay."

Howie, apparently unsatisfied with Joe's lackluster concern, pressed further. "This can be quite serious, Joe. It's also the second lunar eclipse of the year, which makes it doubly powerful."

"Why?" Joe asked.

"Because it's double."

"Gotcha."

"Blood moons can mean danger," Howie explained. "Although cosmic super events can always go either way. Do us a favor and keep us posted about what you're up to this weekend. I don't mean to act all mama bear, but it's really for the best."

"Sure, sure, Howie. No problem."

Joe had been taking most of Howie's woo-woo, foreboding crap with an even greater grain of salt lately. Other than his alleged aura readings, failed attempts at love potions, and incessant pleas to the Great Goddess Mother, there was absolutely nothing that demonstrated any real magical power. Could the good luck charm Howie had given Joe have been more of a *bad luck charm*? The bar had burned down; he'd lost his bartending job; and worst of all, he'd broken the heart of Fergal—and obliterated what was left of his own heart in the process. At least the Picketty Ruff boys had come through with some catering gigs that would pay his bills through Labor Day. It appeared their only real magic power was as a summer temp agency.

"We'll be at the party the whole day tomorrow if you need us," Howie said. "We're on wristband check between eleven and one, and then the last two hours we'll be working security, making sure no one dies of an overdose or is too flagrant with their drug use. Between one and four we'll be dancing near the first big speaker on the ocean side of the dance floor. Okay?"

"Yeah, yeah, sure," Joe said.

After doing his dishes and showering, Joe headed over to the beach to volunteer for the party setup. The party area had been cordoned off with orange plastic fencing. Dozens of shirtless young men with power tools buzzed around, flirting. Joe and Ronnie, having been asked to help set up the big tent over the stage, had also doffed their shirts and were holding up two tent poles while two other men set the canvas tarp atop the frame.

Just like the ACT UP benefit (and every big party), rumors were circulating that the surprise performer that year "just had to be" either Madonna or Whitney. The other big topic of conversation was that Frankie Fabulous, that poster boy of Fire Island fun, would not be able to attend the Morning Party, because, after drinking too many Absolut and cranberries, he had jumped off the Taj Ma Homo's ten-foot-high deck and landed headfirst in the sand, breaking his neck. The severity of which no one knew, but all were certain Frankie Fabulous's shinning summer of '89 had ended with a terrible thud.

"That's some serious bad news for the party," Ronnie said. "A Morning Party without Frankie Fabulous is like a gay porn scene without penises."

"Poor Frankie," Joe said, flinching at the thought of the accident.

"At least the summer's almost over." Ronnie shrugged. "The good news is, he'll have enough time to get his physique back by next year's Pride, or maybe even for the Winter Party in Miami. I mean, if he can walk and all."

"For real, Ronnie? You know you—"

Joe was just about to tell Ronnie how profoundly shallow his worldview was, when Ronnie kicked him in the calf muscle and whispered, "Hey, Joey, heads up. That muscle-ginger over there is giving you the eye." He tossed his head to a group of volunteers building the dance floor. "Do the 'oops-you-caught-me' flirt I taught you."

"I'm not in the mood," Joe said.

"Come on, buddy boy! It'll be good practice!"

Joe shot a glare at Ronnie. "If I try, will you leave me alone?"

"Yep. Just give it a shot, and we can call it a day."

Ronnie's "oops-you-caught-me" flirt technique involved Joe acting like he got caught looking at the muscle-ginger, quickly looking down shyly, then slowly looking back up, but with a huge sexy grin on his face. Joe followed through, but just as he was forcing a smile at the muscle-ginger, Fergal (the only man wearing a shirt on the beach) walked right between them, seeing everything. Joe quickly dropped his smile, but it only made it worse. Fergal, barely masking his disgust at Joe, began stacking crates of Absolut in the bar tent.

"Fuck," Joe whispered to Ronnie. "Why did he have to see that?"

"Just ignore him," Ronnie said.

"Maybe I should skip the party."

"Don't you dare. It's your last chance to achieve what I've been visualizing for you all summer."

"Really, Ronnie." Joe shook his head. "Even you admitted your visualizing got us a big goose egg."

"Not at all. I was just down the day I said that. In fact, I'd say my visualizing has an eighty percent success rate."

"How?" Joe pressed. "You're not marrying anyone rich and you're still cleaning toilets. As for me, I got two heartbreaks to deal with, no real job, no plans to take the MCAT, and still haven't had sex. I don't know even where I'll be living in September. How do you call that eighty percent?"

"Well . . ." Ronnie thought about it. "For one thing, Scotty Black is finally giving me a chance at bartending Sunday night at the Promethean after-party."

"With only two weeks left until we leave?"

"Better late than never." Ronnie scrunched his face. "Also maybe Vince isn't rich now, but I bet he will be. And better yet, I don't have to pretend to be in love with him. As far as you go . . ." He shook his head. "Okay, fine, fuck it. So, it's not eighty percent, but I'm really happy for once." His eyes filled with a swoony glint. "I'm nuts about Vince. That's something. And look at it this way, you still have this weekend and Labor Day weekend to get laid, right? And at least now we know your heart still works well enough to get broke. That's kinda sorta a success, right?"

Ronnie wasn't wrong. Joe's heart did work. Maybe too well. He couldn't stop thinking about Fergal. But going back was impossible— Joe was neither strong nor brave enough to be with someone as good and sensitive as Fergal. He'd make Fergal's life as miserable as he'd made Elliot's, to the point where Fergal would rather die alone than have Joe in his life.

When he looked over at Fergal, he felt that iron knot of pain wad up in his stomach again. When was this going to stop? Would it take as long as it was taking to get over the pain of Elliot? Just then, Fergal looked over in Joe's direction. Joe, hoping even a brief connection might put a dent in the awkwardness, waved and smiled. Fergal's face froze before he rolled his eyes and turned away.

"Did you see that?" Joe's voice cracked as he placed his hand on his stomach, where an invisible knife had been plunged. "That does it. I'm going to make him talk to me."

"Don't embarrass yourself, bud," Ronnie warned, grabbing his arm. "He's just not ready. You hurt him pretty bad. Give the poor guy some space. How about you focus on the man buffet this weekend instead. Maybe that Gladiator Man will be there . . ."

"It's not fair," Joe said, even though he wasn't sure he believed it. "I know I didn't handle it well, but he doesn't need to treat me like I don't even exist."

"Come on, Joey—"

"Hey, Fergal!" Joe shouted, still holding onto the tent pole. "Can you come here for a minute? I want to talk to you!"

Fergal didn't respond but walked over to the muscle-ginger and started flirting himself. The muscle-ginger reached into the collar of Fergal's shirt to tousle his little patch of chest hair.

"Fuck that!" Joe released the tent pole he was holding, causing the entire structure to collapse. He furiously trudged over to where Fergal was standing. All eyes watched, anticipating either tears or fists between the hot ex-lovers—potentially more thrilling than the finales of *Dynasty, Dallas,* and *M*A*S*H* combined.

"Is it so hard for you just to say hi?" Joe's voice wavered, despite trying to sound controlled. He wanted to say so much, but he mostly just stammered, knowing that there really was nothing to say, yet somehow hoping saying something would change the course of the heartbreaking awfulness. "You . . . you know . . . so, we broke up and. . . . well, it sucked and . . . well . . . you don't need to be a dick!"

Fergal's neutral expression vanished as his blue-blue eyes swirled with what looked like hatred. For a split second Joe thought Fergal might strike him—and he wished he would. At least the physical pain might briefly distract from the emotional agony. But a moment later, any threat of violence evaporated as Fergal's face turned sad.

Without responding, he picked up his backpack and left the party area, leaving Joe standing there on the hot beach, his entire body numb with despair, the last hope of repair set adrift forever on an arctic sea.

40.
Confessions, Part 1

"Sing your deepest darkest secrets loudly to the universe. If you keep them hidden, they will devour you with their teeth."

—*Disco Witch Manifesto #33*

On the day of the Morning Party, Howie awoke with an even darker feeling than all the other dark feelings he had already awoken to that summer. With Max on the brink of death, Lenny having spotted the egregore in the Meat Rack, the blood moon ready to reach its totality at the end of an already cosmically complex weekend, and still no confirmation of who might be the chosen one, the dark event his guts had been prophesying all summer had to be imminent.

Then again, he thought, *it could end up being just a big old bag of bupkis.* The Great Goddess Mother could be unpredictable in her dance with the Great Darkness. Why would she suddenly give Lenny—the schlub who had been doubting their old magic—the individuated power to see the egregore when there wasn't even a quorum on the island? So, even though Howie's gut swarmed with the wasps of ill omen, he knew he and Lenny were capable of getting things laughably wrong. He ruminated on his own misguided prediction of 1969, when his prescient nightmare (in retrospect brought on by eating beef too close to bedtime) caused the entire coven to undergo emergency herbal colonics. And there were other gaffes of magical insight over the years as well, especially when the Disco Witches were far apart from one another.

Of course, Howie's necromancing stomach was more often right than not. Consider the spring of 1981 and his most catastrophically accurate prediction of all: the plague that had decimated legions of holy lovers. But what was the use of speculating whether there was or wasn't an impending cataclysm? Without a quorum of Disco Witches on the island, they were helpless. He prayed his stomach was on the fritz with the rest of his powers. *Let Lenny and me be wrong this time, Great Goddess Mother. Let us be the most wrong we have ever been.*

"Time to snap out of it!" Howie commanded himself. He then jumped from his bed, threw on his favorite Hawaiian birds-of-paradise caftan, and stared into his closet. After all the recent terrible news, he decided to break his fashion fast and bring some necessary light to the island. *I should make a new hat. Something that reminds people of their holy place in the world.* Of course, with things as they were, there would be no inherent magic—it would only be for show. *Still, something silly and colorful might at least brighten the mood.* As a frontline volunteer at the Morning Party, he would be seen by everyone at least once. (This would also allow him to keep an eye on Joe, just in case the boy found himself overwhelmed.) As he was about to go make sketches of a joy-inducing hat for the party—silver Mardi Gras beads, bows, and tinsel; a disco dinosaur perhaps?—he heard loud banging coming from the attic.

"Joe!" Howie ran to the living room and clambered up the ladder. "Are you all right?"

As soon as his head popped over the lip of the attic hatch, he saw Joe sitting on the floor. His right hand wove dramatically through his wavy dark hair while his left held his stomach as if he had been punched. His drawers had been emptied. Clothing was strewn across the floor as if it had been ransacked.

"Joe, you scared me!" He grasped the neck of his flowered caftan like a six-foot-three femme fatale. "I thought you had injured yourself!"

"I can't find it." Joe's voice cracked with emotion.

"What did you lose?" Howie stepped up into the attic.

"It's this mixtape I listen to all the time. It's really important to me."

"It's awful to lose things," Howie said. "Can't you recreate it? I mean we have thousands of albums and a state-of-the-art (give or take a few states) record-to-tape console downstairs—"

"No!" Joe snapped. "You don't get it! Someone else made it for me. It can't be recreated."

Joe dipped his head between his arms. He wasn't crying, but Howie knew that was probably because he was there. Looking over to the top of the bureau, Howie noticed the cassette's empty jewel case with the handwritten title in blue marker ink: *Love Songs 1*, with a tiny smiley face and a three-word note. *Love you forever. E.*

"Oh, I see," Howie whispered. "Your Elliot made you the tape?" Joe nodded, mumbling something into his forearms. "I'm sorry, Joe, I couldn't hear you. What did you say?"

Joe lifted his head. His aura was illuminated by despondent dark blue, a sickly green, and speckles of somber red and grayish pink. Rippling underneath everything was that unresolved and bitter black that had been present since day one. Only now it appeared twice as pervasive. Howie looked away for a moment, his sensitive retinas unable to behold that hue of wretchedness for long periods.

"When we first met," Joe said, "Elliot made me a bunch of mixtapes. This was the only one I had left."

Howie recognized the razor-sharp center of Joe's pain. He, himself, had had nine romantic heartbreaks in his own life, not to mention the scores of beloved friends and comrades he had lost over the last eight years. He knew so many who were, at that very moment, in the process of losing a lover. Joe's pain was ... not worse, but different. Confused, yearning, incomplete.

"Did you look inside the Walkman?" Howie asked, taking his hand from his own heart, where he had been holding it.

"Of course. I looked everywhere. After Fergal and I broke up, I took it to the beach to listen to it, and walked halfway to Water Island. I dunno—maybe I changed the tape on the way back and left it on the steps at Sail Walk. But when I went back to look ..." He shook his head.

"I see." Howie attempted to make sense of what he didn't know. The indigo of clarity suddenly illuminated Howie's own eyes as a jab of insight poked his intestines. *Elliot. Fergal. Elliot. Fergal. Lost tape.* "Joe, you and Elliot—was there something unfinished between you?"

"I don't know what you mean," Joe gruffly mumbled to the floor. "We loved each other, then he got sick and died." He lifted his head, but not his eyes. "No. That's a lie. Did Fergal tell you?"

"No, not at all." Howie placed his large warm hand on the middle of Joe's back. "You don't need to tell me if you don't want to."

"I'm tired of lying." Joe's whole heartbreaking story suddenly spilled out. All of it, from falling in love with Elliot, to learning of his HIV infection, to Elliot's refusal to talk about it, through their fights, all the way until Elliot cut Joe off and then disappeared forever.

Howie visualized the entire relationship both mentally and viscerally. He relived Joe's agony, the regret still lacerating his soul. And just when it became unbearable, Howie saw the light blue of truth breaking through Joe's aura, fighting to overpower that putrescent green.

"I didn't even find out he had died until weeks after." Joe's reddened eyes looked to Howie. "I don't blame you for judging me. I get it. You and your friends stood bravely by while all your lovers died in your arms, and mine kicked me out because I couldn't handle it. And then I go around lying to everyone about it. I just felt so embarrassed and angry at myself. He was all I ever wanted, and I couldn't even . . . Anyway, that's why I broke up with Fergal."

Howie raised his eyebrows. "So Fergal is . . . ?"

Joe nodded. *This* was what Howie had been subtly intuiting for months. He just hadn't wanted to believe it. So many of the most kindhearted of the island's demigods had fallen victim to the plague. "That poor, sweet boy."

"What really sucks is"—Joe's words fought their way out—"I'm completely in love with him. Great, right? I came out here to get over Elliot, and I fell for Fergal—someone else who has the virus. But at least this time I knew the relationship would be doomed. I'd lose my shit again. I won't do that to him too."

"I understand," Howie said gently. "Of course, there is the minuscule possibility it might be different this time. You've grown so much."

"I don't think I have. And what happens if he dies? Huh? It would just hurt so bad. I'd rather be alone forever . . ." Joe choked on a small gasp of air and pressed the heels of his hands into his eye sockets to stem any seepage.

Howie sat next to him and pulled Joe's head to his chest. "It's all so confusing and awful," he said. "Holding all that inside, not being able to talk with Elliot . . . of course that made it impossible. And that wasn't only your fault. But to lose your first great love like that . . . so unfinished. It makes absolute sense to be scared to love again. How can we even begin to love without the delusion of forever?" He stroked Joe's hair. "It was almost two years ago that your Elliot left us?" Joe nodded. "And you're twenty-four now, which means you were only a child when all this—"

Joe lifted his head abruptly off Howie's chest. His aura flashed an angry red.

"I didn't mean to imply your feelings weren't valid," Howie said. "I just meant that no one as young as you should have had to go through that. None of us should. And if you still believe that it's somehow your fault, that you're damaged beyond repair, please stop. The Great Goddess Mother loves you, Joe. She loves all of us passionately. You need to trust me on this. I'm not going to tell you it will work out with Fergal. I can't know that. But you mustn't control your heart too much or you'll end up bitter. Just look around." Howie gestured widely to the room, the island, the world. "So many people who have lists of limits for who is and is not worthy of their love—and they wonder why they are alone. We need to give the Great Goddess Mother the freedom to do her matchmaking work."

"Her matchmaking work?" Joe said, bitter poison drenching his words. "Is her *work* always forcing me to fall in love with someone who's dying?"

Howie held his gaze. "We're all going to die, Joe."

Joe's teary eyes squinted into a look of puzzlement. "Is that supposed to help?"

"No," Howie said. "But it's true. That's what makes love possible. While we tell ourselves "forever," inside we know that our time is limited. That's why we embrace our lovers so tightly when we first meet them. The goddess wisdom in our bones understands the brevity of it all. But I also promise you something else, Joe: many of those who have the disease today won't die from it. I just know it. The greatest of the gods and goddesses are on our side."

Joe looked up to face Howie. His dark eyes were ready to challenge. "Do you really believe in all that woo-woo stuff?"

"Most of the time." Howie smiled, using the edge of his caftan to wipe the tears from Joe's cheeks.

Joe's eyes shifted as he jerked his head away. "You know, ever since I got here, I've heard people say crazy stuff about you and Lenny, that you are . . ." He hesitated. Howie saw his embarrassment to even say it.

"Witches?" Howie offered.

"Yeah." Joe rolled his weepy eyes. "Disco Witches, in fact—whatever that means. That you used to perform spells in the clubs—magic and stuff."

"They say that, do they?" Howie feigned being aghast, then chuckled.

"Yeah," Joe said. "It freaked me out. What with you making all that weird potion stuff on the stove, and your reliquaries and charms, and the way you're always talking about the Great Goddess Mother and auras . . ."

"I see." Howie's face began to feel hot.

"So, are you? Are you and Lenny Disco Witches? Do you cast magic spells? Cause people to fall in love? Did you . . . did you set a club in Rehoboth Beach on fire?"

Howie sighed and then laughed a small bitter laugh. "Those silly queens just love to talk. Of course we didn't set anything on fire. That's arson, not witchcraft."

"I knew it was stupid." Joe gritted his teeth guiltily. "I feel like an idiot even bringing it up. But can you just say it out loud? Say, 'No, Joe, Lenny and I aren't Disco Witches.'"

Howie studied the young man's face. Was it the right time to tell him?

"Joe, everyone has a power inside themselves—" he began.

"Oh, bullshit!" Joe spat. "Don't patronize me. Just tell me the truth. I've seen how people react around you." His voice grew softer but insistent. "I told you my secrets. Now you tell me yours."

41.

Confessions, Part 2

"Upon their first Saturn Returns, the chosen one will rise up or fall prey to the Great Darkness. It is the Disco Witches' responsibility to protect them."
  —*Disco Witch Manifesto #122*

"So? Are you going to answer me?" Joe asked, scrunching up his thick eyebrows in a way that made Howie think of the phrase *rolling hills of puzzlement*. "Do you, Lenny, and Dory call yourself witches?"

Howie recalled all the friendships and romantic paramours he had lost over the years when he revealed his true nature. Most gay men had no problem with the most lurid or complex sexual fetish, but tell them you follow an offbeat esoteric spiritual practice that enables you to sometimes levitate while wearing six pounds of ostrich feathers on your head and then boogying to Gloria Gaynor's "I Will Survive" with dozens of other Disco Witches, and within a matter of minutes you'll hear the screen door slamming behind them. Yet, if Howie wanted to make Joe a true friend, he had no choice.

"Yes, is the simple, unmediated answer." Howie sighed. "Some of us are, or were, part of a spiritual cooperative—a dance-centered 'religion' if you will. Our faith is more like Quakerism or Unitarianism in that we all can believe whatever we like. Individually we follow a metaphysical hodgepodge of beliefs—paganism, folk witchcraft, Strega, Santeria, and so on. To be quite frank, most of our solo practices were just a bunch of silly superstitions."

Joe just sat there, expressionless. Howie wasn't sure if he was even listening, but it didn't matter. The truth moved at its own velocity, and *now* was its moment. "It was in dancing together that our magic truly catalyzed itself. We experimented, testing various hallucinogenic infusions, both popular and esoteric forms of dance, all set against this or that track of club music. At first it was just a lot of fun, an extra layer to our creativity and dancing. But then one night we noticed little sparks of true magic happening."

"What kind of sparks?" Joe said, sitting up and hugging his knees. That he spoke at all pleased Howie.

"Oh, nothing that crazy. Altering the flow of electricity to the lights, pepping up the mood of the party, inspiring the DJ to play better music. It was hit or miss at first, but bit by bit our craft matured. Max—who, besides being our best friend, is also our founder and high priest—began compiling a manifesto of our collective wisdom, as well as his private spell book of what worked and what didn't. One of our greatest triumphs was called the Boogie Down Disco Love Ceremony. We'd use incense and this fabulous twenty-three-song disco diva set—Gloria, Donna, Nena, Nona, all the greats. Suddenly, all the 'potential lovers' in a club discovered one another. Of course, spells like that also have their downsides. We used them sparingly."

Howie paused to see if Joe needed a moment to process, but after a few silent seconds, Joe tossed his head—a demand for Howie to continue.

"After a while we started experimenting more with our dance-floor magic—you know, testing out necromancy, psychic prediction, levitation, that sort of thing. And yes, it's true, sometimes during our twirling trance dances we were able to even combust matter, but nothing extremely dense—only softer matter like wood and drywall. Setting fires requires intense concentration and an absolutely off-the-charts DJ set."

"Did you burn down Asylum Harbor?" Joe asked pointedly.

"Absolutely not!" Howie crossed his heart.

"And you swear you had nothing to do with burning down that club in Rehoboth?"

Howie started to deny it again, but then sighed. "Okay, we *might* have encouraged a Wilmington witch, who allegedly had pyrokinetic abilities, to take revenge on that bigot of a club owner. But I swear we had no idea the witch would choose arson. That's just *so* low-rent. Pah! And to be clear, no one died. We aren't murderers. Ours is a craft rooted in peace, love, and dancing. We are *generative*, not destructive. By the way, that awful club owner got rich by opening a TGI Fridays in the ashes of the gay club, so everyone lost."

Joe's aura had become a murky kaleidoscope of emotion and feeling. "Go ahead," Howie said. "Ask me anything. It's okay. I won't be offended."

Joe looked up into Howie's eyes. "So, if I asked you to heal someone who was sick or might get sick, could you do that?"

Howie shook his head sadly. "I'm afraid not. We tried. Of course we tried, but we don't have that power." Joe furrowed his brow, ready to speak, but then swallowed his words into silence. "What is it?" Howie asked.

"I understand you don't have the power to heal people, but a few minutes ago you said you knew for certain not everyone who has HIV will die, so . . ." His eyes grew teary as he struggled to ask the next question. "So, will Fergal be one of those people who will survive?

Howie's heart broke a little more. "I'm sorry, Joe. I can't know that."

"But can you try?" Joe begged. "You said you didn't always know the power you had. Maybe if you tried—"

"None of us ever had the power to predict life or death, Joe. Not even Max. The Great Goddess Mother doesn't allow that ability. Even at our full capacity, we're limited to a handful of powers, like guiding people onto their right path in life or love, inducing healing dreams, intuiting disaster, lending aid to the innocent under threat, and sometimes altering electromagnetic fields and affecting the weather—though that's very rare and not a hundred percent verifiable. Mostly we spent our time helping young people stay out of trouble and turning lousy dance parties into the greatest nights of people's lives. But now we'd be lucky to summon a simple card trick. I will say, my aura reading has been a little sharper of late, but it's probably sun flares."

"I see," Joe scoffed. "So, you used to have magic powers, but you don't anymore? That's convenient."

"Joe, listen. Our sort of magic is never done alone. A certain number of souls are required. Eight years ago, we always had at least thirty-seven Disco Witches on the dance floor at any one time. Then the health crisis began, and suddenly thirty-seven became thirty-one, then twenty-three, then eighteen, then eleven, then eight, and until a year ago we were five. Max, Lenny, Dory, Saint D'Norman, and myself. The despair wounded our ability to dance, but we've tried to persist. Now we've come to a turning point. The one vital requirement of our practice is the need for a quorum of five members present to convene our holy twirling ceremony. If Max dies, it will be the end of us. We've vainly hoped that some previously unknown magical being might appear to restore our ranks, but so far . . ." A moment of light filled Howie's eyes. "You haven't ever noticed that you could predict the future, have you?"

"Nope," Joe said.

"See colors emanating from people's bodies?"

"Uh-uh."

"Good with a Ouija board?'

"Look, I should get going—" Joe began to stand.

"Wait a moment longer," Howie begged. "I want to tell you something. Sometimes certain loves just aren't meant to work out in this life. But the only starting place for moving on is acceptance. The universe of love is large, Joe. Trust an old witch on that."

"You don't get it, do you?" Joe's eyebrows curled petulantly. His lip fought against quivering. "I've only loved two men in my life, and I hurt both so badly that they ended up never wanting to see me again. I'm done."

"Oh, for Chrissake, Joseph!" Howie slammed the table with the flat of his hand. "Can we please save the flagellation for Lenny's sex dungeon?" Taking a deep breath, he began again more calmly. "What I mean to say is, just because a relationship ends doesn't make it any less important. I encourage you to disabuse yourself of that stupid romantic Hollywood notion. It's false and limiting. And to be quite honest, I have a strong sense that neither Fergal nor Elliot ever stopped loving you."

Joe wiped his eyes with the heels of his hands and stood up. "I'm gonna head to the Morning Party now." He crossed to the bureau and pulled a tank top over his head. Then, as he ran a brush through his hair, his eyes caught Howie's reflection in the mirror. "Since we're coming clean about who we are, I might as well tell you, I lied to you and Lenny about something else. I'm not really twenty-four."

"You're not?" Howie said, grateful that Joe was still talking to him, but feeling overwhelmed by the despairing auric fog that had filled the room. "I sensed there was something else off."

"Yeah. Sorry about that. I started lying about my age when I first met Ronnie. He doesn't even know. I actually turned twenty-nine last March."

"Twenty-nine?" Howie's heart filled with a momentary terror. *The rubric!*

But, he reminded himself again, the chosen one had to meet *all* five main prerequisites. And there was no flying heart mole on Joe. He heaved a private sigh of relief and smiled. "Ah yes. That makes such sense. Twenty-nine is your Saturn Returns year. No wonder you're in a muddle."

"What's a Saturn Returns?" Joe asked.

"Oh it's very impactful and can be wonderful or awful. Every twenty-nine and a half years, Saturn returns to the spot in the sky exactly where it was in the year of your birth. I, myself, am in my second Saturn Returns. No wonder I've felt so connected to you. You've probably been feeling the effects. The changes to one's life can be quite significant during our Saturn Returns."

Joe murmured in agreement as he pulled a black fanny pack from his bottom drawer and snapped it around his waist like a gun belt. The gesture puzzled Howie. Next, Joe picked up Elliot's empty mixtape case, briefly looked at the handwritten liner notes, and then tossed it in the garbage. "I guess we all lie to ourselves sometimes, right? Don't wait up for me." Joe began to descend the ladder.

"Joe, if you could just wait one more—"

Before Howie could say another word, he heard Joe walk across the living room and then out the door. The vibrations of his pain lingered in the attic. *That poor, poor boy,* Howie thought as his foggy gaze swept across the ruined room. Something atop the dresser caught his eye: a single photo of a handsome, sandy-haired, dimple-cheeked young man playing the guitar on a beach. In front of him was a dark-haired man—clearly Joe—lying on his side facing him. *This must be Elliot,* Howie thought, taking in how he'd looked down at Joe with such love in his eyes. Why couldn't love last forever? Why couldn't *lovers* last forever?

It was rare for Howie to observe an object's aura, but the photo was practically glowing. It must have meant a lot to Joe. Just before he set it back down on the dresser, he glanced again, and that's when he flung his hand across his own mouth to silence a screaming gasp. There it was. Right there. The winged-heart mole on Joe's back. Just to be sure, Howie wiped his thumb across the photo to make sure it wasn't dirt. It wasn't.

His eyes tore around the discombobulated room once more. It all was becoming apocalyptically clear—the mixtape case in the trash can, the egregore sighting in the Meat Rack, the half-packed suitcase on the bed, the snap of the fanny pack, the blackness of Joe's aura. Howie grabbed Elliot's mixtape case from the trash and stuffed it into the pocket of his caftan. There was no time to waste. He had to find the others and get to Joe as quickly as possible.

As he scrambled down the ladder, his right foot snagged itself in the hem of his caftan. His six-foot-three-inch, two-hundred-forty-two-pound body fell four feet, cracking his head on the hardwood floor. Just before oblivion descended, he imagined himself calling out Joe's name.

42.

The Morning Party

"Dance, dance, dance, as if tomorrow we all shall die!"
—*Disco Witch Manifesto #10*

When Joe walked into the Morning Party at eleven fifteen AM, he was hit with an overwhelming blast of energy from the ecstatic, sun-drenched crowd. Every man, woman, and drag queen was wearing some sort of spangly, skimpy thong, swimsuit, or jockstrap—with or without headdress. Several people wore matching outfits signifying the comradeship of that summer's house share. There were shiploads of sailors in short shorts, blister packs of Judys in various incarnations (Oz or overdose), pools of synchronized Esther Williamses. Former bar patrons shouted:

"Hey, Joe! Yowza! Look at you!"

"Save a dance for me, Joe!"

"If you wanna use the VIP tent with me, Joe, just ask!"

When DJ Michael Jorba blasted "Get On the Dance Floor" the crowd cheered, arms raised, heaving like the ocean.

Joe, however, didn't move. He scanned the crowd to see if Fergal was there. Not that he wanted to see him. Did he? He didn't. He did. He didn't. *What would be the point?* He knew what he was there to do: *Just for one night, do whatever you have to do to get out of your head.*

And then, in the morning, if you make it that far, you'll get your things and catch the earliest ferry from the Grove. Tell no one. Just vanish.

"Looking good, Joe! Love the white shorts!"

"Wow! Someone is looking for trouble!"

"Get a load of you! Now we know why your bar burned down! Hot stuff!"

Joe forced a smile as he swerved and dodged his way to the beach side of the dance floor, longing for anonymity, still searching (but not searching) for Fergal. He steered clear of Dory and Saint D'Norman dancing in their glimmering silver and white costumes near the stage. He saw Ronnie and Vince, wearing wrestling singlets, pouring drinks and joyfully squirting each other with water guns. Next to them were Elena and Cleigh, drinking Tab and bopping to the music. *At least they were able to find love on Fire Island.*

Joe pushed deeper into the crowd, not wanting to be seen by them or anyone he knew. Although that would nearly be impossible since a Who's Who of his Fire Island summer was swirling around him—the Graveyard Girls (with bumpers stuffed into their nostrils), Chrissy Bluebird, Ace Dandridge, Trey Winkle, Tommy Tune, Jerry Herman, a bevy of Brians, a gaggle of Gregs, all shouting their hellos.

"Hey, Joe! Hey!" a familiar but unexpected voice called out.

Joe turned to see none other than Frankie Fabulous with his broken neck.

"What the hell?" Joe muttered as he stared in shock at Frankie, who was wearing a huge metal satellite ring around his head, held in place with metal pins sticking out of his skull and stabilized with a vest around his naked, chiseled chest. Despite the massive, neck-stabilizing headgear, Frankie was shirtless and wiggling his see-through-mesh-covered hips while waving his arms to the music.

Despite being dumbfounded why anyone in that condition would be there, Joe shouted, "Hey, Frankie! Looking good!"

Then a thought flickered across his brain—*Frankie Fabulous looks like the planet Saturn has come to dance. Is this what Howie meant? Saturn returns for all of us. Are you my broken-necked Saturn, Frankie?*

Joe looked around at several attractive men who were staring at him, their half smirks sending an invitational signal. Given another place and time, they might have been worthy of his love—if he were capable of it. Darker thoughts stabbed at his brain. How many of these men would be dead within the next ten years? Would Howie, Lenny, and Saint D'Norman be dead? Would Fergal be? How many times could a heart break until it could no longer be a container for love? *Come on, stop it, Joe, stop it. It's a party. Try and smile. Today you escape from your head, tomorrow you escape for real. No looking back. No quitting now.*

He fished into the black fanny pack that clung around his waist, his fingers caressing the little mottled merman's head from the burned clock. Pushing it to the side, he felt for the three pebble-smooth, brown glass vials and the little baggie he had promised Ronnie he'd throw away weeks before.

So, where would he go if he made it until tomorrow? Move to New York? Or maybe even Los Angeles or San Francisco? *You know you won't go to any of those places, and you won't go to med school or even take the MCAT. You're a coward, Joe. You'll move back into mom's house in Bucks County and get your old job back cleaning toilets at Friends Hospital.* He'd start pretending to be straight again. On weekends he'd go to Philly and hook up with random strangers, checking their bathroom cabinets for AZT, avoiding anyone who might get sick or break his heart any other way. He'd spend his thirties, forties, and fifties remembering this summer and what he could have had with Fergal, and how he'd hurt both him and Elliot. Eventually he'd die miserable and alone, and they'd only find his body because of the smell, and no one would come to the funeral because there wouldn't be a funeral.

"You okay, Joe?" Frankie Fabulous screamed into Joe's ear—or as close as he could get with his satellite neck brace.

"Huh?" Joe realized he had been standing frozen in the middle of the dance floor.

"You look like your dog just OD'd!" Frankie Fabulous wildly wiggled the lower half of his broken body. "This party is tubular! Come on, smile! If I can smile, anyone can!"

Saturn returns! Saturn returns! Saturn returns!

Joe smiled as broad as Frankie Fabulous, then made his way into one of the porta potties and locked the plastic hatch. One by one he pulled the brown glass vials from his fanny pack and checked their contents. Two were half full and one was completely full. There was also the little packet with the star-embossed blue pill. He remembered hearing a Promethean bartender calling X a bliss rocket. That was exactly what Joe needed. He tossed the X into his mouth, making spit to swallow it down. He waited five minutes but felt nothing. *Fuck this!* Joe poured a tiny white mountain of coke onto the meaty part of his hand behind his thumb, exhaled all his breath before snorting the powder as deeply as he could. Zing! A slight burn, a bitter taste, and his nose felt immediately clear. A second later, tiny explosions ignited inside his brain.

"Holy shit," Joe said, carefully shoving the vial back into his fanny pack.

He burst out the door of the porta potty to an entirely different world. All his dark musings had been subdued. *It's really not such a bad party! In fact, it's a really, really nice party!* The music seemed better, the weather seemed perfect, and everyone appeared way more fascinating than only moments before. This shit really did work. He ran back to Frankie Fabulous and started dancing wildly underneath the man's scaffolded neck brace.

"There ya go, Joe!" Frankie cried. "That's the spirit!"

"You're a really great guy, Frankie!" A lightning bolt of bliss surged through his veins. "That you can have that kind of accident and come back and dance! It's incredible! You're such an inspiration!"

"Thanks, Joe! I just *love* to dance!"

Joe blew Frankie a kiss and bounced off deeper into the crowd until he found the perfect spot to dance alone. Fifteen minutes later something felt different—the coke zing grew quieter. Suddenly he was overcome with the most sublime feeling, as if little rays of light were shooting out of his pores. The bliss rocket. He stood on his tiptoes, closed his eyes, and stretched his arms up toward the sun. The warm breeze blew through each hair on his body. When he opened his eyes, the sky was bluer, the sun brighter, the dune grass greener. Everything was sparkling, including him. He grabbed his pecs and biceps. The feel of his own flesh turned him on.

"Yeah, that's right!" he yelled. "I am Falafel Crotch! That is who I am!" He reached into his fanny pack and lovingly grasped the brown vials and empty cellophane baggie in his hands. "Thank you so much!" he told them. "I understand now! I can get through life like this! I can be brave! I can do what I came to do!"

In one giant, loud, harmonious, electronic voice, the vials and baggie began to sing "This Is Acid" by Maurice Joshua. "Bah bah bah-bah bah-bah-bah-bah!" Joe shoved the singing drugs back into his fanny pack and began to dance with his two thousand dance partners, all stomping on the makeshift pool-top dance floor that bounced to the throbbing dance mix. So many hands groped Joe's chest, his cock, his ass. He felt so loved, so happy on his final day. Everyone's eyes sparkled. Why had he waited so long?

"How's it, Joe?"

"You look great!"

"Didn't know you could dance, Joe!"

"Wow, it *is* big!"

Joe's grin strained the edges of his face. He was in love with every single person on the dance floor. One middle-aged dude began rubbing his hand down the center of Joe's sweaty back until it reached his buttocks. Joe's skin leaped to meet the man's touch. He wasn't even attracted to him, though he ruminated on whether he might be the love of his life. *If only the world could feel like this forever.*

"Thank you!" Joe yelled into the man's ear. "I have to go, but I love you very much! But today is the ending! The big finale! And I have to find someone first!"

And it wasn't a lie. Joe intended to find someone ... or rather someone *else*, someone with a big, muscled body and a handsome face. Someone who wanted to have sex with Joe but at the same time hated him. Someone who could never be wounded or hurt.

He had to find the Gladiator Man.

Joe slid around the dance floor as if it were a giant flesh jungle gym, kissing this one, dancing with that one, using all the beautiful bodies like slippery water slides to whatever beautiful man was next. When he finally paused to look up at the sky, the sun had fast-forwarded itself to the far west. How long had he been dancing? He glanced at someone's watch—hours had vanished. He felt a sudden swoop, like an airplane losing ten thousand feet of altitude. He looked around. Nothing seemed to have changed, yet everything had. Eyes no longer sparkled. The music was no longer magical. The groping hands were attached to men he no longer found attractive. Dark, pickax-carrying thoughts floated across his brain. *Is it right to be dancing when so many others are dying? Did Fergal already meet someone else? Will he die without ever finding love? Will Elena? How are you supposed to be brave enough now?*

Joe hoovered his way through the rest of the coke vials, and for fifteen-minute bursts he got a little of his zing back, but then the swoop down would return, the dark thoughts. Finally, he stood stone still in the middle of the dance floor, shoulders slumped, his face a mask of despair. All the brown vials and the baggie in his fanny pack were empty. The Morning Party would be ending in a matter of hours. Howie's blood moon would rise, and all the people would leave for dinner or go to the Promethean, partying until Monday morning, cuddling with someone they were capable of loving. By then Joe would be gone. But before then, Joe needed to find the Gladiator Man—and more drugs—to be brave enough to do what he intended to do, to be brave enough to escape.

He unscrewed each of the empty coke vials and tapped them on his tongue, hoping orphaned grains would fall out. None did. He licked the inside of the X baggie. Nothing. He pulled out the little burned merman's head and looked at his tiny, manly, bearded face, still black with soot. The face that had once looked like Fergal's.

"What am I going to do now, little merman? I'm drowning again, and you don't even have a tail anymore to save me."

The little merman's black dot eyes stared back at Joe coldly.

"Fuck you." Joe tossed the charred head high up into the air over the dancing crowd. Once he saw it drop into their midst, he returned his own head to his knees and prayed for the day to finally *end*. It was the strange vibration of the floor that made him look up.

"What the fuck?" Joe stumbled up from the floor. "Did you feel that?" he asked a man, sweating with a rapturous look on his face.

"Feel what?" the man said, dreamily pulling Joe's hand toward his crotch. "Wanna feel this?"

The floor rumbled louder. It felt as if Fire Island was being hit by an earthquake. He heard the sound of wood splitting. The floor beneath his feet dropped to a tilt. The crowd fell into one another and erupted into screams. Joe, realizing the pool-top platform was collapsing, ran toward the temporary fence that surrounded the party. Just as he landed on solid ground, he tripped and fell, scraping the heel of his hand. When he turned to look back, he saw the entire middle of the dance floor crack, split open, fold inward, and collapse. Bodies fell into one another and then into the pools.

Some people screamed for help, as if they were Shelley Winters in a seven-foot-deep version of *The Poseidon Adventure*. Some people laughed at the absurdity of it. Others whined loudly how the disaster had killed their high. A few simply floated dreamily on the sinking debris, cocktails still in hand. The DJ never stopped spinning.

"Quite a shit show if you ask me," a voice from behind Joe said into his ear. "Wouldn't have happened if I'd been in charge."

Turning around, Joe saw that it was Scotty Black, the person he hated most in the world other than himself. He appeared unfazed by the dance-floor disaster, as if he had seen things like that happening every day.

"What do you want?" Joe said coldly. "Wasn't burning the bar down enough?"

"Don't believe the rumors." Scotty laughed. "Need anything?"

"What do you mean?"

"Party favors," he said, winking and patting his white fanny pack. "You look like you could use something."

"No thanks," Joe said, turning away.

"I know what you think of me," Scotty said, "but I'm on your side. I want hot studs like yourself to have a good time. It's good for business."

Scotty handed Joe what looked like a small conical seashell. But it wasn't a seashell at all. It appeared to be a fancy little glass bumper encased in a highly decorative silver sheath.

"What is it?" Joe asked. "Coke? K?"

"Nope. It's my own special mix. A combo of this and that." He winked again. "Mostly *that*. Not something I do myself, but it helps my staff keep up their energy for long stretches. Better than coke. Makes you forget all the sorrows of our world." He gestured to the carnage in front of them. "It'll also give you some pep. Gotta have pep at a party, right?"

"Will it make me brave?" Joe asked, screwing off the top of the bumper and peering at the mottled yellow-gray powder.

"It will make you the bravest you've ever been. You'll be superhuman for a little while. It'll be fun. I'm gonna open the Promethean early to give these folks a place to party. You should come by and brighten up the place. I promise, you'll have the time of your life."

Normally, Joe would never take anything Scotty Black offered to him. But right then, the thought of staying sober was unthinkable. Before his mind could catch up to his hands, he was pressing the bumper to his nose. "Ow!" The bitter powder burned a fiery trail from his nostril all the way to the back of his soft palate. Every hair on his body leaped to attention. A dark, rushing, sexy sensation rocketed throughout his brain and limbs.

Less than twenty seconds later, Joe's relentless thoughts of yesterdays and tomorrows had been extinguished. No Elliot. No Fergal. No AIDS. No fear of dying or losing others. For the first time in his life, Joe felt truly brave.

"Feels good, right?" Scotty sniggered.

"Something like that." Joe offered the bumper back to Scotty.

"It's okay." Scotty smiled. "Keep it. It's the end of summer. Let loose. Maybe next season you'll be ready to work for me. I better go open the club. See you there in a bit."

Scotty kissed Joe on his lips and walked away. Joe wiped his mouth, then loaded up the bumper and napalmed his throat and sinuses again with the yellow-gray powder. When the pain subsided, his skin felt as if it was liquefying into molten honey while his viscera filled with the most ravenous sexual hunger. *Despair? What despair?*

But where to have his night of abandon before whatever came next? The Promethean? *No, no, no.* He'd know too many people. He didn't want to be reminded of the real world or its heartbreaking inhabitants. With his newfound, drug-induced superpowers, he took a running leap over the beach fence, landing in the warm sand. *The Meat Rack,* he thought. *If Gladiator Man is anywhere, he'll be there.* It was the only answer. Gladiator Man needed to pound the memory of Fergal and Elliot from Joe's body and heart. He'd have his wild, dark Fire Island moment, then be gone forever.

"I will be brave," he muttered. "I will finally be brave."

43.
The Last Premonition

"Whenever there are five or more Disco Witches twirling on the dance floor in the name of the Great Goddess Mother, magic shall be at hand!"
—*Disco Witch Manifesto #3*

The first thing Howie noticed when he opened his eyes was that he had one of the worst headaches of his life. The second thing was the three angels dressed in white sequins and feathers staring down at him. *How strange to be lying on the floor when angels have arrived to accompany me to the Morning Party.* He pictured all the jealous queens watching him strutting through the gate with flashy, decked-out seraphim. It would almost be better than bringing Liza! (Okay, that's an exaggeration.) He'd need to make an extra-special hat of course. *Do angels get into the party free? I wonder if they get VIP drink tickets.*

One of the angels, the Italian American one, in white leather chaps and a harness, started yelling with the most discomforting nasal desperation, "Talk to me, you motherfucker!"

Next, the old female angel, who was Black and wearing a white feather boa and dozens of spangly silver necklaces, spoke in a more soothing voice. "Shh. Calm yourself. His eyes are open. He's going to be okay."

"But he has a bump on the back of his head!" the little Italian angel complained. "What if he has a friggin' concussion? Oh marone!"

"Oh dear," the female angel said. "Maybe we should call for a water taxi to take him to the hospital? Or do you think we'd need to airlift him?"

"Both of you settle yourselves," the third angel told the other two. He was also Black and dressed in what looked like a silver jump suit. "I'm the only one here who was a registered nurse. I'll check him out. Howie, honey, do you think you need to go to a hospital? That fat head of yours nearly busted in half."

So that was the reason for this headache. Howie must have knocked himself out. It wouldn't have been the first time. He took in the view of the very unangelic Lenny, Dory, and Saint D'Norman all standing over him in their spangly Morning Party outfits.

"I don't need a hospital." Howie groaned as he wobbled up to sitting. There was something important he needed to tell them, but what was it? "You look fabulous by the way. What time is it? Are we going to the Morning Party?"

"The party ended hours ago, darling." Dory breathed a sigh of relief.

"Complete shit show!" Lenny said.

"What are you talking about?" Howie felt for the bump on the back of his head.

"He doesn't even know?" Saint D'Norman lifted the pendant flashlight from around his neck to examine Howie's eyes. Did he have dizziness? No longer. Did he have a ringing in the ears? Nausea? Blurry vision? Fatigue or drowsiness? No. No. Just a teeny bit. No and no.

"I'm fine!" Howie demanded, though he still couldn't recall why he had such a sense of urgency in his guts. "Tell me what happened at the party."

Saint D'Norman gave the other two the head nod, clearing the patient.

"It started out lovely." Dory widened her eyes for emphasis. "But then that flimsy dance floor they put up over the pools collapsed, sending the entire crowd into the toilet."

"Oy! The way those queens were screaming," Lenny added, "you'd think someone filled their poppers with pepper spray."

"How awful," Howie said, as images of splashing queens conflicted with the lost information he was trying to drag from his mind meat. *Something about wings. Was it about a butterfly? A mourning dove? Did I feel the need to buy wingtips?*

"They say no one was seriously injured," Saint D'Norman muttered as he examined Howie's head bump.

"But they stopped the party just when everyone's X was peaking," Lenny added. "Talk about a tragedy. Scotty Black is opening the Promethean early for the after-party." Lenny arched his one eyebrow. "The greedy bastard upped the entrance fee by five bucks. We were on our way to Chrissy Bluebird's for drinks, but—"

"But then Saint D'Norman found out some incredible news!" Dory almost squealed, which was unusual for her since she was not a woman who ever, *ever* squealed. "That's why we came to find you!"

"Tell me later." Howie pulled himself to standing with Lenny's help. "There's something very important I need to tell you ... but I can't quite remember ... Where's Joe? I think it has to do with Joe."

"Just fuckin' shut up for a minute!" Lenny lifted his palm to Howie's face. "Listen to Saint D'Norman for one friggin' minute! Please!"

"Fine," Howie groaned. "Go ahead. But please be quick."

Saint D'Norman, burdened with a dozen silver chains around his neck, asked for a chair. To lighten his load, he removed his dazzling, five-pound, rhinestone-studded fez.

"The weight of fashion is just too much for me nowadays." Saint D'Norman sighed and fanned himself. "Perhaps I should have worn a veil instead of the fez."

"Saint D'Norman, darling"—Dory patted the frail man on the back—"tell Howie about your vision."

"Ah, yes..." Saint D'Norman wet his teeth with his tongue, which he tended to do when he knew a long explanation was needed. "Well, because I wanted to go to the Promethean tonight, I left the Morning Party early to take a disco nap, so I unfortunately missed the whole floor-collapsing fiasco. But during my nap I kept waking up to take a pee. I've got a bladder the size of a Japanese beetle's. On the way to the toilet, I was hit with a necromantic nausea. You know the sort. Someone from the other side was trying to contact me."

Howie, suddenly curious, momentarily ceased searching his foggy brain and sat in the chair across the table. He knew never to ignore one of Saint D'Norman's intestinal telegrams from the netherworld. Before the plague years, he had been considered the Ma Bell of necromancy. "So who was it?"

Before Saint D'Norman could speak, Lenny blurted, "It was fucking Lucho!"

"Lucho?" Howie's voice cracked.

Lucho, the poor beautiful young man they had lost to the Great Darkness in Provincetown so many years before, the failure that had haunted all their dreams—especially Lenny's. That Lucho had made an appearance at all was staggering (those taken by the egregore were usually never heard from again), but that he had contacted Saint D'Norman during a disco nap at almost the very moment the dance floor at the Morning Party was collapsing—it couldn't be just a coincidence.

"Did he say anything about Joe?" Howie cried as bits of their recent conversation started to flicker in his mind.

Saint D'Norman shrugged. "He mentioned someone that might have been Joe, but it wasn't clear. You know how gay men are, describing everyone as 'hot.' But he did say whoever it was, they were the chosen one, and that there is indeed an egregore on the island, so we need to be alert."

"Maybe Joe's with Ronnie," Howie said, stumbling to get up. "Help me up!"

"Why are you getting agita about Joe?" Lenny said, pushing Howie back down. "He doesn't match the rubric. He's too young and has the back skin of a Gerber's baby." Lenny turned to Saint D'Norman. "Check his heart again."

As Saint D'Norman pressed his ear to Howie's chest, fireworks went off inside Howie's head, obliterating the last vestiges of mental clouds. It all came back to him. His conversation with Joe, the packed suitcase, Joe's lie about his age. The tossed-away mixtape case. The fanny pack snap. The photo of Elliot. *The winged heart.*

"He lied!" Howie touched the wound on his head again. "That's what I've been trying to tell you! He matches the rubric completely. He lied about his age. He's really twenty-nine."

Saint D'Norman gasped, as did Dory and Lenny (but more subtly).

"Motherfucker," Lenny said. "But what about the—"

"He's got it," Howie said. "Or rather, he had it. I saw it in a photo he took with his late ex-boyfriend Elliot. It was right there, the winged-heart mole on his right shoulder blade. He must have had it removed. *And* he's been blabbering all summer about that hot Gladiator Man. The one Lenny just saw in the bushes."

"The egregore." Dory's eyes grew heavy with fear. "Your instincts were right after all, Howie."

"He's who Lucho was talking about." Saint D'Norman sucked his cheeks knowingly. "He's the chosen one."

"Fuck the Great Darkness and the dragon it rode in on!" Lenny pounded the table with his fist, clearly having overcome any skepticism. "We'll just make sure not to leave Joe's side until he's off the island in September. It's our fucking job."

"It's too late for that." Howie's expression turned desperate again. "Joe packed his bags. He's planning to leave the island without telling us—or maybe do something stupid or—oh, I don't even want to say it out loud. He even threw away Elliot's mixtape case. I'm certain he's at the same breaking point as poor Lucho."

"Well, we have to try something!" Lenny blurted. "Let's put on our fucking dancing shoes!"

"How can we?" Howie's eyes flared at Lenny's ignorance. "You know we don't have any power without a quorum—"

"Tell him now, Saint D'Norman!" Dory demanded. "Quickly, please!"

"That was the other reason for Lucho's visit." Saint D'Norman cleared his throat. "He wanted us to know that we still have a chance for a quorum."

"Is it Max?" Howie smiled, clutching the necklaces around his throat. "Please tell me Max is going to rally."

Saint D'Norman looked into Howie's eyes and shook his head. "I'm sorry, honey. Max will be crossing over anytime now."

"Heshy left a message this morning." Dory wiped away a tear as Lenny gave her a hug.

"Shit," Howie mumbled, his voice wobbling. "And we're not there with him..."

"Heshy and their best friend, Melon Blossom, are there," Saint D'Norman said. "Max doesn't want us to worry. He knows we're needed here."

"So then, how can we have a quorum if it's not Max?" Howie asked.

"That's the thing." Saint D'Norman lowered his tone to sound soothsayer ominous. "Lucho said there's another witch on the island who has the gift."

"Another witch?" Howie shook his head in disbelief. This fact did not adhere at all to what he knew of the history of their order. "Someone we didn't recruit ourselves? Back when we started, Max said—"

"That was then!" Lenny barked. "Stop being a fuckin' nostalgic naysayer. It's 1989! You heard what Lucho said. We have a chance of getting our collective powers back. We just have to find this fifth witch!"

"Or let them find us," Dory added. "With some of our old magic back, we'll have a chance."

"I wonder if that's the additional strangeness I've been feeling?" Howie's voice was almost a whisper. "Since the beginning of the summer, I've felt a presence, a power. My own ability to see auras has been stronger. I thought it was just because of it being my own Saturn Returns year—"

"I felt the same thing," Saint D'Norman said. "I thought it was my medication."

"Count me in." Lenny raised his hand. "I felt it in the Meat Rack when I saw the egregore. And I've had some moments where I've been able to mind-read almost as well as the old days—something I don't recommend when you're cruising Low Tea. Those bitches can be cruel."

Dory raised her finger in an aha gesture. "I do recall feeling a kind of electricity at the ACT UP benefit when we were all there, and once more when the four of us met for lunch at the Leviathan."

"That means this potential fifth witch was near enough to be creating the electro-cranial-magnetic bond," Howie said. "Do you remember who was near us when you felt it?"

Dory shook her head. "There were dozens of other people around. I can't remember anyone in particular."

"I've been trying to make contact with Lucho again all afternoon," Saint D'Norman said. "I get the feeling the Great Goddess Mother wants us to discover the fifth ourselves. We should prepare the sacred circle on the dance floor in our regular spot. My gut says whoever the fifth is, they'll be drawn to us."

"We have to try." Howie stood. "Lenny, go see if Vince and Ronnie can look for Joe?"

"Gotcha," Lenny said.

"I'll see if Elena wouldn't mind helping too." Dory picked up her purse.

"Definitely ask Elena." Saint D'Norman smiled at Lenny and Dory. "It will be good for her to get out and do some service."

"Perfect!" Howie clapped. "We don't have much time. We'll need to do the whole nine yards—our best twirling shoes, hats, a special infusion, everything."

"Yes!" Lenny cried out. "Finally! That's what I'm talking about!"

Howie's eyes glinted in a bellicose twinkle. "My comrades, are you ready to boogie?"

44.

The Fifth

"That passionate desire which frightens you the most, which shocks you to your core, that is the one which shall set you free."

—*Disco Witch Manifesto #89*

As soon as the doors of the Promethean swung open, a rolling disturbance rippled across the club. It didn't matter that the DJ was blasting Karyn White's mega-hit "Secret Rendezvous." Someone or something important had obviously entered the club.

"Is it Madonna?" several club goers muttered.

"It's Jeff Stryker I bet," others insisted.

The younger patrons were horribly disappointed when they discovered that, instead of pop divas or porn stars, the ruckus was ignited by a quartet of bizarrely dressed old people. The more senior club goers, however, began whispering or covering their mouths in joyous shock.

There they were, strutting in single file: Dory, Lenny, and Saint D'Norman, wearing outlandish sparkling headgear with black crepe capes, clearly hiding some sort of spangly outfits beneath. Last to enter was Howie. He too was draped in a black robe, while atop his head he wore a three-foot-high, five-foot-wide, massive, cone-shaped white hat, featuring a replica of the Saint dance floor on its fabled opening night (his holiest of costumes)! Emerging from the very top of the hat was a miniature spinning star machine that projected the Milky Way onto the walls and ceiling of the Promethean in homage to the Saint's famous dance-floor planetarium. The base of the hat's star machine was festooned with bouncy silver wires encrusted with rhinestones and silver star shapes that shimmied with every breath he took. The wide platform brim featured a small army of toy soldiers spray-painted silver and positioned as if they were dancing. There was an added "mezzanine level" around the hat's middle, where the silver soldiers were coupled in various sexual positions in homage to the Saint's nightly balcony orgy. Dripping from the edge of the brim were strands of rhinestone stars in varying lengths. If (and when) Howie twirled, the strands would lift and spread, creating a huge shimmering aura. All four Disco Witches wore their coven's most sacred symbol: a disco-ball cocktail ring the size of a pug's eye, which spun, reflecting the club's lights and lasers. To protect their eyes from the impending dazzle and to dissuade others from asking them questions, all wore the darkest of vintage aviator sunglasses.

As the quartet moved to the center of the room, old-timers, eyes dampened, cried out:

"You're back!"

"We missed you!"

"Can we buy you a drink?"

The four ignored all adulation until they arrived at their spot—middle of the dance floor, ten feet from the mirror.

"Do you feel it?" Lenny shouted over the music.

Indeed, they did. It was an almost nauseating swirl of power igniting itself in every chakra. The fifth had to be nearby. *If only they would reveal themselves!* Moments later, Howie saw Vince and Elena pushing through the crowd.

"We've looked everywhere!" Vince shouted. "We can't find Joe!"

Howie shook his aching head. (A seventeen-pound hat didn't help.) Vince gestured to someone else. It was Ronnie walking toward the group. As he took in Howie's costume, he looked both astonished and appalled. It struck Howie how very vibrant Ronnie's aura appeared—reds, yellows, blues, even purples—but then again so was everyone else's in the club. Howie didn't even need to remove his sunglasses—just like in the old days. Lenny was right. The fifth *had* to be nearby. Howie's intestinal prescience roiled with a salmagundi of premonitions. *Shh!* he bid his own gut. *Shh! I can't concentrate!*

"Has anyone heard more about when Joe left the party?" Howie shouted.

Elena nodded her head at Ronnie, her eyes demanding he speak. "Don't be a dick, Ronnie!" she shouted. "Just tell him!"

Ronnie huffed as he moved Howie's dangling hat crystals and said, "Frankie Fabulous saw Joe doing all sorts of drugs at the Morning Party—which is not like him at all. The last thing Frankie saw was Joe walking alone down the beach toward the Meat Rack. He looked really fucked up. No one has seen him since."

Howie removed his sunglasses and rubbed his eyes. *It has begun—the Great Darkness is making its move.* After relaying the news to the others, he noticed the auric flares of furious red blasting from Ronnie's head. "What else is it, Ronnie?"

"Joey never did drugs before he met you!" he yelled.

"Easy there, Ron," Vince said, his hand gently pressing on Ronnie's forearm.

"No one here would've given Joe drugs," Elena added.

Howie gazed deeply into Ronnie's furious retinas. There was something else, something that caused Ronnie's guts to twist like pulled taffy whenever Howie was around. Could he not let go of his disdain for Howie, even when Joe was in such danger? Was Howie such a shadow for him? A terrifying reminder of his own impending withering? *No,* Howie thought, *it's something more, something even deeper.*

"Ronnie, listen." Howie drew back the strands of crystals. "I promise you, we're on the same side. I don't need you to like me. But I need us to be allies. Joe is in a very bad place. We need to find him and help him before something bad happens. Trust me on this."

Ronnie averted his eyes and took a deep breath. Howie noticed the slightest shimmering of blue in Ronnie's aura—which could mean he was starting to trust, although it could also indicate his need for healing. "All right!" Ronnie surrendered. "I'll ask if I can start my shift later."

As Ronnie ran off, Howie requested Elena to search along Fire Island Boulevard to see if Joe had fallen off or passed out somewhere. "Come back here when you finish," he told her. "We'll need your help." He instructed Vince to go see how Ronnie was doing and come back for directions on where to search in the Meat Rack and on the beaches.

"Got it," Vince said, running off to retrieve Ronnie.

Howie turned back to Dory, Saint D'Norman, and Lenny but found them in the midst of some intense, animated colloquy.

"What are you three jabbering about?" Howie demanded, annoyed. "You should be looking around for the fifth!"

"Didn't you feel it just a few seconds ago?" Lenny grabbed Howie's arm. "It felt like being hit with a Mack truck of energy. Gave me a boner even!"

"You mean—" Howie's eyebrows furrowed.

"The electro-cranial-magnetic waves!" Dory offered. "They're off the charts!"

"The fifth must be inside the club!" Howie said. "But who is it?" He gestured at the two thousand club goers surrounding them.

Saint D'Norman smiled and whispered into the ears of each of his three friends separately. As soon as he finished, each pair of eyes widened with utter shock.

"*Him?*" Lenny shouted. "You can't mean that two-bit Fabio stripper?"

Saint D'Norman nodded his head.

Dory looked to Howie, whose eyes lit up with the fire of the entire club. "Of course it's Ronnie!" Howie howled up at the disco lights. "How did I not see it? That's why he's been so angry with me all summer! When our true nature stares us in the face, it's terrifying!"

"He'll never believe it." Dory sighed through her teeth. "How will we convince him?"

At that very moment, Vince came running back, pulling Ronnie by the arm.

"Thursty threw a fit." Ronnie caught his breath. "But he's letting me start my shift late. I just have to be back by midnight." He looked at the four faces staring at him as if he were standing in a glass specimen box. "Um . . . did something happen?"

Howie grabbed both Ronnie's and Vince's arms. "Change of plans, gentlemen. Vince, you'll need to search the Meat Rack alone. We need Ronnie here to help with something else."

"He's *my* friend!" Ronnie spat angrily. "I want to go look for him!"

Howie nodded toward Dory. She was the high priestess of empathy and benevolent manipulations, with an unbelievable power to get the uninitiated to understand.

"Listen, my dear," Dory said, switching places with Howie to be closer to Ronnie. "Take a deep breath, please." Her old hand caressed his cheek as he did. "You've been caught in a muddle for too long. It's time to locate your true self—the one you've always known was there. Trust us. We don't have much time, and what we're about to tell you will not make sense, but if you do exactly what we tell you to do, we can help Joe. Do you understand?"

Ronnie's anxious eyes glistened in the glow of the four witches' sparkling hats. "Is it going to hurt?"

45.

The Meat Rack

"The Darkness doesn't care."
—*Disco Witch Manifesto #66*

It was hard for Joe to breathe the Meat Rack's balmy air through his powder-caked nostrils. Scotty Black's trail mix had also made Joe so horny and jumpy he felt like leaping out of his skin. Still he wanted to snort more—anything to stay high until he was off the island. The problem was there wasn't a lot left in the bumper. He'd need to ration it.

Not watching where he was going, Joe stumbled down an embankment, scraping his already twice-wounded leg. He touched the reopened scabs and wiped the blood onto his white shorts. He'd need to be more careful.

Without a flashlight the Rack was far more precarious than he'd imagined, like a giant skateboard park with fifteen-foot drops in places, all covered with dirt, vines, trees, and roots. The only light was from the moon peeking through the twisted trees like some lunar pervert. Soon even that would darken with the eclipse. Wanting to get his bearings, he scrambled up the side of a steep dune. From the top he could see the shimmering sea with its glowing white waves, heaving and crashing on the beach.

If only Fergal could see this. *Stop! Don't think about him!* But Joe couldn't help but think about him. He pictured his face that night he told him he couldn't see him—those blue-blue eyes hurt, enraged, and betrayed. Joe never deserved Fergal's love anyway. Fergal was better off without him. Why wasn't the drug working anymore?

Joe fell to the sand, curled into a ball, his body convulsing as he sobbed. Each tear contained the certainty that he'd never be happy again. He filled the chamber of Scotty Black's bumper and snorted the last of the yellow-gray powder. He felt the burn, the whoosh, but this time there was no release from the despair. It was still there, along with his cowardice and the crushing pain of all he had lost. He tossed the empty bumper into the shrub pine. Again, his body shook with his tears. He felt so exhausted yet horribly awake. Without more of the drug, how would he make it through the night? How would he brave enough to make his escape?

"What's going on?" a man's deep voice asked from the shadows.

Joe looked, but only saw a tall shadowy form. Unable to speak without crying, he waved the man away. *Can't he see what a mess I am?* But the man stepped forward from the shadows and angled his body so what was left of the eclipsing moonlight revealed his identity. He wasn't wearing a Titans sweatshirt, but he had that same expression of desire and disdain on his strikingly handsome face. *Gladiator Man.*

46.
Reluctant Heroes

"Healing spells are written upon the wound."
—*Disco Witch Manifesto #24*

"Joseph!" Vince shouted into the darkness of Fire Island Boulevard. "Hey, Joe, where the hell are you?"

Vince didn't fully understand why everyone was so dramatically concerned about Joe. True, Joe didn't have much experience with drugs or the Meat Rack, but he also wasn't a total idiot. But then again, seeing Howie's and Dory's terrified expressions had definitely fueled the fires of Vince's own worry. He'd become very fond of the wee lad and would hate it if something bad happened to him. "Joseph, ya damned numpty! Show yourself or I'm going to knock your furry little—"

Heavy footsteps pounded the boardwalk behind him. As he spun around, fists raised to fight, chilblains shot through the Celtic knot tattoo on his spine. It wasn't until the man was within five feet that Vince recognized his sweaty face.

"Fergal?" Vince barked. "Jesus, Mary, and Joseph! I nearly clobbered you!"

"Elena told me you're looking for Joe!" Fergal gasped for air. "I came to help."

"I thought you weren't talking to him anymore."

"I'm not!" More gasping. "He's a fucking asshole."

"So don't bother, then. I can look myself. Go back and have some fun."

"You don't understand." Fergal bent over, holding a cramp in his side. "If something bad happens to Joe, I'm fucked. I'll never get over him..."

"You're not making sense—"

"It's what drove my mother nuts!" Fergal cried out, the inebriation in his voice becoming apparent. "The bastard who knocked her up just took off without a word. Not even a goodbye. She's spent the rest of her life pining over him, thinking he must've died or something. That's not happening to me. I need to make sure Joe's safe. Then I can hate that selfish dickhead forever and be free."

"Suit yourself." Vince shrugged. "I already combed the beach. We can divide up the paths into the woods. You know your way around the Rack, lad?"

"Not really."

"Ach, then when we go in, you better stay on the Judy Garland Memorial path—the one closer to the foredune. Just keep the ocean on your left, and head toward the Grove. I'll do the Meat Rack circle. That damned eclipse has made it as dark as black pudding in there. If you follow the sand, everything should be fine. I'll never be that far off, so holler loudly if you find him or if you get lost."

As Fergal made his way into the dark thicket, he wore that same scared, desperate look as Howie and Dory. Vince considered demanding to know if there was something they weren't telling him, but opted instead to just do what he was told on that strange night in a strange summer in the strangest of years.

"Joseph!" he called out again, as he would continue to, forty-seven more times.

47.

The Big Guns

"The answer to your specific salvation is always within your reach. You'll know it by the way it sparkles."
—*Disco Witch Manifesto #92*

"Now will you tell me what is going on?" Ronnie demanded. Howie, Dory, Lenny, and Saint D'Norman had avoided his questions as they rushed back to the attic crawl space of 44 and ¼ Picketty Ruff. But as they dug through the glittery costumes, looking for Ronnie's exact size, they outlined what they believed was his "true nature"—how he was born a "holy lover" of "the Great Goddess Mother," and, like them, was blessed to be part of a secret coven whose powers reached their apotheosis when five or more were gathered on the dance floor in "holy ceremony."

Ronnie's head felt like it was about to explode. "So you people actually believe you're dancing witches?"

"Well, that's a bit reductive." Dory pulled down a fabulous white cowboy hat with feathers and rhinestones. "And you should rephrase that to *we* now, darling. Because you're a disco witch too." She placed the hat on his head. "Perfect, right?"

Howie and Lenny nodded with satisfaction.

"Why are you putting this crap on me?" Ronnie peevishly tossed the hat back on the shelf—though he had never felt a hat so perfectly made for him. His scalp longed for its return.

"Look, we don't have a lot of time," Howie said. "So, *Reader's Digest* version." Howie, as fast as he could, explained the entire formation of their dance-floor fellowship. He outlined their successes and their failures, their purpose in protecting certain special young men, always in the time of their Saturn Returns, bearing specific characteristics, whom the Great Goddess Mother put in their path. Howie then demarcated what was within their collective power and what was not. He explained how, at that very moment, Max was dying, and that their only hope was Ronnie, because, as fate would have it, he too had a magical propensity that made him a natural member of their dance coven, thus being the greatest (and only) luck that they'd had in years.

"That's the biggest load of bullshit I have ever heard." Ronnie pushed off the black cape Lenny had just pinned around his neck. "I am not at all like you."

"Just be still!" Lenny slapped Ronnie on his overly muscled trapezoids. "Coglione! You want to help your friend or not?"

"Yeah, of course." Ronnie swallowed his emotion. "Joe means everything to me."

"Then shut your friggin' mouth and let us get you ready."

"It's as simple as this, darling." Dory touched Ronnie's hand, causing an ever so slight jolt of electricity between them. "You're joining us is essential to the process of saving Joe."

"*Saving* Joe? Are you telling me you think Joe is your 'special person' that needs saving?" Ronnie asked, though he already knew. He had envisioned Joe's vulnerability all the way back when they first met in Philly. He, too, had instantly felt an inexplicable need to protect him.

"Yes," Howie began, "and tonight is his apotheosis. He either makes it through . . . or he's lost. Ever since his breakup with Fergal and the burning of the bar, Joe's lost all hope. That is the state the Great Darkness needs to do its worst. I know this won't make sense to you, but you need to trust us—trust that feeling you have in the pit of your stomach. Joe's on a precipice and has lost the desire to live. It's our responsibility to try and help him. We must!"

It was then that Ronnie first noticed the small tingling in his lower abdomen that pointed toward the truth in Howie's words. Yet he still didn't want to believe it. "How can you help Joe with all of this dressing-up crap?"

"For starters, sugar," Saint D'Norman said, "we're bringing out the big guns." He measured a pair of silver satin shorts against Ronnie's bubble butt. "Mm-hmm. Like a glove."

"I'm so confused," Ronnie groaned, putting a hand to his gurgling stomach.

"Just trust us!" Howie fumed. "Things don't always have to make sense to work! But we're not asking you to be different from the way you are. Just allow yourself to see the similarities and the connections. We *are* one!"

Ronnie, still grimacing, touched a rhinestone on the white cowboy hat, and similar to Dory's touch, he felt electricity shoot into his fingers. Images flashed across his brain—the day he'd met Joe; the embrace with Joe on the boardwalk the night they'd became friends again; Joe wandering in a haze through the Meat Rack, not caring if he lived or died. Joe snorting a toxic chemical just to free himself from his bottomless psychic pain. Joe wanting to disappear forever. Ronnie pulled his hand from the hat. "Okay. What exactly would I have to do?"

"First, you'd let us finish dressing you," Howie said. "Then we'd head to the Promethean to do a little ceremony—"

"You know." Lenny spun a panel of silver silk. "A little twirling, a little flagging."

"Fuck no!" Ronnie shouted. "I will not flag. I'll never get laid again!"

"Goddammit!" Dory slammed her bejeweled hand on a metal shelf, causing several urns of ashes to clank together. "You're our only hope! Do you want Joe to live or not?"

Ronnie stared at the four old eccentrics with their aging faces, ridiculous outfits, and pleading eyes begging him to join their humiliating, flagging dance ceremony that allegedly would "save" his best friend. He would become a person he'd never wanted to be. And yet, beneath that sickening feeling, there was a deeper one he struggled to identify. Excitement? Fear? Recognition? *Haven't you already had this nightmare?* And then... *What if this gayest of gay ceremonies really could save Joe? What if you didn't do it, and Joe was lost forever?*

"Okay. Do me up—but I'm not going to like it."

48.
The Gladiator Man

"Be wary of the comedown—it is like a dark veil on our joy. Be wary of the high—it deludes us into loving the liar. Seek the Great Balance between."
—*Disco Witch Manifesto #52*

"You found me," Joe said, his voice barely a whisper, his skin shivering at the very presence of the gorgeous god towering over him. His gaze slid across the Gladiator Man's huge, glistening pectoral muscles, then down to his tight athletic shorts that strained against his massive crotch pouch and mountainous ass, then back up to those terrifying eyes. *Are they black? Are they blue? Why does he want me this much? Why does he hate me this much?* Even if the Gladiator Man was just a byproduct of Scotty Black's burning powder, Joe didn't want to waste this moment. He threw his arms around the giant man's hairy tree trunk of a thigh. "Please, let's just do it!"

"What the hell?" the Gladiator Man barked in his sonorous, otherworldly voice. "Get off me!" He shook Joe from his leg as if Joe were an amorous Jack Russell terrier. "What are you on?"

"Almost everything," Joe mumbled. "It's my first time."

"Right," the Gladiator Man scoffed. "We all say that." He lifted Joe to his feet and inspected him. "Not bad, except the snot coming out your nose. Haven't I seen you before?"

"Yeah," Joe said, wiping his face on his own forearm. He wanted to ask if the Gladiator Man did, in fact, hate him or desire him. But instead, the words in his drug-filled head scrambled, and he simply shrugged and muttered, "So, you wanna fuck me?"

"You're a real charmer." The Gladiator Man grunted and offered his hand. "I'm Glen."

"Glen?" Joe smiled at how silly and wrong it sounded. "Gladiator Glen?"

"Huh?"

"Nothing. I'm Joe."

"Is that so?" Gladiator Glen's lips spread in a most chilling smile.

Joe felt another wave of weeping coming on, and at the same time his desire for the sexy but terrifying man intensified. *No, no,* he thought. *It's not desire you're feeling.* It had never been that. Gladiator Man was why he'd come to the island—not to fall in love, but as the vehicle for his escape. *He is your penance.*

"You can even fuck me raw," Joe said, still snuffling. He undid his fanny pack and yanked off his shorts, leaving both on the ground. "This is what the Meat Rack is for, right? I don't even care if you're a ghost with AIDS. Just fuck me, okay? Please."

Gladiator Glen's snigger was like slow bullets. "It doesn't matter if I'm a ghost with AIDS, hmm?" His eyes combed Joe's naked body. "Nice cock." He gestured for Joe to turn around. "Nice butt. You'll do." He lowered his mouth to Joe's and kissed him. The roughness of Gladiator Glen's beard; the turgidity of his lips; his hot, wet tongue exploring. His breath tasted old, sour. It didn't matter since this wasn't about pleasure anymore. His hand moved to Joe's ass.

"Ow!" Joe's teeth gritted as he felt Gladiator Glen's finger roughly penetrate him. "Lube please. I'll also need another bump of something. I need to stay brave."

"Brave? What for?" Gladiator Glen scoffed. "To get raw-dogged by a stranger you met in the Meat Rack?"

"Sure, and other things. I'm in the process of escaping. I don't know to where . . . but I need to be brave."

"Whatever toots your whistle, stud. I left my backpack in a spot farther back. It's a ten-minute walk from here, and a lot more private. I got lube there, and something else that might relax you—and make you brave at the same time." He lifted Joe's chin, forcing him to confront his now colorless eyes. "You really wanna do this, boy? You're not going to waste my time, are you?"

Joe looked up at the moon, which was nearing its full eclipse. It was far more orange than blood red. Another of the island's disappointments. "Lead the way."

49.

The Last Dance

"At the end of the world there will be suffering, there will be chaos, there will be death. But still, there will be dancing. Dancing is the only hope to overcome the Great Darkness. Dance, Disco Witches, dance!"
—Disco Witch Manifesto #157

THE DANCE FLOOR—9:46 PM

The five Disco Witches entered the Promethean covered in their black capes. As "Pump Up the Jam" by Technotronic blasted, they began strutting toward the center of the dance floor, their arms folded across the tops of their chests *I Dream of Jeannie* style. Silver silk flags dangled from their left hands while disco-ball rings sparkled on their right. Some men sniggered at the sight of Ronnie in his flowing robe, his head topped with the rhinestone-covered cowboy hat, his face, like the four others, painted with black, white, and silver semi-runic, semi-Mayan symbols, partially masking the crimson of his embarrassment.

"Woo-hoo, Ronnie! Didn't know drag was your thing!"

"Ronnie, what are you supposed to be? A Christmas tree cowgirl?"

"Isn't that Trey Winkle's ex–boy toy? Someone find Trey! He's gotta see this!"

Ruined, Ronnie thought. *I'm ruined.* His years of carefully curating his "hot blond jock" image lay crushed under the soles of his silver, sequined cowboy boots.

"Just ignore them!" Howie shouted over the music. "Our job is not about impressing a bunch of self-hating homo-assimilationists. We're here to help Joe! Hold your head up. You look fabulous!"

Ronnie looked at all the gawkers, seeing neither lust nor envy in their eyes. He had become a sexless, campy part of the scenery. Even his "sexy stud sneer" could barely be seen through his makeup. *What a fucked-up summer!*

Surrendering, Ronnie dropped the sneer, un-sucked his gut, and allowed his perpetually flexed biceps and pectorals to relax. *What's the point? No one will ever forget this.* And then it hit Ronnie—if his reputation was already ruined forever, then he no longer needed to prove himself to anybody. A wave of peaceful energy surged throughout his body while that strange prescient feeling in his stomach got even stronger than before. He looked ahead at Howie, Dory, Lenny, and Saint D'Norman. Their hats and rings shimmered in the disco lights, shoulders pulsing to the beat, strutting toward the center of the dance floor. A mischievous smile erupted across Ronnie's face. He too began to strut like the others, rooster-flapping his black cape with his elbows.

THE JUDY GARLAND MEMORIAL PATH—9:47 PM

The path along the dunes was more difficult to navigate than Fergal had hoped. He kept getting trapped by dead ends and frequently needed to empty sand from his boat shoes. If it weren't for the brambles and used condoms, he would have gone barefoot. Because of the darkness, he had to get extra close to any correctly shaped silhouette—whether alone or in the midst of an embrace—and whisper, "Joe? Is that you?" Awkward misunderstandings abounded, inspiring contrite apologies and the batting away of groping hands.

At one point, he was ninety-nine percent sure he saw Joe having sex with two men under a canopy of shrub pine. Enraged, he charged the ménage. "So this is where you've been!" he shouted, kicking sand. "Don't you know people are going nuts looking for you?"

The rutting triumvirate, horrified, unknotted their amorous tangle. "What the fuck?" the jock-strapped bottom cried out, throwing an empty bottle of poppers. "Back off, ya pervert!"

Fergal flushed with embarrassment. "Sorry, I just thought you were someone else."

"No wonder whoever you're looking for is avoiding you! You're pathetic!"

Apologizing again, Fergal continued his quest, exercising more caution in his inspections of coupling men. A few minutes later he spied a discarded fanny pack and a pair of glowing white shorts on the pathway. *Wasn't Joe wearing white shorts?* On closer inspection, he found the fanny pack contained Joe's wallet and empty drug vials. Then he saw the smear of blood on the front of the shorts. His insides exploded with a dozen feelings at once, the most prominent being panic and heartbreak. The emotion he longed to feel toward Joe, *hatred*, was nowhere to be found.

"Vince!" his hoarse voice cried out. "Vince! I found something! Vince!"

THE DANCE FLOOR—10:04 PM

While Ronnie waited anxiously for his next instructions, Elena ran up to Howie, looking frazzled.

"Elena, my dear," Howie said. "Thank you so much for helping!"

"So, what do you need me to do next?" Elena said. "I promise not to ask too many questions. Dory already warned me."

"Perfect!" Howie handed her a pair of very dark, vintage Chanel sunglasses caked in rhinestones. "Wear these. We don't want you to hurt your eyesight."

Elena, following her vow not to ask, shrugged and put on the sunglasses as Howie whispered more directions. A moment later she, the most ravishing bodyguard, began moving people away from the area where the five intended to dance.

Ronnie waved for Howie. "Can someone please give me some instruction here? Is there specific choreography? Do I chant something?"

"My dear," Howie said, "I can't go into great detail at the moment. Just do exactly what we do. When the twirling begins, keep your eyes focused on your nose. Never look out. Okay? First, we drink this." He pulled five capped tincture bottles from his fanny pack, handing one to each of the quorum. "This one with the *L* on it is for Lenny. It's alcohol free."

"What is it?" Ronnie asked.

"Just a little ancient preparation to help us with the twirl. It's fermented. Augments strength and focus."

"Cool." Ronnie grabbed for one, always happy to try out a new party cocktail.

"Places, please!" Howie shouted, directing Ronnie to stand exactly five feet from him, with Lenny five feet away on the other side. That's when Ronnie noticed the giant pentagram that had been drawn in chalk on the floor. Each of them was to stand at a pinnacle.

"DJ Susan always plays it right after this song," Howie said. "When I give the signal, then we all drink and"—his voice became almost inaudible as he mouthed the word—"*dance*."

Seconds later, layered under the end notes of Donna Summer's "On the Radio," the intro to Sylvester's "Do Ya Wanna Funk" began.

"There it is!" Howie lifted his tincture to the others. "The Call to Magic!" Ronnie remained silent as Dory, Saint D'Norman, and Lenny recited the words from memory: "Covenant of the Saint, Communion of the Sacred Dance Floor, Sisters of the Twirl. Knuf annaw uoy OD? Em htiw knuf annaw uoy OD? We do!"

The four swallowed their tinctures; Ronnie followed suit. It was nothing like he had ever tasted before—fizzy flavors of flowers, musk, cucumber, cinnamon . . . life and death.

"Is this where we start flagging?" Ronnie's viscera vibrated with a newfound energy.

"That's for later." Howie tucked his flag in his belt. "As I said, watch . . . then do!"

The four older Disco Witches folded their arms atop their chests again, closed their eyes, and bowed. Ronnie copied them. Then they slowly opened their arms and let their black robes fall to the floor. Beneath their robes they wore floor-length, weighted white skirts shimmering with mirror sequins. The entire dance club exploded with the light reflecting off their costumes. Their various blouses, more individuated, were equally bedazzling. The club erupted into cheers as the four kicked their black robes away from their feet, bowed one more time, focused their eyes on the tip of their noses and, one by one, began to slowly spin. After several turns, they raised their arms—their right slightly higher than the shoulder, palm up toward the ceiling, their left lower than the shoulder, palm facing down. As their turning escalated, their skirts opened up like shimmering upside-down calla lilies. Their heads were tilted slightly, as if they were listening for something, their eyelids so low they looked closed.

Ronnie watched, enthralled by the four sparkling disco dervishes. He took a deep breath, dropped his black robe and, as they had done, focused his half-closed eyes on the tip of his nose as he began to spin in place, right foot over the left. As he got into the rhythm of the spin, he lifted his right palm to the ceiling and turned his left palm to the floor, turning faster and faster. His skirt began to rise, escalating his spin as if it were being moved by some external force. *This is amazing!*

Wanting to see the others, he focused his opened eyes outward and promptly tumbled to the floor—just like Howie had warned. He jumped up, got his bearings, and began to turn again, this time keeping his eyes nearly closed, blurred, and aimed at his nose. As his speed increased, he began to feel small gusts of wind from the spinning skirts of his companions. He again lifted his arms: right palm facing up connects to the heavens; left palm facing down shoots energy to all of humanity. He could have sworn he felt sparks between himself and the others—like they were fomenting their own singular electrical weather system.

Sylvester's song seamlessly mixed into Donna Summer's "This Time I Know It's for Real." Ronnie heard the whoosh of the whirring strands of beads whipping off Howie's hat, and then the clacking and buzzing sounds of all their collective spangles. It was as if a host of swarming seraphim had alighted onto the dance floor. Was that a merging with the others he was feeling? Was this what melting into the fabric of time and space felt like? Was he letting go of every pretense of being a successful gay he had ever believed and becoming part of something greater?

Then it happened. He felt his feet lifting from the floor. It was only an inch or two, but it was really happening—that same feeling he'd had as a child in his dreams, flying over Northeast Philadelphia and nearby parts of Jersey. The only things holding his body and the others aloft were energy, air, and the music. They were five paper whirly toys set loose into the cosmos and at the same time lovingly held close by the Earth.

Free, Ronnie thought. *I'm finally free.*

A CLEARING IN THE MEAT RACK—10:13 PM

Gladiator Glen's hiding place was under a thicket of chokeberry. It was in a small hidden clearing several feet off the regular path on the bay side, near where the solid ground turned soft and became marsh. In the time it took to walk there, Joe's high had severely dissipated again. While his body still buzzed from the copious quantity of drugs he had ingested, soul-crushing lucidity was catching up to him, shining a sick green spotlight on all he had lost and all those he had hurt. Meanwhile, Gladiator Glen's attractiveness was flickering on and off like a broken lightbulb. One moment he'd be as handsome as when Joe had first seen him, and the next his muscles seemed to deflate, and his face grew jowly, his teeth twisting and yellowing. It was as if Gladiator Glen's otherworldly beauty was evaporating from his skin with each moment Joe's own high grew weaker. Not that any of that was giving Joe second thoughts about what he was there to do. He just needed to get totally fucked up again.

"How's it going?" Joe's voice twitched with desperation, annoyed at how long it was taking Gladiator Glen to move a slab of rotted plywood from atop his hiding spot and pull out a large leather backpack.

"All good here." Gladiator Glen said, digging through the backpack. "So, you got a boyfriend?" He said the words almost mockingly—like a very large schoolyard bully. His low sonorous voice sounded much higher and far more nasally than before.

"No," Joe said, trying to sneak a glimpse into the backpack. "You really have something that will get me high in there, or—"

"Look, I told you"—Gladiator Glen growled—"I'll take care of you, boy. So just shut up, okay? There's plenty of other faggots that wanna play with me."

Joe fell silent as fear filled his chest. If he had been totally sober, he might have left upon hearing Gladiator Glen use that awful word. If Joe were a better person, he might have said something. But that moment wasn't about being a better person. And fearing Gladiator Glen felt right. Joe knew he had never deserved someone good or caring like Fergal or Elliot. That was what he'd really wanted from the Gladiator Man, from that very first day—the capacity to not care, the inability to be hurt, the willingness to hurt others. The willingness to hurt Joe.

"Here we go." Gladiator Glen pulled a plastic bottle filled with a Windex-blue liquid.

Joe's heart sank. He wished it looked like one of the drugs he had taken earlier—a pill or a powder, something he knew had worked. Glen unscrewed the lid and offered Joe a sniff. It smelled like nail polish remover mixed with something sweet. "You sure that's a drug?"

"Oh, it's a drug, all right," Gladiator Glen said. "I get it from the health food store. It's called Blue Nitro and helps to build muscle when you sleep, but it also gets you high as a kite—makes you feel real sexy too. Just sip a little, though—it's powerful stuff."

Ignoring the warning, Joe lifted the bottle and took a huge gulp, as if the sheer quantity would burn away all the feelings.

"What the fuck are you doing?" Glen grabbed the Blue Nitro back. "That's too much!"

"I don't feel anything!" Joe protested, hoping for an immediate burn or whoosh.

"You did enough to get an elephant high." Gladiator Glen took a tiny sip from the bottle. "You're supposed to pace yourself. Now come here."

He wrapped his thick, hairy forearm around Joe's neck like he was about to choke him or throw him down. Joe had fantasized about this moment all summer, but then he started to compare Gladiator Glen's embrace with Fergal's. How Joe loved when Fergal held him from behind, his breath in his ear, and his lean, muscular forearms—strong but gentle, warm, devoid of hatred. Joe abruptly turned and thrust his mouth onto Gladiator Man's, sucking at his giant, sluglike tongue, wanting his saliva to wash away Fergal's memory. A deep, dense wooziness hit Joe all of sudden, and then another, deep, dark, sexy urge—just like Gladiator Glen had said. Once again, the man's body, face, and voice morphed into every dark fantasy Joe had ever had.

"You're feeling it now, right?" Gladiator Glen's low, rumbly voice asked in between thrusts of his tongue.

"I think so."

"Wanna get fucked now?"

"Yeah," Joe said numbly.

"You still want it raw?"

Questions, questions, questions. Enough with the questions. After all, Joe wasn't asking him questions, like whether Gladiator Glen had a boyfriend, or if he knew his HIV status, or if he was afraid of loving anyone for fear of them dying, or if he wanted to escape and/or die like Joe did. It didn't matter anyway. Joe groggily reached down to remove his shorts but realized he was already naked, that he had left his shorts and fanny pack somewhere back on the pathway and had walked through the Meat Rack completely bare-assed. *What would Vince have said? An embarrassment to Asylum Harbor. Oh, wait, that's right, Asylum Harbor burned down, just like everything else I loved.* He was annoyed by the whiny interference of his mind, but then a deeper and darker wave of the drug washed over his brain. His eyelids dozed as he wobbled.

"Easy there," Gladiator Glen said, pulling him up. "Better just bend over, and I'll take it from here."

Joe did as he was told and flopped over. His fingers touched the sand and the prickly holly leaves on the ground. His vision blurred. He turned his head, peering up at the orange glow of the blood moon, which was spinning, along with his eyes. Sickness began to bubble in his stomach as Gladiator Glen stepped behind him and started pulling at his cock. "Mmm," he said. "Nice little bubble butt you got." Joe looked back through the Blue Nitro fog. Gladiator Glen was indeed the man in all those photos in Howie and Lenny's attic. And now, close up, Joe saw just how much Gladiator Glen truly did hate him—and it was perfect.

"Jus' do it already," Joe demanded, slurring his words, his eyelids feeling heavy as bricks. "Fuck me!"

"Bossy little bitch bottom, aren't we?" Gladiator Glen barked. "Stay still!"

All those years of protecting himself and fearing for those he loved. *Finally* Joe would feel the ultimate pain and then, hopefully, oblivion. He felt Gladiator Glen's huge hands spread his cheeks, he felt the tip of the burning hot cock press against his hole, he felt the large hairy hand reach around his throat. And that would be the last thing he remembered before the blackness.

If Joe could have seen himself the very next moment, he would have seen his body jolt from pain as his insides heaved. He would have seen his face lose all color as his body fell to the ground. He would have seen the man whom he had called Gladiator Glen turn utterly mortal and cowardly. He would have seen the terrified man grab his things and run away through the beach forest as Joe lay in the prickly, dry holly leaves on the ground, mouth foaming, eyes rolling back inside his head, body convulsing violently. Above him, he would have seen and heard a large flock of mourning doves in the trees begin to scream.

THE DANCE FLOOR—10:16 PM

They had been twirling their heads off for over ten minutes. Sweat sloshed off Ronnie's body, encircling him in a mist. Twirling was physically harder than any workout he had ever experienced—though none made him feel so glorious. Then, just as DJ Susan was mixing the end of Janet Jackson's "Miss You Much" with Madonna's "Express Yourself," something snapped. All five Disco Witches faltered in their spin and tumbled to the floor. Howie managed to catch Dory, and Lenny stabilized poor Saint D'Norman, who was shaking.

"What the hell happened?" Ronnie stood up, huffing and puffing. "Did we help Joe?"

The others looked completely devastated and exhausted.

"It's not working," Lenny shouted over the music. "Something is missing."

"If we only had Max's spell book." Howie squeezed his fist to his head.

"We have to keep trying. We can do this!" Dory rubbed a sore elbow. "Let's get the flags out!"

Saint D'Norman, knees buckling, leaned his body full force onto Lenny. Elena ran to the group with bottles of water. Kneeling next to Saint D'Norman, she wiped sweat from his brow.

"Are you okay?" she asked.

"I'm fine, sweetie." He ignited his phosphorescent smile. "Just a little cramp."

"I'm not exactly sure what the hell you guys are up to—"—she nodded her head to Saint D'Norman—"but maybe it's time to take a rest?"

"No, no, baby doll." Saint D'Norman patted Elena's cheek. "This old gal is just thirsty. I'm having a good ol' time. Do me a favor, honey. Go run and get this fabulous ol' queen an orange juice and a banana? The potassium will help. There ya go."

Elena looked angrily at Howie and then ran off to do Saint D'Norman's bidding.

"Maybe she's right," Ronnie whispered to Howie. "Saint D'Norman doesn't look great, and Dory's pretty old. Maybe we could try flagging sitting down?"

Howie, with a wild look in his eye, grabbed Ronnie's arm aggressively.

"Okay!" Ronnie said. "Easy! It was just a suggestion!"

"That's not it!" Howie shouted. "I know what's missing!" He pulled a slip of paper and pen from his fanny pack and scribbled something. "Quick, Ronnie. Take this to the DJ. I need her to play this right away. Get back here as fast as possible. Hurry!"

With the note in hand, Ronnie yanked up his costume and jammed his way through the crowd. Not a single man tried to grope him, which helped with speed. He was nearing the stairs to the DJ booth when he felt something catch the hem of his dervish skirt.

"What the fuck?" He spun around to find Scotty Black holding a fist full of the white sequined cloth in his hands.

Scotty was flanked by Thursty and the shortest Graveyard Girl. All three were sucking on ethyl chloride rags, which hung from their mouths like gray lizard tongues. Scotty removed his rag. "Where the hell are you going?"

"Sorry, Scotty," Ronnie shouted. "Just asking the DJ to play a special request for Howie. We're kind of doing a little ceremony—"

"Not on my dime!" Scotty barked. "And I don't hire drag queens to bartend at the Promethean! Now, get out of that getup and get back to work, or you're fired."

"He's just having fun with the Picketty Ruff boys," Thursty said. "You know they always put the crowd in a great mood. It's good for business."

"My businesses don't need anyone's help!" Scotty snapped, then turned to the shorter Graveyard Girl. "If he's not back to work in five minutes—shirtless and looking like a man—I want all his shit emptied from his room immediately, and he can sleep on the beach, for all I care.

"Please, Scotty," Ronnie begged. "I just need thirty minutes more, okay?"

"You heard me!" Scotty turned to Thursty. "And you, whose side are you on? Remember who pays your check!"

"I just think—" Thursty began.

"Like I care what a bloated overgrown K queen thinks!" Scotty scoffed and shoved his ethyl rag into Thursty's hand. "Now, fill me up. And don't be stingy. I paid for it!"

Thursty began digging in his fanny pack for the can of ethyl chloride.

Ronnie felt an odd tapping inside his brain, almost like a mental Morse code from Howie and the others. *Time is running out.* If he didn't get that playlist up to the DJ quickly, there'd be no hope of helping Joe.

"Okay, then I quit." Ronnie snatched his skirt from Scotty's tight claw.

"You can't quit, since you're fired!" Scotty screamed, grabbing Ronnie by the neck of his shirt. "That means you're trespassing on my property." He turned to the Graveyard Girl. "Get security to get him out of here now!"

"What was that?" The Graveyard Girl cupped his ear, acting like he didn't hear. "Come again?"

"Oh, Scotty!" Thursty sang out, as if he were oblivious to the melee. "Try this! It's a whopper. I think you'll like it!"

Thursty shoved the ethyl rag to Scotty's nose and mouth and held it there until Scotty released Ronnie's collar. Then Scotty smiled, latched onto Thursty's arm, and sleepily crumpled to the floor.

"Girl down!" the short Graveyard Girl sang out.

"*Big* girl down!" Thursty devilishly smiled at Ronnie. "Oh dear," he deadpanned. "I sure hope I didn't accidentally go too heavy on the dose, knocking him out *for at least thirty minutes or more*. Now, honey, you go do whatever those glorious Disco Witches say! Enjoy the ride!"

Ronnie bolted up the steps to the DJ booth, his heart flopping into the mosh pit of his ribs. Discovering the booth locked, he banged on the door, screaming, "Please! Susan! Let me in! It's an emergency!"

When the door opened, DJ Susan looked furious. "What the hell?" She pulled the headphones from her ears.

"I'm sorry!" Ronnie shouted. "You need to play this right away! It's urgent! Please!"

He handed her the folded piece of paper. As soon as she saw Howie's note, the rage drained from her face. "You got it," she said. "Now get the fuck out of my booth!"

Ronnie flew back downstairs to the quorum. Saint D'Norman was just finishing a banana while patting Elena on the cheek. The other three looked like springs ready to be sprung. Howie pulled a rectangular object from his fanny pack. Ronnie recognized it instantly. It was the cassette case for Elliot's mixtape *Love Songs 1*.

"Quick!" Howie shouted. "Each of you touch this to your heart and then your forehead. Focus your thoughts on it!" They all did exactly as he instructed. "Perfect! It will center all the deities of light onto Joe's heart." He then motioned for Elena to come over and warned her not to look at the five while they danced. "Or you'll need reading glasses before you're forty. Okay?"

Elena nodded and returned to her bodyguard position.

"Everybody get back in place!" Howie's expression was trapped somewhere between terror and excitement. "We're going longer and harder, and we may see a lot of unusual things. Don't be afraid." He looked deeply into the eyes of all his comrades. "We've only tried a spell of this size once before. This time, we can't let it fail. Everyone ready?"

"Ready!" Dory said.

Saint D'Norman gave a languid thumbs-up and winked.

"Sure!" Lenny barked. "Let's fucking do this thing!"

"Okay." Howie looked to Ronnie. "Sweetie, this is where the flagging comes in. Okay?"

Ronnie nodded, pulling the silver silks from his belt. Howie then placed a shiny red flag in the center of the pentagram and took his place back at the pinnacle. As the thunder-laden, opening chords of the Weather Girls' "It's Raining Men" blasted through the sound system, Howie began to spin. This time he lifted Elliot's *Love Songs 1* jewel case to the sky in his right hand and the silver flag in the other.

Ronnie and the others began their twirl. When up to speed, they spun their flags into silver swirling balls of lightning. Once again Ronnie felt himself lift off the ground as the Weather Girls belted their anthem to sopping wet men. As he twirled faster, faces suddenly appeared in front of his blurred eyes. He didn't know to whom the faces belonged, yet they seemed deeply familiar. His brain filled with extraordinary memories of events he had never witnessed, places he had never visited, and old lovers he had never met, all boogying through the disco ball of his brain. He recalled throwing a brick through the window of the Stonewall. Making love to a Guatemalan man in the dunes of Herring Cove Beach in Provincetown, dancing on an East Village rooftop with a gorgeous Black opera singer in the 1940s, and on and on; a parade of lovers reaching back through time. Each memory, a mirrored fractal reflecting the mind of every twirling, magical being that ever was or would be.

Suddenly, in the center of the pentagram, right where Howie had left the red flag, a brown-skinned drag queen appeared, wearing a sparkly dress and blonde wig. Ronnie understood this was Max De Laguna, the high priest of the Disco Witches, in his religious drag-queen attire. His body, slim and translucent, flickered between flesh and vapor. The glowing specter picked up the red flag and looked at it quizzically.

"Max is transitioning," Howie called out.

"It's his time," Dory whispered.

Just as Max's spirit began to spin the red flag, an explosion of actual thunder struck the very foundation of the old wooden dance club. Howie's mind commanded them: "Don't stop twirling! There! Look at him! There's Joe!"

In his mind's eye, Ronnie saw his best friend, lying on the ground, his body jerking violently, his mouth foaming, his lungs unable to take in air. Joe was dying.

A CLEARING IN THE WOODS—10:19 PM

"There's no point, lad!" Vince gasped for air as he indicated for Fergal to slow his desperate trudge. "We've looked everywhere. Hopefully, he's back at home."

"He's not," Fergal said, clutching Joe's bloodstained white shorts and fanny pack. "I have a really bad feeling."

"Then we'll head back and contact the police—"

A huge flash of lightning lit up the sky. When Fergal looked up, there was a massive flock of mourning doves all flying northwest toward the Great South Bay.

"Isn't that that the queerest thing," Vince said, gawking at the sky. "Wasn't even a cloud a minute ago, and would you look at that." He pointed to a colossal cumulus cloud moving directly over the island, blocking the eclipsing moon. "Let's make a run for it—"

"No," Fergal yelled. "This way!" He left the path, heading in the same direction as the birds. Another bolt of lightning lit the sky.

"Feck it!" Vince cursed before taking off after Fergal. "I'm right behind you, lad!"

THE DANCE FLOOR OF THE CLUB—10:20 PM

While the five Disco Witches continued to twirl and flag, Max's spirit swooped through the Promethean's ceiling. Thunder clapped. Lighting cracked. Wind slammed the balcony windows open and closed.

"What is happening?" Ronnie shouted.

"It's working!" Howie cried out.

"I'm weakening," Saint D'Norman warned.

"Keep twirling!" Dory pleaded.

"We're almost there!" Lenny hollered.

Sweat splashed halos around their bodies as they levitated what Ronnie believed to be nearly three inches above the dance floor. Most people in the club assumed the five had slipped on even taller platform shoes or had stepped onto a box. Others, who were dancing closer, would later credit the phenomenon to their party drugs and what a singular night of dancing it had been. Elena, obeying Howie's warning, did not look back, but would later speak of the energy in the room and the bewildered and ecstatic expressions of the onlookers' faces—those who, unbeknownst to her, were mesmerized by the blur of the crazed Disco Witches twirling and flagging between the worlds of the living and the dead. No one saw the bulge of their crossed eyes behind their lowered lids. No one saw their bluish flush under the disco lights. No one saw how close they all were to their own demise. If they only could spin their magic a little longer. They had the wind, they had the lightning. All they needed was the rain.

"Please!" Howie begged. "Please, Great Goddess Mother, help us!"

OFF THE PATH NEAR THE GREAT SOUTH BAY—10:21 PM

Now. Right now. The present. Tense.
What's happening? You'll see.
I'm confused. Just wait.

Joe floats over his convulsing body. *Am I dead? I must be dead. I saw an interview once with someone who claimed they had died and gone to heaven. It was on* Phil Donahue—*or was it* Oprah? *But I don't feel dead. It must be a dream. Is it a dream?*

A thought pops into Joe's brain: *Feeling brave doesn't make you want to escape the world. Bravery makes you want to stay.* A sense of absolute bliss like he has never known fills his heart. He looks around and notices the Meat Rack looks different—foggy yet sparkly, like the mist is made of diamonds. Gladiator Glen is gone. *Thank the goddess.* Hovering above the clearing, at the top of the birch tree are five twirling silvery balls of fire.

"Where am I?" Joe calls out, but there is no response. "Hello?"

"Hello," a voice whispers.

Joe turns and standing over him is Fergal, face illuminated by the five twirling balls of fire. Joe gazes up into his blue-blue eyes, which are now fluctuating in tone, one moment Frostie Blue Cream soda, another moment indigo hydrangeas and then a shade of blue Joe has never seen before. And now he knows what he needs to know, what he has always known.

"You still love me," Joe states matter-of-factly, surprising himself with his own brazenness. "There's still a chance."

After lifting Joe to standing, the vision of Fergal flies up, merging into the five balls of fire that spin into a vortex of swirling disco lights. Joe, still earthbound, feels the kiss of each dapple of light, like a promise.

There is a tap on his shoulder, and he turns, hoping it is Fergal. Instead, it's Elliot, his late ex-lover standing before him as Joe had known him when they first met, so beautiful and wise with his green eyes, sandy brown hair, and enraptured smile.

"Elliot!" Joe throws his arms around him and is about to beg forgiveness for not having been a better partner, for not having been able to handle Elliot's illness better, for not being brave when he needed to be brave.

"Don't," Elliot says before Joe can speak. Then, without saying a word, he relays a message to Joe's heart, the contents of which are what Joe has always needed to know. Then Elliot places something in Joe's hand—it's the lost mixtape, *Love Songs 1*. He embraces Joe in the warmest, deepest hug before rising up, like Fergal, into the fiery disco light vortex and disappearing.

Joe, feeling the deepest, most satisfying warmth in his chest, yells to the balls of light, "Take me too!"

Inside the belly of the celestial flaming vortex, he sees the faces of Howie, Lenny, Dory, Saint D'Norman, and Ronnie; Max is there too, dressed in drag like in the photo in Howie's room.

"You're brave now, Joselito," Max whispers down to him. "You're brave now. What would you really do with your life if you were truly brave?"

Visions of all he would do suddenly fill Joe's brain with an astounding clarity. There is no plan to escape, there is no plan to return to Philly or to die a lonely and sad death because of regret and a broken heart. He is overwhelmed by a sense that he has seen both the worst that life has to offer and the absolute best—and he is no longer afraid. The universe opens up before him with all the possibilities of joy, meaningful sorrow, and the knowledge that he can handle anything. His head and heart fill with a million longings, loves, and dreams. Fear of losing, his forever bedfellow, is nowhere in sight. All the imprisoning guilt and darkness missing from his heart cause him to feel so unbelievably light, like floating dandelion seeds lifting up into the swarming, twirling, disco-ball conflagration above his head. He flies upward.

"Nope," Max says, laughing. "Not yet, papacito."

Joe feels a force pushing him back down to the earth.

"You look thirsty," Howie says. "Would you like a drink?"

"Not now!" Joe yells, laughing. "I've never been this happy! I feel like I could fly to the sun! Please tell me this isn't a dream! Look, Elliot found the mixtape!"

"He's had enough now," Dory says.

"I hope we didn't go overboard," Saint D'Norman adds. "He's definitely thirsty."

"Have some water, Joe!" Lenny tips a long-nosed watering can over Joe's head.

Joe tilts his head up and opens his mouth wide. The water from Lenny's can begins pouring into his mouth. It's sweet and delicious. But then Lenny tilts the can more and the sweet water gushes down Joe's gullet. He tries to close his mouth and pull away, but he can't. He drops the mixtape. He's drowning. *Why would they drown you when you just found out how to be happy?*

OFF THE PATH NEAR THE GREAT SOUTH BAY—10:22 PM

The next crack of lightning sliced open the belly of the cumulus cloud, releasing the downpour onto the Meat Rack. Fergal saw the flock of mourning doves alight on the top of a tall birch tree. Leaping off the regular path, he bulldozed straight through the bayberry and holly. The spiked leaves and thorns tore at his skin. Between thunder claps he heard Joe's choking, causing him to run so fast it was as if he were doing the butterfly stroke through the gushing rain, arms slapping at branches, legs barely touching the ground, desperation crushing his lungs. Finally, there Joe was, lying on the ground, naked, wet, shivering, and coughing in a puddle of his own sick. *But he's alive.*

"Joe!" Fergal dropped to his knees, pulled his wet T-shirt from his own back, and used it as a blanket over Joe's naked chest as he helped him back into his white shorts. When Joe stopped coughing, he looked at Fergal and smiled, not with any sort of contrition, but like he was happier than he had ever been. "What the fuck happened to you?" Fergal shouted, shaking Joe by the shoulders. "Everyone's been crazed looking for you! I thought you were dead!"

Joe pointed up at Fergal's face and laughed. "Would you look at that?"

"Why are you laughing?" Fergal's fists punched his own legs. "You are the most selfish piece of—"

"Sorry!" Joe blurted. "It's just your eyelashes. They are so thick and beautiful and have these little waterfalls falling off them." He squinched his face, failing to suppress another happy giggle. "I'm so sorry. Seriously, I am."

"Well, you should be!" Fergal raged. "Why are you still smiling?"

At that very moment Vince showed up, having fallen way behind Fergal. His face was Pepto Bismol pink from the effort, and he was shivering from the cold rain.

"Well, there you are, lad," Vince said to Joe, relief palpable in his voice. "You had us all mad with worry. For a minute I swore I saw young Fergal here lift off the ground and swim through that storm to get to you. Anyway, where have you been?"

"I got pretty sick on some stupid party drugs," Joe said, as if it might be a slightly humorous anecdote. "I also maybe died a little. But I'm not sure."

Fergal glared at Joe, then clenched his fists and stormed over to the edge of the small clearing. Rivulets of raindrops slid down his astoundingly beautiful, shirtless back.

"I guess I better stick to beer from now on, huh?" Joe chuckled nervously. "Hey, I'm sorry, but . . ." He let his voice trail off, seemingly stuck on what to say next.

Fergal, without looking back, snorted with derision. Then he picked up an old piece of rotted wood and hurled it into the Great South Bay. For almost a full minute the three men stood speechless in the rain, Joe looking at Fergal's back, Vince looking awkwardly at the two men. The downpour suddenly slowed to a mere drizzle while jelly bean–size drops still plopped down from the forest canopy.

"Maybe I should leave you two alone for a bit," Vince said. He pointed to the sky. "Would you look at that? Clear skies with a moon, full and white like a boiled potato. You'd never know there had been an eclipse, nor a flash storm. What a thing!" He looked for a response from the men, but none came. "Well, despite it all, you're looking well, Joseph. I'll see you back in the harbor, I hope. Try not to get into any more trouble, will ya?"

"Sorry about everything, Vince," Joe said.

"That's all right, lad. We all have our bad nights. I'll go and tell the others the good news." He crossed to Fergal and patted him on his back. "Ya did well, son."

For a long time neither Joe nor Fergal spoke. The wind blew through the wet trees. The flock of birds flew off one by one. Joe's joyful heart quieted as he finally absorbed the level of Fergal's distress. *How to make him understand?*

"Would you mind walking with me to the beach?" Joe finally asked Fergal. "The mosquitos are killing me here. I need to tell you something important—about what happened. But I think I want to tell you by the ocean. Also, it will give me a chance to clean myself up."

Fergal grunted and, without even looking back at Joe, began to walk. By the time Joe got to his feet, he was twenty paces behind. After ten minutes of walking, he found Fergal already sitting at the ocean's bubbling edge, fiddling with a twig of driftwood. Joe first washed Fergal's shirt of the mucky sick, then dove into the frothy waves and scrubbed himself clean, gargling with the saltwater. When he was done, he handed Fergal his wet shirt back and sat a foot away. He really wished to take Fergal into his arms and warm him with the heat of his newfound bravery. But the ferryman still wouldn't look at him.

"So, what happened?" Fergal finally asked, his voice low and cold.

"Well, I was kind of a mess, so I got really fucked up on this trail-mix drug Scotty Black gave me. Made me all hyped up and crazed. Then I met the Gladiator Man... er... this guy, and he had this Blue Nitro stuff—"

"Who or what is a Gladiator Man?" Fergal wrenched the wet T-shirt between his fists, wringing the water into the sand in front of him. "You dating him now?"

"God, no." Joe sniffed. "He was a total douchebag. Just some homophobic muscle head. At one point I thought he was hot. But I'm different now." He looked at Fergal, hoping he'd look back, but he didn't. "That's the thing. Something crazy happened to me back there. I know no one is going to believe me, but I have to tell someone, and I want it to be you."

"Why?" Fergal finally turned to look at Joe. His eyes were like blazing blue switchblades. "We're *not* friends, Joe."

Fergal's words would have stung if it wasn't for the ring of brilliant light encircling Joe's heart. "I know I hurt you," he said, "and I don't expect you to forgive me, but can I tell you?"

"Go ahead."

And Joe told him everything that had happened that night. He told him about his plan to escape the island without telling anyone, about doing all the drugs he could find and not caring if he lived or died. He told him of going with Gladiator Glen because the man seemed to hate Joe as much as he hated himself. And then Joe told Fergal about the dream—if it was a dream. He told him how he thought he might have died, but it didn't matter, because either way he felt something miraculous had happened. He told him about seeing Elliot and the others, and how he had come to a new understanding about what had happened and could finally forgive himself.

He considered explaining how he also saw the end of time and how the ability to feel peace, joy, and bravery had been instilled permanently in his heart, but he was wise enough to know that no one, not even Fergal, would fully comprehend the momentous shift in consciousness he had experienced. Even he didn't understand it, but he knew it was true.

So, instead, Joe jumped to the result, saying how he no longer wanted to escape or die and how he was excited by life again and was less fearful of the future, and planning to start pursuing his dream of going to med school as soon as he left the island. Then he explained how the rain saved him by making him choke and vomit out all the Blue Nitro. He watched Fergal's face for signals—belief, disbelief—but there were none.

"So why are you telling me all this?" Fergal finally said.

Joe took a deep breath and dug his feet into the sand. "Because, well, I'm in love with you, Fergal. I think I have been from that first moment I saw you swimming in the ocean like a wild, insane dolphin with those weird webbed feet. I know you may not feel the same way right now, or like you did in my dream, but if there is anything like love for me left inside you—and I know there is, so you don't have to lie—I'm asking you to give me another chance. I think we can make each other happy—or happy enough . . . but in a really deep and meaningful way."

Fergal's arms remained locked around his hairy knees while his blue-blue eyes fixed themselves on the farthest edge of the sea. He finally turned to Joe with a seriousness that prepared Joe for the worst—and still Joe wasn't afraid, because he knew, with his new self, he could handle anything. "You hurt me so bad, Joe."

"I know, and I'm sorry. It's a lot for me to ask you to trust me. I get that. And I guess there's always a chance we'll hurt each other again. But I'm willing to risk it if you are. I'll try my best, but all I ask is that I'm allowed to talk about it with you if I get afraid again—that we talk about everything. That we do this thing together."

Fergal turned toward Joe, his lips parted like he wanted to say something, but also like he was afraid to say it. Joe knew what he was thinking because he was thinking it too; whatever words came out of Fergal's mouth at that moment would change everything for them forever. For several more agonizing seconds they sat there, staring at each other in suspended animation, Fergal about to say something, Joe waiting and breathing into what he had learned in the dream. *Whatever happens, it's just the path. I can handle anything.*

Suddenly, as if the ocean could no longer bear the suspense, a heavy and unexpected wave leaped up over them, bowling them over into each other's arms and sending them tumbling into the shallow surf. When they stopped laughing, their eyes met.

"Okay," Fergal said. "I'm in." He leaned over and kissed Joe's wet lips. As the kiss deepened, they fell back, Fergal on top of Joe, hearts pounding, tongues wrestling, hands grasping, pelvises thrusting.

"Let's move up the beach a little," Fergal said, standing up and offering his hand to Joe. "I don't want you to drown while I'm kissing you."

As they settled on a spot about ten feet above the surf line, Joe gave a little eyebrow wiggle. "You wouldn't have any of those condoms on you, would ya?"

Fergal fished into the soaked back pocket of his board shorts, first pulling out a small bottle of lube and then a string of three condom packets, each decorated with an ancient helmet. "I hope you prefer Trojans over Gladiators."

"I do." Joe laughed. "I really do. But let me clean some of the sand out of my . . . you know, *the important spots*."

Joe awkwardly pulled his sandy, drenched white shorts off past his aching erection and then swam to a deeper spot to get cleaned up. Fergal watched and smiled until Joe stumbled back onto the beach. There appeared to be no diminishment in excitement for either man.

"My turn," Fergal said as he laid out his wet T-shirt on the softer, dryer part of the sand. "Meanwhile you can lie down here." He started for the water, and just as he was nearing the line of bigger waves, he called out, "On your stomach please!"

Hearing those words made Joe's entire body vibrate with excitement. He tried to act calm as he laid himself down belly first, butt up to the stars, easing his too-hard erection to the side for comfort. Then, craning his neck and shoulders, he watched Fergal yank down his board shorts, his perfect cock snapping to attention, its unhooded tip yowling at the moon. Smiling back at Joe, he did one of his almost acrobatic dives under a wave, disappearing for a disturbingly long time and then joyously rocketing out of the water, just like he had done that first morning Joe saw him on the beach. Joe inhaled and exhaled slowly, trying to calm his throbbing heart, trying to comprehend everything the dream had taught him and how everything that had happened in his life had led him to this exact moment, about to make love to Fergal. *This is right, this is good, this is how it should be.*

Fergal, having finished washing up, trudged up onto the beach. For a moment he simply stood there in the surf, completely naked and dripping, hairy and hard in all the right places, the ocean crashing behind him, the warm wind blowing across his long, lean body; the white moons of his muscular, untanned butt cheeks the brightest thing on the beach. The way Fergal was looking out over the water reminded Joe of someone who was praying. After a moment he turned and slowly walked up to where Joe was lying on his stomach and then fell to his knees and, like he had done that night in the attic, spread Joe's ass cheeks and began using his mouth, tongue, fingers—and whatever other mysterious appendage might be available to him—to make Joe's body swoon and shiver.

Like before, Joe's mind dove beneath the surface of Fergal's blue-blue sea, only deeper than before. With each magical maneuver of Fergal's mouth on Joe's body, sea creatures began floating across Joe's brain: pods of smiling dolphins and whales; undulating manta rays; schools of glittering fish; seahorses the size of Labradors; and finally, as he neared the ocean floor, a small group of stunning creatures, half-human, half-fish, with muscular bodies, long flowing hair, and iridescent green and blue fishtails. They nodded knowingly at Joe, as if they were the only beings that could truly understand the depth of what he was feeling at that moment.

After what could have been fifteen minutes or an hour (he had lost track of time), Joe came out of the trance as Fergal stopped what he was doing and whispered, "Flip over. I need to look at that face."

Joe complied as Fergal tore open one of the condom packets and stretched the latex sheath over his cock, rubbing it with a thick layer of lube. He then lifted Joe's muscular legs so that his ankles rested on Fergal's shoulders. Joe's body shook from the slight chill in the air, but more from the anticipation.

"You all good?" Fergal asked.

"So good," Joe said, meaning it. "I've never wanted something more."

Fergal took a deep, smiling breath and pressed the tip of his cock inside Joe. Joe winced a little at the pleasurable pain of it. Fergal's raised eyebrows signaled for Joe to let him know how he was doing. Joe nodded encouragingly. He wanted more. Fergal went a little deeper, then a little more, but before it went any further, Fergal stopped, which made Joe's heart jump in a momentary panic.

"Is something wrong?" Joe asked.

"Just making a little adjustment I think you'll like." Fergal lowered one of Joe's legs to the ground, while keeping the other on his shoulder. This allowed Fergal to lean his long torso over Joe so he could both warm him and press his mouth to his. Joe moaned in pure gratitude, both for the warmth and for how well Fergal already understood him. Fergal slowly moved deeper until, with an extra deep kiss, Joe's insides opened and closed around Fergal, embracing him as if he was always meant to be there.

Lifting his lips only slightly from Joe's, Fergal whispered, "Your dream didn't lie. I love you, Joe."

"I know," Joe whispered back. "I always knew."

They fell back into their kiss, which grew deeper and wetter, as if all the Earth's oceans were flowing back and forth between their bodies, connecting them completely, fully, fearlessly.

They made love for hours until, utterly spent, they lay pressed against each other at the edge of the surf, the sea's frothy tongue tickling their toes. Joe's head made a pillow of Fergal's bicep while one leg flopped over Fergal's thigh to keep him warm. They breathed in the scent of each other's sticky, sweaty flesh, felt the tickle of each other's body hair, swallowed the sweet and salty spit from each other's mouth. The Atlantic roared its approval, the wind whispered words of thanks, the screeches of the seagulls called out hallelujahs. And Joe knew, down to his bones, that if anything tried to tear them apart again, be it Gladiator, disease, or self-doubt, it wouldn't stand a chance.

THE BALCONY OF THE PROMETHEAN—5:43 AM
Monday morning

Beethoven's Fifth poured from the Promethean sound system—DJ Mike's closing signature. It had been hours since the sudden storm had ended. The quorum lay on the club's outdoor balcony, skirtless and completely spent. The gold of divine guidance and wisdom encircled all of them with white flashes of light—a perfect connection to the cosmos. The Great Balance had begun to be restored.

"So, we're one hundred percent certain?" Ronnie asked. "Joe is gonna be all right?"

"We've told you a dozen times already." Howie took Ronnie's hand. "He's better than all right. He and Fergal are now up in the attic, all curled up in each other's arms."

"Thank the Great Goddess Mother," Ronnie said, which still felt strange. Who exactly the Great Goddess Mother was, he still wasn't quite sure, but he knew she had something to do with what had happened on the dance floor and in helping Joe home safely.

"You're one of us now, Ronnie," Dory said. "What do you think?"

He closed his eyes to tap into that same connected brain thing he had experienced earlier. It took him almost a minute to find the link, but when he did, he once again felt that whoosh of his mind quintupling in its expanse of what it could perceive. "This shit's crazy." He laughed before disconnecting from the others so he could think and speak as one individuated being. "How long does this disco witch thing take to get used to?"

"Oh, a little while." Howie's eyes suddenly lit up. "Wait! Listen!"

Inside the club, the DJ was transitioning from Beethoven into Natalie Cole's "Miss You Like Crazy," reminding the stragglers who hadn't gotten his classical clue that the club was closing.

"The DJ chose that song for Max," Howie said, and then sighed. "I say we all head home, take a few hours' nap, and then catch the twelve fifteen ferry. We'll need to help Heshy with memorial arrangements in the city."

"Max's ashes can finally be placed in the reliquary," Lenny said.

"Of course," Howie confirmed. "But maybe only a third. The rest I think we should spread in P-town and the Ramble in Central Park. Oh, and at least a thimble for the base of the Guatemalan volcano where he was born. He'd get bored being in one place."

All five nodded, allowing Natalie Cole to sing the sad song of their hearts. The first ferry of Monday morning blew its horn announcing its arrival. Then, as if the five Disco Witches were of one mind, they leaned back against the wooden bench, sighed, and gazed up to watch the moon do her walk of shame across the early morning sky.

She's beautiful.
She is.
I wonder where she left her crimson cape?
Somewhere in the Meat Rack, no doubt.
Does she even remember what she did last night?
Oh, most certainly. But she won't tell anyone. It will be our secret.

Epilogue

"Disco Witches find magic everywhere."
—*Disco Witch Manifesto #1*

Labor Day weekend of 1989 was the fourth high holy day of Howie's summer calendar. For the seasonal renters it meant packing up, settling bills, and a final clawing for any scrap of romance in which to wrap themselves during the long, cold New York City winter. A few would succeed. Most wouldn't. Some of the disappointed would vow to never return. But then, after a bitter winter of overly clothed mortals, amnesia would set in. By January the same failed romantics would be desperately seeking a "full share" and vowing to be "really ready this time" to have their perfect summer of love.

On his final day on Fire Island, Joe was still living in the glow of bravery and a newfound outlook on life. The effective dream's epiphanies clung to him like glorious armor. He no longer feared having his heart broken again. It was merely another part of life, framing what was important and pointing one toward ways to grow. And while the AIDS epidemic was never far from his mind, he continued to explore the depths of his love for Fergal. Their conversations grew more passionate, inspiring, and relentless by the day. They'd spend long hours cuddled in bed after making love, speaking of their dreams, their fears, and their intentions to be warriors together in whatever fight the universe laid before them.

These were just some of the thoughts Joe was having as he stood in line for the four thirty PM ferry back to Sayville. It had been hard saying goodbye to Elena, who had left the island the week before. She was planning on applying to law school, and wanted to get settled in a recovery program near where she lived in Manhattan. Cleigh went with her for support. Elena had finally told Dory of her HIV status. Though Dory was distraught, she confessed she had suspected as much, and was already preparing to join Elena's fight for improving women's access to experimental HIV medications. Elena told Joe she didn't know whether she and Cleigh would end up in a relationship after she got a year sober. But then, in her very next breath, she repeated what Dory always told her: "If you're doing life right, you should allow it to surprise you."

"It looks like the exodus from gay Saigon!" Lenny shouted, trudging toward Joe, carrying a picnic basket big enough for ten. "I brought some snacks for your road trip!"

"Holy heck!" Joe gave a teasing weightlifter's grunt as he lifted the basket. "You do know they serve food on the plane to Honolulu, right?"

"Airplane food is garbage," Lenny snarled. "You'll also need to keep your figure in Waikiki if you wanna make good tips. This oughta hold you for the first two days at least. I included some cured meats that should last at least until you locate a good Italian deli."

Joe swallowed the emotional lump clogging his throat. "Thanks, Lenny."

"Basta!" Lenny took a deep tremulous breath. "Now don't get me started. Where's Fergal?"

"I'm meeting him on the ferry. He wanted to work this last crossing with the—"

"Hey! Hey!" Howie shouted, trotting across the dock, dressed in his bathrobe and baseball cap. Not far behind followed Vince, Dory, and Ronnie. Instead of his usual jock outfit, Ronnie wore a loose-fitting, tie-dyed hippie shirt with a beaded and feathered necklace.

"Sorry, we're late," Dory said, catching her breath. "These lovely gentlemen had to help me with a last-minute errand."

"Lenny!" Howie pointed at the picnic basket. "You told me you were gonna just pack a couple of sandwiches."

"They're flying all the way to the other side of the world. You want they should eat each other? And not in the good way?"

Dory kissed Joe on the cheek. "Thank you for what you did for our bar. You are a wonderful bartender and will be a marvelous doctor one day." She slipped a fat envelope into his hand. "This will get you started in Honolulu. I'm also setting up a tuition fund for both of you."

"Oh, Dory, no," Joe said. "We can't—"

"You don't want to offend her," Howie warned with a raised eyebrow. "Just take it."

Joe stuck the envelope in his duffel and hugged Dory very tight. She slid her hand atop his head, looked deeply into his eyes, and blessed him.

"Now I need to get back to the house," she said. "Elena is calling me at five from her new place, and I don't want to miss the call." She turned to those who would be remaining. "Saint D'Norman and I shall see you three for the equinox ceremony on the twenty-second, yes?"

Howie and Lenny nodded their heads in that strange knowing way of theirs. Ronnie copied them awkwardly. Talk about life being surprising—Ronnie, the man who'd vowed never to be "one of those freaks who lived year-round on Fire Island," was indeed planning to live year-round on Fire Island with Vince, a decidedly non-rich, non-famous boyfriend. Best of all, Ronnie appeared more content than Joe had ever seen him.

"You guys are gonna take care of my buddy Ronnie, right?"

"We'll do our best," Howie said, pulling Joe into his huge arms and hugging him so his face was crushed into the plush of the maroon bathrobe.

"I'm so, so glad you spent time with us," Howie whispered over Joe's head. "I have something for you too." He fished into his fanny pack and pulled out Elliot's mixtape *Love Songs 1*, complete with case and cassette.

Joe momentarily couldn't breathe. "You found it?"

"No," Howie said. "I *recreated* it. We had every song in our collection already. I just followed Elliot's beautiful handwritten list. You can share it with Fergal on the drive across."

"Thanks, Howie." Joe stared at the newly reconstructed mixtape in his hand. Saying goodbye to the others was hard enough. But saying goodbye to Howie without turning into a mess seemed impossible, so Joe just smiled and nodded.

"I need to tell you something." Howie sniffled and lowered his voice. "It's not always gonna be smooth sailing. You know that, right? Just remember that life goes fast. That doesn't mean it's not wonderful. So don't waste too much time worrying about the ending. I'm not a mystic—that was Max's job, and a little bit of Saint D'Norman's. But like I once told you, not everyone who has you-know-what right now will die from it. I truly believe that. With your help we *will* triumph over the Great Darkness. 'An army of lovers cannot fail.' Ronnie knows what I'm talking about, don't you?"

Ronnie smiled and held Vince's hand tighter. The ferry horn blasted.

"Now you better not miss your boat," Howie said. "That handsome ferryman of yours is ready to take you away."

Joe pulled both Howie and Lenny into his arms and hugged them tightly. Their combined scent of leather, patchouli oil, and cleaning chemicals filled Joe's nose and swirled around his heart. "Thanks for the mixtape," he whispered. "Thanks for saving my ass, and thanks for . . ." He could say no more.

Howie wiped his own wet face on the sleeve of his bathrobe. Then he herded Lenny and Vince ten feet away to give Joe and Ronnie a moment to themselves. At first, the two best friends stood facing each other awkwardly.

"I can't believe you're staying, and I'm leaving," Joe said.

"Can't second-guess the Great Goddess Mother." Ronnie winked.

"I also can't believe you just said that." Joe's tear ducts unleashed. "I love you, my big brother."

"I love you, my little brother. You'll be thirty years old next time I see you."

"At least." Joe snuffled and smiled. After using his T-shirt hem like a handkerchief, he said, "And it's only another twenty-nine years until my next Saturn Returns, so . . ."

The ferry blasted its horn again. The rush of other straggling passengers pushed past Joe and Ronnie, to avoid missing the soon-to-be-removed gangplank.

Joe picked up his duffel. "Maybe you can come visit us in Honolulu this winter when it's quiet. Fergal will be in school full time, but I'll just be taking organic chem, bartending, and studying for the MCATs, so I'll have time to hang out."

"I'd love to, but not this winter." Ronnie cracked his knuckles nervously. "We got big plans for the new Asylum Harbor now that Scotty gave us a new deal on the space."

"I still can't believe he agreed to it," Joe said, shaking his head.

"Yeah." Ronnie nodded with a mysterious wink. "You never know what'll change people's minds. Anyway, it's gonna be a lot more work being a co-owner and rebuilding, so I'll need to stick pretty close for a bit."

"Yeah, well, sometime, then," Joe said.

"Yeah, for sure," Ronnie answered, his voice growing froggy. "Do you remember everything I taught you about being a good gay?"

Joe laughed as they walked together slowly to the gate. "Of course," he said.

"Good. Then forget it." Ronnie's lower lip quivered. "It was bullshit. But remember the stuff I taught you to about how to dress and work out. That advice was solid."

They hugged like two straight boys after a game of touch football, which was both awkward and unsatisfying. While they knew they'd see each other again, they also were aware that this period of friendship neither would nor could ever be repeated.

"Hey, Joe!" Fergal called from the edge of the ferry door. "You coming or what? We got a Pan Am 747 waiting for us at JFK!"

Joe and Ronnie smiled sadly, then simultaneously threw their arms around each other—this time like the long-lost brothers they truly were. It was Ronnie who finally broke the embrace and wordlessly (for he couldn't speak) shoved Joe through the gate.

"Goodbye, you feckin' eejit!" Vince called out. "You best learn how to make a decent Blue Hawaiian! And don't bring shame on the bartender who taught ya everything!"

"Don't worry!" Joe slapped the side of his duffel bag. "I stole your *Mr. Boston*!"

Joe ran to Fergal, and without a second thought, they fell into a shameless passionate kiss. All who saw, passengers and crew members alike, broke out into cheers, as if they had been waiting for that moment all summer. Seconds later, the gangplank was pulled up, the moorings untied, the ferry door slid shut, and the engine revved.

As he watched the passengers on the upper deck wave to those left behind, Howie could already feel the pull of the impending autumn equinox. They had made it through another summer. Magic had happened, spells had been cast, love and progress toward the Great Balance achieved once more. The Great Goddess Mother had once again bestowed her blessings. They'd saved Joe's life. He would go on to do great things.

As the ferry chugged its way past the hook, then into deeper water, it whisked the saltwater into a long, foamy trail, like some glorious Ziegfeld girl strutting across the Great South Bay.

What next summer would bring was really anyone's guess.

Author's Note

While *Disco Witches of Fire Island* is a work of fiction, it's partially inspired by my own life events during the early years of the AIDS crisis in America, when I fell in love for the first time with a wonderful man and lost him to the virus. More specifically, the novel is about the aftermath of that devastating heartbreak and the summer I spent working as a bartender in Fire Island Pines, a queer community on a barrier island off the coast of New York's Long Island. It was the early '90s, still at the height of the epidemic. During that summer I moved into the attic of a house on Picketty Ruff, which was inhabited by three older gay men who had come of age in a time before AIDS. They shared their stories with me, often dressed in what I thought were outlandish costumes, while '70s disco music played all day and night from their living room stereo system and they cooked, um, let's just say "interesting substances" on their stovetop. I had always wanted to write something about that summer and about the challenge of trying to find love when the world was on fire and all seemed hopeless. The result was this novel. I thank you for reading it and wish you many magical dances on your journey.

Discussion Questions

1. *Disco Witches of Fire Island* is set in 1989 Fire Island during the height of the HIV/AIDS crisis. What did you know about the AIDS epidemic before you read this book? What didn't you know? Did anything surprise you?

2. The novel is a mix of realistic romance with magic and subtle witchcraft. What do you think was the purpose of pulling magic into the story? How is magic used as a metaphor for that period in history? For Joe's struggle to be able to fall in love?
3. While the romances in the novel are "queer" romances, how can someone who doesn't identify as queer or LGBTQ+ relate to this story? What does the author mean by the term "holy lover"?
4. Disco Witch Manifesto #29 indicates *"Love is not the cause of happiness—it's a symptom of it."* This seems to imply that one can't find true love until they're happy with themselves. Do you agree or disagree? How does this sentiment relate to those not in a relationship or who don't want one at all? Does this idea also apply to friendships? Why or why not?
5. What are the different forms of love and family represented in the novel? How does your life mirror this or differ in terms of friendships and love?
6. Disco Witch Manifesto #17 says, *"In the time of the Great Darkness, we search for the truth. Upon finding it, we rejoice ... except when we don't."* There are many truths and many lies in the novel. Joe lies a lot—to others and to himself. Does this make Joe a less likeable character or a more relatable character?
7. Elena and Cleigh's same-sex relationship in the story marks a dramatic shift for Elena and her identity, and she seems surprised by it, since she's previously only been attracted to opposite-sex partners. Does this seem believable? Can someone change that dramatically in a summer? Or does everyone live on a spectrum of sexuality?
8. *"Healing spells are written upon the wound."* What does this quote from the Disco Witch Manifesto mean to you? Was there ever a time in your life where you were hurt so badly, but later learned you benefitted from the hurt or have come to appreciate it in some way? How can emotional, spiritual, physical "wounds" guide us?
9. A straight woman of color like Dory would typically be considered an "outsider" in a gay-male dominated world like Fire Island Pines. What does she gain by being an outsider? Is being an outsider ever the more comfortable place to be? What

are your thoughts on non-queer individuals spending time in queer spaces?
10. Disco Witch Manifesto #26 states, "*To get home, Disco Witches often go in the completely wrong direction.*" What in the heck does that mean? Which characters' journeys embody this sentiment?
11. Joe has an "affective dream" near the end of the novel which changes him psychically. According to interviews with the author, this dream was based on real experience he had. What did you feel about this moment? Have you ever had a dream that affected you greatly? If you had the ability, for just a year, to be struck "unafraid" what would you do in that year?
12. If you could have a coven of beloved friends, who would be in your coven? Who would be the high priest? What spells would you cast?
13. How would you define the Great Goddess Mother?
14. How is aging talked about in the novel? Who is the most age positive character? Disco Witch Manifesto #221 states that "Aging . . . will alter the topography of love. To remain on the playground of Eros means knowing one's niche." Does this dictum hold true in the world at large?

Lenny D'Amico's "Love (or Beloved Friendship) Tea" Recipe

Hibiscus tea base
Coriander
Honey
Dash of vanilla
Lemon grass
Cinnamon

A few dried rose petals, preferably from your own pesticide-free garden (or purchase the roses, wash, dry, then sleep with them under your pillow for one night before adding them to the mixture)

Drink this tea at least three times per week while traveling to somewhere you've dreamed of traveling, doing volunteer work, and/or doing something you've always longed to do that has always scared you. Talk to strangers about what you adore. Stay open.

Howie Fishbein's "Good Luck Charm" Recipe

Fill a small pouch or sachet with the following ingredients:

Cinnamon
Jasmine
Comfrey
Lavender
Mint
Ginger
One small tiger's eye gemstone (optional)

Take a walk or hike to your favorite spot and look on the ground for something that fills you with joy and throw that into the sachet.
Next, carry the sachet in your pocket while taking a big next step in your life. Take a class, ask for a raise, visit a city you've always dreamed of living in, talk to at least three people you're attracted to in a bar even though you're scared. The Great Goddess Mother doesn't drive parked cars.

Resources

- *The Evans Symposium: Witchcraft and the Gay Counterculture and Moon Lady Rising* by Arthur Evans
- *The Faggots and Their Friends Between Revolutions* by Larry Mitchell, illustrated by Ned Asta
- *The Green Witch's Guide to Magical Plants & Flowers: 26 Love Spells from Apples to Zinnias* by Chris Young, illustrated by Susan Ottaviano

Acknowledgments

First, there are so many people to thank, it's hard to know where to start. I suppose the best place to start is with my weekly writing group, made up of the genius writers Marian Fontana, Louise Crawford, Jennifer Berman, Kent Shell, and Aaron Zimmerman. Their ongoing support and inspiration are what keep my fingers stabbing away at the keyboard week after week

None of my books would ever see the light of day if it weren't for my brilliant and patient agent, Doug Stewart at Sterling Lord Literistic, whose guidance and feedback on my writing is invaluable. Thanks to the Goddess (and to James Hannaham) for bestowing such a smart-as-hell agent upon me.

I also need to thank my first readers. The glorious photo-artist and writer Gary Jones who always offers such inspiring and encouraging comments. I won't even think of publishing a book without first consulting Gary. Then there's my good friend David Ciminello, who, along with being one of my first readers on this book, has written his own brilliant debut with *The Queen of Steeplechase*

Park. David's inspired notes truly helped me make this a better book, not to mention helped me zhuzh up the sex scenes.

And a special thank-you to Maria Bell, my agent's former assistant, who now is off on another continent to work with nonliterary animals. She took my way-too-long manuscript and brutally and brilliantly showed me how to cut it down to make it something readable.

Also, I need to acknowledge those other blessed souls who either read the whole thing (Bruce Ward) or parts (Ivy Arce) and offered their expertise on the subject of AIDS or shed their light on that difficult period of the 1980s.

And an emphatic thanks to my good friend (and ex-husband) Colin Lentz, one of the smartest people I know, who is always ready to offer grammar advice or let me test out a sentence or passage on him (even after our divorce, I might add). Our connection is a complicated one, but that's also one of things I love about us, and he certainly continues to inspire me both in life and in my fiction.

And much love and gratitude to the brilliant painter Alberto F. Murillo, who was also one of my first readers as well as a Spanish language advisor, an inspiration, and my most avid cheerleader during the last two years of this novel's creation. I love you very much.

And holy crap, can we talk about the apotheosis of romance editors? Jess Verdi, my editor at Alcove Press, is all I could have hoped for. She's smart, funny, incisive, and so, so, so supportive and affirming. She knows how to cheer one on as she subtly squeezes that extra sex scene from you or convinces you that a secondary character you were once in love with is just no good for you anymore. (And she can do this all while un-braiding her daughter's hair.) Although I sometimes balked at the work she asked me to do, it was such a fun challenge, and I am so glad I got to do it with her.

And thanks to the other angels at Alcove Press: Rebecca Nelson, Thai Fantauzzi Perez, Dulce Botello, Mikaela Bender, Stephanie Manova, Megan Matti, Doug White, Matt Martz, Cassidy Graham, Monica Manzo, and cover artist Jim Tierney.

One can't write a book about witchcraft without talking to some witches. And so I want to thank the witchy advice from two of my favorite Wiccans. First, my good friend, phenomenal artist, and member of my soul-team, Enrico Gomez. One long conversation with Enrico changed the soul of this book, and I can't express how grateful I am for all that he is and all the magic he's done for me as a friend. I'm also grateful for The Green Witch's Guide to Magical Plants and Flowers, written by my good friend Chris Young along with his illustrator and fellow green witch Susan Ottaviano. And to the other members of my soul team, you know who you are, but with a special shoutout to Bryan, Patrick, Jimmy, John, Bill, Vinnie, Carolyn, Cynthia, Julie, Jillian, David, Sandy, Sarah, and Jamie.

Although this book is a work of fiction, it is inspired by events that occurred in my life during the worst years of the AIDS crisis, and by those I've met along the way. I would never have conceived the characters of Howie and Lenny without getting to spend a summer living in the attic of the incomparable Frank Corradino and the late Gerry Cervellino in Fire Island Pines. The voices and spirits of those two wonderful men echo throughout this book, and I'm so grateful to have met them. I also have to thank my running (away) companion during that first summer—Jeff Palumbo, who, while I was writing this book, graciously reminded me of some of the people and events I had forgotten. There are so many other people from that summer and since who have inspired me (Dave Sumrak, I'm looking at you!). All of them live somewhere between the sentences of this story, and I encourage you to use your imagination and necromancing powers to discover who they might be. An extra special thanks to a bodhisattva, the late Donald Norman from Los Angeles, whose spirit I've hopefully honored with my fictional homage.

And finally, I need to acknowledge two men who are no longer with us because of the AIDS pandemic and subsequent (and continued) government inaction and neglect. One is the late Stephen Gendin, ACT UP fellow and friend, who once confided in me how he longed to start a religion based on his spiritual experiences on the dance floors of Manhattan. The disco witch manifesto is for him. I also want to acknowledge the late Alan Contini, whom I met while working together on ACT UP's media committee. Alan encouraged me as a writer even while he was dying, and even still, long after his death. On the day before he transitioned, he told me that he wished he still had the strength to work on his play because, being so close to his end, he finally saw clearly what he wanted to say.

And lastly, Brian James Smith, a holy lover who once lived on Keswick Avenue in Glenside, Pennsylvania, and went to Bishop McDevitt High School and got his BA in communications from Temple University and liked Swedish fish and Fleetwood Mac. (I specify all this since he left us long before the internet and has such a common name.) Brian was my first great love, and my first utterly devastating heartbreak. His memory and influence are all over this book, and all over my life. I thank him.